Clements R. Markham

Life of Christopher Columbus

Clements R. Markham

Life of Christopher Columbus

ISBN/EAN: 9783743330658

Manufactured in Europe, USA, Canada, Australia, Japa

Cover: Foto ©Raphael Reischuk / pixelio.de

Manufactured and distributed by brebook publishing software
(www.brebook.com)

Clements R. Markham

Life of Christopher Columbus

LIFE

OF

CHRISTOPHER COLUMBUS.

BY

CLEMENTS R. MARKHAM, C.B.

LONDON:

GEORGE PHILIP & SON, 32 FLEET STREET;

LIVERPOOL: 45 TO 51 SOUTH CASTLE STREET.

1892.

CONTENTS.

LIST OF ILLUSTRATIONS.

PORTRAITS OF COLUMBUS.

LIST OF MAPS.

* PRINTED IN COLOURS.

LIFE OF
CHRISTOPHER COLUMBUS.

—-•+—-

CHAPTER I.

THE HOME AT GENOA.

THE city of Genoa was still a mighty power in the
Mediterranean when the great discoverer, Christopher
Columbus, was born, towards the middle of the fifteenth
century. Its highest state of prosperity passed away
with the fall of Constantinople, when its factories in
the Crimea, at Pera, and in the Levant were lost or
weakened. But the Republic, though forced to seek
protection alternately from France and Milan, continued
to be powerful by reason of the enterprise and maritime
skill of her sailors, the ability of her merchants, and
the credit of her bank of St. George. Less formidable
and less independent than in the previous two centuries,
the beautiful city was still the chief centre of Mediterranean trade, and was never more full of intellectual
activity. But since 1421 the Republic had been under
the protection of the Duke of Milan. The Genoese were
thus drawn into the contest for the succession of Naples,
Milan and the Pope supporting Louis of Anjou against

A

King Alfonso of Aragon. Genoa fringes the sea, and
the green Ligurian Alps, cleft by narrow fertile valleys,
rise up behind the palaces and churches of the city.
The Republic derived its strength not only from the
citizens, and the sailors whose homes were in the sea-
ports of the Riviera, but also from the sturdy farmers
and artisans in the valleys of the maritime Alps.

In one of these valleys, to the eastward of Genoa,

HOME OF THE FATHER OF COLUMBUS AT TERRAROSSA.

called Fontanabuona, there lived a farmer named Giovanni Colombo, with his son Domenico, in the hamlet
of Terrarossa, near Moconesi. They moved to a little
fishing village, called Quinto al Mare, about four miles
east of Genoa, where Domenico adopted the trade of
a cloth weaver. He had a brother, Antonio, and a
sister, Battistina, married to one Fritallo; all settled
at Quinto. Antonio had three sons, named Giovanni

Antonio, Mateo, and Amighetto, of whom we shall hear again in the course of the story. Domenico throve so well that in the year 1439 we find him established as a citizen of Genoa, and engaging an apprentice named Antonio de Leverono. A few years afterwards he was in a position to marry and support a family.

Domenico Colombo sought a wife in the valley of the Bisagno, a stream which finds its way to the sea close to the eastern wall of the city. The long valley through which the Bisagno flows is very fertile, and is gemmed with hamlets, villas, and gardens. The peasantry of the Val di Bisagno were loyal subjects of Genoa, but they clung to their local liberties. Every year, on Christmas Eve, they elected their new "Abbot" or Governor. The people assembled on the banks of the river, and two large stones were placed close to one another. The retiring Abbot, attired in his toga and beretta, stood on one, the newly-appointed Abbot on the the other. Then the latter received from his predecessor the standard of St. George. In the evening the Abbot and people proceeded to Genoa to pay their respects to the Doge in his palace. In the midst of the procession was a cart dragged by a yoke of oxen, containing a huge tree hung with wreaths of flowers. The tree was dragged into the courtyard of the palace, and the Abbot of Bisagno went up to pay his respects to the Doge, and make this customary offering. He and his people went home rejoicing, with a present of money; and in the night the Doge and his courtiers made a bonfire of the tree, and poured wine into the flames.*

Among these inhabitants of the Val di Bisagno, there was a silk-weaver living in the village of Quezzi, named

* Bent's Genoa, p. 12.

Giacomo di Fontanarossa, who had two sons, Goagnino and Guglielmo, and a daughter, Susanna. Thither came the young cloth-weaver, Domenico Colombo; and in due time Susanna became his wife, with a dowry consisting of money, and some land in the neighbouring hamlet of Ginestrato.

The young couple naturally took up their abode in the weavers' quarter at Genoa, outside the old gate of San Andrea. The monks of San Stefano held a considerable extent of land outside this gate, divided into lots, which were let out to weavers, carders, and fullers. Domenico held two small houses under them, one near the Porto dell' Olivella, and the other, where he lived with his wife, between the gate of San Andrea and the lane or Vico di Mulcento. The walls of Genoa were built in 1155 as a defence against the Emperor Frederick Barbarossa, and the gate of San Andrea was flanked by two round towers. Thence a street called Vico Dritto di Ponticello led to the church of San Stefano, and the Vico di Mulcento branched from it, parallel to the city walls. The house of Domenico Colombo was in the Vico Dritto, between the gate of San Andrea and the Vico di Mulcento, on the left hand side, coming from the gate. It is now No. 37, and was bought by the municipality of Genoa in 1887, who have placed an inscription on its wall. The neighbours were Antonio Bondi on one side, and Giovanni Pallavonia on the other. The ground floor was occupied by the loom where Domenico and his apprentices worked, and behind there was a garden extending to the city walls.

The first child of Domenico Colombo and Susanna Fontanarossa was born at Genoa,[1] almost certainly in this house, in the year 1446 or early in 1447,[2] when

Raffaele Adorno was Doge of Genoa. He was named Cristoforo. The next child was probably born in 1448,

HOUSE OF COLUMBUS AT GENOA.

and was named Giovanni Pellegrino. Bartolomeo was born in 1450. Then there was an interval. The only sister, Blanchineta, was born in 1464, and the youngest child, Giacomo, in 1468. The place of baptism of the children of Domenico Colombo was the church of San Stefano, at the end of the Vico Dritto, where the weavers had their special altar. Founded in 1258, it had a picturesque campanile, and a marble façade in alternate white and black courses, a mode of building only permitted for churches, and for the palaces of a few of the chief noble families.

The Vico Dritto ending near the church of San Stefano, the old gate of San Andrea with its flanking towers, and the garden bounded by the city walls, were the first things that became familiar to the eyes of little Cristoforo Colombo and his brothers. The weavers established special schools for their children in the San Andrea quarter, and in one of these Cristoforo received his first lessons in writing, arithmetic, and geography. He was then apprenticed to his father, and his chief work for many years was the carding of wool and the weaving of cloth. But the boy from a very early age indulged in day dreams, and his young mind was filled with thoughts which took him far from the work of his trade. His aspirations could not be restrained. He first went to sea at the age of fourteen, and voyages to all parts of the Mediterranean broke the course of his ordinary life as a cloth-weaver in his father's workshop.

When Cristoforo passed into the city, through the gate of San Andrea, he was within a few minutes' walk of the busy harbour. Standing under the shadow of the stately edifice occupied by the bank of St. George, he feasted his eyes on the ships and war galleys in the harbour; and if he ascended the heights of Sarzano or Carignano, he could watch them until they became tiny white specks on the horizon. When he was ten years old, Genoa was placed under the protection of the King of France, and the expedition of the gallant young John of Calabria, son of King René, was fitted out in the harbour, and sailed for the recovery of Naples on the 4th of October 1459. Cristoforo was then a red-haired boy of twelve, with bright blue eyes and florid complexion. How eagerly he must have gazed at the ten stately war galleys, forming the fleet of the French adventurer, as they lay at anchor with all their flags and pennons fluttering in the breeze. How he must have longed to be taken on board one of them, and how his young heart must have beat with excitement, as he saw them sail away. We may still, with the aid of Sanutus and Colonel Yule, picture to ourselves what Cristoforo saw. These war galleys were 120 feet long and very narrow, not more than $15\frac{1}{2}$ feet beam, but the width was increased by an outrigger deck projecting beyond the ship's side, and supported by timber brackets, to give room for the fighting men. A castle rose up amidships, and the battery was in the bows. There were from twenty-two to twenty-eight benches for rowers on each side, placed diagonally, so that each rower could handle a separate oar, while using the same *portella* or rowlock; and along the centre line of the deck, fore and aft, there was a raised gangway, called *corsia*, to afford a passage clear of the oars. The galleys were built for war purposes and for speed, but they were very low and could not keep the sea in rough weather. Even with a smooth sea the toil of rowing was excessive, yet the work was performed by freely enlisted men, *galeotti assoldati*, and it was not until the following century that slaves were employed, several tugging at a single large oar. The Genoese merchant

ships were of a very different build, with much more
beam in proportion to their length, **and** supplied with
masts and sails.

Columbus himself tells us that he first went to sea **at**
the age of fourteen, that is in the year 1461, but whether
in a merchant ship or in a war galley is left to conjecture.
In March of the same year the Genoese rose against the
French, killed many in the streets, and forced the rest to
take refuge in the castle of Casteletto, which was surrendered in the following July. The Doge, Prospero
Adorno, defeated a French invasion; but the Fregosi,
who succeeded, found that the Republic was too weak to
stand alone, and placed it under the protection of Francesco Sforza, **Duke of** Milan, **in 1464.** It was during
these stirring times that the future discoverer made his
first voyage out of Genoa, and he continued to lead a
seafaring life until he became a thorough sailor, while
he worked at his father's trade during the intervals on
shore. We have scarcely any details of these voyages,
but he must have visited all parts **of** the Mediterranean,
and we know that he was at the island **of** Chios, and in
Sicily.[*]

Young Cristoforo did not content himself with a knowledge of practical seamanship. He must have been **a**
zealous student of cosmography and history, for it is
certain that he acquired his knowledge in these early
years, as well as his remarkable skill as a penman and a
draughtsman. In those days there was no better place in
the world for such studies than Genoa. Forzio had written
the history of the Chioggian war with Venice, Bracelli
had narrated the naval victory over Alfonso of Aragon
in a style which was compared with Sallust, and at

---

[*] Navarrete, i. 41.

least two members of the ducal family of Fregoso were authors and poets as well as statesmen. Above all, Andalone di Negro, the poet, mathematician, and astronomer, and the master of Boccaccio, lived well into the fifteenth century, and wrote a treatise on the use of the astrolabe, which was printed at the very time when Columbus was completing his studies, before finally leaving his home. Genoa also rivalled Venice and Ancona at this time in the production of *portolani*, or beautifully executed sea-charts of the Mediterranean and western coasts of Europe and Africa. The Portolano Mediceo, now at Florence, was executed a century earlier; but Grazioso Benincasa was in the height of his fame as a draughtsman at Genoa during the youth of Columbus. He was a native of Ancona, but he was working at Genoa when Columbus began his sea life, and it is more than probable that the quick-witted and talented boy found employment in the workroom of the great draughtsman. There he would see delineated the "Insula del legnana," Antilla and Brasill far out in the western ocean, and thus the first germ of his mighty thought would be implanted in his young mind. The planisphere of Bartolomeo Pareto, drawn at Genoa in 1455, which shows St. Brandan, Antilla, and Royllo on the verge of the unknown, might also have been familiar to him. Over a score of the maps of Benincasa are still in existence, two or three in the British Museum; and as we admire their beautiful workmanship, we may reflect that the boy Cristoforo may well have gazed upon them too, while his teeming brain indulged in a day dream which the maturity of his genius would convert into a reality.

These conjectures respecting the training of Columbus

cannot be far from the truth, because we find in him
such matured knowledge so soon after his departure
from Italy, that it can only have been acquired by long
study, and in Genoa. Las Casas tells us that Columbus
received part of his education at the university of Pavia.(?)
He would not have gone there to study any subject
bearing on the seaman's art, for Genoa would be the
place for that; but a knowledge of Latin was needful
for him in the perusal of works on the sphere, and it is
not at all unlikely that, as a young man, he may have
gone to Pavia to acquire latinity. It is clear from the
knowledge shown by Bartolomeo afterwards, that his
younger brother was the companion of Cristoforo in his
studies. It is most probable that the grand idea of
Columbus had found a birth in his mind, and impelled
him onwards to his destiny, before he finally left his
home.

In 1470, when Cristoforo had attained the age of
twenty-three years, the affairs of home called for a
closer attention to business on the part of all the sons
of Domenico Colombo. The industrious weaver had
thriven and become a substantial citizen. He resolved
to move to Savona, and to extend his business in various
ways, while still retaining his house in the Vico Dritto.
He was evidently a man of an enterprising spirit and
more than average capacity. In order to provide capital
for his new venture, he sold the little property at Gino-
strato in September 1470. The consent of his wife
Susanna to this sale was necessary, and as all the sons
were under age, her brothers and other relations were
summoned to give formal sanction to her consent,
which was registered in the following May. Meanwhile
Domenico Colombo had established himself at Savona,

not only as a weaver ("Textor pannorum"), but also as a tavern-keeper ("Tabernarius"); and in March 1470 he engaged an apprentice from his native valley of Fontana-buona, named Bartolomeo Castagneti. In this under-taking Domenico needed all the help that his three grown up sons could give him. Many and many a time must Cristoforo and his two brothers, now stalwart young men almost of legal age, have walked over the distance of twenty-six miles from Genoa to Savona while the change of abode was proceeding. The road skirts the seashore, and Cristoforo must have cast many a longing glance over the deep blue sea to the white sails on the distant horizon, while engaged on this work of piety. In 1469 he was witness to the will of a young comrade named Nicolo Monleone at Genoa. In 1472 and 1473 his father was buying wool on credit, and by a deed dated Savona, August 16, 1472, Cristoforo guaranteed one of his father's debts. More capital was needed, and Domenico Colombo sold his house at Genoa, near the Porta dell Olivella. The consent of his wife Susanna was again necessary, to be given with the sanction of her nearest relations of legal age. Her two eldest sons had now attained their majority, and the document was signed by Cristoforo and Giovanni Pellegrino Colombo, on the 7th of August 1473. This is the last time that Cristoforo Colombo appears as a wool-weaver ("Lanerio"), and the last piece of evidence of his presence in Italy.

Cristoforo had seen his family comfortably established at Savona. He had zealously and efficiently assisted his father in all the business involved in the change. He was now free to follow his own great destiny. By his own exertions and talent he had become not only an excellent practical seaman, but also a cosmographer and a draughtsman. He had acquired this knowledge subject to long interruptions, and while following the trade of a weaver. The difficulties in his way must have been such as only a youth of extraordinary genius and strength of will could have overcome. He was deeply imbued with the religious spirit of his age and country. **From** a child he had belonged to one of the religious guilds, and all the acts of his life were tinged with devotional feeling. I cannot doubt that, even at this **early period,** he had the germs in his mind of the great enterprise of his life. He had reached the age of twenty-eight when he left his native land and the home of his youth, and made his way to the country which, **of all** others, seemed to him most likely to afford the means of fulfilling his destiny. Columbus left Genoa **and** went to Portugal **in** 1474.[4]

Soon after the departure of Cristoforo, his next brother, Giovanni Pellegrino, died. The last documentary evidence of the presence of Bartolomeo at Savona is dated June **16, 1480. He** probably joined his brother at Lisbon in the latter part of that year. The only sister, Blanchineta, married a cheesemonger named Giacomo Bavarello. **The** father of Bavarello had a house near the San Andrea gate, and Giacomo had probably known the young Colombos, and played with them in the Vico Dritto from infancy. The only child of the Bavarelli, named Pantaleone, was born in 1490. The mother of the great discoverer, Susanna Fontanarossa, died at Savona in about 1483. Then the business of Domenico began to fail. He no longer had grown up sons to help him. So he resolved to abandon **the enterprise** at Savona, and to return to Genoa. His youngest child, Giacomo, was sixteen, and his father apprenticed him to a weaver at Savona, named Luchino Cademartoni, for twenty-two months. When he had served his time he joined his father at Genoa, and remained with him until the wonderful news of his brother's great achievement reached him, when he hurried to Spain to share the prosperity of his family. The old father was left alone. On the 31st of March 1492 he gave up the old home in the Vico Dritto to his son-in-law Bavarello, and his last years were probably passed with his daughter Blanchineta. He lived to extreme old age, long enough to be gladdened by the news of the great discovery, to receive help from his illustrious son, and letters from his grandsons. Domenico Colombo was a man of enterprise, and of great physical activity. The formation of the establishment at Savona is a proof of his spirit of enterprise; and his frequent journeys to Savona, down to the year 1492, are evidence of his activity. Domenico Colombo and Susanna Fontanarossa were good types of the Ligurian peasantry, and their fine qualities helped to form the character of their illustrious son. They were worthy to be the parents of the greatest maritime genius of the fifteenth century.

NOTES.

(1) *Date of the Birth of Columbus.*

Columbus was certainly born in the city of Genoa, for he himself said, "De la ciudad de Genova sali, y en ella naci"—"I came from the city of Genoa, and in it I was born."

(2) The date of the birth of Columbus is fixed by various statements incidentally made by himself in his letters, which all harmonise with each other, and by legal documents at Genoa. The first statement was that when he first went to

sea he was fourteen, and that when he came to Spain in 1485 he had led a sailor's life for twenty-three years. This makes 1447 the year of his birth. The next is in a letter dated 1501, where he says that it is forty years since he first went to sea. He went to sea at the age of fourteen, and was therefore fifty-four in 1501. This again makes 1447 the year of his birth. The third is in a letter dated July 7, 1503 (*Navarrete*, i. 311), where he says, "Yo vine a servir a veinte y ocho años"—"I came to serve at twenty-eight years of age." He refers to the time when he first devoted his services to the great discovery, and came to Portugal in 1474. Once more 1447 is shown to be the year of his birth.

The evidence at Genoa consists of two documents in which the mother of Columbus consented to the sale of property by her husband. For the first deed, dated May 25, 1471, the judge summoned her brothers and other relations to authorise her consent. The second, dated August 7, 1473, is signed by her son Cristoforo. This shows that he attained the legal age of twenty-five between the two dates, and makes 1447 the year of his birth. There is another document, dated 10th September 1484, binding the youngest brother, Giacomo, apprentice at the age of sixteen. Giacomo was therefore born in 1468. If, as some authorities contend, Columbus had been born in 1436, the mother would be over fifty when Giacomo was born, which is impossible.

The only ground for the contention that Columbus was born in 1436 is the statement of Andres Bernaldez, a Spanish priest, who knew the Admiral in his later years (*Historia de los Reyes Catolicos*, cap. cxxxi.), that he was seventy years of age, a little more or less, when he died. Bernaldez had no knowledge of the date of his birth, and merely judged from his worn and aged appearance.

The reason that the authorities who advocate the earlier date wish to make Columbus older than he was, is that a passage in Las Casas, and in the "Historie" of Fernando Columbus, translated by Ulloa, may be reconciled with facts. In a letter to King Ferdinand, dated January 1501, not now in existence, Columbus is alleged by Las Casas, and in the "Historie," to have made the following statement with reference to the use of the compass: "It happened to me that King René, whom God has taken to Himself, sent me to Tunis to take the galley

Fernandina, and being off the island of San Pedro in Sardinia,
I heard from a despatch boat that there were two ships and a
carrack with the said galley. On this the people who were
with me determined not to go on, but to return to Marseilles
for another ship and more men. I saw that, without some
artifice, I could not force their wishes, so I consented to their
demand. Changing the compass card, I weighed at dusk, and
next day at sunrise we were off the Cape of Carthagena, when
they all made certain that we were at Marseilles."

In 1461 the Genoese rose against the French, and from that
time King René was the enemy of Genoa; but he never attempted any expedition in the Mediterranean after the failure
of his son in 1460. The event must, therefore, have taken place
before 1461. If Columbus was born in 1447, he was thirteen in
1460, and could not have commanded one of King René's ships
of war. If he was born in 1436, he was a young weaver of
twenty-four, and the conferring of such a command upon him
would be almost as improbable. A captain of a war galley
would be an officer of rank and experience. But as late as
1473, in legal documents, Columbus is called "Lanerio di
Janua" (weaver of Genoa), not "Capitano di Galea."

The statement, as it stands, cannot therefore be true. Fernando Columbus, from whose notes Ulloa and Las Casas copied,
quoted the passage from memory, attributing to Columbus
himself an incident which he doubtless referred to, as having
happened to one of René's officers. Fernando (cap. iv. of "Historie") fully admits his liability to error owing to inattention to
such matters in his youth.

Muñoz, Robertson, Spotorno, Harrisse, D'Avezac, and Major
rely upon the statements of Columbus himself, and adopt the
date of 1446 or 1447. Navarrete, Humboldt, Lamartine, Washington Irving, Roselly de Lorgues, and Asensio rely upon the
vague guess of Bernaldez that Columbus was about seventy
when he died, and place his birth in 1436.

(9) *Student at Pavia.*

Fernando Columbus, as rendered both by Las Casas and
by Ulloa in the "Historie," states that his father was at the
university of Pavia. "Dico adunque che nella sua piccola
eta imparo lettere e studio in Pavia tanto che gli bastare
per intendere i cosmografia." Mr. Harrisse doubts the story.

Pavia taught philosophy and medicine, not cosmography, and a weaver apprentice would not be sent to cross the Apennines alone, in the fifteenth century, **to** learn cosmography, which was better taught at Genoa. There is nothing **in the** archives of the Pavia university on the subject; **and** Nicolo Scillacio, a Professor of Pavia, who published an account of the second voyage **of** Columbus, dedicated to Ludovico il Moro, says not a word about Columbus having been there. If he had been, Scillacio would almost certainly have mentioned it on such an occasion.

(4) *Story of Columbus having swum on shore in* **Portugal.**

Las **Casas** has a story (i. p. 51) that there **was** a famous corsair named Columbo **Junior, who** commanded a great fleet against Venetians, infidels, **and other enemies** of his nation. Cristopher Columbus **determined to join him,** and serve **under** him for a long time. **This Columbo Junior,** hearing that four Venetian galleys **had gone to Flanders,** waited for their return between Lisbon and Cape **St. Vincent. A** desperate naval action followed, the **vessel** on **which** Christopher Columbus served, was burnt, **and** with the **help of an oar** he **reached** the shore. Las Casas quotes **as** his **authority for** this event the chronicle of Sabellico (Lib. S, Dec. **10, p. 168). This** is **the way** in which Columbus is **said to have found his way** to Lisbon. Unfortunately for this story, **the naval action in** question is known **to** have taken place on **August 22, 1485,** more than ten years after the arrival **of** Columbus **in** Portugal. The "Columbo Junior" was really a French corsair named Casaneuve. The story must be rejected as apocryphal.

CHAPTER II.

COLUMBUS IN PORTUGAL.

SAN STEFANO, at the end of the Vico Dritto, was the parish church of the Colombo family. On one of the marble courses of its façade were inscribed the names of the Admirals of Portugal of the Genoese family of Pessagni. Cristoforo had seen them. He had also seen the flag of St. George marked on the *portolani*, where Genoese had made discoveries in command of Portuguese ships. It was quite natural that, in seeking to work out his destiny, he should make his way to Portugal.

In truth, the Genoese had been closely connected with Portuguese maritime affairs for more than a century. In 1317 King Dinis secured the services of Emanuele Pessagno of Genoa to fill the post of hereditary Admiral of the Portuguese fleet, with the undertaking that he would find twenty experienced Genoese captains to command the ships. Portuguese ships, with Genoese commanders, rediscovered the Canary Islands in 1341. The Isle of Lanzarote was discovered by Lanzarote Melocello. On the *Portolano Mediceo* at Florence, which was drawn in 1351, the shield of Genoa is painted by the side of the island of Lanzarote, and a legend also records the discovery on the planisphere (1455) of Pareto. Lancelot Pessagno succeeded his father Emanuele in 1357, and the office of Admiral of Portugal continued to be held

17   B

by members of this Genoese family until 1448. The enterprises of their captains were not confined to the voyage to the Fortunate Islands, which is mentioned by Petrarch. They also discovered the Azores early in the fourteenth century, although those islands were not colonised until long afterwards. They are shown on the Laurentian map of 1351.

Prince Henry of Portugal was despatching vessels to discover the coast of Africa, from 1420 to 1460; and one of the explorers of his time was a Genoese, named Antonio Uso di Mare, who sailed beyond the Gambia with Cadamosto in 1457. Another Genoese, named Antonio di Noli, was with Diogo Gomez when the Cape Verde Islands were discovered in 1460; and Noli obtained the captaincy of the Island of Santiago, which he held until his death.

The disappearance of the name of Cristoforo Colombo from the notarial records of Genoa and Savona in the autumn of 1473 points to 1474 as the year of his arrival in Portugal. At this time he and his brother Bartholomew were known as Colombo di Terrarossa, from the birthplace and original home of their father. When Cristoforo reached Lisbon, Prince Henry the Navigator had been dead fourteen years. The state of geographical knowledge was represented by the map which the Prince's nephew, Affonso V., had caused to be constructed, so that all the new discoveries might be placed on record. The King intrusted the commission to Fra Mauro, of the Camaldolese Convent of San Miguel di Murano at Venice, assisted by a well-known draughtsman, several of whose *portolani* are still preserved, named Andrea Bianco. The completed work, which was an elaborate planisphere, was sent to Portugal in April 1459.

The west coast of Africa had been explored from Cape Bojador to the Cape of St. Catherine, which is over a hundred miles south of the equator. But all to the westward of the Azores and the Canaries was so utterly

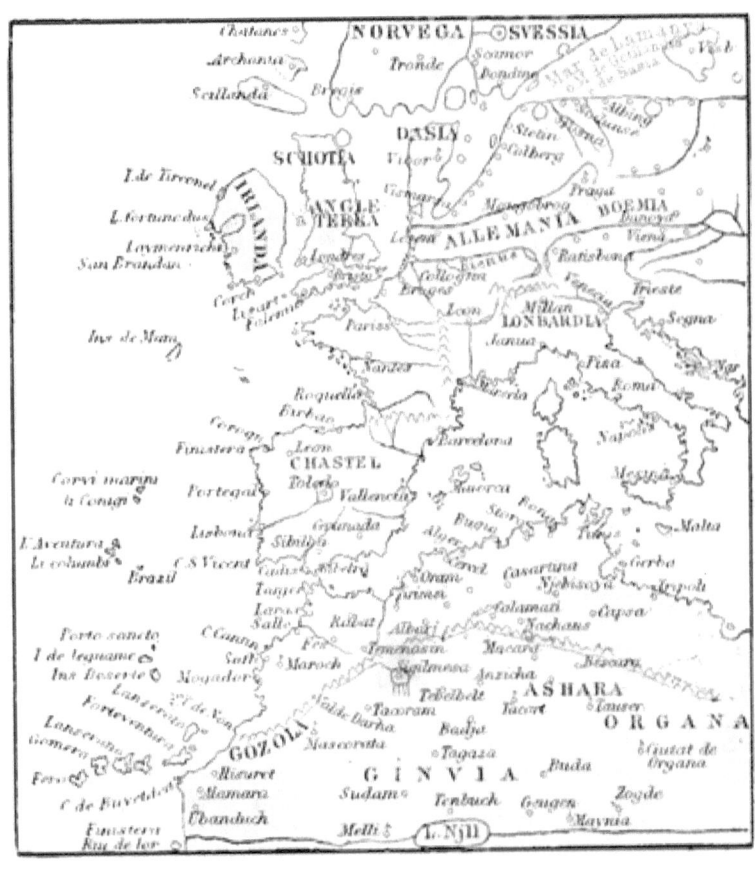

WESTERN PART OF THE CATALAN MAP OF THE WORLD, 1375.

dark and unknown, and progress to the west seemed so impossible, that the idea of penetrating in that direction had not even entered into men's minds. One youthful genius had alone conceived a settled plan. It had been born in his gifted brain before he left his home at

Genoa. For its sake he had come to Portugal, and while eagerly acquiring all the new knowledge respecting the African coast, it was to the western limit of the charts that he most frequently turned his anxious gaze.

The fabulous western islands of the Atlantic almost seem to have been put on the old charts to lure mariners to the unknown west. The largest was called "Antilia," and first appeared on a portolano of 1425. It is placed on the chart of Andrea Bianco of Venice, bearing date 1436, in 25° 35'. W. But Ruysch, in his important map, which was engraved after the death of Columbus, removed it further west. "Antilia" here appears in 17 W. and 40° N., and the legend informs us that it was discovered long ago by Roderick, the last of the Gothic Kings of Spain, who took refuge there after his defeat by the Moors. Another tale was that two archbishops and five bishops escaped to Antilia, after the fall of Don Roderick, and that they built seven cities there. Hence it was sometimes called the Isle of the Seven Cities. Another fabulous island of the Atlantic was called Brazil. It is shown on the Catalan chart of 1375, which was drawn for Charles V. of France, as one of the Azores. Andrea Bianco has it on his chart of 1436. On the chart of Benincasa, dated 1469, which Columbus may have seen at Genoa, the isle of Brazil is placed to the westward of Limerick, and it has the same position on the chart of 1476 by the same draughtsman. The name may be derived from the Genoese word "braze" for wood, converted by the Portuguese into brazil. The position of this island on the charts, away to the westward of the British Isles, attracted the attention of English mariners; and William of Worcester, in his Chronicle, relates that in July 1480 some ships sailed from Bristol

in search of the island of Brazil, under the command of
a scientific master-mariner named Thlyde. After being
battered by the storms of the Atlantic for nine months,
they returned to an Irish port without having seen any
signs of Brazil. The legend of St. Brandan, derived
from an Irish source, caused the appearance of another
mythical island in the western Atlantic. Uso di Mare,
in his journal, tells how, in the sixth century, St. Brandan, Abbot of Ailech, who had 3000 monks under him,
went to sea in company with St. Malo, in search of an
island which always moved away from him. It appeared
on the planisphere drawn at Genoa by Pareto in 1455,
far away to the westward of the Canaries, and continued
to retain its place on maps and charts throughout the
two following centuries. Other fabulous islands occur
on ancient charts, which were probably due to the fertile imaginations of the draughtsmen. "*La Caparia*"
figures on the famous Hereford mappe-monde, which
was drawn in the end of the thirteenth century, and
"*L'Oro*" is on the Laurentian portolano. The island of
"*Royllo*" has a place with Antilia and St. Brandan on
the planisphere of Pareto; and Benincasa, in 1476, has
"*Isola di Man*" and "*San Giorgio*."

The mythical islands of the western Atlantic, Antilia,
Brazil, St. Brandan, Royllo, San Giorgio, were realities
to Columbus and his contemporaries. A mystery hung
round them, but there they were on the portolani and
planispheres of the most learned cosmographers, delineated as lands which might be reached through the daring
and skill of resolute explorers. They were of special
importance to the genius who had conceived the grand
idea of a western voyage to India, for they appeared
as stepping-stones on his route. The predecessors of

Columbus had made known to him and his contemporaries the whole eastern side of the Atlantic, from the Equator to the Arctic Circle, with the groups of islands; and the map-makers seemed to lure the illustrious Genoese on his destined path, by strewing the unknown ocean with the isles of legend and fable.

Columbus had heard of these things. He came to Portugal with the object of acquiring a personal knowledge of all that had been discovered. He was to pass through a long and hard apprenticeship, to become the foremost of living seamen in experience and knowledge, before he could secure acceptance for the mighty scheme which was already fermenting in his mind. Very little is known of the events of his life during the years that he spent in Portugal. It is believed that he earned a livelihood at first by drawing maps and charts. He made voyages along the African coast, and was at Madeira and Porto Santo. The first certain date is 1477, when he made a voyage to England and Iceland.

The passage respecting the visit of Columbus to Iceland is in the "History of the Indies," by Las Casas, and also in the "Historie" of Fernando Columbus. It professes to be a quotation from a letter of Columbus, but it bears evidence of, at least, two explanatory interpolations of later date. "In the month of February, and in the year 1477, I navigated as far as the island of Tile [Thule], a hundred leagues (whose southern part is 73° from the equator, and not 63°, as some say: and it is not within the line which includes the west, as Ptolemy says, but much further to the west), and to this island, which is as large as England, the English, especially those of Bristol, go with merchandise, and at the time that I was there the sea was not frozen over, although there were very high tides, so much so that in some parts the sea rose twenty-five *brazas*, and went down as much, twice during the day. (It is quite true that the Tile of Ptolemy is where he says it is, and this land is called Frislandia by the moderns)."

The passages in brackets are clearly interpolations. Las Casas began his work in 1527, and finished it in 1561. In the interval the map of Nicolo Zeno had been published in 1558, on which he placed an island which he called Frislandia, in 63. This accounts for the second bracketed passage, which contradicts the first. Both must be omitted, in reading what Columbus really wrote, which was that he sailed a hundred leagues to the island of Thule in February 1477 ; that the island is as large as England ; that the English, especially those of Bristol, traded there ; that the sea was not frozen over when he was there, and that the rise and fall of the tide was twenty-five *brazas*.

It is very improbable that Columbus, during a short visit, should have heard of the discoveries of Norsemen sailing from Greenland more than three centuries before, and if he did, such information would not have furnished him with any argument for his proposed voyage westward to the Indies. In the time of Columbus, Greenland was believed to be a peninsula of the continent of Europe, and it is so delineated on every map of that period without exception. If the great navigator did hear of Greenland, and of the wooded isles of Markland and Wineland, to the south of that promontory, he would think of them as a European peninsula, and as off-lying European islands. They would not appear to him to be of any significance with reference to the westward voyage to the Indies. His arguments are all recorded, and the existence of wooded islands south of Greenland is not among them.

In the course of these three years, from 1474 to 1477, the talents of the young Genoese must have been recognised. No doubt he had become known as a cosmographer and a seaman of distinguished ability, and had won a certain position in Lisbon, when he made his Iceland voyage. On his return he was a man of some distinction, with courteous manners and noble bearing. He was above the middle height, with well-knit and vigorous limbs. Las Casas remembered him well, and described his face as oval, with a pleasant expression, the nose aquiline, the eyes blue, the complexion fair and inclined to ruddiness. Oviedo calls it somewhat fiery red and freckly. It was a fair complexion that turned red, rather than bronze, from exposure to the sun. The hair was red. Las Casas adds that he was agreeable and cheerful, and a good speaker. It must have been very soon after his return from Iceland, in the spring of 1477, that the handsome Genoese won the heart of Filippa Moniz. This noble lady was attached to the convent of All Souls at Lisbon, where Columbus was accustomed to hear mass. They met. Friendship ripened into love, and they were married. The date of the marriage is indicated by the birth of their son Diego. He was about the same age as Don Juan, the son of the Catholic sovereigns, who was born on June 30, 1478. If Diego was born at about that time, his parents were probably married towards the end of 1477. Filippa Moniz was a granddaughter of Gil Ayres Moniz, secretary to the famous Constable Pereira, in the days of João I., who founded the chapel of "Piedad," in the monastery of Carmen at Lisbon.

In this chapel the Moniz family had an exclusive right
of interment.

Isabel, a daughter of Gil Ayres Moniz, and aunt of
Filippa, was the second wife of Bartolomeu Perestrello,
who received a grant of Porto Santo in 1425, and died
in 1457. Isabel had an only child, also named Bartolomeu, who was too young to assume the captaincy of
the island at the time of his father's death. But the
widow was tired of living in such a lonely place. She
therefore ceded the captaincy of Porto Santo to Pedro
Correa da Cunha (who had married a daughter of her
husband by his first wife) in 1458, and returned to Lisbon. The younger Bartolomeu succeeded his brother-
in-law in command of Porto Santo in 1473. It is likely
enough, as is stated by Las Casas, that this connection
of his wife with the widow of such a man as Perestrello
may have led to the acquisition of much valuable information relating to maritime discovery, which would be
useful to Columbus in his study of arguments for the
western voyage.

It is an interesting and curious coincidence that the
lives of Christopher Columbus and Martin Behaim almost exactly coincide. Born in the same decade, they
achieved the great work of their respective lives in the
same year, and died in the same year. Behaim was a
learned young Nuremburger, who, after passing some
time in Portugal, found his way to Fayal in 1486, lived
there for several years, and married a daughter of Jobst
van Hueter, the Flemish governor of that island. The
great services performed by Behaim to nautical science
connect his career somewhat closely with the labours
and studies of Columbus. Behaim devoted his talents
to the improvement of that science of navigation, on the

development of which the success of the scheme of Columbus depended. The former was born at Nuremburg in 1436, and was a pupil of Regiomontanus, the great German astronomer, who died at Rome in 1475. Behaim was a merchant as well as a learned cosmographer and maker of instruments. Arriving at Lisbon in 1479, he was employed during the following year in adapting the complicated astrolabe of astronomers for use at sea. Two learned natives of Portugal were associated with him in this service, named Master Rodrigo and Master Joseph, a Jew. There is no record of the fact, but it can scarcely be doubted that Columbus, who was settled at Lisbon, was also consulted on a subject of which he had such special knowledge. It was at this time that he was joined by his brother Bartolomé, as we gather from the fact that the last notarial record of Bartolomé at Genoa bears the date of June 16, 1480. The two brothers had studied together, and there was the warmest attachment between them, which remained unshaken through life. Cristoforo was not only a cartographer, but, as Las Casas tells us, he wrote so good and legible a hand that he might, and probably did, earn his bread by it. Bartolomé possessed the same accomplishments in a scarcely less degree, and was an invaluable assistant to his brother.

The need for an instrument by which the latitude could be ascertained began to be felt as soon as navigators ceased to creep along the coast, and stood away out of sight of land. Diogo Gomez rightly attached much importance to his observations with a quadrant, when he discovered the Cape Verde Islands in 1460. The quadrant was a copper or brass triangle, one side being an arc graduated to 90°. The other two sides met at an apex where there was a ring, and whence a plumb line hung across the arc. Two sights were fixed on one side, and the observer held the instrument loosely by the ring. As soon as the two sights were on with the sun, the arc was read off at the point where it was intersected by the plummet line, which gave the altitude. This simple instrument differed from the astrolabe which was adapted by Martin Behaim and his coadjutors in 1480. The astrolabe used by astronomers was a complicated instrument, covered with confusing circles crossing each other and indicating points not required by plain seamen. A treatise on its use, which needs a good deal of close study for its mastery, was written by our own Chaucer. The problem referred to Behaim was the simplification of the astrolabe for use at sea. The sea astrolabe was a metal circle from 8 to 9 inches in diameter, and of some thickness in order to give it weight, for, like the quadrant, it was necessary to hold it by a ring in order that it might hang perpendicular to the horizon, when used for observing. It was crossed by two metal lines, one from the ring to the opposite side of the circle, called the zenith line, and the other crossing it, and called the horizon line. The circle was graduated to 90° from the horizon line to the zenith. A movable limb, called the *alidada*, worked over the circle, and a line was drawn down its centre—the "*linea fiducia*." Two sights were fixed on the *alidada*, which was moved until the sights were on with the sun. The point where the "*linea fiducia*" cut the arc showed the altitude. The observer was instructed to sit down and place himself with his back against the mainmast, hold the astrolabe by the ring hanging on the second finger of his left hand, and move the *alidada* up and down with his right, until the sun was on with both sights.

The adaptation of instruments for observing the meridian altitudes of **heavenly** bodies, for use at sea, was a very important event **in the** history of maritime discovery. It brought the great scheme of Columbus **nearer to** maturity, **for he** knew that a long voyage across the ocean **could not be** undertaken without such **aid.** The arduous **task of** guiding **a** ship over the ocean, **when nothing is** seen but sky and sea for many **days,** would **not be possible,** unless astronomical **ob-servations could be taken.** As old Cortes wrote in **his art of** navigation, **the** guidance **of** a ship makes it **necessary to** keep **the eyes on the** heavens—"poner les **ojos en** el cielo." **The** improvement of navigation was, **as** Columbus well knew, **an** essential part of the pre-paration for **his** great achievement. Expert in every department **of his** profession, **he** constructed his own instruments, **as well as his** nautical **charts.**

To find the latitude, **the** meridian altitude is only one **element in the calculation.** It is also necessary to have **the sun's** declination for **each day** of the year. **The publication, for** the first time, **of** tables of declination was contemporaneous with the adaptation of the astrolabe **by Behaim.** His master, Regiomontanus, completed his "Calendarium **No**vum" in 1475, which contained tables of the sun's declination calculated for the years **from** 1475 to 1566 inclusive.

The mariner's compass **had** been long in use, **and the** properties of the load-stone were well known to the learned as early as the thirteenth century. Roger Bacon was acquainted with them, although he nowhere mentions the use to which they might be put, and, indeed, super-stition and fear of witchcraft probably delayed and hindered the first use of the compass. Flavio Gioja of

Amalfi, early in the fourteenth century, appears to have made some great improvement in the practical arrangements connected with the use of the magnet, if he did not, as is asserted, actually introduce it on board ship.(²) Further improvements were adopted, and in the time of Columbus the magnetic needle had become a serviceable instrument. A card was painted with the thirty-two points, a *fleur-de-lys* for the north, and a cross for the east. A steel pin was fastened to the back of the card, of the same length as its diameter, and touched at each end with the *iman*, or load-stone. The centre of the card was made to work on a pyramid of brass, fixed in a circular box covered with glass; and the box rested on the metal circles, which swung with the ship, and kept the card steady.

The sea chart was the fifth, and not the least important aid to navigation. Although the charts were drawn as if the world was a plane and a century would elapse before an improved projection would be invented, still they had been brought to great perfection; they were more accurate in outline than the maps produced at the same period by learned professors, and the execution of the portolani of Benincasa and Pareto, the probable masters of Columbus, is exceedingly beautiful.

Columbus had acquired a profound knowledge of the construction and manufacture of all the scientific machinery of a navigator—the astrolabe, quadrant, compass, and plane chart; and he was expert in the use of the declination tables, as well as in all calculations for the solution of problems in navigation, as they were understood in his time. He found his longitudes by observing eclipses of the moon. He also studied with enthusiastic interest the few works on the sphere, and on the Ptolemaic system of the universe, which were then in existence. The "Opusculum Sphericum," by Johannes de Sacrobosco, was the most popular manual of the principles of astronomy and cosmography in those days, and it was well known to Columbus. But the work to which he devoted his closest attention, and from which he derived his knowledge of Aristotle and Strabo, was the "Imago Mundi," written by Cardinal Pierre d'Ailly. The book was so familiar to him that his own copy, still preserved in the Colombian Library at Seville, has the margins annotated in his handwriting. Here he entered many things he had collected and read elsewhere. The "Imago Mundi" was finished in 1410, but not printed until seventy years afterwards; so that it can only just have reached the hands of Columbus during his residence at Lisbon, and perhaps it is more likely that he first obtained it in Spain. D'Ailly quotes largely from the "Opus Majus" of Roger Bacon and other authors, and fully discusses all the cosmographical theories of the time. Some of these, such as the uninhabitability of the torrid zone, Columbus was able to refute from his own experience, and he did so in the marginal notes.

The studies of Columbus confirmed him in his great idea that India might be reached by sailing westward. His mind was made up on this point, after years of study and reflection; but he left no stone unturned, and his inquiries were directed to every quarter. For he not only had to satisfy his own reason, but also to convince others. In the very year of his arrival in Portugal he had addressed a letter to a learned Florentine seeking for information. Paolo Toscanelli was born in 1397, and was the most celebrated astronomer of that age. He is

specially known for the gnomon which he constructed in
the Church of Santa Maria Novella at Florence. As a
reply to the request of his Genoese correspondent, whom
he evidently took to be a Portuguese, from the Lisbon
address, Toscanelli sent him a copy of a letter and of a
chart which he had previously despatched to a Canon of
Lisbon who had made similar inquiries.

Toscanelli held that the way to the spice-yielding
Indies by sailing westward was the shortest, and he
demonstrated his conclusion on the chart which formed
an enclosure to the letter. On this chart he showed,
on one side, all the coasts from Ireland to Guinea, with
the islands; and on the other side, the continent and
islands of the Indies, with the distance that must be
traversed to reach them. He then referred to the great
trade of the Indies. In the port of Zaiton alone, which
is one of the most beautiful and famous in the east, he
said that there were a hundred ships laden with pepper
at one time, without counting those laden with other
spices. Zaiton was a famous seaport of the Chinese
province of Fokien (Chwanchau-Fu), between Fuchow
and Amoy, and Toscanelli took this statement about
the pepper trade from the eighty-second chapter of
Marco Polo. He went on to say that the country was
large and populous, and that it was under the dominion
of a prince called the Grand Khan, whose usual residence
was Catay. In the time of Pope Eugenius IV. (1431–
1447), Toscanelli said that the Grand Khan sent an
ambassador to Rome, with whom he had conversations;
and that this ambassador dilated upon the greatness
of his country, where two hundred cities might be seen
with marble bridges built over the same river. Toscanelli then referred to his map again, where there were

twenty-six spaces divided by meridional lines, between Lisbon and the famous city of Quisay, and he said that each space measures 150 miles. He thus only allowed a distance of **less** than 4000 miles. **The Quisay** of Toscanelli is **the** Kinsay of **Marco Polo**, fully described in his chapters lxxvi. and lxxvii., and **now** called Hangchau, **south** of Shanghai. He said that **it** was in the province of Mango near Catay, and that it was twenty-five leagues round, the **name**, **as Marco Polo said**, meaning "City of Heaven." **Toscanelli** went on to say that from the island of Antilla **to that of** Cipango there were ten **spaces, equal to 225** leagues, **and** that Cipango so abounded in gems and **gold** that the temples and palaces **were covered** with **golden plates. The** letter is **dated** June 25, 1474.

In another **letter to Columbus the Fl**orentine astronomer encouraged **his** design **of** sailing westward, and **felt su**re that his **former** letter **had** demonstrated that **the voyage** was **not** so difficult as **was** supposed. He assured his **correspondent** that he would find populous **and** wealthy **cities, and** provinces abounding in riches, **and that the princes who reign in those** distant parts would **welcome the** opening **of** communication with **them.**

The **original of the** Toscanelli letter, **in** Latin, was **found in 1860, in the** Colombian Library at Seville, in the fly-leaf of a book which had belonged to Columbus, entitled, "Historia rerum ubique gestarum," by Eneas **Silvius.** Previously it **had only** been known in the Spanish translation of Las Casas, and **in the** Italian of **Ulloa.** The map is unhappily lost.

The letters from Toscanelli made a deep impression on Columbus, and confirmed him in **the** ideas he had

PORTRAIT OF LAS CASAS.

formed from a detailed examination of charts and books, and from an investigation of the geographical bearings of the question. But his studies did not interrupt those voyages by means of which he sought to increase his knowledge of maritime affairs. It is certain that he visited the Cape Verde Islands and Sierra Leone. We also know that he was at San Giorgio da Mina, the most remote settlement on the Guinea coast. He could not have been there before 1482, as in that year the settlement was first founded by order of King João II. It seems probable that he actually accompanied the expedition which sailed in December 1481, under the command of Diogo d'Azambuja. It consisted of nine caravels, and two merchant ships with stores and building materials. Arriving in January 1482, the troops were landed, and the fort of La Mina was immediately commenced. In twenty days the walls and tower were completed, and the fort was dedicated to St. George. This settlement was very successful, and considerable sums of gold were annually collected and sent to Portugal. On his return from the coast of Guinea, Columbus resolved to submit his matured scheme to João II., King of Portugal, and to propose to him the despatch of an expedition westward.

The arguments he put forward were explained long afterwards by his son Fernando, in an essay which was inserted by Las Casas in his History of the Indies. The first argument was that as all the earth and water in the world constitutes a sphere, and is consequently round, according to the opinions of several philosophical authorities, it was possible to go round it until men on one side stood foot to foot with those on the other. The second argument was that, as the greater part of this globe has been navigated and travelled over, the whole was now discovered except the space between the eastern end of India, of which Ptolemy * and Marinus had notices, and the isles of Cape Verde and the Azores. The third argument dealt with the distance. Columbus maintained that the untraversed portion could not be more than a third of the whole circumference. For Marinus had described fifteen hours out of the twenty-four in the eastern parts; but as he did not commence his description so far west as the Cape Verdes, there could not be more than eight hours between those islands and India. His fourth argument was a continuation of the third. He urged that Marinus had not included the most eastern part of the lands of India in his fifteen hours, and that, therefore, the distance was even less than eight hours from Portugal westward to the Indies, which might easily be sailed across in a short time. He fortified this last argument by the testimony of Ctesias in Strabo, of Nearchus, and Pliny, respecting the vast extent of Asia. He relied also on the authority of the learned Arab astronomer, Alfraganus, who held the length of a degree to be not more than $56\frac{2}{3}$ miles, which was his fifth argument. This was the origin of the cardinal error of Columbus respecting the earth's circumference; and his conclusions may have been unconsciously influenced by the wish to shorten the distance. The early Greek astronomers rather exaggerated the true circumference, and Ptolemy was not very far from the truth. But the later Arab writers, including Alfraganus, held the circumference of the earth to be only 20,400 miles, which would give 56 miles to a degree. According to Abulfeda this con-

* See Plate for Ptolemy's map.

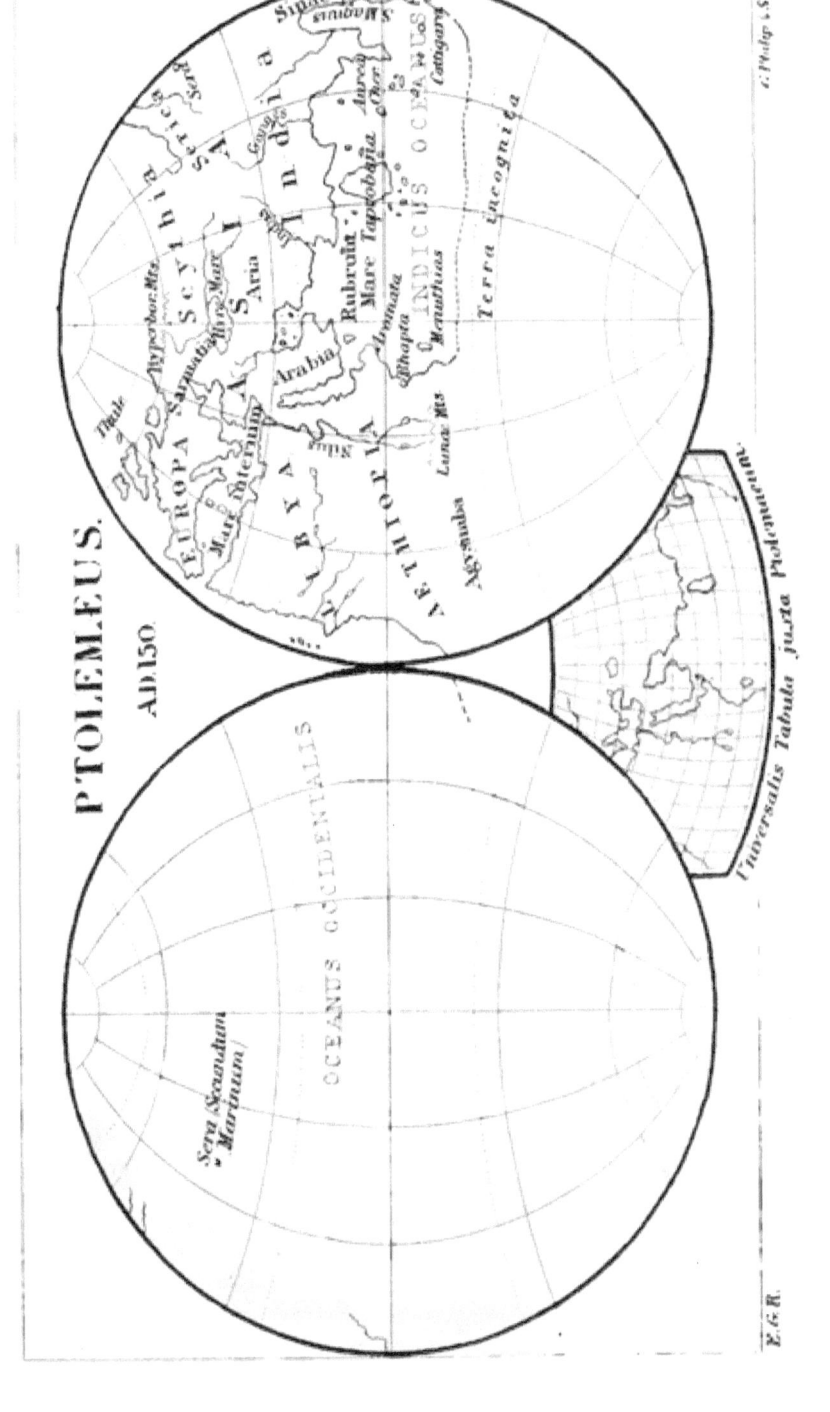

PTOLEMEUS.
A.D.150.

OCEANUS OCCIDENTALIS

Sera Secundum Marinum

EUROPA
Thule
Hyperbor. Mts
SCYTHIA
Sarmatia
Albis Mar
Seres
Seres
Mare Miterum
Mare
Aria
ASIA
Gangua
India
Sigae
Magnus S.
Aurea
Cher.
Catigara

Arabia
Rubrum
Mare Taprobana
Armata
Ethapta
Menuthias

LIBYA
Silua
Lunæ Mts

INDICUS OCEANUS

AETHIOPIA
Agysimba

Terra Incognita

Universalis Tabula juxta Ptolomæum.

G. Philip & Son.

E.G.R.

clusion is derived from the careful measurement of a
degree on the plain of Lingar, by order of the Khalifah
Almamun, in about A.D. 800. It was adopted by
Columbus, and was the main cause of the error in his
calculations.

The principal arguments were carefully drawn up by
Columbus, and submitted to João II., who referred the
question for decision to D^r. Diogo Ortiz Castellano,
Bishop of Ceuta, Dr. Calzadilla, Bishop of Viseu, and
the two physicians, Rodrigo and Joseph the Jew, who
had been joined with Behaim in his work connected
with the adaptation of the astrolabe. They unanimously
reported against Columbus, and his proposal was rejected.
The Bishop of Ceuta, however, advised that the illustrious Genoese should be amused with negotiations,
while a caravel was secretly despatched to test the correctness of his arguments. She encountered a gale and
gave up the attempt, returning to report that the voyage
was impossible. This treachery came to the ears of
Columbus, and he resolved to break off all correspondence with the Portuguese Government, and to seek for
sympathy and countenance elsewhere.

Columbus, alike in his voyages and his studies, had
been wrapped up in the work of maturing his great idea.
He had the two gifts which constitute genius, a vivid and
brilliant imagination and the power of taking trouble.
But gain was indifferent to him. He was as poor when
he left Portugal in 1484 as when he arrived in 1474.
Indeed he was poorer, for he had contracted debts to
some of his countrymen at Lisbon, debts which were all
honourably paid in after years. His wife had died, and
was buried in the chapel of Piedad, a place of interment
exclusively reserved for the Moniz family. Columbus

was left with his little son Diego.(1)   He resolved to **turn his steps to Spain**, and begin the whole labour of persuasion **over** again, with the same ardour and enthusiasm.   His wife's sister, **Violante**, or Brigulaga, **was** married to a certain inhabitant **of** Huelva named **Don** Miguel Muliarte.   He would place **Diego in** safe keeping with his aunt, while he went forth **to renew his** battle with the world.   Leaving his affairs at Lisbon **in** charge **of** his faithful friend **and** brother Bartolome, he set **out on** the long journey with **his** little son, penniless and **on foot.   He** was about to present the priceless gift of **his genius** and **his discovery to the crowns** of Castille and **Leon**.

NOTES.

(1) *The Marriage **of** Columbus in Portugal, and the Fables based on it.*

There is **much confusion** in the reference to the marriage of Columbus by his son, Fernando Columbus, as quoted in the "Historie," and by Las **Casas.**   They say that Filippa Moniz was **a daughter** of **Bartolomé Moniz** Perestrelo, **who was** then dead, **and that Columbus went to live** with his mother-in-law, who furnished **him with** charts and other sources of information from the effects of **her late** husband.   **Diego, the** son and heir **of** Columbus, also **told Las Casas some further** particulars, which he **wrote down from memory many years** afterwards. These were **that Columbus inherited** property **in** Porto Santo, and went there **to live with his wife;** and that as Madeira and Porto Santo **were** places **to which all the** Portuguese discovery ships resorted, he thus collected **much** information.

In the will **of** Diego his mother is called Moniz only, and **the name** Perestrelo is not mentioned.   Fernando Columbus had **a** confused idea about the Perestrelo relationship, taking the **wife** of Perestrelo to be the mother, whereas she was the aunt **of** the wife of Columbus.   Fructuoso, and the Portuguese

genealogists, tell us that Bartolomé Perestrelo had an only
child by Isabel Moniz, named Bartolomé, and that, far from
living at Porto Santo, she gave up her rights and left the island
thirty years before the marriage of Columbus. This is strong
evidence against the wife of Columbus having been a daughter
of Bartolomé Perestrelo, and in favour of her Moniz parentage.
Filippa, the wife of Columbus, was buried in the chapel of
Piedad, a place of interment reserved exclusively for the Moniz
family. She could not have been buried there if she had been
a Perestrelo. With the assumed Perestrelo connection all the
stories about the inheritance and the residence at Porto Santo
fall to the ground, together with a growth of fable that had
gathered round them. The memory of Las Casas, taxed to
record events of which he had been told many years before, no
doubt played him false. The fable, first noticed by Oviedo as
a rumour without foundation, that a pilot had been driven
across the ocean to an island of the new world, who gave
Columbus the information that enabled him to make the
voyage, rests on the other fable that he lived at Porto Santo
or Madeira. Gomara copied the story from Oviedo, omitting
the important fact that Oviedo believed it to be false. He
asserts that the pilot died at the house of Columbus in Madeira,
leaving him a chart, a journal, and observations. As soon as
the pilot and his companions were dead, Columbus proposed to
go in search of the land they had discovered, but concealed the
source of his information. If Columbus was silent, how, it may
be asked, did Gomara obtain his information, if not from his
own inventive brain? For Oviedo only alluded to the story
as a rumour, while Gomara states it as a fact. Gomara, however, admits that the name of the pilot was unknown. Acosta
and Mariana refer to the story, but without the name of the
pilot. Acosta indeed remarks that the name continued unknown in order that God might have all the honour. Benzoni
alluded to the tale as an envious fabrication of Gomara. Garcilasso de la Vega, writing 120 years after the event, gives the
most circumstantial version. Such fables usually grow and
thrive as the distance from the time increases. Garcilasso even
gives the name of the pilot, which was unknown to all the contemporaries and to all writers of the next generation. According
to him it was Alonzo Sanchez of Huelva. Invented to detract
from the merit of Columbus, the fable took shape under the

envious hand of Gomara, **and** grew until the anonymous pilot received a **name more** than a century afterwards. It is inexpressibly the **most** absurd **tale** that got into circulation among the detractors of the great Genoese, and the most unworthy. It **may** safely be assumed **that** no such person as Alonzo Sanchez ever **existed**, although **a modern street** has been named after him at Huelva.

(2) *The Compass.*

Two passages relating to the introduction of the use of the compass by **Flavio Gioja have been quoted from** Antonio **Beccadelli**, surnamed **"Il Panormita,"** (1374–1471), who was a Latin versifier, and author of a life of Alfonso of Aragon. One of these passages **is given** by **Henricus** Brencmannus **in his** *Dissertatio de Republica* **Amalfitana, and is** to the following effect: **"Prima** dedit **nautis usum** magnetis Amalphis." The other is cited **by Klaproth : "Inventrix praeclara** fuit magnetis Amalphis." **But Mr.** Major says that **he** has sought through the **pages of Beccadelli** for these **passages** in vain ("Prince **Henry,"** p. 59, *n.*).

(3) *Mention* **of** *Wife and Children by* *Columbus.*

In one of his letters, **Columbus makes** use of the following **expression : "*Yo dejé muger y fijos* que jamas vi ; *por ello*"—"I left wife and children whom** I never saw, for **it,"** *i.e.*, **for this** service. **This might be** interpreted that he **had** at **least two children** besides **Diego, and** that they and his wife **were** not dead when **he left** Lisbon, **but** died in his absence. There is, **however, a more** probable explanation. He may allude to **a second wife, namely, to** Beatriz Enriquez, and to his two sons, Diego and Fernando, whom he never, or scarcely ever, saw owing to his long absences. **He** does not say that he never saw them *again.* He uses the word *jamas* (never), but his knowledge of Spanish was imperfect, at least not that of a native, and he probably intended to say, hardly ever.

CHAPTER III.

COLUMBUS IN SPAIN.

HALF way between the Guadalquivir and the Guadiana there is an estuary formed by the two rivers Odiel and Tinto, which drain the Andalusian province of Huelva. The town of Huelva is on the Odiel, Moguer and the port of Palos on the Tinto. On the promontory to the east of the Tinto rose the old Franciscan monastery of Santa Maria de la Rabida. It was an irregularly-built pile, with no architectural pretensions, consisting of two cloisters with upper stories, a refectory, and a small church. But it is a conspicuous landmark out at sea, and is in a commanding position. The rocky promontory on which it stands is half covered with a gloomy pine forest, and a few cypress trees appeared over the wall of the convent garden.

On an evening of January 1485 a wayfarer was seated at the foot of the stone cross in front of the convent gate, which is still preserved, and a little boy rested on his knee. Columbus had toiled across the mountains of Aracena, and down the valley of the Rio Tinto, only to find that the Muliartes were not known at Palos. They appear to have moved to Seville. Without friends or resources, Columbus wandered up the sandy road from Palos to the lonely convent of La Rabida, sometimes leading the child by the hand, sometimes carrying him

. in his arms. After resting for a little while on the
steps of the cross, he rang the convent bell, and asked
for a glass of water and a little bread for his son.
When the doors were thrown open the monks were
struck by the noble presence of the wayfarer, and
invited him to bring the child into the convent.   Among

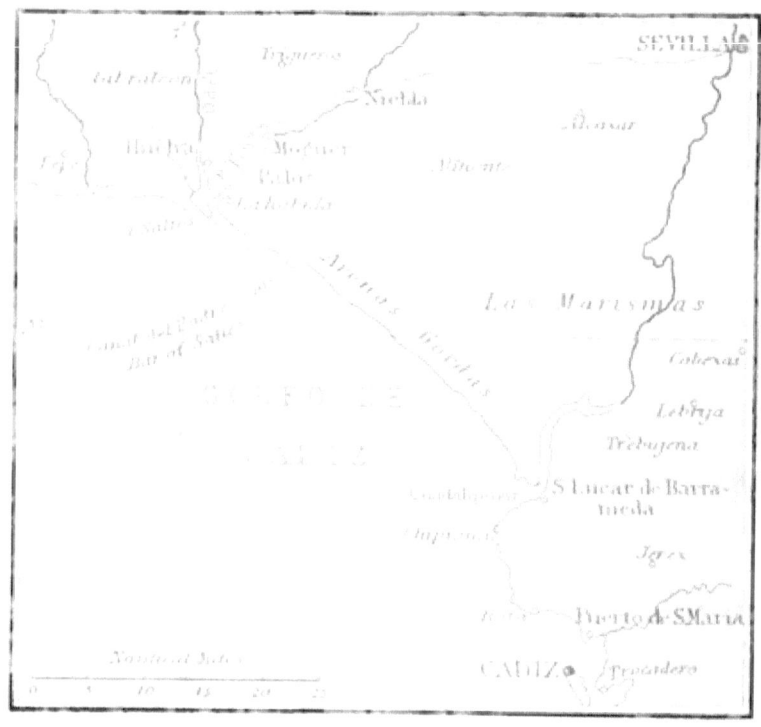

MAP FROM HUELVA TO CADIZ.

the brotherhood there was a young monk named Fray
Antonio de Marchena, who took a special interest in
the stranger, and entered into conversation with him.
Columbus afterwards spoke of this newly found friend
in most grateful terms.   He was induced, by the kindly
interest the young monk took in his affairs, and the un-
usual knowledge he displayed of astronomy and kindred

sciences, to explain to him the great project of the western voyage. Marchena listened with the closest attention, fully accepted the conclusions of Columbus, and entered warmly into all his hopes and aspirations. "He alone," declared the great discoverer in after years, "never treated my ideas with ridicule." Marchena even appears to have imparted a higher tone to his aspirations, and to have filled his mind with the grand thought of conveying Christianity across the ocean, and of saving millions from perdition. Henceforward this religious aspect of the enterprise ever held a leading place in the mind of Columbus.

The brotherhood of La Rabida gladly took charge of little Diego until other arrangements could be made for him; and the father, relieved of anxiety for his child, prepared to face the ridicule and contempt of the world, and to urge his scheme on the acceptance of the Spanish authorities. But he first had to find the means of earning his daily bread.

Taking a hopeful farewell of his little son, and of the kind-hearted monks of La Rabida, Columbus set out for the city of Seville. Assuming a Spanish form for his name, he henceforward called himself Cristoval Colon. We are told by Father Bernaldez * that Columbus got a living at Seville by the sale of printed books. But he soon formed the acquaintance of men of learning, such as his countrymen Antonio and Alessandro Geraldini. They probably obtained for him an introduction to the Count of Medina Celi, one of the greatest noblemen of Spain.

The founder of the house of Medina Celi was a gallant knight who came to the help of Henry of Trastamara

* *Historia de los Reyes Catolicos*, cap. cxviii.

with 250 lances, and was rewarded with the title of
Medina Celi in 1371, and with the hand of the Princess
Isabella de la Cerda. The fifth Count of Medina Celi *
was Don Luis de la Cerda, whose mother was a Mendoza, and heiress of Cogolludo, and whose wife was a
princess of Aragon. He entertained the illustrious
Genoese with generous hospitality at his lordship of
the port of Santa Maria, near Cadiz, and warmly encouraged him in his project. Indeed, this enlightened
nobleman was ready to fit out an expedition himself;
but he considered that so great an enterprise ought not
to be undertaken by a subject. He therefore resolved to
introduce Columbus to persons at court who could pro-
cure for him an interview with the Queen, and an
opportunity of explaining his scheme to their Catholic
majesties. When Columbus returned after his first
voyage, the Duke of Medina Celi wrote to the Cardinal
Mendoza, his uncle, on the 19th of March 1493, explaining the part he had taken in befriending the
Admiral at a time when he most needed friends. He
said that he entertained Columbus for a long time in
his house when he first came from Portugal, and when
he was meditating an appeal to the King of France.
The Duke wished to undertake the enterprise himself,
despatching Columbus from the port of Santa Maria with
three or four caravels. But he felt that such a business
was one for the Queen, and not for him. He therefore
wrote to her from Rota, a little town at the north entrance of the bay of Cadiz, submitting the matter for
her judgment, but offering to take part in it. She
replied that she wished Columbus to be sent to court,
where he was to be placed in charge of Alonzo de Quin-

* The Dukedom of Medina Celi was not created until December 1491.

tanilla. In another communication she caused the Count of Medina Coli to be informed that she did not look upon the matter as very certain, but that if anything came of it he should take part in the enterprise.

This was the occasion of the first arrival of Columbus at the court, which was then at Cordova, and of his presentation to Queen Isabella in the spring of 1486. The Queen was in the meridian of her life and of her reign when she first met the great seaman with whom she was destined to share the glory of the discovery of the new world. There can be no doubt that she was a woman of more than ordinary cleverness and force of character. She had passed through a long period in her brother's lifetime during which she had been exposed to extraordinary risks and dangers. She had avoided the one and overcome the others by the exercise of her own judgment, frequently acting against the advice of her councillors. She had not only maintained her position, but had dethroned her own niece, and had ascended the throne of Castille with the consent of the people. Her sole right was the will of the nation expressed by its representatives in Cortes. Her marriage with her cousin of Aragon was another serious risk, and their married life reflects great credit on the judgment and wisdom both of Ferdinand and Isabella. Their positions were most difficult, yet they succeeded in making the arrangement work harmoniously and without friction throughout their married lives. Isabella took for her share of the work the civil administration of Castille, and the provision of men and supplies in time of war. She conducted these affairs with remarkable ability. In her war with Portugal, from 1475 to 1479, she was completely successful: and since 1481 the joint sove-

reigns had been engaged in successive campaigns against
the Moors in Granada, which were only to close with
the expulsion of the Muslim from the Peninsula. In
1486 Isabella was in her thirty-seventh year, and she
had been twelve years on the throne. Her descent was
not wholly Spanish. Her grandmother on her father's
side, and her great-grandmother on her mother's side,
were Englishwomen. Hence she inherited a fair complexion, auburn hair, and blue eyes. She was above
the middle height, with a countenance full of animation
and intelligence, and an impulsive disposition kept under
control by the long practice of self-restraint.

Columbus, when he arrived at Cordova, was at once
befriended by Alonzo de Quintanilla, a knight of an
ancient family in Asturias, who held the high official
post of Minister of Finance for the kingdom of Castille.
Quintanilla relieved the Genoese stranger's needs, and
supplied him with meals from his own table. He also
introduced him to the Archbishop of Toledo, the great
Cardinal Mendoza, under whose powerful auspices an
interview with the Queen was arranged.

Isabella liked the illustrious Genoese from the first
time they met. His candour and obvious sincerity, his
earnestness, and the interesting character of his conversation touched her heart while it riveted her attention.
She at once decided that his extraordinary project at
least deserved careful investigation. The sovereigns
ordered that a committee, presided over by the Queen's
confessor, Fray Hernando de Talavera, the Prior of the
monastery of Santa Maria del Prado, near Valladolid,
should examine and report upon the arguments of Columbus. The sittings of the committee were held at
Cordova, while Ferdinand and Isabella were occupied

with the Moorish campaign, which in that summer comprised the siege of Loja.

The Prior of Prado was a man whose virtues had raised him from the humblest condition. He was an ecclesiastic of exemplary piety and the strictest probity, and had acquired great influence over the Queen. In any matter relating to the doctrine and discipline of the Church his judgment was sound, and his advice was always sure to be honest; but he was about as fit to give an opinion on the arguments of Columbus as the mule on which he rode. He was learned, pious, and amiable; and in after years, when he became Archbishop of Granada, he endeavoured to convert the Moors by argument and exhortation rather than by violence. He had read many a tome full of theological lore, but his narrow mind could not comprehend the novel ideas, so far outside the sphere of his thoughts, on which he was to sit in judgment. They would seem to him no better than the ravings of a madman. Dr. Rodrigo Maldonado, of the royal council, and other learned persons, including some versed in marine affairs, were joined with Talavera, but they could not enlighten him, and it was a case of the blind leading the blind.

Talavera's committee reported against Columbus. His arguments, they thought, were absurd in themselves, and were unsupported by any high authority. They were at variance with the expressed views of some of the Fathers of the Church, and the good Prior was not quite sure whether some of them had not a taint of heresy. Columbus was bitterly disappointed. He paced the streets of Cordova absorbed in thought, finding sympathy from very few, and exposed to the ridicule of the crowd, who thought he was mad. Boys in the streets ran after him, with their fingers pointed to their foreheads.

In this time of sadness and depression he found a most valued friend. Diego de Deza was Prior of the Dominican convent of San Estevan at Salamanca, Professor of Theology in the University, and tutor to Prince Juan. He was a man of the world, and was struck by the earnestness and intelligence of the Genoese, to whom he took a great liking. He resolved to befriend him, and he shrewdly foresaw that the most effectual way of doing so would be by affording opportunities of discussing the questions raised by the stranger, and of thus ventilating them and making them known to men who were more capable of forming a judgment than Talavera and his colleagues. Ferdinand and Isabella had been called into Galicia to suppress a disturbance raised by the Count of Lemos, and they intended to pass the winter of 1486-87 at Salamanca. Deza arranged that Columbus should also pass the winter at Salamanca. At that time the famous Spanish university was an important centre of learning. With its walls overlooking the river Tormes, a tributary of the Douro, its ancient bridge of many arches, and its numerous towers, the Spanish Oxford is a grand place even in its decay. The colleges and convents clustered round the solid romanesque cathedral of the twelfth century, with its beautiful central dome. The later renaissance cathedral by its side had not then been begun. The cloister on the south side was the place where the schools were held until the fifteenth century, and on one side of it is the ancient chapter-house. Within a very short walk from the cathedral was the convent of San Estevan with its richly-ornamented facade and great hall of "De Pro-

fundis," while other conventual and collegiate buildings
gave an academical tone to the old city, thronged as it
then was with professors and students. The professorial
chairs were not devoted exclusively to theology and other
priestly learning. Mathematics, physics, natural philosophy, and astronomy were also studied; nor were
Strabo, Pliny, and Ptolemy exclusively taught. The
works of Alfraganus and Regiomontanus were included
in the course, and Pedro Ciruelo, a graduate of Salamanca, had written a commentary on the *Sphæra Mundi*
of Sacrobosco. Aguilera, another graduate, had composed a work on the astrolabe. So that Columbus was
coming to a place where his reasoning would have some
chance of being appreciated.

The Prior of San Estevan determined not to lodge his
guest within the city, but in a country farm or grange
called Valcuebo, which belonged to the Dominicans, and
was at a short distance from the walls. It is described
as having been situated on a slight eminence, surrounded
by pretty rural scenery, and as well adapted for study
and meditation.* Hither the Dominican brethren came
to converse with their guest on the great deductions he
had drawn from a study of scientific books, and on the
reconciliation of his views with orthodox theology.
Sometimes the monks were accompanied in their walks
to Valcuebo by learned professors, and even by persons
of distinction attached to the court. Later in the winter
Deza and his monks received company in the hall of
their convent, called "De Profundis," when Columbus
would come into the city and hold conferences with men
of learning, at which numerous courtiers were present.
These assemblages for discussion, sometimes in the quiet

* Asensio, i. p. 117.

shades of Valcuebo, at others in the great hall of the convent, excited much interest both among the students and at court. The kindly object of Deza was secured. The question was thoroughly ventilated, and even those who withheld their assent admitted that it was a fitting subject for discussion. Ferdinand and Isabella left Salamanca for Cordova on the 29th of January 1487, and by that time Columbus could count among his friends and advocates the Cardinal Mendoza, the Count of Tendilla; Alonzo Quintanilla the treasurer of Castille; Luis Santangel who held the same office in Aragon; Gabriel Sanchez, the King's Treasurer; Diego Deza, the Prior of San Estevan; Don Andres Cabrera, and, perhaps most important of all, his wife, Beatriz Fernandez de Bobadilla, the Marquesa de Moya, and the Queen's oldest and dearest friend. Thus it was that accounts of the conferences held in the convent of San Estevan reached the ears of the King and Queen, and when they left Salamanca the ill effects of the report of Talavera were quite removed from their minds. Columbus followed the court to Cordova in March 1487, having during the winter made a great step towards the fulfilment of his aspirations. Thanks were chiefly due to the unfailing kindness and sagacious management of Diego Deza, the future Bishop of Palencia and Archbishop of Seville. It is difficult to realise that this very man was also the successor of Torquemada as Grand Inquisitor of Spain. We, however, need only know him as the generous and enlightened friend of the great Genoese. When this peaceful oasis in his stormy life came to an end, Columbus must have felt regret at leaving his quiet home at Valcuebo. The humble grange still stands at a distance of about three miles to the westward of Salamanca,

The country people have a tradition that, on the crest of a small hill near the house, now called "Tero de Colon," the future discoverer used to pass long hours conferring with his visitors or reading the Holy Scriptures in solitude. The present proprietor, Don Martin de Solis, has erected a monument on this site, consisting of a stone pyramid rising from a masonry substructure, and surmounted by a globe.

In the spring of 1487 Ferdinand commenced the siege of Malaga, while the Queen remained at Cordova to superintend the transmission of stores and provisions to the army. She had not forgotten Columbus, but caused it to be intimated to him that, as soon as the exigencies of the public service permitted it, she would give detailed attention to his representations. Meanwhile he was to consider himself to be attached to her court, and he received a payment of 3000 maravedis * on May 5th, and a similar sum on July 3rd. He was ordered to join the camp, and was present at the surrender of Malaga on the 18th of August. In October he received a third royal donation of 4000 maravedis. But no further progress was made. The sovereigns went to pass the winter at Zaragoza, and Columbus was left inactive at Cordova, where he found some consolation for his numerous disappointments and his long and weary waiting.

The noble family of Arana was established in the city of the Khalifahs, but, although of ancient lineage and highly connected, its members were not rich in this

34 maravedis = 1 real.
8 reals = 1 duro (dollar), 1 ounce of silver 4s. 6d.).
490 maravedis = 1 castellano (of gold).
393 maravedis = 1 ducado.

world's goods. Columbus was hospitably received in the house **of the** Aranas at Cordova, having probably brought introductions to them when he first arrived **from** Seville in 1486. They were delighted with their guest, were interested in his story, and the male members of the family formed for him a lasting friendship. **Diego** de Arana was one of the officers in his first **voyage, and Don Pedro** commanded a ship in the third. Another member of the family was a beautiful sister of Don Pedro, named Beatriz. **Her** sympathies **were** at once excited **by the** history **of the illustrious Genoese.** She conceived a passion for the **great** man, **who was** many years older than herself; **she** keenly felt his disappointments, **and** had an **enthusiastic** belief in his genius. When the dishearteni**ng** judgment of the Prior **of Prado became known, she** animated her lover in his **despondency, sustained his droopi**ng spirits by words of comfort and hope, **and at len**gth aroused a corresponding feeling **in** his heart. **During** the whole winter of 1487-88 they were thrown together, and in the course of the **long months she** consoled and encouraged **him, and** was his constant companion. **It** is still a disputed **point** whether **the** love of Columbus and Beatriz was **ever** sanctioned **by the** benediction of the Church.(1) On the 15th of August 1488 a son was born, and named Fer**nando.** There **was a** difference of ten years between the ages **of the** two sons; but Diego, who **had** probably been entrusted to **the** Muliartes at Seville, now found a second mother **in** Beatriz at Cordova, and remained there until he became a royal page in 1492.

The patience of Columbus was nearly exhausted. Year after year slipped away. He had found many kind and sympathising friends, but no progress was **made.** He began to think that his sole reliance must not be on Spain, and that if his great aspirations were ever to be fulfilled it behoved him to seek aid elsewhere. We have no exact information, but it seems probable that his brother Bartolomé had remained at Lisbon. If so, Columbus would naturally turn to him for counsel in his difficulties. This would explain the reason for his having obtained a safe conduct from the King of Portugal, dated at Avis on the 20th of March 1488, which is otherwise inexplicable. Early in the autumn of 1488, after the birth of Fernando, the two brothers conferred together at Lisbon. It is probable that Cristoforo made a final overture to the King of Portugal at this time; for, in one of his letters, he speaks of having urged the matter on that sovereign's attention for fourteen years—that would be from 1474 to 1488.* Cristoforo had made so many powerful friends in Spain, and the Queen had shown such favour to him on several occasions, that it was decided to be unwise to abandon all hope from that source. Cristoforo was therefore to return to Spain, while Bartolomé proceeded to London, and endeavoured to induce the King of England to undertake the project. Failing him, similar help was to be solicited from the Regent of France.

Bartolomé Columbus is described by Las Casas as a man of great valour, combined with prudence, more astute, and not so simple-minded as his brother Cristoforo. He was experienced in the affairs of the sea, and he had studied cosmography, and acquired the art of a draughtsman. The two brothers read and worked together. Bartolomé had less genius and more worldly wisdom than Cristoforo. He embarked for England.

* Letter to King Ferdinand, May 1505. Navarrete, iii. p. 526.

but his ship was captured by Easterling pirates, and he was detained for weeks and reduced to great poverty. At length he reached London, where he prepared a *mappemonde* with the intention of presenting it, when he should obtain an audience of King Henry VII. It was accompanied by a copy of Latin verses, also said to have been composed by Bartolomé, for it is signed by "the Genoese named Bartholomeus Columbus de Terrarossa, who executed this work in London on the 10th of February 1489." Oviedo * tells us that Henry ridiculed all that Columbus said, and looked upon his words as foolish. This is exactly what might be expected from that shrewd and clever, but narrow-minded and unimaginative usurper. Bartolomé consequently left England, and endeavoured to secure his brother's interests at the court of Anne of Beaujeu,† who then governed France for her young brother Charles VIII. There he remained until he was summoned to Spain in 1493.

Cristoforo was still at Lisbon in December 1488, for he saw the return of the expedition of Bartolomeu Diaz in that month, from the discovery of the Cape of Good Hope, and witnessed the reception of Diaz by the King of Portugal. He referred to these events in a marginal note in his copy of the *Imago Mundi* by Pierre d' Ailly.(2) The note concludes with these words " in quibus omnibus interfui :" referring to the arrival of Diaz and his presentation to the King. But he appears to have returned to Spain soon afterwards, and to have been at Cordova again, in the spring of 1489. For an order was given by the Queen on the 12th of May that Columbus should receive board and lodging

---

* Lib. i. cap. iv. i. p. 16.

† Harrisse, "Colomb," ii. p. 102.

in the towns through which he passed in his journeys.
In the same month Ferdinand revived the war against
the Moors, and began the siege of Baza; a difficult
and tedious operation, involving much hard fighting.
Columbus served in the besieging army, but the place
did not surrender until December.

Early in 1490 the court arrived at Seville, where
the sovereigns took up their residence for several
months. But Columbus failed to obtain attention to
his plans. The Queen was busily engaged in making
arrangements for the marriage of her daughter Isabella
with Affonso, the son of João II. of Portugal, and could
attend to nothing else. Then followed festivities and
tournaments which lasted until May. Columbus not
only continued to retain the friends he had made at
Salamanca, but he had secured many more. Nevertheless, he could not obtain another interview with the
Queen. In November she bade farewell to her daughter,
and at the opening of 1491 nothing was heard of but
preparations for the siege of Granada. At length the
patience of Columbus was exhausted. Years had been
wasted in Spain, and he seemed to be no nearer the
goal of his wishes than when he crossed the frontier.
He resolved to join his brother in France, and quitted
the court of Seville without communicating his intention
to a soul. But he would first bid farewell to his warm
hearted friends in the convent of La Rabida. Sadly
and wearily he set out on the road to Huelva, and he
rang the convent bell with a feeling of despondency,
almost of despair. His young son Diego was again his
companion. It was nearly seven years since he left
those gates, buoyant with hope, and confident that his
great destiny would be fulfilled. He stood before them

again with all his hopes crushed, and his plans frustrated —almost broken-hearted.

La Rabida proved the turning point of his life story. Here lived the men who had been true to him, through good report and evil report, who had never doubted him, never ridiculed his idea. He found Fray Antonio de Marchena as full of enthusiasm as ever, and refusing to entertain the idea of failure. Hope revived as the weary traveller crossed the threshold. The aged Guardian of the convent, Fray Juan Perez, was as cordial as the younger monk; and, moreover, he had the power as well as the will to help. Perez had been an accountant of the royal revenues in his youth, and, before he retired to La Rabida, he had preceded Talavera in the important and confidential post of confessor to the Queen. The conversations of Marchena had impressed him very favourably, and he was strongly inclined to give Columbus his cordial support. But before finally deciding, he resolved to give the extraordinary proposal of the great Genoese his full consideration. He therefore summoned to his counsels a learned physician of Palos, named Dr. Garci Hernandez.()

There was a very full discussion of all the arguments put forward by Columbus, and the old Guardian was convinced of the correctness of the calculations, and of the vast importance of the proposed enterprise. Perez resolved to write a letter to his old friend Queen Isabella, in which he urged her, in the strongest possible terms, not to abandon the grand project by which not only her kingdom would be aggrandised but her God would be served, through the agency of the learned stranger who was about to leave the country, but whom he detained at La Rabida until her answer arrived.

The letter was entrusted to a pilot of the little port of
Lepe, to the west of Palos, named Sebastian Rodriguez.
Ferdinand and Isabella were besieging Granada, and
they were so resolved never to raise the siege until the
Moors surrendered that they had converted their camp
into a town, which was named Santa Fé. Rodriguez
did not let the grass grow under his feet. He returned
with a reply from the Queen within fourteen days of
his leaving La Rabida.

Isabella ordered her old confessor, Juan Perez, to
come to her at once. The Guardian lost no time. He
borrowed a mule from one Juan Rodriguez Cabezudo
of Moguer, and set out alone that very night, without
regard either for the difficulties of the road or the
rigours of the season. The Queen had never forgotten
the favourable impression made upon her by Columbus,
and his numerous friends at court had kept his project
in her mind. It really only needed a strong stimulus,
such as was supplied by the impressive letter of her
old confessor, to re-awaken her interest, even when
engaged in such absorbing work as the final destruction
of Muslim power in Spain. The presence and per-
suasions of Juan Perez clinched the matter. Columbus
had not long to wait for the result of his friend's mission.
In a few days Diego Prieto, one of the chief magistrates
of Palos, rode up to the convent door. He brought
orders from the Queen that Columbus was to proceed
at once to Santa Fé, and a sum of money. 20,000
maravedis in florins, with which he was to buy a mule
and a suitable outfit to enable him to appear at court.
There was also a letter from Perez to the physician
Garci Hernandez, and another to Columbus, which was
as follows :—

"Our Lord has listened to the prayer of His servant
The wise and virtuous Isabella, touched by the grace of
heaven, gave a favourable hearing to the words of this poor
monk. All has turned out well. Far from despising your
project, she has adopted it from this time, and she has summoned you to court to propose the means which seem best to
you for the execution of the designs of Providence. My heart
swims in a sea of comfort, and my spirit leaps with joy in
the Lord. Start at once, for the Queen waits for you, and I
much more than she. Commend me to the prayers of my
brethren, and of your little Diego. The grace of God be with
you, and may our Lady of La Rabida accompany you."

On the arrival of Columbus at Santa Fè he found that
Perez and his other friends had been very active, and
he had several encouraging interviews with the Queen.
He learnt from her that she was determined to undertake the enterprise, and she was not deterred by the
concessions he demanded. They must have appeared
enormous to ordinary men when coming from a poor
stranger. But they represented, from the point of view
of Columbus, the greatness and importance of the enterprise, and he firmly refused to abate them. Satisfied
with the assurances of Isabella, he readily consented to
the reasonable delay rendered necessary by the exigencies
of the siege, and he himself took part in the various
combats outside the walls, giving proofs of the valour
which was the accompaniment of his prudence and of
his lofty aspirations. At last Granada fell on the 2nd
of January 1492.

The concessions demanded by Columbus then came
before the royal council; and their acceptance was
strongly opposed by Talavera and others, who looked
upon such demands from a penniless adventurer as extravagant, and indeed preposterous. They reported that

it was impossible for the Crown to surrender prerogatives and rights of such importance in perpetuity. Columbus could not be induced to recede from his position. When he was informed of the decision, he mounted his mule and left Granada by the Cordova road, intending to join his brother, and submit his project for the acceptance of the King of France.

This famous act in the life of Columbus needs careful study. To the Talaveras of all time there only appears an arrogant adventurer, without modesty or moderation, who was making extravagant demands for his own personal advantage in payment of services the value of which he presumptuously exaggerated, and which he had not performed. But to the careful historian, who tries to gauge the motives which actuate great men in critical moments of their lives, this is a superficial and an erroneous view. Columbus had been working with untiring enthusiasm for many years to secure the realisation of his ideas. His studies and his experience taught him that those ideas were based on solid facts. He knew that his project would lead to results of supreme importance affecting the whole world. He not only did not exaggerate those results, but his measurement of them fell far short of the truth. He knew that they would be great, but he did not know how great. He had faced ridicule, poverty, and hardships for the sake of his grand convictions, and he was ready to do so again. Poverty or riches were nothing to him, and could be nothing. But he saw, with the unerring prevision of genius, that the enterprise must be undertaken with a full acknowledgment of its supreme importance. The government or the sovereign that refused so to recognise its significance was unworthy to undertake it. The privileges and the dignities he demanded were **not for himself** but **for the** achievement he represented; and **that achievement** would not be worthily done, **if** it was not **done in** this spirit. It **cannot be doubted** that he had pondered the matter long and deeply, and **that his conduct in** leaving Granada **was the** result **of a resolution taken** long **before,** and **from which nothing would divert him.** His **was** the **master-mind.** He worked **for his** fellow-men **and** for **his God, and the instrument he used** must either be **fashioned by** his hand, **or give place to one of** better and truer **metal.** Some such **view as this** was, no doubt, the **one taken by** Columbus. He believed that he was called to a great wor**k by the Divine** Will, and that **the full** recognition **of its greatness was** incumbent on those **who were to assist him. His conduct** was not that of an adventurer **seeking paltry gain for** himself. It was **that of a** great **man, destined to be** one of the lights **of the** world, acting **from a supreme sense of** duty.

The departure **of Columbus caused the** greatest consternation among all the true friends **of** their country. The Marquesa de Moya immediately sought an interview with the **Queen,** and **entreated her to** recall **the great** navigator **and concede his demands.** Her entreaties **were seconded** by those **of Luis** de Santangel. Isabella had **not thought the** demands excessive. This noble woman **was able** to appreciate the **lofty** motives of her petitioner, **and in some** measure **to** comprehend the workings **of his mind. The work, she** decided, should **be the work** of Castille **alone. But** the great difficulty **was to find** the **means of** despatching an expedition. The exhausting war had been a terrible drain on the **treasury. When her** mind was made up she was resolved that no difficulty in raising the funds should form an obstacle. She declared that she would give up her own jewels, but Santangel obviated this sacrifice by finding the needful supplies from another source. To the great joy of his friends, Isabella announced her resolution that the expedition should be despatched, and that the concessions demanded by Columbus should be granted.

A messenger was despatched to recall Columbus. He was overtaken near a bridge called "Pinos," which was celebrated for the many chivalrous feats of arms performed by Moors and Christians round its approaches during the recent war. It is six miles from Granada. He turned his mule's head, rode back to Santa Fé, and immediately had an interview with the Queen. In concert with her husband she gave the necessary orders, and the capitulation, prepared by the secretary, Juan de Coloma, was signed at Santa Fé by their Highnesses on the 17th of April 1492. In return for his discoveries, Columbus was created Admiral of the Ocean in all those islands and continents that he might discover. The title was granted to him for his life, and to his heirs for ever, with the same rights and prerogatives as were enjoyed by the Admiral of Castille. Columbus was also appointed Viceroy and Governor-General of all the lands he might discover. He was also to have a tenth of all the precious metals discovered within the jurisdiction of his Admiralty, and he had the privilege of receiving an eighth part of the profits made by any ship to the equipment of which he had contributed an eighth share. On the 30th Columbus received the grant of his titles, inscribed on parchment, with a leaden seal pendant from silken threads, and signed by the King and Queen. On the same day the citizens of Palos were ordered to supply the two caravels, which they had been condemned to furnish for the Queen's use without pay during twelve months, as a punishment for certain acts of theirs committed at some former period to the injury of the royal service. Columbus hastened to La Rabida to make preparations for the equipment of his expedition, kissing hands and taking leave of their Highnesses at Granada on the 12th of May 1492.

NOTES.

[1] *Question of the Marriage of Beatriz Enriquez.*

Some of the biographers of Columbus believe that his intercourse with Beatriz Enriquez was unauthorised by the Church. Others maintain that they were married.

The arguments against the marriage are as follows. It is alleged that there is no mention of a wife in the transactions of the Admiral's life after he left Portugal. In his will he recommended Beatriz to his son Diego not as his wife, but as a person to whom he had been under great obligations, and respecting whom his conscience was burdened, for a reason which he did not think it right to explain. Las Casas said that Columbus "instituted his son Diego his heir-general, and if Diego had no children, then his heir was to be Don Fernando, his natural son" (iii. 194). In a letter dated 1500 Columbus said, "I left my wife and children whom I never saw," and it is assumed that he referred to his Portuguese wife. Also, when he was expecting to be lost in the storm, on his return from his first voyage, he expressed his anguish at leaving his sons orphans "both of father and mother."

On the side of the marriage it is urged that Beatriz was of noble birth, and that an improper connection would have been resented by her family. This was so far from being the case that her male relations continued to be among the Admiral's most steady friends. Her cousin, Diego de Arana, was in the first voyage of Columbus; and her brother, Pedro de Arana, commanded one of the Admiral's ships in the third voyage. The boy Fernando became a page of the Queen, an honour which would not have been conferred on a bastard. When Columbus wrote, in 1500, "I left my wife and sons for this service, whom I never (*jamas*) saw," he could not have referred to his Portuguese wife, because she only bore him one child. He must have referred to Beatriz Enriquez as his wife, and to his sons Diego and Fernando. So that there is mention of her by the Admiral as his wife. He uses the word *jamas*, which would mean *never* if taken literally : but Columbus, as a foreigner, may well have used the word in the sense of *hardly ever*. The sentence written during the storm that he would leave his sons orphans of father and mother would have been true as regards Diego, but not as regards Fernando. Beatriz was the mother of Fernando whether she was married or not. To imply that Fernando had no mother was a slip of the pen, either on the part of Columbus when writing in a gale of wind, or of Las Casas, who made the abstract from his journal. If Beatriz had not been his wife, he would have charged her own son, Fernando, who was well off, with her maintenance ; but he imposed this duty on his eldest son as heir-general, because the maintenance of his widow ought to come out of his entailed estate as Admiral. In his instructions to his son Diego before he sailed on his third voyage, the Admiral charged the young man to look upon Beatriz Enriquez as his mother (Asensio, i. 105). In his instructions to Diego before he sailed on his last voyage in 1502, he again charged his son to treat Beatriz as his mother. Las Casas did not necessarily use the word "natural" in the sense of illegitimate. In those days it was used for sons of the body, whether illegitimate or not, in contra-distinction to sons-in-law or step-sons. Pantaleone Bavarello is officially called "fillius *legitimus et naturalis*" in a deed dated in 1517, contemporary with Las Casas.

All the arguments against the marriage are thus disposed of, except the curious wording of the Admiral's will, which is per-plexing. The explanation may be that Columbus was married to Beatriz Enriquez, but that some ecclesiastical obstacle sub-sequently caused the marriage to be dissolved. The obstacle may have been a pre-contract to a person named Enriquez, for the maiden name of Beatriz was Arana. This would explain everything. The Admiral's conscience may have been uneasy because he did not sufficiently assure himself before marriage that no obstacle existed.

(2) *Question respecting the Voyage of Bartolomé Diaz.*

The marginal note is on folio 13 of the copy of the *Imago Mundi* in the Columbine Library at Seville, as follows : " Nota quod hoc anno de SS in mense descambri apulit in ulixbona bartolomeus didacus capitaneus trium caravelarum quem miserat serenissimus rex portugalie in guinea ad tentandum terram et renunciavit ipso serenisimo regi prout navigaverat ultra quan navigatam leuch 600 videlicet 450 ad austrum et 150 ad aquilonem usque uno promontorium per ipsum nominatum cabo de boa esperança quem in agesinba estimamus quodque in eo loco invenit se distare per astrolabium ultra linea equinociali gradus 45 quem ultimum locum distat ab ulixbona leuche 3100 quem viagium pictavit et scripsit de leucha in leucha in una carta navigacionis ut oculi visui ostenderet ipso serenissimo regi in quibus omnibus interfui."

Las Casas declared that this note was in the handwriting of Bartholomew Columbus, which he knew well, and he therefore assumed that Bartholomew was in the expedition of Diaz. But this is not possible. Diaz returned in December. Bartholomew Columbus finished his great map in London early in the following February. This gives little over a month for him to land at Lisbon, embark for England, be captured by pirates, be detained several weeks, find his way to London, and complete the drawing of an elaborate *mappa-monde*. It is impossible.

Varnhagen, who was well acquainted with the handwritings, declared that Las Casas was mistaken, and that the marginal note is in the hand of Christopher Columbus. Ascensio, another expert, came to the same conclusion. It can be proved that Christopher was in Spain during part of the time occupied by the voyage of Diaz. But the words "in quibus omnibus interfui" do not imply that the writer was in the voyage with Diaz, but merely that he took part in his reception and was present at his landing. Christopher Columbus was probably in Lisbon at that time. Bartholomew Columbus could not have been there.

(3) *The Visits to La Rabida.*

The authority for the visits of Columbus to La Rabida, and for the story of his asking for bread and water for his little boy, is Garci Hernandez, the physician of Palos. He gave evidence at the trial instituted, with permission from the Crown, by Diego Columbus to recover the viceroyalty inherited from his father. The evidence reads as if there had only been one visit to La Rabida. This led Mr. Harrisse to think that there was only one visit, namely, that in 1491. But the evidence is given as a statement, whereas it was really a series of replies to questions. Closer scrutiny shows that some sentences refer to the first and others to the second visit. One proof that the first visit is also referred to appears in the fact that Hernandez calls young Diego a little child (*niño*). This would be a correct description of him in 1484, but not in 1491. Las Casas mentions the first visit to La Rabida with the child (i. p. 227).

A curious confusion has also arisen between Antonio de Marchena, the monk who received Columbus on his first visit, and the guardian, Juan Perez, who befriended him in 1491. Many authors have mixed them together, and made them into one monk named Perez de Marchena. Marchena was a young monk versed in science, Perez was the aged guardian of the convent. Columbus speaks of them as distinct individuals.

CHAPTER IV.

THE FIRST VOYAGE.

COLUMBUS was forty-six years of age when he at length obtained the fulfilment of his life-long aspirations. His hair had become prematurely grey. Naturally quick-tempered, he had subdued this feeling by the practice of self-restraint. He was a man acquainted with adversity, and his countenance wore a somewhat melancholy expression when at rest; but he was eloquent in discourse, engaging and affable with strangers. His magnanimity and inborn courtesy, joined to long intimacy with courts, gave him a noble and dignified bearing. Yet there was still much in common between the enthusiastic young wool-comber of Genoa and the venerated Admiral of the Ocean Sea; the same love of kindred and of home, the same industry and close attention to details, the same kindliness of heart and consideration for comrades.

During the third week of May, Columbus remained at La Rabida in close consultation with his friends Marchena and Perez, and with the good physician Garci Hernandez. They sat in the courtyard, under the shade of fig trees, and discussed measures for obtaining ships, and the still more difficult task of obtaining men.

The little town of Palos lies in a hollow among hills, a quarter a of mile from the right bank of the Rio Tinto. It consists of two streets of humble white-washed houses, and there is a ruin of a large house which once belonged to the Pinzons. Just above, on the crest of the hill, are the ruins of an old Moorish castle. On Wednesday, the 23rd of May, it was publicly notified in the church of St. George at Palos that the town was to furnish the Admiral with two caravels. This old church, which was originally a mosque, stands on the brow of a hill outside the town, with a view along a little valley to the river. The same image of St. George and the Dragon stands over the high altar as was there in the time of Columbus, when the people crowded out of the church on that Wednesday in May. They must find the two caravels in obedience to the royal order, but no man was forced to sail on board of them. This was a mad voyage, sailing away into the mysterious unknown never to be seen again ; and as the sailors of Palos and Moguer discussed the matter the terrors of the undertaking seemed to increase, and they became more and more reluctant to ship with Columbus. This difficulty in persuading men to join the expedition was fortunately overcome owing to the Admiral having secured the good will of the most influential family in Palos.

The Pinzon family was highly esteemed in the district, owing to the enterprise its members had shown in commercial ventures, to their credit and wealth, and to their probity. The three brothers—Martin Alonzo, Vicente Yanez, and Francisco Martin Pinzon—were pilots and shipowners. The guardian of La Rabida, Fray Juan Perez, applied to Martin Alonzo, the elder and most influential of the three. While he appealed to his patriotism, he also stimulated him by the hope of gain, and as soon as he was duly impressed he introduced the pilot to Fray Marchena and Columbus. After a few conferences in the old cloister, Pinzon was convinced

E

by the eloquence of the Admiral. He and his brothers
entered heart and soul into the enterprise. They proved
to be excellent recruiting agents, and, by their powers
of persuasion and coercion, they soon altered the aspect
of affairs. Provisions and stores were collected, two
caravels were fitted out, and men were entered from
Palos, Moguer, and Huelva, as well as from the little
port of Lepe to the westward, and from Ayamonte, still
farther west on the Portuguese frontier. A third vessel
was at length secured, much larger than the other two,
apparently called the *Santa Maria* or *Marigalante*, but
Columbus himself only mentions her as the *Capitana*.
Her owner, who was to go in her as master, was a young
pilot named Juan de la Cosa, a native of Santoña, on the
north coast of Spain.

The *Santa Maria* was called a "nao" or ship, and
she was of about 100 tons burden. She was built with a
deck, a high poop, and a forecastle. Two of her masts
had square sails, but the mizzen was lateen rigged. On
the mainmast was the mainsail (*maestra*) and a main-
topsail (*gabia*). The foremast had a foresail (called
trinquete), and there was a spritsail (*cebadera*). The
courses were enlarged in fair weather by lacing canvas
to their leeches, called *bonetas*. The mizzen lateen sail
was called *metana*. The armament consisted of the
small guns used on board ship in those days, called
lombards. The crew numbered fifty-two men all told,
including the Admiral and the principal officers of the
expedition. But while the crews of the two caravels
were all natives of Palos and the neighbouring towns,
the Admiral's ship's company came from various parts
of the Peninsula. Two were natives of Santoña, followers of Juan de la Cosa, and all those who hailed

Oceanica Classic

OCEANICA CLASSIS.

From Leandro de Cosco's Latin version of the Admiral's letter (Rome, 1493).

CRISTOVAL COLON

ALMIRANTE MAYOR   *DEL MAR OCCEANO,*
Virrey y Governador   General de las Yndias,
su Descubridor   y Conquistador.

from the north of Spain were probably known to him, and attracted by his presence.

Among these it is very interesting to find an Englishman from Lajes, a small place in Galicia, not far from Coruña. He is entered in the list as Tallarte de Lajes (*Ingles*). An English mariner trading to Coruña may well have married there and settled down at Lajes until his love of adventure was aroused by the news from Palos. Tallarte would be the Spanish form of Allard or Alard, a corruption of Aethelwald. The first English admiral was Gervase Alard of Winchelsea in 1306, and there were Alards for several generations, afterwards, who were sailors of Winchelsea. It is not improbable that one of them was among the first discoverers of the new world, and a companion of Columbus. There was also an Irishman among the crew, one William of Galway.

The chief magistrate, or master-at-arms, was Diego de Arana, a near relation of the lady, whether wife or not, at Cordova, with whom the Admiral left his sons. Young Diego had been nominated as page to Prince Juan, the heir-apparent of Castille and Aragon, on the 8th of May, with a salary of 9,400 maravedis a year, but he remained at Cordova for a time with Beatriz Enriquez to complete his education. The complement of the *Santa Maria*, officers and men, was as follows :—

Admiral	Cristoval Colon.	*Overseer*	Rodrigo Sanchez of Segovia.
Master and Owner	Juan de la Cosa of Santoña.	*Secretary*	Rodrigo de Escobedo.
Pilot	Sancho Ruiz.	*Master at Arms*	*Diego de Arana of Cordova.
Boatswain	Maestre Diego.		
Surgeon	Maestre Alonso of Moguer.	*Volunteer*	*Pedro Gutierrez. (*A gentleman of the King's bedchamber.*)
Assistant Surgeon	Maestre Juan.		

Volunteer . .	{ *Bachiller Bernar- do de Tapia of Ledesma.	*Diego — of Mamblas.
		*Diego de Mendoza.
		*Diego de Montalvan of Jaen.
Steward . .	Pedro Terreros.	
Admiral's Servant .	} Diego de Salcedo.	*Domingo de Bermeo.
		*Francisco de Godoy of Seville.
Page . . .	Pedro de Acevedo.	
Interpreter .	{ Luis de Torres. (A converted Jew.)	*Francisco de Vergara of Seville.
Seamen .	Rodrigo de Jerez.	*Francisco —— of Aranda.
..	Garcia Ruiz of Santoña.	*Francisco Henao of Avila.
..	Pedro de Villa of Santoña.	*Francisco Jimenes of Seville.
..	Rodrigo Escobar.	
..	Francisco of Hu- elva.	*Gabriel Baraona of Belmonte.
..	Roy Fernandez of Huelva.	Gonzalo Fernandez of Segovia.
	Pedro Bilbao of Larrabezua.	Gonzalo Fernandez of Leon.
..	*Alonzo Velez of Seville.	*Guillermo Ires (of Galway).
..	*Alonzo Perez Osorio.	*Jorge Gonzalez of Trigueros.
Asceer and Silversmith	} *Castillo of Seville.	*Juan de Cueva.
		*Juan Patiño of La Serena.
Seamen	*Antonio of Jaen.	*Juan del Barco of Avila.
..	*Alvaro Perez Osorio.	
..	*Cristoval de Alamo of Niebla.	*Pedro Carbacho of Caceres.
..	*Diego Garcia of Jerez.	*Pedro —— of Talavera.
..	*Diego de Tordoya of Cabeza de Vaca.	*Sebastian of Majorca.
..	*Diego de Capilla of Almeden.	*Tallarte de Lajes (Ingles.)

The second vessel was commanded by Martin Alonzo
Pinzon, who had done so much towards the equipment of
the expedition. Señor Asensio truly observes that if
"Colon was the head, Pinzon was the right arm." His
caravel of about fifty tons was named the *Pinta*, and
was owned by Gomez Rascon and Cristoval Quintero.

who were on board as seamen. Another seaman was
Juan Bermudez, the future discoverer of Bermuda.
One of Pinzon's brothers was with him as master. The
Pinta was strongly built, and was originally lateen
rigged on all three masts. She was the fastest sailer
in the little squadron. Her complement numbered
eighteen, as follows :—

Captain	. Martin Alonzo Pinzon.	*Seamen*	Juan de Sevilla.
Master	. Francisco Martin Pinzon.	,,	Garcia Alonzo.
		,,	Gomez Rascon (*owner*).
Pilot	. . Cristoval Garcia Sarmiento.		Gristoval Quintero (*owner*).
Boatswain	Bartolomé Garcia.		Diego Bermudez.
Surgeon	. Garci Hernandez.		Juan Bermudez.
Purser	. Juan de Jerez.		Francisco Garcia Gallegos of Moguer.
Caulker	. Juan Perez.		
Seamen	. Rodrigo Bermudez de Triana of Alcala de la Guadaira.		Francisco Garcia Vallejo.
,,	Juan Rodriguez Bermejo of Molinos.	,,	Pedro de Arcos.

The third vessel, a caravel of forty tons, was owned
by the Niño family of Palos, three of whom sailed in
her. Hence she was called the *Niña*. She was commanded by Vicente Yanez Pinzon, and had a complement of eighteen men.

Captain	. Vicente Yanez Pinzon.	*Seamen*	Diego de Torpa.
		,,	Francisco Fernandez.
Master and Part Owner	} Juan Niño.	,,	Hernando de Porcuna.
		,,	Juan de Urniga.
Pilots	. . . Pero Alonso Niño.	,,	Juan Moreillo.
	Bartolomé Roldan.	,,	Juan del Villar.
Seamen	. Francisco Niño.	,,	Juan de Mendoza.
,,	Gutierrez Perez.	,,	Martin de Logrosan.
,,	Juan Ortiz.	,,	Pedro de Foronda.
,,	Alonso Gutierrez Querido.	,,	Tristan de San Jorge.

Total of the three ships eighty-eight souls. (Those with an asterisk were left behind at Navidad.)

Throughout the months of June and July the greatest activity was displayed, and Palos had never seen so busy a time. The funds supplied to the Queen by Santangel were altogether insufficient, but the necessary sums were obtained through friends of the Admiral, or well-wishers of the expedition, on the personal guarantee of Columbus. It has been suggested that Pinzon advanced what was needed. On this point there is no reliable information; but one thing is certain, all loans were honourably repaid.

Columbus held many consultations with his friends at La Rabida, and with Pinzon, respecting the route. He relied for guidance chiefly on the chart that had been sent to him by Toscanelli. But he was about to enter a new and unknown world, where no existing chart would be of any avail. All that was known of the old world could be of no use to him there. It is fortunate, however, that in this very year stock should have been taken of geographical knowledge up to 1492. Then Columbus began the great work of his life, the discovery of the new world; and in the same year Martin Behaim completed the great work of his life, his terrestrial globe.

The globe of Martin Behaim, still preserved at Nuremburg, is now the oldest terrestrial globe in existence. It is drawn on parchment, beautifully illuminated and ornamented, and stretched on a sphere 20 inches in diameter. Its great importance consists in the fact that it is an exact representation of the geographical knowledge of the period immediately preceding the first voyage of Columbus. As the map of Toscanelli is lost,

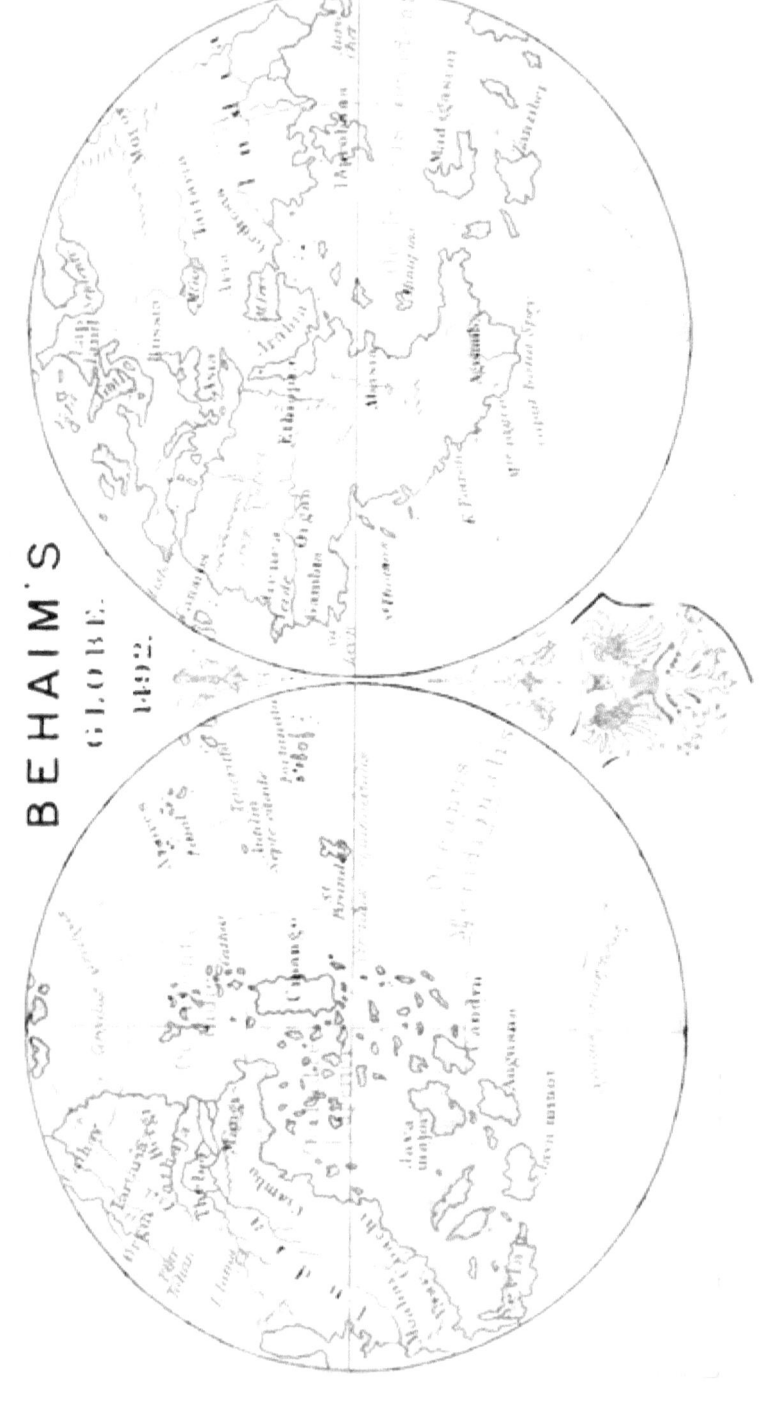

BEHAIM'S GLOBE. 1492.

the Behaim globe is the only extant document which does this. For the first time the two hemispheres are clearly shown, with the route round the Cape to India, and the discoveries of Marco Polo. The western edge of the Western Hemisphere is fringed by the Azores, Canary Isles, and Cape Verdes. West of Ireland is the island of Brazil, and west of the Cape Verde Isles is the fabulous Isle of St. Brandon, bordering on the equator. Then, with no very great width of ocean between, Zipangu and a labyrinth of smaller islands stretches across the torrid zone and far into the temperate zones on either side, occupying the centre of the hemisphere. The eastern side is occupied with a continental mass, having Cathay marked on it, and other names made known by Marco Polo. Behaim's globe should be well imprinted on the reader's mind before accompanying Columbus across the Atlantic; for it represents the state of geographical knowledge when he sailed, and shows exactly the nature of his expectations. The map of Toscanelli must have closely resembled that of Behaim, with the addition of the island of Antilla in mid ocean ; and the names of Zaiton, Quisay, Mango, Catay, conspicuously shown on the eastern continent. With the map of Toscanelli, Columbus took with him the materials for drawing plane charts, the declination tables of Regiomontanus, and the work of Pierre d'Ailly. The quadrants, astrolabes, and compasses were prepared under the personal supervision of the Admiral, who paid close attention to every detail.

At length everything was ready. It was the 2nd of August. Columbus and all his men assembled in the little church of St. George, at Palos, and received the Holy Communion. Fray Juan Perez exhorted them to trust in God and in their Admiral, and dismissed them with his benediction, and a solemn prayer for success and prosperity to the expedition. The majority were natives of the district, and these went from the church to bid a last farewell to their families. On the same day vessels of the State passed down the river, laden with all the Jews in the province of Huelva, to be taken across and landed on the coast of Africa. Cruel bigotry and scientific research were brought, as it were, face to face.

Half an hour before sunrise, on Friday the 3rd of August, a great crowd was assembled along the banks of the Odiel. As the sun appeared over La Rabida the three little vessels weighed their anchors. The Admiral displayed the standard of Castille, and let fall his mainsail, on which was painted the sign of the redemption. Fetching way, the squadron sailed over the bar of Saltes, men waving their caps and women their handkerchiefs until the white lateen sails looked like the wings of gulls hovering over the sea. Few ever expected to see them again. The adventurers seemed to be going to certain death. It was a memorable event, and it was felt to be so, but none knew how great. Looking back at all that has grown out of it in the four centuries that have since elapsed, we now know that the sailing of those three little boats over the bar of Saltes was, since the fall of Rome, the most momentous event in the world's history.

The Admiral shaped a course for the Canaries—the *Pinta* leading, the *Santa Maria* next; but the *Niña* proved a bad sailer, owing to the defective cut of her lateen sails. Columbus reckoned his distances run in Italian miles, of which there were four to a league; and he calculated that on the first day he ran sixty miles before sunset with a fresh breeze from the land. On the 6th, when there was a chopping sea, the rudder of the *Pinta* came unshipped without any apparent cause, suspicion falling on Rascon and Quintero, the owners, who were serving on board, and are supposed to have repented of the agreement they had made. Pinzon managed to rig a temporary makeshift, and in that plight they reached Grand Canary. Here the *Pinta* received a thorough overhaul, the rudder was repaired, and her rig was altered from lateen to square sails on the fore and main masts. The little squadron then proceeded to the island of Gomera, anchoring there on the 2nd of September. In passing Teneriffe they observed a great column of flame issuing from the peak—a magnificent sight, which might have been considered as a commemoration of the voyage, but which the sailors rather perversely looked upon as a bad omen.

Gomera is the most westerly of the Canary Islands, and the little squadron found a sheltered anchorage in the bay on the north-east side, off the town of Palmas. Some days were occupied in getting the ships ready for sea, and filling them up with water and provisions. In the morning of the 6th of September Columbus sailed from Gomera, but for two days he was becalmed between that island and Teneriffe, and on the 8th there was a head sea; but on Sunday the 9th the ships were fairly on their voyage. The men at the helm, however, steered badly from want of experience, and the Admiral had occasion to reprimand them several times for letting the ship's head fall off. The people were fearful of the unheard of character of the voyage. Many were timid and credulous; so the Admiral arranged that the reckon-

ing for their inspection should make the ship's runs
shorter than the real estimate entered in his own journal.
If the voyage proved to be a long one, they would have
so much less cause for alarm and panic. This was a precaution fully justified by the circumstances.

On the 13th of September Columbus first observed
that the variation was westerly. He had crossed the
line of no variation, which was then in about the longitude of Flores, the westernmost of the Azores. By the
17th the variation had increased to a point westerly,
and the strange phenomenon excited and alarmed the
sailors—

> " The compass, like an old friend, false at last,
>   In our most need, appalled them."

The Admiral, with unwearied patience and kindness
of manner, laboured to allay their fears. After thinking the matter over in his own mind, he hit upon a
probable cause, which he carefully explained to his
people. The conduct of the needle had been detected
by observing the bearing of the pole star. It was not,
however, the needle, but the pole star that was in an
abnormal state. It was describing a circle in the
heavens, while the compass was as true as ever. This
satisfied the men. The proposition was correct. The
pole star really does move in a circle; but this movement was very far from being equal to the change
observed in the direction of the needle. Columbus did
not discover the variation of the compass on this occasion. It is scarcely credible that variation had not
been remarked by the numerous intelligent seamen who
had long used the compass in navigating the Mediterranean from end to end. What Columbus did discover

was far more important. This was the change of variation from easterly to westerly after crossing a point of no variation.

Columbus was now in the region of the trade-wind, always blowing his ships westward in exquisite weather, and a smooth sea, generally like the river at Seville, so that the men often bathed alongside. The sunrises and sunsets were indescribably lovely, and sometimes the clouds on the horizon formed themselves into such close resemblance to islands that the most experienced eye might have been deceived. The lonely adventurers watched every sign with eagerness and anxiety. Antilla or St. Brandan might rise above the horizon at any moment. Many birds were seen, and sometimes a ship's boy knocked one down with a stone. The direction of their flight was carefully noted. Columbus mentions a *garajao*, the name for a tern in the Canary Islands, and *rabia de junco*, which means literally "tail of a rush." This is the boatswain-bird, which breeds at Bermuda and in the Bahamas. The two long projecting central tail feathers are never seen separated and seem to form one, like a marlin-spike, whence the name. Another bird frequently seen is called an *alcatraz* by Columbus. The word means a pelican, and was also applied to the largest bird in the southern seas, our word *albatross* being a corruption of it. But the *alcatraz* of Columbus was a dark-brown gannet very common in the tropics, called a *booby* by sailors. They also saw the *rabiforcado*, "which makes the *alcatraz* throw up what it has swallowed and eats it itself, living on nothing else. There are many at the Cape de Verde Islands." *Rabiforcado* is the frigate or man-o'-war bird, which breeds on the Bahamas and goes far out to sea: but this robber gull must be the long-tailed skua of the Canaries, which ranges over the Atlantic as far as the Cape of Good Hope. *Pardales*, or sandpipers, were also seen. In the sea, playing round the ship, there were many fish, and they caught *toninas* and *dorados*.

Soon after the panic about the conduct of the needle had been appeased, the ships began to pass quantities of weed, and soon the sea seemed to be covered with it. A fresh alarm arose. They were sailing into a sea of weed, which would get denser and denser until the ships would become immovable, and they would all perish. Columbus reasoned with them, and explained away this imaginary danger also. Yet it was a strange sight even to himself. He examined the gulf weed, which looked so golden and beautiful as it floated in masses on the deep blue sea, and noticed that it was covered with small balls like berries. This Sargasso Sea, first described by Columbus, is midway in the Atlantic, between the Azores, Canaries, and Cape Verdes. Andrea Bianco, in his map of 1436, gave it the name of " Mar de Baga," from the vesicles on the gulf weed (*Fucus natans*), like berries, or *bagas* in Portuguese. The northern border of the weedy sea is near the Azores, and its existence must have been reported to Bianco through some of the early Genoese discoverers of that group. Columbus was being introduced to the mighty oceanic phenomena which his acute intellect would enable him to grasp in part, but it would be centuries before they would be pieced together and understood as one harmonious whole. Maury likens the Atlantic, with its Gulf Stream, to a basin of water to which a circular motion has been given. Any floating substances put into the basin will be found crowding together near its centre where there is the least motion.

"Just such a basin is the Atlantic Ocean to the Gulf Stream, and the Sargasso Sea is the centre of the whirl."

A great cause of alarm to the sailors was the constant easterly wind, always blowing day after day, a source of anxiety which increased as day succeeded day. It made them think that they would never be able to return home. Fortunately there was a contrary wind on the 22nd of September. The Admiral observed that "this foul wind was very necessary for me, for my people had become much excited, thinking that no winds blew in those seas that would carry the ships back to Spain." He doubtless made much capital out of that one day of westerly breezes.

After they had been three weeks at sea, the Admiral began to think that Antilla should be near at hand. He closed with the *Pinta* to compare notes with Martin Alonzo Pinzon on the 23rd, and to converse about certain islands on the chart of Toscanelli, and the chart was sent from one ship to the other on a line. Both agreed that they must be very near Antilla. At sunset Martin Alonzo hailed the *Santa Maria*, and with great joy announced that he saw land. He turned the hands up, and repeated the "Gloria in excelsis Deo." Columbus did the same. The crews manned the rigging in all three ships, and declared that it was land. A course was shaped towards it over a smooth sea, but it was soon found that they had been deceived by the fantastic shape of clouds on the horizon. For the next few days the air was soft and mild, and the sea smooth as a river, with much weed floating on its surface. On the 4th of October the best run was made during the voyage, upwards of 200 miles. But the great length of the passage across was telling upon the spirits of the men, and the

frequent false alarms made them doubt whether land
would ever appear, and caused irritation. A mutinous
spirit became more and more manifest. The Admiral
tried to encourage them by assurances that land was
close at hand; but he added that "whether they com-
plained or not, he would go on until he found the Indies,
with the help of God." This was on the 10th of October.
The standing order was that the *Pinta* and *Niña* should
close the Admiral at sunrise and sunset.

On the 11th the sea was rougher than at any other
time during the voyage, but there were several signs
that land was close at hand. A green rush floated past;
and the *Pinta* saw a cane and a pole, and picked up a
small stick with marks of having been cut. The *Niña*
reported having seen a small branch with berries on it.
Sunset was at 5.41 P.M., when the course was altered
from W.S.W. to west. Orders were given to keep a very
sharp look-out; and the *Pinta*, being the best sailer,
went ahead.

At 10 P.M. the Admiral was on the poop of the flagship with other officers, gazing intently into the dark-
ness, the moon not having yet risen. Suddenly he saw
a light with an uncertain motion, and he called to Pedro
Gutierrez, who also saw it. He asked the overseer,
Rodrigo Sanchez, whether he saw it; but he did not
make it out, owing to his not being in a position whence
it could be visible. The Admiral saw the light again
once or twice, like a wax taper raised and lowered. He
made certain that land was in sight, but determined to
keep the same course until daylight, under very easy
sail. While the Admiral was conversing with his officers
about the light, a seaman on the forecastle, a native of
Lepe, saw it also, and cried out, "A light! land!" Sal

cedo, the Admiral's servant, told him that the Admiral had seen the light; and Columbus himself replied that he had seen the light on shore already.[1]

It had been full moon on the 5th of October. On the night of the 11th the moon rose at 11 P.M., and at 2 A.M. on the morning of the 12th the look-out man on board the *Pinta*, whose name was Rodrigo de Triana, reported land in sight. At that hour the moon was 39° above the horizon on the 12th of October 1492, and would have been shining brightly on the sandy shores of an island some miles ahead—the moon being in its third quarter, and a little behind the look-out man. The ships clewed up all the sails, except the courses, and hove-to until daylight. They then anchored at the eastern end of the south shore of a moderate-sized island.

Columbus went on shore in an armed boat, with Rodrigo de Escovedo, the secretary, and Rodrigo Sanchez, the overseer, followed by Martin Alonzo and Vicente Yanez Pinzon, the captains of the two other ships. The Admiral sprang on the beach, bearing the royal standard of Spain, knelt down and returned thanks, solemnly taking possession of the land in the name of the King and Queen. The two captains each carried a banner with a green cross, and on either side of it the letters F and Y, surmounted by crowns. A crowd of natives stood round as spectators, and the Admiral presented them with caps and strings of beads. Afterwards many of them swam off to the ships with parrots and skeins of cotton, which they bartered for hawks' bells and beads. They wore no clothing, and had fine well-shaped bodies, good faces, and coarse hair like a horse's mane, cut short. Their only arms were spears tipped with fish bone, and, seeing some with the marks

F

of wounds, the Admiral concluded that parties from the
mainland came to hunt and capture them. No women
were visible. They had dug out canoes, some very large
and capable of carrying forty or forty-five men, others

LANDFALL OF COLUMBUS.

From " La lettera delle isole che ha trovato nuovamente il Re di Spagna
(Florence, 1493).

smaller, which they managed very skilfully with a
paddle. The island was a good size (*bien grande*) and
very level, bright with green trees, with plenty of water,
and a very large lagoon in the centre.

Thus was the mighty enterprise achieved, mighty in
its conception, still more important in its results.
Columbus believed that he had discovered a new route
to the Indies. He had done infinitely more. He had
discovered another continent, and the consequences of
his discovery would be vast beyond what it was possible
for the greatest genius of the fifteenth century even to
conceive. The probable distance run, between Gomera
and the newly discovered island, was 3105 miles, or an
average of 105 miles a day in thirty-five days, the course
W. 5° S. The longest run was 200 miles, or eight knots
an hour, the average rate four knots. The difference
of latitude between Gomera and the new land was 235
miles, and Columbus noticed that the colour of the skins
of his islanders was the same as that of the natives of
the Canary Islands, which he attributed to their abode
on nearly the same parallels.

The Admiral supposed that he was near the Zipangu
of Toscanelli's chart, and was anxious to continue his
voyage. He determined to remain at anchor until the
afternoon of the second day, and then to steer to the
south-west, for he had seen some small gold ornaments
worn by the islanders, and had understood their signs to
mean that there was a king to the south who possessed
much gold. At dawn on the 14th the boats were sent to
explore the eastern coast of the island by rounding the
south-east point. It was found to trend N.N.E., and the
people came out to the boats swimming and in canoes,
bringing them food and fresh water, and saying that
they had come from heaven. A reef was found to
encircle the island, with perfectly smooth water between
it and the shore. The Admiral, looking for strategic
points, observed a peninsula which could easily be con-

verted into an island, where a strong fort might be
built.

Returning from this boat expedition, the Admiral got
under weigh the same afternoon and resumed the
voyage, taking with him six of the natives to learn
Spanish and act as guides. The native name of the
island was Guanahaní, with the accent on the last
syllable, as Las Casas informs us. The Admiral gave it
the name of San Salvador. It is identical with the
modern Watling Island, one of the Bahamas, as I propose to demonstrate in the next chapter.

On leaving San Salvador the cloud appearances on the
horizon so closely resembled land that Columbus believed he was in sight of a great number of islands, and
he even hesitated towards which he should shape his
course. The wind was light from the eastward, and
soon carried his ships across to the only real island,
about five to seven leagues distant. He found it to be
five miles long on the side facing San Salvador, and ten
miles * east and west. He sailed along the south side to
the westward until night, and, observing another larger
island to the westward, he clewed up the sails and
anchored off the western point. As he was resolved not
to pass any island without taking possession, he landed
at dawn on the 16th of October, and gave the island the
name of Santa Maria de la Concepcion. It is the Rum
Cay of modern maps. The wind came round to south-east
while he was on shore, so he hurried on board again,
and the squadron was under weigh by 10 A.M. Two of
the natives of Guanahaní, who had been carried off,
here effected their escape from the *Niña* by swimming

* Las Casas has leagues, an obvious clerical error

to a large canoe. When another native came with skeins
of cotton to barter, the Admiral gave him several presents and allowed him to depart with his canoe, that
his favourable report might counteract the contrary
accounts of the fugitives.

The island seen from Santa Maria appeared to be very
long, and its northern end bore west about nine leagues.
It was low, and trended north-west and south-east for
about twenty-eight leagues. The Admiral named it Fernandina. Navigating all that day, with calms and light
winds, he succeeded in edging away to the south, and at
dawn on the 17th he anchored at its southern end, near
a village. Fernandina is the Long Island of modern
charts. Having taken in water, the Admiral weighed
at noon, with the intention of sailing round Fernandina,
the wind being south. He came off a remarkable harbour with two entrances divided by a rocky islet, both
very narrow. Within there was ample room for a
hundred ships if there had been sufficient depth. He
sent the water-casks to be filled, and occupied the time
in strolling among the trees and observing their differ-
ences, how some resembled palms, while many others
were different from any he had ever seen. Shaping a
course north-west, he came to a part of the coast where
it trended more to the west, but here the wind shifted
and blew from north-west. The Admiral therefore abandoned his plan of circumnavigating Fernandina, and
sailed south during the night, anchoring again at the
south-east end of the island.

Columbus had been told by the natives of an island
called Samoete to the southward, where there was said
to be much gold. At dawn on the 19th he made sail in
search of it, scattering the ships to make more certain

of sighting the **land**. Sailing south-east, he ordered the *Pinta* to hold an east, and the *Niña* a south-south-east course until noon, and then to close. After three hours an island was sighted, and all three ships arrived at its **northern point** before **noon**, where there is a rocky islet and **a reef** of rocks outside. The men from **Guanahaní** called **this** new island Samoete, and Columbus **named it** Isabella. It bore east from Fernandina, **and is the** modern Crooked **Island**. The coast trended from the islet westward **for twelve** leagues to a promontory named **Cabo** Hermoso. Here he anchored, and **found** the land to be the **most beautiful he had yet seen, while a** delicious scent **of flowers was wafted** from **the shore.** He landed **and saw** many **natives, who brought balls of** cotton and small **spears to barter, but** he **could find** no king, and **the gold** appeared **to be a** delusion. Tidings **were received of countries called** Cuba **and** Bohio, and **on October 24th the Admiral weighed, with the intention of** proceeding **to Cuba. It came on to blow very** hard with rain, and the squadron was obliged to lie to, but on the 25th a good run was made with a west-south-west and west course, until **a** group of **islets** was sighted and named " Las Islas **de** Arenas." This is now called Ragged Isles. Here t**hey** anchored, and on the **27th** they ran fifty-eight miles south-south-west until land was sighted. On Sunday, the 28th of October, Columbus **entered the** mouth of a fine river where there was safe anchorage, and gazed **upon** a land the most lovely his eyes had ever rested **on. It** was a river in Cuba, which **he named** San Salvador, now known as Puerto Naranjo. **He gave the name** of Juana to the island of Cuba, in honour of the young Prince **of** Spain.

NOTE.

Reward for Sighting the Land.

The Queen had intimated her intention of giving a reward to the man who first sighted land. No one doubted that the light was on shore, nor was any such doubt expressed for the next three centuries. This having been universally accepted, the Admiral himself was undoubtedly the first who saw it. He pointed it out to Pedro Gutierrez. The story of a sailor from Lepe having seen it from the forecastle is told by Oviedo, who adds that Salcedo, the Admiral's servant, told the man at once that Columbus had already seen it. There was no question about the look-out man of the *Pinta*, who reported land four hours afterwards, because all believed that the light was on shore. The name of the look-out man is doubtful. It was reported to the Admiral at the time that his name was Rodrigo de Triana. Oviedo gives the same name; but one of the sailors of the *Pinta*, named Francisco Garcia Vallejo of Moguer, in a deposition taken on 1st October 1515, speaking from memory twenty-two years after the event, gave evidence that the look-out man's name was Juan Rodriguez Bermejo of Molinos. Two witnesses who were not in the expedition, and who spoke from hearsay, probably from what they had heard from Vallejo, also said that the name was Juan Bermejo. Navarrete has suggested (iv. p. 613) that Rodrigo de Triana and Juan Rodriguez Bermejo of Molinos were one and the same name, Columbus, as a foreigner, mistaking Rodrigo for Rodriguez, and that he put Triana because the man was known there, though a native of Molinos. This conjecture is scarcely admissible, and is disposed of by the fact that both names occur in the list of the *Pinta's* crew. The Admiral, making the entry at the time, was no doubt right.

When the narrative of the voyage, including these facts about sighting the land, came before the Queen, she could have no doubt that her reward belonged to the Admiral. The appearance in the form of a light kindled her religious enthusiasm, for she held it to be a sign of the Gospel's light accompanying the ships across the ocean. Under such circumstances it would have been very difficult and most ungracious for the

Admiral to have declined her reward, in order that it might be given to a man who had not earned it. It consisted of a pension of 10,000 maravedis, secured on dues from the shambles at Cordova, and he at once transferred it to Beatriz Enriquez. Oviedo says (lib. ii. cap. 5) that the seaman from Lepe, who saw the light after the Admiral and Gutierrez, was so disgusted at not receiving the reward that he went over to Africa and became a renegade. Oviedo got this gossip years afterwards from Vicente Yanez Pinzon and Hernan Perez Matheos. The latter was not in the expedition. The story was probably untrue. If the man became an apostate his not getting the reward certainly could not have been the pretext for he had no ground whatever for expecting it, and no right to it. Navarrete, in referring to Oviedo, assumes that it was the look-out man of the *Pinta*, and not the man from Lepe who saw the light, that turned renegade. And other writers have followed him. But the words of Oviedo are quite clear : "Aquel marinero que dixo primero que veia *lumbre* en tierra, tornado despues en España, porque no se le dieron las albricias, despechado de aquesto, se paso en Africa y renego de la fé."

A charge of unfairness has been made against Columbus in this matter. Such a charge is unfounded and absurd. It is true that, with our later geographical knowledge, many of us are now convinced that the light must have been in a canoe and not on shore. But this does not affect the fact that, at the time, the light was universally believed to be on the land, and that the Queen, in that belief, decided with perfect fairness.

CHAPTER V.

THE LANDFALL.

It is an interesting point to ascertain, without doubt, the landfall of Columbus by the identification of the island of Guanahani or San Salvador. The materials for a decision are to be found in the description of the island, and in the course taken thence to Cuba, which are given in the full abstract of the journal of Columbus by Las Casas, as well as in the authoritative maps of the pilot, Juan de la Cosa, and of Herrera. If the course is traced back from Cuba with close attention to the words of the journal, an island will be reached which will agree with the description, and which must needs be Guanahani. The maps of La Cosa and Herrera will afford corroborative testimony. Yet, in spite of these unerring guides, the highest authorities have differed on the subject : the controversy has extended over a hundred years, and the landfall has been claimed for at least five different islands. Discussion has at least cleared the ground, the disputants have ably exposed each other's fallacies, and to such an extent that an inquirer is now able to investigate the question with an assurance of ascertaining the actual landfall of Columbus.

The journal of Columbus kept during his first voyage is lost ; but a full abstract, in the handwriting of Las Casas, was found among the archives of the Duke of

Infantado in 1791. It is written on parchment in a
small folio volume of seventy-six leaves. It was examined by the learned Don Juan Bautista Muñoz, the
cosmographer of the Indies, and author of the *Historia
del Nuevo Mundo*, and was published by Navarrete in
1825.* This is the sole authority for the position
of the landfall, and all arguments must be based
on it.

But some side light is thrown on the question by
early maps with details derived from the great navigator's original charts. No charts under his own hand
have come down to us, but a map drawn by Juan de la
Cosa, the pilot and owner of the *Santa Maria*, is still
in existence. It was drawn in 1500 by that very able
draughtsman, who was the companion of the Admiral on
his first and second voyages. After having been lost
for centuries, the map of La Cosa was found and identified by Baron A. von Humboldt in 1832, in the library
of Baron Walchenaer at Paris. At the sale of that
library in 1853 it was bought by the Queen of Spain,
and is now in the Naval Museum at Madrid. It is
drawn on ox hide, 5 feet 9 inches long by 3 feet 2
inches, and is illustrated by a picture of St. Christopher
bearing the infant Christ across a river, in allusion to
the achievement of Columbus. The Bahama Islands
are shown as discovered in 1492, with one or two additions derived from information collected afterwards.
On the map of Juan de la Cosa the complete Bahama
group is not shown, Guanahani being the most northern

---

* The journal of Columbus was translated into English and published by Samuel Kettell (Boston, 1827) at the suggestion of Mr.
Ticknor. It was also translated in part by Admiral Becher, and
published in his "Landfall of Columbus," London, 1856.

of the outer islands. Samana and Mainana (Mariguana) appear as islands to the south of, and distinct from, Guanahani.

In 1600 a more complete and accurate map of the Bahamas was published by Antonio de Herrera, the official historian of the Indies. Herrera had access to every available source of information. He had the charts drawn by Columbus himself, the map of Juan de la Cosa, and all the results of subsequent visits to the group. He was thus able to correct the La Cosa map, and to add the islands to the north of Guanahani. The map of Herrera retains the old native names, most of which have disappeared from modern maps. Guanahani, Yumay (for Long Island or Fernandina), Someto or Xumeto, Samana, and Mayaguana, occur both on the map of Juan de la Cosa and on that of Herrera.

A comparison between the map of Herrera and a modern chart will show that Herrera gives all the islands, and that the relative positions are correct. Consequently it is quite clear that no other island can be Guanahani (the landfall) which appears on Herrera's map, where Guanahani also appears. Neither Samana nor Mayaguana can be themselves and Guanahani at the same time. It is also clear that the landfall must be in the same relative position with reference to the other islands as is given to Guanahani by Herrera. The shapes of the islands are distorted, but their relative positions are correct on his map. An inspection of it shows that Guanahani is the fifth of the outer islands of the Bahamas, counting from the north. Then turning to a modern chart, it will be found that the fifth island is the one now called Watling Island.

Herrera.	*Modern Chart.*
1. Yucayoneque.	Abaco.
2. Cigateo.	Eleuthera.
3. Curateo.	Little S. Salvador.
4. Guanima.	Cat Island.
5. Guanahani.	Watling Island.
6. Triangula.	Rocks near Samana.
7. Samana.	Samana.
8. Mayaguana.	Mayaguana.
9. Amana and Caicos.	Caicos group.
10. Canciba.	Turks Island.

Herrera's map establishes one requirement that must be satisfied in deciding to which island belongs the honour of being the true landfall of Columbus. It must be the fifth of the outer Bahama Islands, counting from the north. There are twenty-three other requirements contained in the journal of Columbus, and all twenty-four must be satisfied by the island which is to be identified as the landfall :

1. It must be the fifth of the outer Bahamas, counting from the north.
2. It must be of moderate size. *Bien grande*, also *Isleta*.*
3. A very large lagoon in the centre.
4. The south half of the east side trending N.N.E.
5. Encircled by a reef.
6. Quite flat.
7. A tongue of land, like an island, yet not one, forming a harbour at the south part of the east side.
8. The second island bearing south-west, distant seven leagues.
9. The side of the second island approached from Guanahani trending north and south.
10. Length of one side of the second island five miles, of the other ten miles.

* 11th October 1492 and 5th January 1493 of Journal.

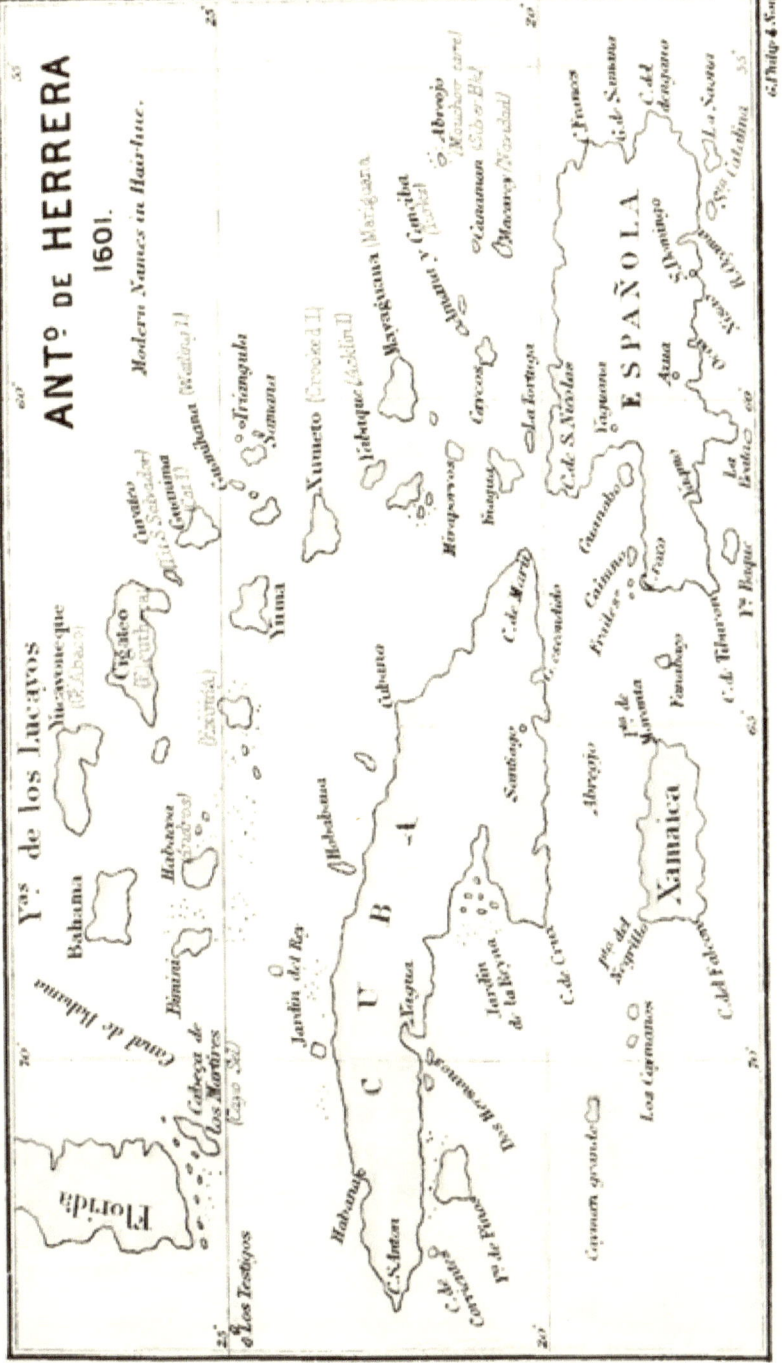

11. The third island in sight from the second.

12. Third island eight leagues from the second, bearing west.

13. Trend of the third island N.N.W. and S.S.E., twenty leagues long.

14. A large shallow harbour on the south-west side of the third island, with two entrances.

15. Part of the west coast of the third island trending east and west.

16. The native name of the fourth island must be Samoete.

17. Fourth island not in sight from the third.

18. Fourth island east of the third.

19. A rocky islet at the north end of the fourth island.

20. Fourth island higher than the others.

21. Coast of fourth island makes an angle, and seemed to form two islands with an islet between them.

22. Twelve leagues from the rocky islet at the north end of the fourth island to the South Cape.

23. Fourth island fifty-seven miles north-east from the "Islas de Arena."

24. Cuba in sight after sailing fifty-one miles S.S.W. from "Islas de Arena."

Navarrete, Kettell (the translator of the Journal of Columbus), Mr. G. Gibbs, who had resided some years on Turks Island, and Mr. Major, in the first edition of his "Select Letters of Columbus," contend that Turks Island was the landfall. Turks Island is the tenth of the outer Bahama Islands on Herrera's map, while Guanahani is the fifth, so that the authority of Herrera is against them. This little island is indeed the most southern of the Bahama group. It is true that it possesses two of the requirements. It has large lagoons, and is surrounded by a reef. Navarrete was induced to fix upon Turks Island because he erroneously assumed that Columbus always shaped a westerly course in sailing from island to island. He therefore thought that

Guanahani must be the most easterly of the Bahamas, in order to make room for sufficient westing in the rest of the voyage to Cuba. He thought that the second island was Caicos, the third Inagua Grande, the fourth Inagua Chica. But the course from Turks Island to Caicos would be north of west, while the course of Columbus to the second island was south-west. The third island of Columbus was in sight from the second. Inagua Chica is not in sight from Caicos. The third island of Columbus was sixty miles long. Inagua Chica is only twelve miles long. The fourth island of Columbus bore east from the third. Inagua Grande bears south-west from Inagua Chica. For these reasons Turks Island cannot be Guanahani.

Washington Irving, Humboldt, De la Roquette in a voluminous note to his French translation of Navarrete, and José Maria Asensio, the latest biographer of Columbus, maintain that Cat Island (called San Salvador on some maps of the seventeenth and eighteenth centuries) was the landfall of Columbus. Irving and Humboldt satisfactorily disprove the theory of Navarrete, but their own is still more untenable.

Cat Island is the fourth of the outer Bahama Islands on Herrera's map. Guanahani is the fifth. The principal argument relied upon in support of Cat Island is that it was named San Salvador on maps of the seventeenth century. Washington Irving says : " Established opinions should not be lightly molested. It is a good old rule that ought to be kept in mind in curious research as well as in territorial dealings. Do not disturb the ancient landmarks." But Cat Island is not an ancient landmark. It was first called San Salvador on the West India map in Blaeu's Dutch Atlas of 1635

for no earthly reason but the caprice of the draughtsman.
The same map was published at Leyden by Joannes de
Laet. D'Anville copied in 1746, and so the name got
into some later maps. It represents no tradition, and
has no title whatever to be called an ancient landmark.

Cat Island does not meet a single one of the requirements of the case. Guanahaní had a very large lagoon
in the centre; Cat Island has none. Guanahaní was
low; Cat Island is the loftiest in the Bahamas. Guanahaní had a reef round it; Cat Island has none. The
south part of the east side of Guanahaní trended N.N.E. :
on Cat Island it trends N.N.W., and there is no peninsula forming a harbour as on Guanahaní. The two
islands could not be more different.

It is suggested by Washington Irving that the numerous islands which Columbus thought he saw when he
sailed from Guanahaní were the "Cadena" or chain of
rocks extending northwards from Exuma Island. But
these rocks are not in sight from Cat Island, the nearest
being thirty-six miles away.

Columbus makes his second island south-west twenty-
one miles from Guanahaní. Irving makes him steer S.S.E.
to Concepcion Cay, which he adopts as the second island;
but it is much too small, only 2¼ miles long by 1¾ wide.
Irving's third island is Exuma, but it is not in sight
from Concepcion Cay, while Columbus says that the
third island was in sight from the second. The fourth
island, according to Irving, is Long Island; but there is
no navigable route from Exuma to Long Island south
of the north point. From Long Island, Washington
Irving takes Columbus across all the mass of reefs and
rocks awash on the Great Bahama Bank to the Mucarras
Reef, an impossible piece of navigation. He makes the

Mucarras Reef to be the Islas de Arena of Columbus. But Mucarras is only twenty-six miles from the coast of Cuba, while Columbus sailed fifty-four miles from the Islas de Arena before he even sighted Cuba. For these reasons it is impossible that Cat Island can be the landfall.

Unsatisfied with the theories of Navarrete and Washington Irving, Don Francisco A. de Varnhagen sought for a landfall elsewhere. He published his theory in favour of the island of Mariguana, or Mayaguana, at Santiago de Chile in 1864.[*]

Mayaguana cannot be the landfall, because it is shown with that name both on the maps of Juan de la Cosa and Herrera, with Guanahani, the real landfall, far to the north.

The starting-point in the argument of Varnhagen is that the fourth island of Columbus, which he called Isabella, and the native name of which was Samoete, is Crooked Island, because Crooked Island retains the name of Samoete. On this point he is undoubtedly correct, and with this true departure he tries to work back, and he properly identifies Long Island with Fernandina, or the third island of Columbus. But then he runs off the track of Columbus, who came from the north. Varnhagen takes him east to Acklin for the second island, and he chooses Mayaguana for Guanahani. This island is twenty-three miles long, east and west, and from two to six broad. It has no large lagoon in the centre, and is not surrounded by a reef. A

---

[*] *La verdadera Guanahani de Colon. Memoria por Don Francisco A. de Varnhagen ... impresa en el tomo xxvi. de los anales de Chile (Enero, 1864), with the text of the Journal of Columbus, and map, pp. 107.*

narrow peninsula forms a shallow harbour, but it is on the north, not the east coast. The many islands said to have been seen by Columbus on leaving Guanahani are proposed by Varnhagen to have been Caicos, Planas, and Samana. But none of these are in sight from Mayaguana. Acklin cannot be the second island, because the course and distance to it is W.N.W. forty miles, while the course of Columbus from Guanahani to his second island was south-west twenty miles. The third island of Columbus was in sight from his second, but Long Island is not in sight from Acklin Island. Mayaguana meets none of the requirements, and therefore cannot be the landfall.

The most careful and elaborate monograph on the landfall of Columbus was written by the late Captain G. V. Fox, Assistant Secretary of the United States Navy.[*] He had himself visited the Bahamas, and his memoir bears evidence of deep and scholarly research. Captain Fox selected the small islet of Samana, called also Attwood's Cay, for the landfall of Columbus.

It is impossible that Samana can be Guanahani, because both appear as separate islands alike on the maps of Juan de la Cosa and Herrera. Captain Fox tries hard to escape from the evidence of the maps. He appeals to map-makers of the seventeenth century and later, whose evidence is of no value against Juan de la Cosa and Herrera. He suggests that the Samana on Herrera's map was an inside island, one of the Crooked

---

[*] Report of the Superintendent of the United States Geodetic Survey, Appendix No. 18. "An Attempt to Solve the Problem of the First Landing-place of Columbus in the New World," by Captain G. V. Fox, Assistant Secretary of the Navy, 1801 60 (Washington, 1882), pp. 340 411. Republished in an epitomised form in the "Magazine of American History."

Island group, while the present Samana was Guanahani. But Crooked Island is called Someto by Juan de la Cosa. Xumeto **by** Herrera, evidently the same as Samoete, **while** Samana appears outside, in its present place. **Then he** attempts to identify the rocks east of Samana, **called** Triangulo **on the** map of Herrera, with Watling **Island.** He has **found** "**Triangulo** or Watling" on a map of 1730 in Charlevoix, **by** D'Anville, and on **Jeffery's Atlas of 1794.** But Triangulo, as the name implies, **means three islets or** rocks, not one island like Watling. It **clearly** represents the rocks to the east **ward** of Samana.

Samana is $8\frac{1}{4}$ **miles long by** $1\frac{1}{2}$ broad, with **no** lagoon in **the** centre, and the eastern end terminates in a long **point, so that there was no east** side to explore. This **is extremely** unlike **the description** of Guanahani by **Columbus.** Samana, **however,** has a **reef.** Fox makes **Crooked Island the second island of** Columbus, and **Long Is**land the **third. But** Long Island is not visible **from** Crooked Island, while the third island of Columbus **was visible** from the second. Approaching the south end **of Long** Island from Crooked Island, Columbus could **not** see that **the** former was twenty leagues **long. But he** approached the south end of Long Island from **the** north. **Indeed,** none of the requirements of the case **are met,** with Samana as the landfall.

Watling Island **is** identified **as** Guanahani by **the** learned Muñoz, by Admiral Becher **in his** "Landfall of Columbus," **by** Professor Oscar Peschel of Augsburg, by Mr. Major in the second editi**on of** his "Select Letters of Columbus," by Lieutenant **J. B.** Murdoch of **the** United States Navy, and by Don **Juan** Ignacio de

Armas in his elaborate article published in *El Pais*, a periodical of Havanna, in 1889.

On the map of Herrera the fifth outer island of the Bahama group, counting from the north, is Guanahaní. On a modern chart the fifth outer island, counting from the north, is Watling Island, which, on the evidence of Herrera's map, is thus identified as the landfall of Columbus.

The Bahama Islands, or several of them, received names from the buccaneers of the seventeenth century, some of which found their way into our charts. That of Watling, no doubt, came from a famous buccaneer of that name, when the Bahamas were frequented by those worthies. In 1681 John Watling was elected a leader of the buccaneers in the Pacific, and he was killed in the same year, while leading an attack on Arica in Peru. His connection with the Bahamas must have been at an earlier period of his career.

Watling Island is in 74 28' W. longitude, and the south-east point is in 23° 55' S. It is thirteen miles long and from five to seven broad, so that it may be called a pretty good size (" bien grande "), and at the same time only an " Isleta." Guanahaní was flat, so is Watling Island, except that there is a hill 140 feet high, which would not, however, be visible from the anchorage of Columbus. Guanahaní had a large lagoon in the centre, so has Watling Island. Watling Island also has several smaller lagoons and ponds, " muchas aguas," as Columbus says. But the water is brackish, and Columbus could not fill up with water until he reached Fernandina, the third island. Guanahaní was surrounded with a reef; so is Watling Island. The southern part of the east side of Guanahaní trended N.N.E.: so does the

southern part of the **east side of** Watling Island.   On
this eastern side Guanahani **had a narrow** spit of land,
like an **island, but not one,** forming a harbour; so has
Watling Island.   There is no requirement in the description of Guanahani **or** San Salvador which **is not fully**
met by Watling Island.

The Journal **tells us** that the **Admiral took the boats**
to see the side **of the island round the** east point, where
the coast **trended N.N.E.   To have done this he** must
have started **from a point** on **the south coast to the**
westward of the east point.   His anchorage must, **there-**
fore, have been on the south coast of the island, sheltered
from the north-east trade, which **was blowing fresh, by**
the south-east point.   This is Mr. Major's argument,
and it seems conclusive.   Mr. Major was thus the first
to indicate with accuracy the first anchorage of Columbus in the New World.

Columbus sailed twenty miles south-west from Guanahaní to his second island, which he named Santa Maria
de la Concepcion.   Rum Cay is twenty **miles** south-west
from Watling Island.   Rum Cay **is therefore** Santa
Maria de la Concepcion.   The **third island was** in sight
from **the second.   Long** Island **is in** sight from Rum
Cay, **consequently the third** island, or Fernandina, must
be **Long Island.   Admiral** Becher and Mr. Major follow
Columbus quite correctly to Rum Cay, but here they
lose the track through a mistranslation.   Columbus
said : **"As** I saw another island to the west I clewed
up the sails, having gone all that day until night, for I
could not otherwise have reached the west point, where
I anchored at sunset." *   Becher's translation is, " As

---

* " Y como desta isla vide otra mayor al Oueste, cargue las velas por
andar todo aquel dia hasta la noche, porque aun no pudiere llegar

from the island I saw another to the westward. *I made sail, continuing on until night*, for as yet I had not arrived at the western cape." This interpretation caused great confusion in Admiral Becher's theory. Instead of remaining with sails clewed up at the second island, Columbus is sent westward all night, until he reaches Exuma Island. Having got him so many miles off his course, Becher and Major, at the cost of some violent treatment of the text of the journal, get Columbus back on his course again at the south end of Long Island, and then continue on the right route to Cuba.

One of the most recent essays on the landfall of Columbus and on his route through the Bahamas was written by Lieutenant J. B. Murdoch of the United States Navy, and was published in 1884.* Lieutenant Murdoch had the advantage of all the research and argument which had been devoted to the subject by his predecessors. If they did not establish their own theories they were quite successful in confuting those of their opponents. Lieutenant Murdoch made good use of his advantage, and in tracing out the route he alone has succeeded in meeting all the requirements of the journal of Columbus.

The method of Lieutenant Murdoch is to trace the route of Columbus backwards from Cuba. Columbus left the Islas de Arena at sunrise on the 27th of October, and saw the land of Cuba before nightfall, having then run seventeen leagues S.S.W. In making this

andado al cabo de Oueste, y cuasi al poner del sol sorgí acerca del dicho cabo" (Navarrete, i. p. 25).

"Cargue las velas" is a technical expression for clewing up the sails (*Diccionario Maritimo Español por Lorenzo*, Madrid, 1864). Becher thought "Cargue las velas" meant "I made sail."

* "Proceedings of the Naval Institute," Annapolis, April 1884, pp. 449-486.

run he was crossing a strong current that sets to **the**
W.N.W. along the north coast of Cuba. Allowing it an
average strength of two miles an hour, the bearing of
his anchorage at sunrise would have been north-east,
and the distance at sunset fifty-eight miles. The coast
of Cuba was then **in** sight, and not more than twenty
miles off. This would make the point reached in Cuba
seventy-five miles north-east from the anchorage **at sunrise.** Columbus says that this anchorage was on the
south side **of his** Islas de Arena, **which** were seven or
eight islets extending north and south, while the water
was shallow for five **or** six leagues on the southern side
of the **islands.** The Ragged Island chain answers to
this description, and is seventy-five miles from the Cuban
coast. This places Columbus **at** anchor south of the
Ragged Island chain, which he named Islas de Arena,
on the morning of the 27th **of October.**

The course from Isabella, the fourth island, **to** Islas
de Arena is stated to have been **W.S.W.,** and the **dis-**
tance from Cape Verde, the southern end of Long
Island, **to** the point at which the Islas de Arena were
sighted, was fifty-six miles W. ½ S. The distance of the
islands, when first seen, is given as five leagues. **The**
position at sunset on the 24th was, **therefore,** about
sixty-five miles E. ½ **N.** from Isabella. This position
would be south-east **from** Cape Verde, and W.S.W.
from the rocky islet **at** the northern **end** of Isabella.
These bearings point **to** Long Island as the second island,
or Fernandina, and **to** Bird Rock **at the north end** of
Crooked Island as the rocky islet at **the north** end **of**
Isabella. Crooked and Fortune Islands are thus identified as the Isabella of Columbus and **the** Samoete **of** the
natives.

Long Island meets all the requirements of Fernandina. It trends N.N.W. and S.S.E., and is twenty leagues long. It has a shallow harbour on the east coast, called Clarence Harbour, with two entrances, and part of its east coast trends nearly east and west.

Both the fourth island, Isabella, and the second island, Santa Maria de la Concepcion, are described as being some leagues east of Fernandina, Isabella being east of its southern, and Santa Maria of its northern end. Isabella has been shown to be Crooked Island, which is some leagues east of the south end of Long Island. Rum Cay must, therefore, be Santa Maria de la Concepcion, which is some leagues east of the northern end of Long Island.

The second island of Columbus is said to be five leagues (a misprint for miles) long north and south, and ten leagues (miles) east and west.* Rum Cay is five miles by ten miles. Columbus tells us twice that the third island was in sight from the second. Long island is in sight from Rum Cay. This is not the case, as regards the second and third islands, in any of the other theories.

Santa Maria de la Concepcion was twenty-one miles south-east from San Salvador. Rum Cay is twenty-one miles south-east from the anchorage at the south-east point of Watling Island, which is thus identified as the San Salvador of Columbus, or Guanahani.

The landfall is thus found by tracing the route of Columbus backwards from Cuba, and we are conducted

---

* The same error in putting leagues for miles occurs in the journal on December 21, 1492. Columbus was at the bay of Acul on the north side of Hayti. The statement is there made—" the distance from the entrance to the bottom is about five leagues." It is really about five miles.

to Watling Island, which resembles the description given
of Guanahani by Columbus in every particular, and
answers the requirement for Guanahani on the map of
Herrera.

Watling Island is proved to be Guanahani, and is the
true departure from which alone the requirements of
the journal of Columbus are fully complied with.   On
leaving San Salvador (Guanahani), Columbus sailed south-
west seven leagues to the second island. This course
and distance brought him to Rum Cay. As it was dark
before the island was reached, he stood off and on, and
was carried some distance by the current. It took him
all next day to reach the west point of Rum Cay, where
he clewed up his sails and anchored at sunset. The
third island of Columbus was in sight from the second.
Long Island is in sight from Rum Cay. The course
steered after leaving the second island is not precisely
mentioned, but it is clearly indicated. He had heard
of an island called Samoete where there was gold, and
that it was some distance to the south. He therefore
shaped a southerly course (" toeaba de sur "), making as
much southing as light variable winds would permit.
He sailed down the east side of Long Island during all
the afternoon of the 16th, and all night. This is quite
clear, as he could not otherwise have ascertained that it
was twenty leagues in length, which is correct. On the
morning of the 17th he anchored about two leagues
south of Clarence Harbour. Long Island is therefore
Fernandina, the third island of Columbus. The Admiral
weighed at noon on the 17th, and as there was a foul
wind for Samoete, he went north for two leagues to
Clarence Harbour, which he describes correctly as a

shallow harbour with two entrances. Later in the afternoon he examined the part of Long Island coast beyond Clarence Harbour, which trends east and west for a few miles. The wind then veered to the north, and he steered E.S.E. and south-east during the night, anchoring at Cape Verde, the south point of Long Island, on the morning of the 18th.

On the 19th Columbus steered easterly in search of Samoete, there being no land in sight. The ships made the land at about noon at a rocky islet off the northern extremity. The Admiral describes it so accurately as to leave no doubt that his rocky islet is Bird Island, off Crooked Island. The Cabo Hermoso of Columbus is the present Fortune Hill. The remark of the Admiral that Cabo Hermoso appeared to be on a separate island from Samoete, with another small island between, exactly coincides with the modern chart. The fourth island of Columbus, or Isabella, is identified with Crooked and Fortune Islands. Islas de Arena are identified with the Ragged Group by the bearings and distances from Cuba as well as from Crooked Island.

It will be seen that the evidence for Watling Island having been the landfall of Columbus is overwhelming. It answers to every requirement and every test, whether based on the Admiral's description of the island itself, on the courses and distances thence to Cuba, or on the evidence of early maps. Out of the twenty-four requirements taken from the Journal of Columbus, Watling Island fully complies with all, Turks Island complies with two—the lagoon and the reef, Samana with one —the reef, Mayaguana with none, Cat Island (wrongly called San Salvador) with none.

The question of the first landfall of Columbus in the
New World is so interesting that a full discussion of
the various theories respecting it is worth the needful
attention. For we are able to reach a final and satisfactory conclusion, and our time is not therefore wasted.

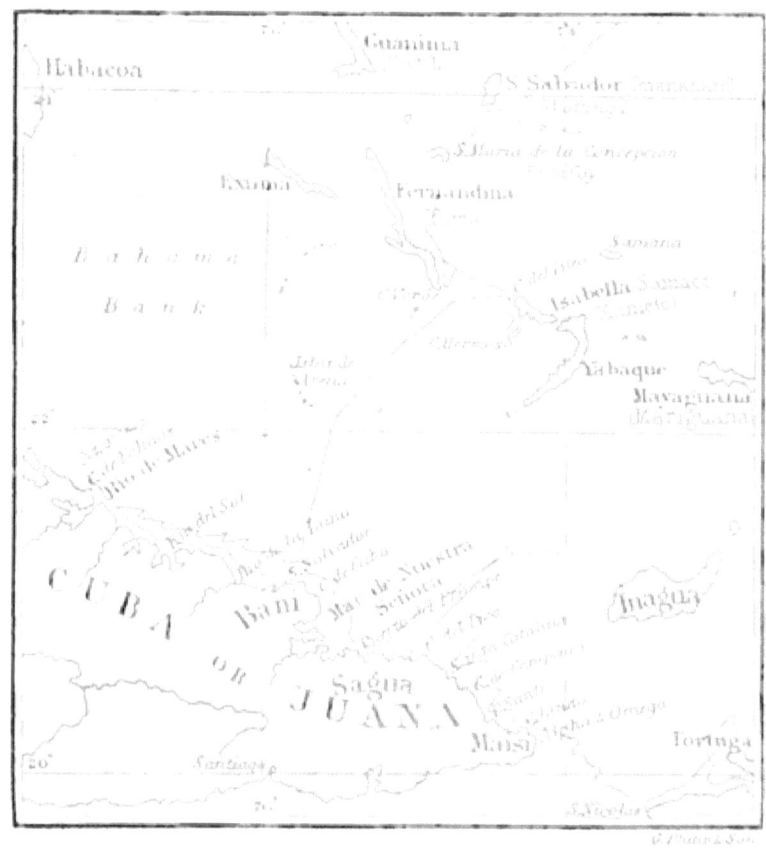

COURSE OF COLUMBUS FROM GUANAHANI TO CUBA.

We have the satisfaction of being able to look back on
that momentous event in the world's history with the
certainty that we know the exact spot. When the great
discoverer sprang from the boat, with the standard waving over his head, it was the shore at the south-east

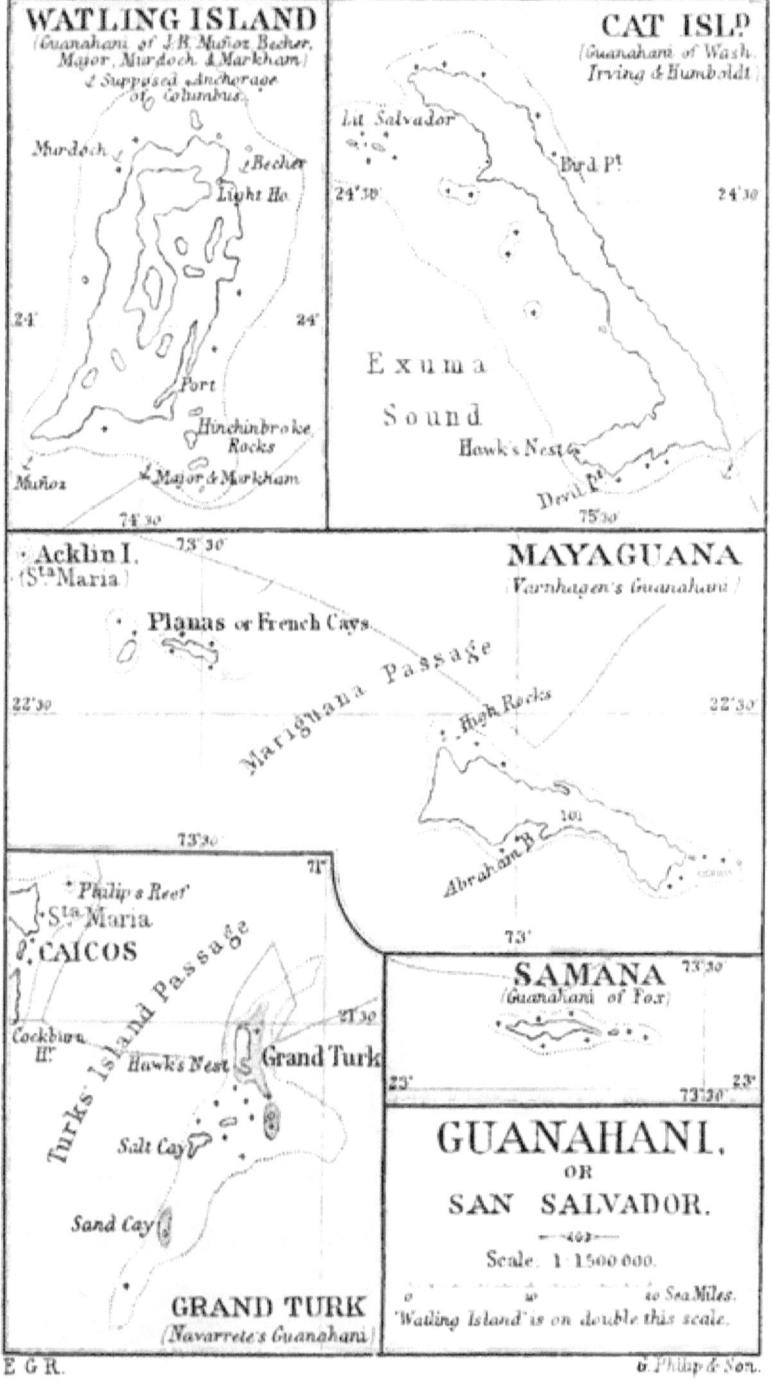

WATLING ISLAND
(Guanahani of J.B. Muñoz, Becher,
Major, Murdoch & Markham)
↓ Supposed Anchorage
of Columbus.

Murdoch
Becher
Light Ho.

24′

24′

Port
Hinchinbroke
Rocks
Muñoz
Major & Markham
74°30′

CAT ISL.ᴰ
(Guanahani of Wash.
Irving & Humboldt)

Lit. Salvador

Bird Pt.

24°30′

24°30′

E x u m a

S o u n d

Hawk's Nest

Devil Pt.
75°30′

Acklin I.
(Stª Maria)
73°30′

MAYAGUANA
(Varnhagen's Guanahani)

Planas or French Cays

22°30′

Mariguana Passage

High Rocks

22°30′

101

Abraham B.

73°30′

71°

73°

Philip's Reef
Stª Maria
CAICOS

Turks Island Passage

Cockburn
H.ᵗ
Hawk's Nest
Grand Turk

21°30′

23°

SAMANA
(Guanahani of Fox)

73°30′

23°

73°30′

Salt Cay

Sand Cay

GUANAHANI,
OR
SAN SALVADOR.

Scale. 1 : 1500 000.

0   10   10 Sea Miles.
"Watling Island" is on double this scale.

GRAND TURK
(Navarrete's Guanahani)

E. G. R.

b. Philip & Son.

angle of Watling Island where his feet first pressed the ground of the New World, and where his knees first made their impress when he offered up thanks for the achievement of the great work of which he was the chosen instrument.

CHAPTER VI.

DISCOVERY OF THE NEW WORLD.

ON Sunday, the 28th of October, the Admiral entered a river of Cuba, where there was good anchorage, clear of all dangers. It was a land of enchantment. The shores were lined with beautiful trees, with flowers and fruit, and all different from anything they had ever seen before, while birds of all kinds sang sweetly among the branches. Columbus observed a great number of palmtrees, which were different from those he had seen on the coast of Guinea. The leaves were very large, and were used for thatching the houses, two of which were visited by the Admiral. The inhabitants fled, and he allowed nothing to be taken away. There were fishing nets and lines and various ornaments. Proceeding up the river in his boat, he was enchanted with the beauty of the scenery. The interior appeared to contain high mountains, and he compared it to Sicily. The vessels were anchored under a height which reminded the Admiral of the " Peña de los Enamorados," near Granada. He described it as two hills, and on the summit of one there was a rock, which looked like a mosque at a distance. The depth of the river at its mouth was twelve brazas, and it was wide enough for a vessel to beat out. Puerto Naranjo is the only port on this part of the coast of Cuba which answers to the description. It

THE WEST INDIES.

COLUMBUS

has a depth of twelve fathoms at the entrance, is wide enough for a small vessel to beat out under sail, and there are two hills rising from the shore, one of which is called " Loma del Templo," because another rock rises up on its summit. Puerto Naranjo is then the first anchorage of Columbus on the coast of Cuba, to which he gave the name of San Salvador.

On the 29th the expedition weighed, and proceeded along the coast to the westward, passing the mouth of a river which was named " Rio de la Luna." The Admiral understood from the Guanahani guides that there was a city ruled over by a king to the westward, and he judged, from the description in the letter of Toscanelli, that he was approaching the dominions of the Grand Khan.

Sailing westward the Admiral came to the largest river he had yet seen, which he named " Rio de Mares." Here he communicated with the land, and found it to be fertile and well wooded. Houses of considerable size were scattered about, which contained small birds kept as pets, and many figures carved in wood. After proceeding on the same course for fifteen leagues, Columbus named a point of land covered with palm-trees the " Cabo de Palmas." At this juncture Pinzon reported that the Guanahani guide on board the *Pinta* was understood to say that there was a river beyond the point, and thence to the city called Cuba was four days' journey; also that the king of that city was at war with another king named Cami. whose city was called Fara. Pinzon further suggested that Cami was really the Grand Khan mentioned in the letter of Toscanelli. The squadron beat up against a foul wind for some time, but on the 1st of November the Admiral returned to " Rio de Mares."

Two of the observations for latitude, taken by Columbus with his quadrant, are recorded by Las Casas in his abstract on the 30th of October and the 2nd of November. **Las Casas** gives the result at 42° **N. ; but he** adds **that there** must have been an error in copying from the **original manuscript.** For the latitude found by Columbus **must have been** about 22° N. Navarrete offers a **strange and quite** inadmissible explanation of the mistake. **He says** that **the** quadrants of those days **measured** the altitude **double,** and that **therefore the** latitude **came out double.** The quadrants **of** those days certainly **did** nothing **of the kind, and if they had** made the altitude double **the resulting latitude** would not have been **double. The explanation is** much more simple. **The clerk who copied the document mistook** 2 for 4.

When the people got accustomed to the ships, and **found that one of their** number **had been** on board and **had returned without hurt,** several canoes came round **the** *Santa Maria* **with balls** and skeins of cotton. The **Admiral** ordered them to be given **to** understand that what he sought was gold, the word for which was thought **to be** *mucay* **in** their language. **He** believed that he was **now about a** hundred leagues from the cities of Zaiton and Quinsay, mentioned in **the** letter of Toscanelli. He resolved **to send an embassy to the** city called Cuba to gather **more** intelligence from **the** king respecting the dominions of the Grand Khan. According to Las Casas the name given to Martin Pinzon was not that of **a** city, but **of a province** called Cubanacan, near the centre of the island, which was rich in gold mines. *Nacan* is a word in the language **of the** islanders meaning the middle, and *Cuba* **is** territory or province—" the central province." The Admiral selected for **the duty** of attempting to reach the supposed city a seaman named Rodrigo de Jerez, a native of Ayamonte, who had been on the coast of Guinea, together with a converted Jew named Luis de Torres, who had been a servant of the Governor of Murcia, and could speak Arabic and other Eastern tongues. They were to be absent for six days. They were accompanied by two Indians, one of whom had been brought from Guanahaní, and the other was a native of Rio de Mares.

The anchorage was in a large basin formed by the mouth of the river, with deep water and a good beach clear of rocks and stones. The Admiral therefore took this opportunity for careening his ships and cleaning their bottoms, heaving them down one at a time so as to guard against treachery. But the people were very gentle and friendly, and numberless questions were asked them respecting the country and its products, the existence of spices, and the locality of gold mines. Their answers were very imperfectly understood, as there had been no time to acquire any knowledge of the language ; and the stories about men with one eye, and others with dogs' noses were, no doubt, the imaginative interpretations of unintelligible signs.

On the 6th of November the envoys returned, and reported that they had marched twelve leagues and had reached a place where there were fifty houses and about a thousand inhabitants, for a large number lived in one house. The Spaniards were received with great ceremony, and were very hospitably treated. They saw many people on the road, and observed that the men always had a half-burnt roll of leaves in their mouths which they smoked. These rolls were made of the dried leaves of a certain plant. They lighted it at one end, and drew the smoke into their mouths at the other, which caused **a** drowsy **feeling,** and prevented the smoker from becoming **fatigued.** They called these rolls **of** dried leaves *tabacos.* **This was the** first occasion **on** which Europeans became acquainted with **the fragrant** weed. We are **not** told **whether Rodrigo de J**erez and the converted **Jew** tried **an experiment and smoked** cigars themselves, or whether **the habit was not acquired by** Europeans **until** afterwards. **But the discovery of** tobacco **was one of the direct results of the first voyage of** Columbus.

From his own observations, as **well as from the** reports **of the envoys, the Admiral came to the conclu**sion **that the land was exceedingly fertile, producing a great number of fruits and** vegetables previously un**known, and that the people were** innocent and well **disposed, and** ready **to be converted to** Christianity. **They wore no clothing of any kind, but** had great quan**tities of cotton, and slept in nets** suspended from **the trees called** *hamacas.*

On the 12th of November the Admiral sailed **from Rio de** Mares **to find an island where he** understood there was much **gold,** called Babeque, **to reach which the course was supposed to be** E.S.E.

In reporting on the products of Cuba, Columbus **mentions a quantity of mastiche at the** Rio de Mares, **the trees being like those** described **by** Pliny. The **Admiral had seen them in the** island **of** Chios, hitherto **the only source of supply, where** they yielded, if his **memory did not** mislead him, **a sum of** 50,000 ducats at **9s. 2d.** He was probably correct, **for** in the next century **the** value **of** the mastiche exported **from** Chios was **30,000** ducats. The resin ducts are in the bark of the stems **and** branches, **and Columbus** caused many trees to be tapped in Cuba to ascertain whether they exuded in the same way as at Chios. This is one out of many examples of the closeness with which the great discoverer observed all natural objects which surrounded him in his new discovery, of his attention to details, and of the readiness with which he brought the knowledge he had acquired in his numerous voyages to bear on the matter before him. It was at Rio de Mares that the Admiral detained six Indian youths on board with the object of taking them home with him, teaching them the Spanish language, and instructing them in the Christian faith. After working to the eastward for two days against light winds, the exploring squadron approached the western end of Cuba, having passed a great number of islands covered with trees. On the 17th two of the captive youths made their escape. The foul wind obliged the Admiral to keep his ships on a bowline, and to make long stretches to the northward, in order to gain any headway to the east. At this time Martin Pinzon, being on board the *Pinta*, and being able to outsail the Admiral, parted company in order to visit the island yielding gold, of which his native guides had told him, thus basely deserting his comrades.

The *Santa Maria* bore up and anchored in a harbour which was named Santa Catalina, now called Cayo Moa, near the east end of Cuba. Here the trees grew straight and to a great height, which enabled the *Niña* to be supplied with a new mizen-mast. The Admiral reported the country to be exceedingly beautiful, with rich vegetation and abundant supplies of pure and excellent water. On the 5th of December he reached Punta de Maise, the eastern extremity of Cuba, and

H

standing across the channel, the explorers soon sighted
the high land of Haiti.

The *Niña* was sent ahead, and anchored in the harbour
of St. Nicholas Mole, at the north-western extremity of
Haiti. The mountains in the background were lofty
and rugged, but the intervening land seemed to be less
thickly wooded than in Cuba ; small clumps and single
trees were scattered over the green open slopes, and it
reminded them more of their own homes than any land
they had yet seen. The *Santa Maria* followed the
Niña, but it was late next day before she came to an
anchor. The present harbour of St. Nicholas Mole at
first received the name of Puerto Maria from Columbus,
which he changed to St. Nicholas. Points of land to
the east were named " Cabo del Estrella," " Cabo del
Elefante," and " Cabo del Cinquin ; " and the island off
the north coast received the name of Tortuga. All the
natives concealed themselves, so the Admiral left St.
Nicholas on the 7th of December, and encountering a
northerly gale, he took refuge in a bay sheltered by the
island of Tortuga, which he named " Puerto de la Concepcion." Here the open plains still more reminded
them of home, and the island received the name of
Española. At this place some Spaniards, who were
taking a stroll on shore, ran down a native girl after a
long chase and brought her on board. The Admiral
caused her to be treated with kindness, loaded with
presents, and returned to her people. In this way
communication was established with the Indians, and
they soon took courage to surround the ship with their
canoes and come on board.

The two little vessels had moved to a port a short
distance to the eastward, and in consequence of the

friendly intercourse with the people, the Admiral named it Puerto de la Paz. He was delighted alike with the beauty of the scenery and with the innocence and gentleness of the natives. The 18th of December was the Annunciation, and was celebrated by a salute from the lombards and a display of flags. At dinner-time the chief of that part of the island came on board with many attendants, and seated himself at the table under the poop where the Admiral was dining. He received several presents, and departed with demonstrations of pleasure and friendship. It was found that the name for a chief or king, in the native language, was *cacique*. In an anchorage, now called "Bahia de Acul," a little further to the east, the natives came in crowds and presented provisions of all kinds, treating their visitors with the greatest frankness and cordiality. Columbus was filled with joy and delight at his new discoveries. He exclaimed, "I had navigated the sea for twenty-three years, and had seen all the east and west, and from England in the north to Guinea in the south, but in all those parts I had never found so perfect a land as this, nor such harbours."

Understanding from the natives that there was much gold on islands to the eastward, the Admiral continued to shape a course in that direction, and on the 22nd a large canoe came alongside with an invitation from a chief named Guacamagari to visit his country. The ships were soon surrounded by 120 canoes, all loaded with bread, fish, and fresh water in earthen jars, and over 500 natives swam off, although the ships were nearly a league from the shore. The Admiral was informed that there was a great quantity of gold at a place called Cibao, which he mistook for Cipango.

Proceeding with little wind on December the 24th from the harbour of Santo Tomas, or Acul, towards Punta Santa, the Admiral kept a look out on deck until 11 o'clock in the first watch. He had had no sleep for two days and a night, so he went below, leaving the deck in charge of the man at the helm. As it was quite calm the man intrusted the tiller to a boy and went to sleep, a proceeding which the Admiral had strictly forbidden throughout the voyage, whether it was calm or not. The orders were that the helm was not to be intrusted to the boys on any pretence whatever. A current carried the *Santa Maria* on to a sandbank at about two in the morning, and she touched so lightly that it was scarcely perceptible. The boy felt the rudder touch and heard the rush of the sea along the ship's side. He cried out, and the Admiral was on deck in a moment. Columbus had piloted the ship past many dangers from rocks and sandbanks during the previous days and nights, and if he had not been fairly worn out with fatigue and want of sleep the disaster would not have happened. The current continued to force the ship further on to the bank, and she gradually heeled over. She became deeply imbedded in the sand. It was the master's watch and he ought to have been on deck. When he came up the Admiral ordered him to lay out an anchor to haul the ship off. The boat was launched over the stern, and the master and others got into her. Columbus thought they were going to obey his orders, instead of which they pulled off to the *Niña*, which was half a league away. They were not allowed on board, and came back; but meanwhile the opportunity was lost. The Admiral tried every other plan. Masts were cut away and the ship was lightened, but all was of no avail. If the anchor had been laid out according to the Admiral's orders, the ship would probably have been saved. Diego de Arana and Pedro Gutierrez were sent to the chief, Guacanagari, whose settlement was a few miles distant, to ask for help. Large canoes were immediately despatched, which assisted in landing the stores and provisions and everything of value during the following day. The warm-hearted chief placed two large houses at the Admiral's disposal, and was anxious to assist him in every way in his power. It was clear that the little *Niña* could not possibly take the crew of the *Santa Maria* as well as her own across the Atlantic, and the necessity for forming a settlement became apparent. The Admiral resolved to build a fort, store it with a year's provisions, and leave in it some artificers and as many of the men as desired to stay, with the ship's boat. As the wreck took place on Christmas Day, the fort was to be called " La Navidad." Guacanagari promised that plenty of gold should be brought from Cibao, and that more should be collected during the Admiral's absence and given to the Spaniards in the fort.

Columbus wrote of the chief and his people with warm gratitude. " He and all his people wept for us. They are a loving race and without covetousness, well disposed in all things; and I assure your Highnesses that I do not believe there is a better people or a better land in the world. They love their neighbours as themselves, and their conversation is gentle and kindly and always cheerful. They go as naked as they were born, both men and women, yet they have very good customs. Their chief keeps marvellous state, and has a manner so composed that it is pleasant to see it. They have good

memories, like to see everything, and inquire what each
article is, and for what it is used." Columbus understood that the province was called Caribata, and that
the native name of the island, which he had called
Española, was Bohio. According to Las Casas, the name
of the province was Marien.

On the 26th Guacanagari visited the Admiral on board
the *Niña*, and afterwards entertained him at dinner on
shore with cassava bread, yams, game, and other viands.
The meal was not hurried; and Columbus was surprised at
the cleanliness and good manners of the chief while at
table, and at the way in which he carefully wiped his
hands afterwards with certain herbs. They exchanged
many presents, and the native chief proved himself to
be a true and faithful friend. He ruled over a happy
and contented people, and the only drawbacks to their
existence were the attacks of a cruel race of savages
called Caribas. The Admiral promised that the sovereigns of Spain would order him to subdue and punish
these invaders.

The fort of Navidad was completed, and it was arranged
that forty-four souls should remain behind—thirty-four
belonging to the *Santa Maria*, and ten to the *Niña*.
Diego de Arana, the cousin of the Admiral's wife, Beatriz
Enriquez, and his steadfast friend, was to be Governor;
with Rodrigo de Escobedo, the secretary, and Diego
Gutierrez, as his lieutenants. They were introduced to
the *cacique* Guacanagari, who undertook to supply all
their wants. All the articles for barter were left with
them, biscuits to last for a year, wine, ammunition, and
the ship's boat. Among those who remained at Navidad
were the Englishman Alard (Tallarte de Lajes), and the
Irishman from Galway.

The Admiral, master, pilot, and fifteen of the crew of the *Santa Maria*, returned home in the *Niña*. Out of her own crew of eighteen ten remained at Navidad, so that twenty-six people were crowded on board this little caravel of forty tons, besides several natives. Columbus bade farewell to those who remained behind, strongly enjoining friendly treatment of the natives, and the preservation of discipline, and promising to return in the following year. Guacanagari parted with the Admiral most unwillingly.

The *Niña* sailed on the 4th of January 1493, and proceeded along the coast to the eastward, giving the name of "Monte Cristi" to a high mountain on the coast having the form of a tent; and a point twenty-four miles further east was named "Cabo del Becerro." There were beautiful undulating plains along the coast, and behind the ranges of mountains rose one above the other into the clouds. In the afternoon of the 6th the mast-head man, who was keeping a sharp look-out for rocks, reported the *Pinta* coming down to them, with the wind aft, and all sail set. The Admiral returned to Monte Cristi with the *Pinta* in company, and anchored. Martin Alonzo Pinzon then came on board the *Niña* to pay his respects. He excused his desertion by saying that it was caused by reasons over which he had no control, and that it was not intentional. The Admiral was not deceived. He knew that Pinzon had parted company in order to obtain the gold of which he had heard, and then return home first. He had utterly failed, and now came back to his chief, who could no longer trust him. But for the good of the expedition Columbus refrained from fully expressing his thoughts. On the 7th the men were sent on shore for wood and water, and the vessels were caulked and refitted.

The *Pinta* and *Niña*, once more in company, weighed from Monte Cristi on the 9th of January; and, when sailing eastward, three syrens or mermaids were seen, which rose well out of the sea, but the Admiral remarked that they were not so beautiful as they are described, though in other respects they had a human form. He added that he had seen others on the coast of Manegueta, in Guinea. The syrens of Columbus are the dugongs which are found on the west coast of Africa; but their cogeners, the manatis, though still met with in the great South American rivers, have disappeared from the sea that surrounds Española. Their resemblance to human beings, when rising in the water, must have been very striking. They have small rounded heads, and cervical vertebræ which form a neck, enabling the animal to turn its head about. The fore-limbs also, instead of being pectoral fins, have the character of the arm and hand of the higher mammalia. These peculiarities, and their very human way of suckling their young, holding it by the fore-arm, which is movable at the elbow-joint, suggested the idea of mermaids or syrens.*

Still sailing eastward they reached the mouth of a river to which the Admiral gave the name of " Rio de Gracia," where the *Pinta* had already been, while separated from her consorts, Pinzon hoping to collect gold. He had seized four men and two girls from among the natives by force; but the Admiral ordered them to be clothed, released, and sent back to their homes. He had himself caused some natives to be taken, because he considered it to be necessary for the King's service, but

* See supplementary note on the dugong, by Mr. Delmar Morgan, in the " Voyage of Leguat," edited by Captain P. Oliver (Hakluyt Society, 1891, ii. p. 370).

he would not allow this to be done indiscriminately and without urgent cause. Leaving this anchorage at midnight on the 11th they passed a high mountain, and as its summit was hidden by fleecy clouds, the Admiral named it "Monte de Plata." It was here that a monastery of Dominicans was afterwards built, in which Las Casas began to write his "History of the Indies," in the year 1527.[*] Columbus had now resolved to make the best of his way back to Spain, to report the unprecedented results of his memorable expedition.

On the 12th they were sailing along the north coast of the peninsula of Samana, at the eastern end of Española. Reaching the eastern point, it received the name of "Cabo del Enamorado," while a loftier and grander headland beyond reminded the Admiral of Cape St. Vincent in Portugal. Between them there was a magnificent bay, the Gulf of Samana, where the Admiral, who carefully studied all the prognostications of the almanacs, prudently anchored his two little vessels. An eclipse of the sun was expected on the 17th, and the opposition of Jupiter with the conjunction of Mercury was believed in the old world to betoken heavy gales. With such small vessels he thought it well to be cautious, and to remain in port until these planetary movements and their supposed consequences had passed away.

Sending a boat on shore, communication was opened with a very different people to those that had hitherto been encountered. The men at Samana were armed with bows and arrows, their faces stained black, and their hair adorned with parrots' feathers. The Admiral judged them to be the Caribs of whom he had heard, who harassed and plundered the more peaceful race of

---

[*] Las Casas, iv. p. 254.

islanders, and were said to be eaters of human flesh.
One of these Caribs came on board, and told the Admiral
that there was much *tuob*, which was supposed to mean
gold, in islands to the eastward, called Matinino and
Goanin, but the man was very imperfectly understood.
Las Casas says that there were never any Caribs in
Española.   A boat's crew went on shore afterwards to
barter, and, owing to some misunderstanding, there was
a collision, resulting in the wounding of two natives and
the flight of the rest.   When the boat came off the Admiral said that it was well that these people should know
the power of the white men, still the collision caused
him some anxiety, lest it should give rise to a feeling
of hostility against the settlers at Navidad.   Next day
some chiefs came on board, and received presents from
the Admiral.

Both the caravels had been very indifferently caulked
at Palos, and were making much water.   The Admiral
therefore abandoned his intention of discovering the
islands to the south-east, and resolved, in accordance
with the wishes of his people, to shape a direct course
for Spain.   He calculated this course to be N.E. ¼ E.,
and weighing on the 16th of January he proceeded in
that direction, continuing on the same course day after
day.   The *Pinta* now delayed the *Niña* owing to her
mizen-mast being sprung, and it was said that if Martin
Pinzon had been as diligent in getting himself a new
mizen-mast as he had been in his insubordinate and
useless search after gold, they would have made a better
passage home.   The temperature soon became cooler,
and in the fine weather they succeeded in catching some
fish, including an enormous shark   These additions to
the larder were important, for the ordinary provisions

were reduced to biscuits and wine. On the 3rd of February the Admiral observed that the pole star was as high in the heavens as it is at Cape St. Vincent, but owing to the motion caused by the waves he could not take an altitude either with his quadrant or astrolabe. On the 7th the reckoning of the Admiral made them seventy-five leagues south of the island of Flores, those of the pilots being much further to the north and east. On the 12th the wind rose to a gale, with a heavy sea, and if the little caravel had not been very carefully repaired, through the Admiral's diligence, when on the coast of Española, she would probably have been lost. Next day there was a fearful sea, and the *Niña* lay to under bare poles until evening, when she began to run before it, showing the smallest rag of a sail. On the 14th the wind increased in violence, there was a terrific sea, and the frail boat was in great danger. Columbus ordered that lots should be prepared, consisting of beans shaken up in a cap, on one of which a cross was cut. All were to draw, and he who got the crossed bean was to vow a pilgrimage to Santa Maria de Guadaloupe, and to present a wax candle of five pounds weight to her shrine. Columbus himself was the first, and he drew the bean with a cross. They drew again for a pilgrimage to Santa Maria de Loreto, near Ancona in Italy, and the lot fell on a sailor of the port of Santa Maria, near Cadiz, named Pedro de Villa. The Admiral promised to provide money for his journey if they were spared. Next they drew lots for who should watch for a night and have a mass said in the church of Santa Clara at Moguer. The lot again fell on the Admiral. Then the Admiral and all the crew made a joint vow that, at the first place where they landed, they would all march in procession, in their shirts, to offer up thanks-giving prayers in a church under the invocation of our Lady.

They had given themselves up for lost. Owing to the provisions being nearly consumed, the boat was very crank; but the Admiral obviated this danger to some extent by causing the empty casks to be filled with salt water so as to serve as ballast, and he paid the closest attention to the helm. Still every moment seemed likely to be their last. Those who have seen a gale of wind with a heavy sea in the latitude of the Azores, can imagine the critical position of a leaky little boat of forty tons like the *Niña* rising on the top of a huge Atlantic wave, then plunging into the trough, with the mountainous billows foaming around higher than her mast-head, then rising and plunging down again, the slightest inattention to the helm making destruction certain, while green seas washed over her fore and aft.

Columbus was filled with anxiety lest his great work should perish with him. The violent motion of the little vessel rendered it almost impossible to write, but he took a piece of parchment and noted down a brief ac-count of his discoveries, earnestly praying that any one who found it would take it to the sovereigns of Spain. He wrapped the parchment in a waxed cloth, fastening it well, and headed the packet up in an empty cask. No one knew what was inside the cloth. All believed that their leader was performing some religious vow or act of devotion, which they did not understand. The cask was then thrown overboard. Columbus passed some time during the fury of the gale communing with his God, who had beforetime saved him in so many perils, and had allowed his loftiest aspiration to be ful-

filled. He strove to persuade himself that it was the
Lord's will that he should be saved, believing that, in
this great achievement of his life, he was an instrument
in the hands of God. Still his heart sank within him
when he reflected on the extreme danger of his position.
He thought with anguish of his two little boys at school
in Cordova, who would be left fatherless. But as he
prayed hope prevailed over despondency, and when the
wind changed to the west during the night he allowed
himself to regain confidence in his destiny.

On the 15th of February the gale abated, but the sea
still ran very high, and towards sunset land was sighted
on the horizon. The pilots believed it to be the coast of
Spain ; but Columbus knew, from his careful reckoning,
that it was one of the Azores. At sunset it was obscured
by mist, but they hoped to reach it the next day. That
night the Admiral, who had been on deck and without
sleep since the 13th, took a little rest. He was suffering a good deal from his legs, which had been so long
exposed to cold and wet, and from want of food, in
common with the rest of the crew. On the 18th the
Niña was anchored, and a boat being sent on shore, it
was found that they had reached the island of Santa
Maria, the most easterly of the Azores. The governor,
who was named Juan de Castañeda, sent a friendly
message to the Admiral, with a present of fresh provisions. Trusting implicitly in his good faith, the Admiral
arranged that half the crew should go on shore, to perform their vow of marching in procession, in their shirts,
to a chapel of our Lady. On their return he intended
to go himself with the other half. But while the first
half was engaged in prayer at a small chapel on shore,
they were treacherously surrounded by an armed body

of Portuguese and taken prisoners. As the Admiral
could not see the chapel from the point where the *Niña*
was at anchor, he got under weigh when he found that
the boat did not return, and came opposite to the chapel.
Then he saw his people surrounded, and armed men
coming off in a boat to attack him. The governor was
in the boat, but he would not come on board. Columbus
told him who he was, that he held a commission from
the sovereigns of Spain as their Admiral and Viceroy,
that they were at peace with the King of Portugal, that
the seizure of his people would not prevent him from
proceeding on his voyage to Spain, and that the governor would surely be punished for his misconduct.
Castañeda insolently replied that they were Portuguese,
and knew nothing of the sovereigns of Spain or their
commissions. The weather was very threatening, and
Columbus decided upon seeking better shelter at St.
Michael's. He put to sea, but was unable to fetch St.
Michael's, and returned to his former anchorage in the
evening. Then some Portuguese came on board, including two priests. They were shown the royal commissions, and eventually the Admiral's people were released,
and allowed to come on board. On the 24th the *Niña*
departed from this inhospitable island, and, after encountering very severe weather, she reached the Tagus on
the 4th of March, and anchored at the entrance, off the
village of Rastelo. A large Portuguese man of war was
there, and the captain, named Bartolomé Diaz, went on
board the *Niña* in an armed boat, and demanded that
the Admiral should come with him and give an account
of himself. The Admiral replied that he was the officer
of the sovereigns of Castille, that he would give no
account of himself, and that he would not leave his ship

except by force. Diaz then said that he might send the master of the *Niña*, but Columbus refused to allow either the master or any one on board to leave his ship in obedience to a Portuguese order. Diaz then moderated his tone, requested to be allowed to see the Admiral's commission, and offered any help in his power. Crowds of visitors came from Lisbon to see the ship during the two following days, and on the 8th Don Martin de Noronha arrived with an invitation from the King of Portugal. Columbus proceeded to the Valle del Paraiso, nine leagues from Lisbon, where the court then was, and had an interview with João II., who received him very courteously. He was the guest of the Prior of Crato, and remained at court until the 12th, when he took leave of the King, and returned on board the *Niña*. On the 13th the Admiral got under weigh, and left the Tagus. He rounded Cape St. Vincent before sunset on the 14th, and at sunrise on the 15th of March he was off the bar of Saltes. At noon he reached the port of Palos, from which he had sailed on the 3rd of August in the previous year, having been absent seven months and twelve days. The *Pinta* had made the port of Bayona, on the west coast of Galicia, after the gale abated, and proceeded thence to Palos, where she arrived on the same day as the *Niña*. Martin Alonzo Pinzon is said to have died a few weeks after he landed.

The *Niña* must have been seen off the bar of Saltes for some hours before she anchored in the river. All the inhabitants were on the bank to receive the great discoverer when he landed. We may be sure that in front of the crowd were his constant friends from La Rabida, Juan Perez and Alonzo de Marchena. Amidst the ringing of bells, salutes from the lombards, and the cheers of the people. the Admiral went straight to the old church of St. George, the patron saint of his native city, to offer up thanks for his delivery from so many dangers. Afterwards the friars conducted him to La Rabida, where *Te Deum* was sung by the brotherhood in presence of the Admiral, his pilots and officers, and the principal inhabitants of Palos. Next day the ten Indians were landed, six from Guanahani and four from Cuba; together with the animals, plants, and curious objects of all kinds that had been brought home. One Indian had died on the very day that the *Niña* arrived, and three others were too ill to travel further than Palos. The Admiral, after resting for a few days with his good friends at La Rabida, proceeded to Seville towards the end of March.

The discovery of America was one of the most important events in the world's history, and the deepest interest will always be felt in the conduct of the discoverer, and in the details of the voyage. Columbus had prepared himself for his great work during twenty years of study and of practical labour. He had known poverty and adversity, and had learnt patience and prudence, forethought and consideration for others, in a severe school; while at the same time he acquired knowledge and experience. During the voyage he displayed the highest qualities of a commander. He alone was capable of conducting the ships across the Atlantic for the first time, of guiding their course, and of calming the anxieties of their crews. To him alone is due the credit of having steered the little vessels clear of a thousand dangers, and of having brought two of them safely back. Having run down the trades on the way out, Columbus reflected that it would probably be impracticable to return on the same parallels. With wonderful prevision he assumed that there must be a complement to the trades in higher latitudes. He therefore adopted a northerly course, and discovered the region of westerlies. He not only found the New World, but also pointed out the way to go and the way to return. To achieve all this a man was needed who was possessed of profound knowledge acquired by years of study and experience, of untiring watchfulness, and of those unerring previsions which genius of a high order alone produces. There was only one such man in that age.

The first account of the voyage was contained in the letter written to his friend Luis de Santangel, the treasurer of Aragon, by the Admiral himself for the information of Ferdinand and Isabella. It is dated on board the *Niña* on the 18th of February, off the island of Santa Maria, and a postscript announces her arrival in the Tagus on the 4th of March. The letter was despatched from Lisbon, or possibly from Palos. It contains a brief account of the principal events of the voyage.[1]

The journal of the voyage is an abstract, probably prepared by Las Casas; as the only copy in existence, which was published by Navarrete, is said to be in the bishop's handwriting. Unfortunately the original journal and the original charts are lost. The abstract is full, and the very words of the Admiral are occasionally quoted. Still the composition is not that of the Admiral, except where the quotations are specified, and he cannot be held responsible for any obvious errors, especially as regards figures. There is reason for the opinion that Las Casas made his abstract from a copy, and he complains of the illegible handwriting more than once. We

I

must be thankful even for this abstract. It supplies us
with a full and minute account of all the events of the
voyage. It shows with what conscientious care the
great discoverer recorded his proceedings, and with what

WESTERN PART OF THE MAP OF JUAN DE LA COSA.

intelligence and interest he observed the natural objects
that surrounded him in his New World. All were new
to him, but he could compare them with analogous products seen in his numerous voyages, and draw useful

inferences. The fulness of his entries was due to the
rapid working of a vivid imagination, as one thought
followed another in quick succession through his well-
stored brain. So that the journal is a mirror of the
man. It shows his failings and his virtues. It records
his lofty aims, his unswerving loyalty, his deep religious
feeling, his kindliness and gratitude. It impresses us
with his knowledge and genius as a leader, with his
watchful care for his people, and with the redundancy
of his imagination. Few can read the journal without
a feeling of admiration for the marvellous ability and
simple faith of the great genius whose mission it was to
reveal the mighty secret of the ages.

NOTE.

(1) *The First Letter announcing the Discovery of the
New World.*

Two manuscripts are in existence of the letter written by
Columbus on board the *Nina*. One is at Simancas, and was
first published by Navarrete from a copy prepared by the
archivist Don Tomas Gonzalez in 1818. The other manuscript
was found by Varnhagen at Valencia, and published there in
1858. The first is addressed to the "Escribano de Racion,"
the second to Gabriel Sanchez. The Valencia manuscript gives
the date correctly : " Fecha en la carabela sobre la isla de Santa
Maria 18 de Febrero 1493." The Simancas manuscript has :
" Fecha en la carabela sobre las islas de Canaria 15 de Febrero
1493." This proves that the Simancas document is a careless copy.
Santa Maria, written "Stamaria," was read by the copyist as
"Canaria," and 18 for 15. Detractors of Columbus have seized
upon this date " Canaria" to suggest that he was either completely out in his reckoning, or that he was always careless.
The journal proves that he was correct in his reckoning, and
expected to make a landfall at the Azores ; and the Valencia

manuscript proves **that** he did not **date the** letter "Canaria," **but** "Santa **Maria." So** that this **attempt** to discredit the accuracy **of the Admiral utterly fails.**

The letter to the " Escribano **de Racion"** was printed at Seville **in 1493, as has been proved by** Asensio (i. 435), and this **edition is of special interest, because** it is the first printed account **of the discovery of the new world.** Only one copy is known **to exist, now in the Ambrosian Library** at Milan. A **Latin version of the letter to Sanchez, by a** Catalan **named Leander de Cosco, was printed at Rome in 1493** by **Stephen Planck—four leaves in Gothic type. Another version** was **printed at Rome in the same year by Silber.**

The " Escribano de Racion" was Luis de Santangel. **But I incline to think that there was only one** letter addressed to **the " Escribano de Racion" without a name,** and that the name **of Sanchez got inserted by mistake, by some** one who thought **that he was " Escribano de Racion."**

CHAPTER VII.

THE arrival of Columbus created a great sensation in Spain. One year had wrought a marvellous change. The needy enthusiast, ridiculed and insulted, was now Admiral of the Ocean Sea, Viceroy of the Western Indies, the observed of all observers. When he entered Seville by the populous suburb of Triana, on Palm Sunday, 1493, he was preceded by a well-equipped squadron of cavalry, which the Count of Cifuentes, who was the Queen's "Asistente" of Seville, had sent out to meet him. A procession was formed of servants carrying parrots and paroquets of beautiful plumage, spears and other arms, plumes and girdles, and many other wonderful curiosities, followed by the Indians, who attracted more attention than anything else. The Admiral was accompanied by Juan Niño, the master and part-owner of the *Niña*, by the pilots and several seamen, and by citizens who were old friends of the illustrious navigator, and had come out to meet him. Dense crowds thronged the streets; there was no window unoccupied, nor was there a place to be found vacant on the roofs as Columbus passed through the streets of Seville to his lodging in the house of the Count of Cifuentes. The Indians and the curiosities were lodged in a house near the archway called " of the Images," at St. Nicholas, where some favoured persons were allowed to examine them.

In that crowd there was a young man, about twenty years of age, to whose diligence, ability, and truthfulness the Admiral's memory owes almost everything. Bartolomè Las Casas was one of those who were admitted to see the curiosities. In after life he was the courageous defender of the poor Indians, an ardent ecclesiastic, and the most conscientious and truthful historian of that age. To Las Casas we owe the story of the early life of Columbus, the journal of the first voyage, the letter of Columbus describing the third voyage, and the account of this famous entry into Seville, of which he was an eyewitness.

Columbus had reported his arrival and the results of his voyage to the sovereigns of Spain, and waited for their reply at Seville. Nor did he omit to give an account of his discoveries to the aged astronomer at Florence, Paolo Toscanelli, to whose advice and suggestions he owed so much. Toscanelli must then have reached a great age, and it is pleasant to know that the illustrious navigator, in the midst of his triumphant reception, did not forget to gladden the heart of his venerable correspondent with the news that his advice had produced such glorious fruit.[1]

While the excitement at Seville caused by the arrival of Columbus was at its height, a special messenger arrived with a letter addressed "from the King and Queen to Don Cristoval Colon, their Admiral of the Ocean Sea, and Viceroy and Governor of the islands discovered in the Indies." It was dated from Barcelona on the 30th of March, and expressed their sense of the greatness of his services to God, to themselves, and to the country. They told him that they considered it most important that his work should be continued, and that he should commence preparations for returning to his newly-discovered government, and they desired that he would come to their court with as much despatch as possible. They were anxious to receive a full account of his discoveries from his own lips.

Columbus set out from Seville in the middle of April, and travelled by land to Barcelona, accompanied by Pedro Niño and the other members of the expedition, and by six of the Indians. The others were not well enough to leave Seville. Enormous crowds assembled to see the Admiral pass through the towns on his road, and a grand reception was prepared for him at Barcelona. As he approached the famous old capital of the Counts, a troop of splendidly-dressed cavaliers came out to meet the great discoverer, and conduct him to the presence of the sovereigns. Ferdinand and Isabella, with their only son, were lodged, during their residence at Barcelona, in the palace of the Bishop of Urgel, in the Calle Ancha. The building has long since disappeared, but it is here that the memorable reception probably took place. The sovereigns were seated on thrones under a magnificent canopy with the young Prince Juan in a chair by the Queen's side, and were surrounded by nobles and ministers of state. But the arrival of Columbus was delayed by the dense crowd in the streets. He was preceded by the Indians, and by sailors of the *Niña*, carrying tropical fruits and various species of vegetable products, parrots, and many other birds with gorgeous plumage, and animals, including an enormous iguana five feet long, with huge spines along its back. The six Indians carried spears and arrows, and wore golden ornaments.

Columbus himself was distinguished by his stature, his snow-white hair, and his dignified and courteous bearing. Preceded by the mace-bearers of the city and the heralds of Catalonia, he was conducted to the presence. Ferdinand and Isabella, as if by a sudden and spontaneous impulse, rose to receive their Admiral, an unprecedented act of condescension. After kissing hands, he was invited to sit on a chair under the canopy, and to narrate the events of the voyage. Nobles, prelates, ministers, and pages stood around, and among the latter was Gonzalo Fernandez de Oviedo, the future historian. In words of moving eloquence Columbus related the anxieties of the voyage, the landing at Guanahani, and the discovery of Cuba and Española. He described the magnificent scenery, the new and varied products, and the gentle character of the natives, and showed the sovereigns how God might be served, and their realms enriched, by a wise and judicious use of the new world his genius had presented to them. When he ceased to speak there was profound silence for some minutes. Then the sovereigns threw themselves on their knees, and returned thanks to God, the whole court following their example. A number of priests and choristers of the chapel royal entered the hall solemnly chanting the *Te Deum*, while the vast crowd outside sent up rounds and rounds of applause. It was a most impressive ceremony. At its conclusion the Cardinal Archbishop of Toledo conducted the Admiral to his lodging, to be his guest during his stay at Barcelona. On the following and several successive days Columbus had interviews with the sovereigns, lasting several hours. Active preparations were ordered to be commenced for a second expedition on a large scale, and negotiations were set

on foot with the Pope to secure the new possessions of
Castile from molestation on the part of the King of
Portugal.

It was resolved that Dr. Bernardo de Carbajal, the
Bishop of Cartagena, should be despatched on an embassy to the Pope, with a present of some of the first
gold brought from the Indies, and instructions to represent the vast consequences to Christianity that were
likely to accrue from the new discoveries. Pope Alexander VI. was an Aragonese, and had been a subject of
Ferdinand. It was found that Pope Martin V. had
already conceded a Bull to the King of Portugal, giving
that country the sovereignty from Cape Boyador to the
East Indies; and the concession had been recognised by
Spain in a treaty signed in 1479. Alexander VI., by a
Bull dated May 4, 1493, made a still greater concession to Spain. In order that the possessions of Spain
and Portugal might be clearly distinguished, the Pope
drew a line over the ocean from the Arctic to the An-
tartic Pole, situated as regards longitude at a distance of
one hundred leagues to the westward of the Azores. The
Pope granted all lands that had been or might be discovered, to the westward of this line, to the sovereigns
of Spain and their heirs for ever.

Columbus was treated with the highest distinction
during his residence at Barcelona. He frequently rode
out with the sovereigns and Prince Juan, and was always greeted with loud acclamations by the people. On
the 3rd of May, when the Indians were baptized, the
King and Prince stood as sponsors; and in many other
ways favour was shown to the Admiral, and to all that
concerned him. All the titles, honours, and precedence
granted in the capitulation of Santa Fe were confirmed,

and he was further invested with the title of Captain-
General of the fleet which was to be fitted out at Seville
for the Indies, in accordance with a royal order of May
28, 1493. In recognition of his great and distinguished services, and for perpetual memory of his achieve-

ARMS OF COLUMBUS.

ment, he was granted a special coat-of-arms on the 20th
of May. The shield is quarterly : first, a castle on a field
vert ; second, a lion rampant *purpure* on a field *argent ;*
third, islands of the sea *or* on a field *azure ;* and in the
fourth, the assumed family arms of Colombo. Subse-

quently five anchors *or* on a field *azure* were placed in
the fourth quarter, and the family arms were removed
to the middle base, in the same way as the pomegranate
appears in the royal arms of Spain. A motto was
allowed to encircle the shield as follows: "*Por Castilla
é por Léon Nuevo Mundo halló Colon,*" but this was
after the Admiral's death. Ferdinand also presented
the Admiral with a splendid suit of Milanese armour,
which is still preserved in the royal armoury at
Madrid.

The anecdote of the egg is said to have reference to
this period—"in Spain after he had discovered the
Indies"—and although it was first told fifty years after
the Admiral's death, it may quite possibly be founded
on fact. Benzoni * says : "Columbus being at a party
with many noble Spaniards, where, as was customary,
the subject of conversation was the Indies, one of them
undertook to say, 'Signor Cristoforo, even if you had
not found the Indies, we should not have been devoid of
a man who would have attempted the same that you
did, here in our country of Spain, as it is full of great
men, clever in cosmography and literature.' Columbus
said nothing in answer to these words, but having desired an egg to be brought to him, he placed it on the
table, saying, 'Gentlemen, I will lay a wager with any
of you that you will not make this egg stand up as I
will, naked, and without anything at all.' They all

---

* Girolamo Benzoni was born at Milan in 1519, and started for the
New World when he was twenty-two. After fourteen years he returned home in 1556, and in 1565 he published his *Historia del Mondo
Nuovo* at Venice, dedicated to Pius IV., second edition 1572. It was
translated into English for the Hakluyt Society by Admiral Smyth,
in 1857. See p. 17 of this translation for the anecdote of the
egg.

tried, and no one succeeded in making it stand up. When the egg came round to the hands of Columbus, by beating it down on the table he fixed it, crushing a little of one end: wherefore all remained confused, understanding what he would have said, that after the deed is done everybody knows how to do it, and that they ought first to have sought for the Indies, and not laugh at him who had sought for it first, while they for some time had been laughing, and wondered at it as an impossibility."

No one was more deeply impressed with the greatness of the achievement, and with its far-reaching consequences, than Columbus himself. But far from giving rise to any feeling of pride, it caused in him a deep sense of his own unworthiness. He believed that he was the chosen instrument in the hand of God to fulfil His designs, and accomplish much that had been prefigured in the prophecies. His whole life was tinged with devotional feeling, and his imaginative mind turned to the prophetic books of the Old Testament and to the Apocalypse for words that foreshadowed the great events in which he was the chief actor. His heart overflowed with gratitude at the thought that he, the humble Genoese weaver, should be the chosen instrument of the Almighty. He longed to signalise this feeling by some act worthy of the favour he had received. Among other aspirations Columbus conceived the idea of going on a crusade to rescue the holy sepulchre from the power of the infidels, when his work in the west was done. The spirit of knight-errantry was closely interwoven with the love of scientific speculation in the mind of this extraordinary man. His thoughts were also full of home, and of his kindred, and the old house in the Vico

Dritto was never forgotten in the midst of all the honours showered upon him at the Spanish court. Oviedo tells us that he sent help to his aged father as soon as he arrived at Lisbon, and from Barcelona he wrote to ask his two brothers to join him. The letter was long in reaching Bartolomè, and he did not arrive in Spain until after the departure of the Admiral. But young Giacomo came at once from Genoa. He had just reached the age of twenty-five, and was proud to follow the fortunes of his illustrious brother. Adopting the Spanish form of his name, he became Don Diego Colon, and accompanied the Admiral on his second voyage.

Columbus took his leave of the sovereigns and arrived at Seville early in June, and at Cadiz he selected the vessels best adapted for the voyage to Española. The fleet was composed of three ships and fourteen caravels, and the number of volunteers was far greater than the vessels could hold. Ferdinand and Isabella determined to create a department at Seville, charged with the duty of superintending the manning and equipment of the expeditions to the Indies, and with the guardianship of the royal interests and rights. It all depended on the character of the head of such a department whether it would work harmoniously and without friction; and unfortunately a worse selection could not have been made. Juan Rodriguez de Fonseca, the Archdeacon of Seville, was a man of noble family, and was known to the sovereigns as an administrator of considerable ability in a subordinate position. But he was an official of the worst type—proud, envious, and revengeful. Jealous of the great man whom he was bound to help in every way in his power, he gratified his jealousy by all the arts of circumlocution so well known to the official who is bent

on obstructive ways. The subordinates soon found that
insolence to the leaders of the expeditions, and the
practice of circumlocution, was the shortest way to favour.
Juan de Soria was appointed accountant and auditor,
while Francisco Pinedo was treasurer; and with these
three officials the Admiral had to deal in fitting out his
expedition at Cadiz. On this first occasion their obstruction was not so bad as it afterwards became when
they were more firmly established in office. Still the
accountant, Soria, appears to have been so insolent as to
call forth a severe reprimand from the sovereigns on the
5th of August, and Fonseca had to be reminded that he
was to further the wishes of the Admiral by all means
in his power.

A disastrous belief had spread abroad that rapid
fortunes were to be made in the New World; and the
very worst class of men, spendthrifts of good family
who hated work, and speculators of all kinds, crowded to
Cadiz as volunteers. The men really required were
hard working artizans and labourers, and the proportion
of these was insufficient. Over 1400 men were embarked, and it is said that, when the ships had got fairly
out to sea, as many as a hundred stowaways made their
appearance. About twenty horses were taken out, stores
of all kinds, seeds, and implements of husbandry.

The Admiral was accompanied by his brother Diego,
a virtuous and discreet young man, as Las Casas describes him, always very soberly dressed, almost like a
cleric. The other principal leaders in the expedition
were carefully selected. Don Antonio de Torres, a
brother of the nurse of Prince Juan, described as a
prudent and able commander, was to go out with the
Admiral, and return with some of the ships. The

accountant of the colony was Bernal de Pisa, and the overseer Don Diego Marque. The father of Las Casas went out as a councillor, and his uncle, Francisco de Peñalosa, as one of the commanders of the troops.

The first priest who went to the New World was Fray Bernardo Boil, a Catalonian, born in Tarragona, who entered the Benedictine fraternity very early in life as a monk of the monastery of Montserrat. He was specially selected by King Ferdinand to accompany the expedition, and his appointment was approved by the Pope. His bearing towards the Admiral was at first friendly and cordial, but afterwards he allowed feelings of pride and jealousy to influence his conduct, which resulted in open disloyalty to his chief. Three friars accompanied him. Another subject of King Ferdinand, who became one of the chief officers of the expedition, was Mosen Pedro Margarit, an Aragonese of good family, who distinguished himself in the war of Granada as an able and at the same time a cautious officer. But Margarit and Boil, the two Aragonese specially chosen by King Ferdinand, turned out to be disloyal and insubordinate.

Dr. Diego Alvarez Chanca, a physician of Seville, with a high reputation for skill and learning, was ordered to join the expedition, not only to take medical charge, but also to report upon the rare and unknown plants of the Indies. The Admiral's journal is lost, and it is to Dr. Chanca that we owe the only narrative of the voyage, contained in a long letter addressed to the Chapter of Seville. He also supplied information to the Cura of Los Palacios, Dr. Bernaldez, which enabled him to give many details of the expedition in his "Chronicle of the Catholic Kings."

But the most striking figure of the second voyage was a young man about twenty years of age, whose acquaintance the Admiral had first made in the house of the Duke of Medina Celi. Alonzo de Ojeda came of a good family in the city of Cuenca, and he passed his boyhood as a page to the Duke. He excelled as a horseman and in the use of arms of all kinds, and he combined a cool head with a fiery and dare-devil love of danger and adventure. Ojeda was of short stature, but muscular and well knit, with a handsome face and a penetrating look in his eyes. In very early youth he performed several acts of daring and valour in the war of Granada, fighting by the side of the Duke his master. A story is told of him when the Queen was at Seville in 1491 which illustrates his coolness and pluck. As the commencement of a solid scaffold for effecting repairs, a large beam had been run out from the top window of the Giralda for ten yards, at a height of 250 feet from the ground. Ojeda, in order to show off before the Queen, walked out to the end of the beam fully armed and accoutred. He then turned on one foot, threw an orange over the top of the tower, and coolly walked back to the window. The very thought of such a feat would turn most people giddy, and the crowd beneath were astounded at the youth's nerve and audacity. Alonzo de Ojeda was destined to play a leading part in the early history of the Western Indies.

Columbus took his brother-in-law, Pedro de Arana, brother of Beatriz Enriquez, as captain of one of the ships; and Juan de la Cosa, the expert draughtsman, accompanied the Admiral again in the capacity of pilot.

Ferdinand and Isabella caused the second expedition to be fitted out with the intention of establishing a per-

manent colony. It would have been wiser if, while im-
posing their sovereignty on the newly-discovered countries,
they had been contented with establishing factories or
trading stations, and had prohibited the advent of a
shoal of useless adventurers thirsting for gold. Such
men came to a country wholly unprepared to receive
them, already occupied by a gentle and unwarlike people,
and destitute of any wealth that could be obtained
without hard and continuous toil. The great majority
of the emigrants were unaccustomed to work, and full of
wild expectations. That they should be useless as settlers, that they should become discontented and insubordinate, and that they should cruelly oppress the natives,
were inevitable results. No leader, be his administrative talents how great soever, could have prevented or
obviated these evils. Columbus entered upon a task
which no administrator could have performed successfully. He had to see that the natives were converted to
Christianity, while they were forced to contribute to the
wealth of the colony ; he had to content the adventurers
and to put them in the way of accumulating riches ; he
had to increase the revenues of the mother country ;
and, at the same time, he had to suppress insubordination
and silence discontent. He was a man of genius, of
warm sympathies, and of great resource. He was prudent, conciliatory, and patient. If he partially failed, it
was because the circumstances rendered failure unavoid-
able.

But the clouds had not yet appeared on the horizon.
All were full of hope and unreasoning expectations when
the preparations were completed, and the order was
given for the expedition to get under weigh. His sons,
Diego and little Fernando, had been with the Admiral

K

at Cadiz, and they were with him when he hoisted his
flag on board the *Marigalante*, a comparatively large
ship, but a slow sailer. He gazed long and anxiously
after the boys as the boat carried them to the shore,
and then turned cheerfully and hopefully to the business
of his high office.

When the Admiral sent for his brother and dearest
friend, he did not know for certain whither to despatch
the letter. In truth, Bartolome had been repulsed by
the English government, and had taken up his abode at
the French court, in the service of Anne de Beaujeu,
who governed the country during the absence of her
brother, Charles VIII., in Italy. Bartolome was probably employed to draw maps and to illustrate works
on cosmography and kindred subjects; and when, after
long delay, he heard of his brother's return, he must
have obtained his dismissal and hastened to Spain. But
he was too late to take part in the second expedition,
which sailed in September 1493. Bartolome does not
appear to have reached Seville until January in the
following year. His first act was to seek out his nephew,
and he presented himself at the court of Valladolid with
young Diego, who had by this time completed his education. The brother and son of the Admiral were well
received by Ferdinand and Isabella. Diego entered
upon his duties as page to the young Prince Juan, with
whom he remained in close attendance until the mourn-
ful death of the only son of the Spanish sovereigns at
Salamanca, on the 4th of October 1497. The deaths of
princes are always referred to by courtiers as national
calamities. But the death of young Juan may really be
considered one, not only to Spain but to the whole of
Europe. If he had lived the fatal inheritance of the

Low Countries would have been avoided, which deluged
Europe in blood for half a century, and crippled Spain,
in men and treasure, beyond recovery.

On April 14, 1494, the sovereigns nominated Bartolomè Columbus to the command of a squadron of
three caravels about to sail for the New World. He
landed in Española on the 24th of June, during the
absence of his brother Christopher on a voyage of discovery; but he found his young brother Diego at
Isabella, whom he had not seen for fourteen years.

NOTE.

(1) *Discovery that Columbus wrote to Toscanelli on his Return.*

The fact that Columbus wrote to Toscanelli from Seville was
recently discovered by Prospero Peragallo. He purchased an
edition of Sacrobosco by Dante di Rinaldi, printed at Florence
in 1571, in which there is a note by the editor on the torrid and
frigid zones being habitable. He says that Cristoforo Colombo
discovered countries within the torrid zone and returned to
Spain, having found that they were perfectly habitable, adding,
" As I have seen from a copy of a letter from the said Colombo,
written from Seville to the very learned and expert mathematician, Messer Paolo Toscanelli, the Florentine, which was
sent to me through Messer Cornelio Randoli" (*Riconferma
dell' autenticità delle Historie di Fernando Colombo per Prospero Peragallo, Genova*, 1885). See Asensio, i. p. 428, *note*.

CHAPTER VIII.

THE SECOND VOYAGE OF DISCOVERY AND THE SETTLEMENT OF ESPAÑOLA.

On the 24th of September 1493 the *Marigalante*, with Columbus on board, gave the signal to weigh anchor, and the squadron of seventeen vessels sailed out of the bay of Cadiz. The Admiral was now in a ship of 400 tons. He had with him his brother Diego and three old comrades of the first voyage. These were the pilot, Juan de la Cosa, who was now entered as chief draughtsman ("Maestro de hacer cartas"), Francisco Niño of Moguer, who took his son Alonzo with him as a ship's boy, and the Admiral's steward, Pedro de Terreros. On the 5th of October the squadron anchored at Gomera, where it remained two days to fill up with water and purchase live stock. The Admiral embarked eight pigs, bulls and cows, sheep and goats, fowls and pigeons, seeds of oranges, lemons, and other fruits, and all kinds of vegetables. On the 13th the island of Ferro disappeared below the horizon, and a pleasant voyage was commenced across the Atlantic. It was the intention of Columbus to discover the islands of which he had heard to the east of Española, and he therefore shaped a more southerly course than on the first voyage. There was a great contrast between that first voyage, when the minds of the sailors were constantly filled with suspicion

and terror, and the second, where all was joyful and
eager anticipation.   Alonzo de Ojeda, Messer Pedro
Margarit, Father Boil, and Dr. Chanca, forming a sufficiently agreeable party, were the messmates of the
Admiral and his young brother.   The *Marigalante* was
a slow sailer, and the rest of the squadron had frequently
to shorten sail in order to keep station.   When, according to his reckoning, the land was near at hand, the
Admiral made the ships and caravels follow in line, and
ordered a very sharp look out to be kept.   Early in
the morning of the 3rd of November the look-out men
reported land ahead, and when the sun rose a lovely
island was in sight, clothed with trees to the summits
of its lofty peaked mountains.   It was Sunday, so the
Admiral gave the name of Dominica to the island.   He
sailed along its northern shore for a short distance in
search of a harbour, but seeing none, he stretched across
to a small well-wooded island that was in sight to the
northward, which received the name of " Marigalante,"
after the Admiral's ship.   Here the squadron anchored.
If they had continued to stand on for a short distance
farther along the coast of Dominica, they would have
come to the beautiful anchorage at the north end of the
western coast, now called Prince Rupert's Bay.   Columbus, with all the principal officials, landed on the island
of Marigalante, and took formal possession in the name
of the Catholic sovereigns.   They were all deeply impressed by the magnificence of the vegetation, so different
from anything they had ever seen before, and almost
spontaneously they threw themselves on their knees
and offered up thanksgiving to God.   There were no
signs of any inhabitants, so the voyage was resumed,
and a much larger island with lofty mountain peaks

almost immediately came in sight. A magnificent cascade, appearing to fall from the clouds, was seen to pour down the side of a mountain and disappear in a mass of foliage. Columbus named the island Guadalupe, in memory of the famous sanctuary of Our Lady in Estremadura.

The Admiral anchored the squadron in a convenient bay, and sent several parties on shore to open communications with the natives. They came to large houses amongst the trees, some of them built in squares round open spaces. They found quantities of cotton in the houses, and some large parrots kept as pets. All the people fled at their approach, except some boys and women, who were captured, and who said that they were prisoners brought from other islands. This circumstance, and the sight of human limbs prepared for food, led the Admiral to the conclusion that he had reached one of the islands inhabited by the fierce man-eating Caribs, of whom he had heard at Española. His skill as a navigator is shown by his having sailed from Europe with the intention of discovering these unknown islands of the Caribs, and having made the landfall exactly.

One remarkable discovery made by the Spaniards at Guadalupe was the pine-apple, the most delicious fruit they had ever tasted, and which excited their enthusiasm for the New World and its vegetable as well as its mineral treasures. There were other new fruits and multitudes of trees and flowers quite unknown to them, but the pine-apples were more pleasant to the taste and more fragrant than anything else among the wonders of this enchanting island. Six women and two boys, who were prisoners to the Caribs, were allowed to come on board as a refuge from their captors.

When the other parties returned to their respective vessels it was found that the overseer, Diego Marquez, who also commanded one of the caravels, was missing, with eight of his men. Trumpets were sounded and lombards discharged, but the missing party did not return. At last the Admiral sent Alonzo de Ojeda in search with forty men, but they returned without finding any trace. The Admiral was on the point of abandoning all hope, when, on Friday the 8th of November, Marquez and his men came down to the beach half dead with hunger and fatigue. They had lost their way in the dense forest, and had been wading streams, cutting their way through dense foliage, and scrambling over rocks for four days, always with the abiding terror that the ships would have sailed if they ever reached the seashore again. Abundant evidence was collected that at least three of the islands were inhabited by a ferocious race of cannibals called Caribs, who made war on their peaceful neighbours with the object of capturing prisoners for the purpose of eating them, after having first treated them with barbarous cruelty. The native names of these islands were Ayay, Turuqueira,* and Ceyre, which the Admiral named Guadalupe and Dominica.

Having filled up with water and fresh provisions, the squadron got under weigh on Sunday the 10th of November, and steered a north-east course in the direction of Española. The Admiral was becoming very anxious to reach Navidad, and learn the condition of the settlement, which he had left well stored with provisions nine months before. But on the way he had to pass a great number of islands, and the navigation called for all his nautical skill and for incessant watchfulness. Dr. Chanca

* Ayay and Turuqueira being the two islands of Guadalupe.

does not mention the names given to these islands, but
the names of some of them are to be found in Las Casas.
Unfortunately, the chart and journal of the Admiral,
where they would all be entered, is lost. After leaving
Guadalupe, a beautiful wooded island with lofty peaks
came in sight, which reminded Father Boil of his abode
in Catalonia. So it received the name of "Montserrat."
A round islet was seen to the westward, so steep on all
sides that it seemed inaccessible without stairs or ropes
thrown from the top. It received the name of "Santa
Maria la Redonda." The squadron rounded the eastern
end of Montserrat, and the comparatively low island to
the eastward received the name of "Santa Maria la
Antigua." In altering course to the north-westward
a number of islands must have come in sight, including
St. Kitts and Nevis. They are not mentioned, but they
doubtless appeared on the Admiral's chart as "San Cristoval" and "Nuestra Señora de las Nieves." The squadron anchored off an island, which was named "San
Martin," and then altered its course to a little south of
west and reached "Santa Cruz." Here a party was sent
on shore to capture some natives with a view to ascertaining the language. There was a fierce encounter with
some men in a canoe, and the people of Santa Cruz and
San Martin were judged to be Caribs. Passing a count-
less number of islands, to the largest of which Columbus
gave the name of "Santa Ursula," and to the others
"Las 11,000 Virgenes," the modern Virgin Islands, they
came to a large and fertile island, where they remained
for two days. The Admiral named it "San Juan Bautista," now known as Puerto Rico. The inhabitants
fled and concealed themselves, so the Admiral proceeded
on his voyage, and arrived off the east end of Española

on the evening of the 22nd of November. After stopping two days off Monte Cristi, during which several excursions were made up the Rio de Oro or Yaqui, to seek for a good site for a new city, the squadron proceeded to Navidad, eager to meet the settlers.

On Wednesday, the 27th of November, the ships anchored off the port of Navidad, and the Admiral ordered some lombards to be discharged, expecting that they would be answered from the fort. There was an ominous silence on shore. It was late when they anchored, so they remained on board until next morning. All feared that some terrible disaster had befallen the settlers. At last a canoe arrived with a relation of the cacique Guacanagari, bringing presents. When he was asked about the settlers his replies appeared to be evasive and confused. He said that many had died of disease, some in brawls among themselves, and that there had been a war with a powerful chief of the interior of the island named Caonabó, in the course of which Guacanagari had been wounded. It appeared that not one of the Spaniards who had been left at Navidad in the previous January was still alive. Next morning an armed boat was sent on shore to reconnoitre. It was noticed that the natives kept at a distance, and appeared shy and distrustful. The palisade which encircled the fort of Navidad was broken down and burnt. The buildings inside were all destroyed. There was evidence of some great calamity. At length a brother of Guacanagari, with some attendants, ventured to approach the Spaniards, and it was ascertained that all the settlers had perished at the hands of the cacique Caonabó, who first attacked the fort with a large force, destroying everything, and killing every soul within it, and then burnt the houses of

Guacanagari. Many of that chief's followers had been killed in trying to defend their guests, and he himself was wounded.

Next day the Admiral landed with a large number of men, and made a close examination of the site of Navidad and the neighbourhood. The result was that he was forced to believe the worst. Not a single one remained alive of all the forty-four officers and sailors whom he had left there nine short months before. Such was the melancholy end of the first settlement in the New World. Columbus, as soon as the place where Guacanagari resided had been found, went to visit him with all his officers. He found the friendly chief lying in a hammock and disabled by a wound. Guacanagari related all the particulars of the disaster with tears in his eyes, and showed the Admiral a number of his followers who had been wounded in trying to defend the Christians.

Many of the Spanish officers disbelieved the chief's story, and proposed to make an example of him and his chief followers. Father Boil was among the number of those who counselled violence—"the first apostle of the New World!" as this truculent and disloyal monk has been absurdly called. But the large and generous heart of the Admiral at once rejected such advice. He felt no suspicion, and fully acquitted Guacanagari and his people, believing that they were telling the simple truth.

After examining the coast for several days, the Admiral selected a site for the settlement about thirty miles to the eastward of Monte Cristi. It was a smooth stretch of shore between the mouths of two streams, and in rear there was a rocky bank suitable for the site of a fort or citadel. The open space was surrounded by dense forest, but at a short distance there was excellent building stone. The people were delighted to land, after having been so long cooped up in the small vessels, and the work of unloading proceeded rapidly. Temporary buildings were run up to house the stores and provisions, while the Admiral traced out the plan of a city, to which he gave the name of Isabella. The church, government house, and royal warehouses were to be of stone, and were commenced at once. In January 1494 the houses were so far completed that all the settlers were able to sleep on shore; and on Epiphany Sunday the first mass was said by Father Boil, in a temporary chapel.

Very soon after the foundation of Isabella, sickness began to make its appearance, caused by hard work under a tropical sun, and by the disgraceful character of the provisions shipped by Fonseca and his officials. Much of the salt meat and biscuit was bad, and the wine was still worse. Fever was very prevalent, and the people became home-sick and discontented. The Admiral had received intelligence that there were rich gold-mines in the mountains of Cibao, a chain which traverses the centre of the island. Hoping to arouse the people, and draw their attention from their own miseries, he organised some exploring parties, entrusting the command of the two first, consisting of fifteen men each, to Alonzo de Ojeda and Genés de Gorbalän, both young and intrepid commanders. Crossing the coast-range of Monte Cristi they descended into the beautiful valley of the river Yaqui, where they were cordially received by the natives, who brought them presents of food and cotton. After marching about sixty miles they reached the foot of the mountains of Cibao, and, assisted by the natives, they obtained a considerable quantity of gold

dust by washing the sands of the streams. Their return
to Isabella animated the hopes of the settlers, and there
was much less despondency when Antonio Torres, in
command of nine of the vessels, sailed on the return
voyage to Spain, with the first news of the settlement,
on the 2nd of February 1494. Gorbalán returned at the
same time ; and Torres was the bearer of an important
memorial to the sovereigns, in which the Admiral set
forth the needs of the colony.

In this memorial Columbus reported that the parties
under Ojeda and Gorbalán had found that the sands of
several rivers in the interior contained gold in considerable quantities, referring the sovereigns to the latter
commander for a fuller account of these discoveries.
Although there had been much sickness, owing to the
want of fresh and wholesome food, yet the work of
building the city and of surrounding it with suitable
defences was progressing. He represented that the
settlers ought to be supplied with wholesome food until
they were able to gather sufficient crops from seeds
sown in the colony. Some corn and sugar cane had
already been sown, and had come up; but he earnestly
requested that supplies of all kinds might be promptly
despatched, so as to arrive in May.

The Admiral recommended that the savage cannibals
in the other islands should be captured in considerable
numbers and sent to Spain as slaves, for the good of
their own souls and to free the peaceable islanders from
the terror of their cruel invasions. His plan was that
a certain number of caravels should annually be sent to
the Indies laden with cattle, and that the live stock
should be paid for with slaves taken from the Caribs.
The revenue might be benefited by fixing a duty on

these slaves when they were landed in Spain. The memorial concluded with commendations of the valuable services of many of the officers under the Admiral's command, especially mentioning Dr. Chanca, whose letter to the Chapter of Seville was sent home by the same opportunity, and Messer Pedro Margarit.

The practice of defraying expenses by the sale of slaves was adopted by Prince Henry the Navigator, whose captains established a regular traffic along the coast of Africa. It was believed that, while the heavy expenses of the expeditions were reduced by this means, the slaves were not injured, and their spiritual and temporal welfare was promoted. Columbus had seen this traffic regularly established wherever the Portuguese traders went on the African coast, and in those days, and for centuries afterwards, public opinion looked upon it with favour. Ferdinand and Isabella adopted the same course, after the capture of Malaga and other Moorish towns. Las Casas raised his voice against it, and wrote eloquent denunciations nearly three centuries in advance of his time. But that was after the death of Columbus, and at the time when he was surrounded by administrative difficulties at Isabella the impression that slave traffic involved no moral wrong was universal. Columbus, however, was desirous of modifying the Portuguese system very materially. His proposal was confined to the cannibals who devastated the islands of the peaceably disposed Indians, and who, he considered, had placed themselves beyond the pale, and to prisoners taken in war.

The Admiral's activity had been marvellous. He had personally attended to every administrative detail, planned out the city, the fort, and the aqueduct for con-

ducting wholesome water to the houses, had organised
the expeditions, and taken measures for clearing ground
for raising crops. At length, just as Torres was on the
point of sailing, he was himself prostrated by fever.
The loss of his guiding hand was felt at once. Taking
advantage of his illness, the most ill conditioned and
discontented among the settlers, led by Bernal Diaz de
Pisa, the accountant, formed a plot to seize one of the
vessels and return home. The conspiracy was assuming
serious dimensions when the Admiral became convales-
cent towards the end of February. He at once stamped
it out ; but he proceeded cautiously, his sole object being
to establish lawful authority and prevent a repetition
of the offence. The discovery of slanderous documents
containing numerous false accusations on board one of
the ships established the guilt of the conspirators, whose
handwriting was identified. They were committed to
prison until an opportunity offered for sending them to
Spain with a statement of the charges against them.
Unfortunately discontent continued to smoulder among
those whose absurd dreams of immediate gain had been
disappointed, which was a serious element of danger.

The Admiral then turned his attention to the organisa-
tion of an expedition on an adequate scale to the gold-
yielding mountains of Cibao. Intending to establish a
fort, he took with him artificers and tools, and on the
12th of March he set out from Isabella with 400 soldiers
well armed, and all the horses. The government of the
rising city was entrusted in his absence to his brother
Diego and Father Boil. Much difficulty was experienced
in crossing the first densely wooded range of mountains
with horses and heavy baggage. Several youths of good
family, who had seen something of pioneering work in

the war of Granada, volunteered to make the road up
the rocky slopes matted with tropical vegetation, until
they conducted the expedition to a pass between the
hills which, from the rank of the pioneers, received the
name of "Puerto de los Hidalgos." The adventurers
were rewarded for their exertions by being able to feast
their eyes on one of the loveliest scenes in nature. A
glorious view was spread out before them. A plain,
through which numerous streams were flowing like silver
threads on the bright expanse of green, was dotted in
all directions by masses of a darker shade, marking the
numerous groves and gardens. Beyond was the lofty
range of mountains of which they were in search : but
the eyes of the explorers rested longer on the fertile
expanse, to which the Admiral gave the name of "Vega
Real."

The strictest discipline was maintained as the Spaniards
marched across the beautiful plain, and crossed the river
Yaqui in canoes and rafts ; but the simple natives came
in crowds to offer presents of yams and fruit. The
ascent of the rocky mountains of Cibao was difficult, ·
and a halt was made on the banks of some gold-bearing
streams, where several small nuggets were obtained
from the natives. Here a fort was built on a hill almost
surrounded by a stream called Xantigue, and a small
force, under a young captain named Juan de Luján, was
detached to make a further exploration of the mountains. The fort received the name of "Santo Tomas,"
and Pedro Margarit was appointed governor with a
garrison of fifty-six men. On the return of Luján with
a favourable report of the gold washings further west,
the Admiral began the construction of a road from Santo
Tomas to Isabella, a distance of about sixty miles. The

expedition returned, after an absence of seventeen days, on the 29th of March.

At Isabella there was nothing but trouble and anxiety. Illness was prevalent, and there had been several deaths, while the stock of flour was becoming very low. Luckily a large supply of wheat had also been brought out, which was still in excellent condition, and the Admiral set to work constructing water-mills for grinding it. There was so much sickness that it was necessary for all who were well, of whatever rank, to work at the mills. The Admiral very properly ordered that those who would not work could only receive half rations, without excepting priests. Father Boil maintained that ecclesiastics ought to be exempted from the order. He wanted no work and a full belly. The Admiral refused to yield, and the truculent monk from this time became disloyal and insubordinate.

In order to give the men a more healthy mode of life, and to save the provisions, Columbus organised a small army of 400 men and sixteen horses under the valiant Alonzo de Ojeda. He was to march to the fort of San Tomas and take the command there, while Margarit was to place himself at the head of the troops and explore the interior of the island, treating with the people, and impressing the chiefs with an idea of Spanish power by this display of force. Margarit was specially instructed to visit the territories of Caonabó and ascertain the amount of influence possessed by that chief, whose hostility had been so fatal to the settlers at Navidad. He was enjoined to preserve the strictest discipline, to prevent any injury being done to the natives, and to punish all excesses with severity.

The instructions of the sovereigns enjoined the Admiral, after he had established the settlement, to undertake a voyage for the purpose of further discovery. He now, therefore, prepared three caravels, and set sail on the 24th of April. A Commission, presided over by his brother Diego, was nominated to govern the settlement in his absence. The members were Father Boil, Juan de Luján, Pedro Fernandez Coronel, and Alonzo de Carbajal.

Meanwhile Ojeda proceeded to the fort, received the command from Margarit, and handed over the leadership of the exploring force to that officer. But Margarit, instead of advancing into the territories of Caonabó, marched down into the Vega Real, and established his soldiers in idleness among the natives, in direct disobedience of the written orders of the Admiral. He himself indulged in every sort of excess, and encouraged his men to do the same. The Commission at Isabella sent him frequent orders to proceed on the service set forth in his instructions drawn up by the Admiral, but he refused to obey, and his troops became utterly demoralised, robbing the natives, outraging their women, and exciting a feeling of hatred and loathing against themselves.

In the midst of all this license and confusion Bartolomé Columbus arrived at Isabella on the 24th of June, in command of three caravels, well supplied with provisions for the colony. His force of will, and the prestige of his position as a commander sent out by the sovereigns, gave him influence which he used to strengthen young Diego in his efforts to suppress the insubordination of Margarit. That officer, however, had gone too far in his evil course to recede. He had already done incalculable, probably irreparable, injury to the infant colony. He feared to face the Admiral on his return.

L

There were traitors on the Commission who were in correspondence with him, and Father Boil was the ringleader. They arranged to desert their posts, return to Spain, and spread calumnies against the Admiral. Margarit marched to Isabella with a force which the Admiral's brothers were unable to resist, seized the three caravels brought out by Bartolomè, and sailed for Spain in September, accompanied by Father Boil and other deserters. These traitors had brought the colony to the very verge of ruin, by arousing the just indignation of the natives, and entirely destroying their original feeling of cordiality and goodwill. The Admiral had made the best arrangements that an able administrator could devise, and if his orders had been loyally obeyed all would have been well. He could not foresee that an officer like Margarit, of high position and military experience, and enjoying the favour of King Ferdinand, would, when entrusted with an important duty, prove himself to be not only a traitor and a deserter, but an abandoned reprobate. He could not foresee that a priest, who had been specially selected for his piety and devotion, and appointed by the Pope himself to the spiritual charge of the infant colony, would conspire with such a man as Margarit after his true character was known, and desert his post.

While the Admiral was on the spot all went well, but the moment his guiding hand quitted the helm the colonial ship was run upon the sands by its worthless crew. The opportune arrival of Bartolomè saved it; and when the Admiral, worn out with toil and almost at death's door, returned from his terrible voyage on the 29th of September, his faithful brother continued to be a tower of strength.

CHAPTER IX.

THE THIRD VOYAGE OF DISCOVERY AND TROUBLES IN ESPAÑOLA.

COLUMBUS had scarcely recovered from a severe attack of fever, and was almost worn out with the anxieties of his government, when he prepared to sail on what may be considered as his third voyage of discovery. He selected three caravels out of the five that remained at Isabella, and caused them to be overhauled and provisioned for six months. The first was the old *Niña* of the former voyage, on board of which he hoisted his flag, with Francisco Niño as pilot, Alonzo Medel as master, Juan de la Cosa to draw charts, one of the monks, ten seamen, and six boys. Pedro de Terreros was with him as steward, and the notary, Fernan Perez de Luna, accompanied him as secretary. The second caravel was the *San Juan*, with Alonzo Perez Roldan as master, Bartolomè Perez of Rota as pilot, a boatswain, cooper, six seamen, and five boys. The *Cordera* was the third vessel, having Cristoval Perez Niño as master, a Genoese boatswain, seven seamen, and five boys. Including the Admiral there were fifty-two souls in the expedition, and it is remarkable that twenty-six came from the Palos district, evidently a great nursery for seamen in those days, while four were Genoese.

Sailing on the 24th of April 1494, Columbus pro-

ceeded along the north coast of Española to San Nicolas,
and then shaped a course to the southern coast of the
island of Juana, as he had named Cuba in his first
voyage.   He anchored in a good harbour on the south
coast, to which he gave the name of Puerto Grande
It is now called Guantanamo.   Here he obtained a good
supply of fish from the natives, and weighing anchor on
the 1st of May, he continued to sail along the southern
coast of Cuba, gazing on the lofty mountains, noting
the rivers and harbours, and receiving visits from
numerous Indians in their canoes, who brought presents
of cassava bread, fish, and fresh water.   They asked for
nothing in return, but were given glass beads, hawks'
bells, and other trifles.   The Guanahani guide, who had
been to Spain and returned with the Admiral, advised
him to visit a large island of which he had heard from the
natives at some distance to the southward.   Columbus
therefore shaped a southerly course, and the next day,
Monday, the 14th of May, he came in sight of the island
of Jamaica.   He anchored in a bay surrounded by a
beautiful country, with clumps of lofty spreading trees,
and the houses of the natives scattered in all directions,
so that the island appeared to be very populous.   The
Admiral named the harbour "Santa Gloria," the modern
St. Anne, and the island of Jamaica received the name
of "Santiago."   The natives showed such hostility, dis-
charging showers of arrows from their canoes, that at
last an order was given to discharge some arquebuses
among them, on which they took to flight.   The Admiral
landed with his officers and took formal possession of
the island in the names of the Spanish sovereigns.   The
natives then ventured to approach with signs of peace,
and being kindly received, they soon came in crowds

with supplies of all kinds. It had become necessary to careen the vessels, and Columbus selected a port for this operation, which he named " Puerto Bueno." The work occupied three days, the Spanish sailors receiving assistance from the natives. Some of the canoes were observed to be ninety-six feet long, hollowed out of a single tree. Having completed the repairs, the little squadron sailed along the island to the western extremity, where a southerly wind prevented further exploration in that direction. They were accompanied by upwards of seventy canoes of various sizes. The western promontory of Jamaica received the name of " Cabo del Buen Tiempo," and thence the Admiral shaped a course to return to the coast of Cuba.

On the 18th of May the squadron once more anchored off the Cuba coast, near the Cape of Santa Cruz; and in proceeding westward the vessels found themselves among an innumerable number of small islets and cays, necessitating incessant watchfulness to avoid a disaster. It was a perfect labyrinth, some of the islands being mere sandbanks, others covered with trees interlaced with lovely climbing plants brilliant with flowers. It was impossible to give a separate name to each, so the Admiral designated the whole archipelago " Jardin de la Reyna "—the Garden of the Queen. He could have avoided the dangers and anxieties of this intricate navigation by keeping further out to sea, but he remembered the description of the further India, that it terminated with innumerable islands, and he did not wish to keep at a distance from a country which he believed to be near the territory of the Grand Khan.

For more than a month he continued to thread the tortuous channels, on deck day and night. The strain

on a system already sorely tried by a recent attack of
fever must have been tremendous. Having **been** told
by one **cacique that** there was a province far to the westward called Mangon, he came to the conclusion that this
was Mango **or** Mangi, in the territory of the Grand
Khan, **mentioned** in the letter **of** Toscanelli, **and** by
Marco Polo. The great extent **of** the coast he had traversed led Columbus **to think that** Cuba could **not** pos-
sibly be an island, but that it must needs be part of the
continent—perhaps **the "Aureus** Chersonesus" of Ptolemy. He could **think** of nothing else, and **it** preyed
upon his mind. But the provisions were running **short,**
and it was necessary to return **to** Española.

The mind of the Admiral** was overwrought. **It was
worn out by** incessant watching **and want of** rest, and a
fever was actually in his veins. **The tension** was greater
than his frame, enfeebled by his former **illness,** could
endure, and for a time his usually sound judgment for-
sook him. This alone can account for the proceeding
recorded in a document** preserved in **the Seville archives.**
It appears that C**olumbus caused **the** notary, Perez de
Luna, to take the opinions **of all** the officers, **men,** and
boys on board the three caravels **as to** whether a coast-
line of such immense **length** was likely **to** belong to an
island or a continent. **Their** unanimous conclusion was
that it was a continent, and this **was** embodied in a sort
of affidavit **with the whole** of their names attached.
Penalties consisting o**f fines and** slitting of tongues, with
whippings for the boys, were added if any of them recanted.
The document **is** dated **June 12th, and is** witnessed by
the Admiral's steward.*** It** shows that the Admiral was
not himself, owing to sleep**lessness** and **fever, the pre-**

* Navarrete, ii. p. 143.

monitory symptoms of a long and dangerous illness. There is, however, no cause for regret that the document was preserved. While it witnesses to the illness of the Admiral, which relieved him of responsibility for a foolish proceeding, it has, at the same time, preserved the names of all his companions in this trying voyage.

They got in wood and water on the Isla de los Pinos, which Columbus named the " Isla del Evangelista," but their provisions were at a very low ebb. They had only biscuits and a little wine, and the daily rations had to be much reduced, all, including the Admiral, sharing alike. They, however, received yams and fruits from the natives, besides doves, which were excellent, and occasionally they secured a turtle. Returning westward to the Bay of Santa Cruz, the caravels were anchored there on the 6th of July, and the Admiral landed with a large party to attend mass, which was said at a temporary altar among the trees. Great numbers of natives stood round to witness the ceremony, with awe and veneration. Among those who watched the service with closest attention was an aged cacique, who afterwards came to the Admiral and conversed with him through the Guanahani interpreter. The old man said : " You have come to these countries, which you had never seen before, with great power, and your coming has caused fear among all the people. I would have you to know that, according to our belief, there are two places to which the departed go after death, one evil and the other good. If you feel that you must die, and that such as your deeds have been so will be your reward, do not do harm here to those who have done no harm to you. What you have now done is good, because you appeared to be returning thanks to God." The Admiral was surprised

at the grand simplicity of the old man's speech, and
could only reply that he had been sent by the rich and
powerful kings who were his lords to discover those lands,
with no other object than to seek out those who did evil
to their neighbours, that he had heard there were such
people called Caribs whom he would restrain and hinder,
but that he would honour and do good to all who lived
in peace. The answer appears to have satisfied the
chief, but the conduct of Margarit in the Vega Real
was even then belying the words of Columbus.

The caravels had to return to Española in the teeth
of the trade wind, which was blowing fresh. The
Admiral stretched across to Jamaica, and then tried to
beat up along the shore, finding it slow and tedious
work. But he was again enchanted with the beauty
of the scenery, and had very cordial relations with the
people, who followed the vessels in their canoes, and
brought out presents of fresh provisions. At length the
eastern extremity of Jamaica was reached, which was
named " Punta del Farol " (Cape Morant), and the vessels
succeeded in reaching the coast of Española on the 20th
of August. The western point, now Cape Tiburon, was
named by Columbus " San Miguel." Proceeding eastward
along the south coast, they were much retarded by the
frequent recurrence of sudden squalls of wind, which
exposed them to some danger, and called for a very close
look out for the sails. In one of these squalls the San
Juan and Cordera parted company with the Niña,
and were lost sight of for some days, owing to the thick
weather and the deluges of rain. Off the southern
extreme of Española a solitary rock rises from the sea,
resembling, at a distance, a ship under sail. The
Admiral called it " Alta Vela," a name which it still

retains. Some birds and seals were obtained on the
opposite rocky shore, affording a welcome supply of fresh
food, and on reaching the mouth of the Neyva river the
two missing caravels again joined company. The valley
of the Neyva was very fertile and populous, and the
friendly people supplied the vessels with all they needed.
Nine men were landed here, with full instructions as to
their route, and with orders to march to the fort of San
Tomas and report the return of the Admiral. The
three vessels resumed their tedious voyage, still encountering sudden squalls of wind and rain, and beating
against the foul wind. They took shelter under the lee
of Saona or Adamanez Island, and on the 24th of
September anchored off Mona Isle, in the channel between Española and Puerto Rico.

Through all this perilous and harassing navigation,
with failing health and fevered brain, the Admiral had
continued to guide and pilot his little squadron. But
off Mona he completely broke down. The spirit had
fought manfully against the enfeebled body, but nature
at length avenged itself. He became prostrate and
insensible, at times delirious. His people believed that
the great seaman's last hour had come. They made all
possible haste to return, rounding the north-east point
of the island with a fair wind, and anchoring in the
bay of Isabella on the 29th of September 1494. The
Admiral was quite insensible, and so weak that it was
feared he would die before he could be landed. He was
borne on the shoulders of his crew to his house, where
he was tended with affectionate care by his brothers ;
but it was a long and anxious illness, and for some time
he was at death's door. It took five months for him to
reach a state of convalescence. As soon as he recovered

consciousness he found his beloved brother, whom he had not seen for six years, seated by his bed side, and tenderly nursing him through his illness. The joyful recognition must have conduced more than any other remedial measure to his complete recovery.

Bartolomé had come to devote the rest of his life to the service of his brother. The Admiral would no longer be alone when surrounded by envy and treachery. This devoted brother, firm, valorous, and stout-hearted, would now be at his side to counsel and advise, and to carry out his instructions faithfully and loyally. The one brother in some measure supplied what was deficient in the other. Bartolomé had no genius, less imagination, was less impulsive, and was less inclined to overlook the faults and shortcomings of others. He was more practical, and perhaps better fitted to deal with the unprincipled men who had come to the New World to seek their fortunes. Another source of satisfaction to the Admiral was the letter which Bartolomé had brought out with him from Ferdinand and Isabella. It was dated the 13th of April, and expressed the full approval of the sovereigns of all that had been done, as reported by Antonio de Torres. They expressed their sense of the importance of the Admiral's services and of his high deserts.

But, on the other hand, Columbus had to be told of the treachery and desertion of Father Boil and of Margarit, men in whose honour and conduct he had a full right to trust implicitly. Their misconduct was not confined in its consequences to themselves. It had probably done irremediable injury to the colony, for the mischief was still at its height. The soldiers, abandoned by their leader, were spreading dismay over

the country by their licentiousness and exactions, while
not one single order of the Admiral had been executed.
He had to face this disastrous state of affairs when he
recovered from his illness.

The internal state of Española called for immediate
attention. This splendid island, 200 miles long by 100
broad, was endowed with the richest gifts that tropical
nature could bestow. A central ridge of mountains,
now known as the Sierra de Cibao, rises to considerable
heights. It sends down rivers which form fertile valleys to the southern shore, while to the north a coast
range, called the Sierra de Monte Cristi, bars the way
and turns the great rivers Yaqui and Yuma to west and
east. The magnificent plain called the " Vega Real" is
thus formed. The island was densely populated by a
handsome but gentle and peaceful race, whose only arms
were bows and arrows. They belonged to the earliest
and aboriginal people who first reached these islands
from the continent, and multiplied in peace for centuries. But at some time, not perhaps a very long
time, before the arrival of the Spaniards, a second race
had appeared on the scene, whether coming from Florida
or from the Orinoco is uncertain. They were stronger
and better armed than the aborigines, and had occupied
several of the windward islands. Columbus found them
at Guadalupe and Santa Cruz. These Caribs were man-
stealing cannibals, and spread terror in all directions by
their fierce raids and their cruelty. Caonabó, one of
the most powerful of the chiefs in Española, was said
to have been of Carib extraction.

The island was divided between five principal kings
or caciques, with several petty chiefs under each. Guacanagari, the first friend of Columbus, ruled a territory

along the **north coast.** Guarionex, a chief of noble and chivalrous character, **held** sway over the Vega Real, the **region between the** two ranges of mountains. The **country of** Xaragua, in **the** south-west, belonged **to** Behechio, whose people appear **to** have **been somewhat more advanced in** civilisation **than the rest of the islanders.** The central part **of the** island, **with the mountains of Cibao, was** called Mayaguana, **and was the territory of the fierce** Carib named Caonabó, **the destroyer of Navidad, who** was **married to Anacaona, the sister of Behechio.** The **eastern** district, **called** Higuey, **was under a brave chief named** Cotabanama. **These five caciques seem to have** exercised **considerable power over their vassals and** dependents. **But the nature of their government and religion is** very **imperfectly preserved to us.** At their chief residence **there was always a large** house forming **one** room, **with carved images**; but **this was probably a place of assembly rather than a temple.** Their **language is lost,** though some Carib vocabularies exist.

The first event, after the convalescence **of** the Admiral, **was the arrival** of Guacanagari at **Isabella.** He came **to report** that the exactions and cruelties of the soldiers in the Vega had driven **the** inhabitants to desperation, and that the whole **country** had risen **in arms.** The caciques headed **the** movement, **and** Caonabó was **thirsting** to repeat **his victory at Navidad and** exterminate **the** invaders. **One sub**ordinate chief, named **Guatiguana, had** taken vengeance on ten soldiers **not far** from Isabella. Guacanagari offered **to** assist **the Spaniards, and** thus gave an additional **proof of his** good faith. The matter was very urgent. The Admiral **was** not yet sufficiently recovered to take the field **in person.** By virtue of the authority he understood himself to possess as Viceroy, he created his brother Bartolomé—Adelantado, or Governor of the Indies. This title and dignity were eventually confirmed by the sovereigns in a royal order dated July 22, 1497, and Bartolomé held them until his death.

The work thus intrusted to Bartolomé as Adelantado was important and difficult. He worked incessantly to prepare arms and accoutrements, to collect the scattered and demoralised troops, and to restore discipline. At this critical juncture Antonio de Torres arrived with four caravels laden with welcome provisions and stores, and having on board a number of useful artizans and labourers, as well as domestic animals. The Admiral received another letter from the sovereigns, repeating their full confidence in him and their sense of the value of his services. A royal letter was also addressed to the colonists of Isabella, enjoining them to obey the orders of their Admiral as if they had been issued by themselves.

Columbus, much against his will, was dragged into the necessity of making war upon the natives, owing to the misconduct of Margarit. His first step was to inflict chastisement on the chief Guatiguana and his people for the murder of the Spanish soldiers. This brought the over-lord Guarionex, chief of the Vega Real, to Isabella, where he was kindly received. The Admiral explained to him the reason that his vassal had been punished, assured him that the misconduct of Margarit and his soldiers was contrary to the orders they had received. and fully satisfied him. Guarionex was a simple and honourable chief, only desirous of peace for his people. Before his departure his beautiful daughter was married

to the Admiral's Guanahani interpreter, who had been
baptized at Barcelona.

The next operation of the Admiral was to prepare for
an encounter with the powerful Caonabó, who was at
the head of a large force, including all the discontented
natives who had been ill-treated by the soldiers of Margarit. The Admiral's plan was to establish a chain of
forts along the road to Cibao, where the Spanish troops
could rest and take refuge. One called "Magdalena"
was built on the Yaqui, and another larger and more
important station, named "Concepcion," was established
in the Vega Real, under the command of an officer
named Juan de Ayala. Offensive operations were commenced by Caonabó, who suddenly surrounded the fort
of "San Tomas," which was defended by Alonzo de
Ojeda. Guatignana, who allied himself with the ferocious Carib, besieged the fort of "Magdalena," where
Luis de Arriaga was at the head of a small garrison.
Ojeda was in an impregnable position, and easily repulsed the attacks of the besiegers by the use of fire-
arms. Caonabó therefore withdrew his forces beyond
range, and commenced a blockade in the hope of reducing the fort by famine. But Ojeda was not a man to
remain quietly behind the walls of his fort. He made
daily sallies with his men, protected by armour, and
each time caused fearful slaughter among the naked
Indians. His activity and valour spread terror among
them, and, after a siege of thirty days, Caonabó retreated.

Then Ojeda proceeded to Isabella and proposed a
stratagem of so audacious and desperate a character that
it could only have been conceived in the brain of this
extraordinary knight errant. It was worthy of the
youth who performed the mad feat at the summit of

the Giralda. He told the Admiral that he would seize
Caonabó in the midst of his warriors, and bring him
bound to Isabella. His plan had been suggested by the
awe with which the Indians listened to the bells of the
Christian church. They thought that the metal was
speaking, that it was a voice from heaven. They called
the bell *turey*, and its fame spread over the island.
Caonabó was a believer in the virtues of *turey*, and in the
virtues of the metals brought by the Spaniards, especially
of brass. Alonzo de Ojeda prepared some bright manacles,
beautifully polished, which he called *turey de Viscaya*. He
then set out for the residence of Caonabó, accompanied
by nine followers, all well mounted. On being presented
to the warlike chief, Ojeda said that he was the bearer
of presents from the chief of the Christians called *turey
de Viscaya*, which had come from heaven, and were of
marvellous virtue. He proposed to Caonabó that he
should come down to the river at a short distance and
wash, and that then he should put on the *turey de Viscaya*,
get upon Ojeda's horse, and appear before his vassals
adorned and mounted. Caonabó was delighted. Ojeda
put the chief on his horse, fitted the manacles on his
wrists, and sprang up behind him. First making a few
circles in view of the chief's followers, and gradually
increasing his distance, he suddenly galloped away at
full speed, followed by his men, carrying Caonabó off in
the direction of Isabella. When they were safe away
they secured the captive with ropes, and after two or
three days of hard riding brought him into the presence
of the Admiral. The fierce Carib was put in prison, and
he confessed that he had killed Arana and twenty of the
other unfortunate Spaniards at Navidad, and set fire to
their houses with his own hands.

The natives were at first stunned by this sudden blow. But soon they began to form a new league against the invaders, headed by the brother of Caonabó, and his wife Anacoana, sister of Behechio, chief of Xaragua. All the other chiefs joined it, with the exception of Guacanagari. A vast army of natives was assembled in the Vega Real. The Admiral could only muster about 200 infantry and twenty cavalry to oppose it. But every ten men were provided with a trained mastiff. The Admiral, accompanied by his brother and Alonzo de Ojeda, left Isabella with this small force on the 24th of March 1495. He was supported by a large number of the vassals of Guacanagari from Marien. The natives, led by Manicotex, the brother of Caonabó, were 100,000 strong. The Spanish infantry was divided into two divisions, led respectively by the Admiral and the Adelantado, who were to open fire on the flanks of the unwieldy army, while Ojeda led the cavalry to an attack in front. The fire from the arquebuses at once threw the natives into confusion, and when the horsemen galloped down upon them, they fled in all directions. A horrible butchery followed. Without other arms than arrows, clubs, and wooden spears, their bodies naked and exposed, the unhappy Indians could make no defence. The prisoners taken in open war were condemned to slavery.

The Admiral had, in the previous February, despatched Antonio de Torres to Spain with four caravels. All the gold that could be collected was transmitted direct to the sovereigns, and the cargo consisted of dyewood, cotton, and other products of the island. Diego Columbus also went home, in order that, as a member of the government during the Admiral's absence, he might expose the misstatements of Father Boil and Margarit. As many as 500 of the prisoners of war were also shipped, to be sold as slaves at Seville.

It was the anxious desire of Columbus to establish a peaceful government as soon as possible. There was complete submission on the part of the natives after the battle of Vega Real, and the Admiral made a progress through various parts of the island. A tribute was imposed, consisting of a Flemish hawk's bell full of

GOLD WASHERS (from Oviedo).

gold from every adult native of the mining district of Cibao, to be paid every three months, while the natives of other districts were to pay their tribute in cotton. This was a tentative measure. The tribute was found to be too heavy, and it was subsequently reduced, its character also being changed in some districts. Some of those who had to pay the tribute in gold gave information that the valley of the river Hayna, which falls into the sea on the south coast, was richer in gold than the Cibao district. The Admiral sent two Spaniards, named Francisco de Garay and Miguel Diaz, to explore.

M

and afterwards ordered a settlement to be formed on the
banks of the Hayna.

Ferdinand and Isabella retained their confidence in
the sound judgment and integrity of the Admiral, and
were anxious to promote the interests of the colony.
They selected the butler of the chapel royal, Juan de
Aguado, to proceed to the Indies with three caravels
laden with stores and provisions, and to report to them
fully on the state of affairs.   He sailed towards the end
of August 1495, and arrived when the Admiral was
still absent in the interior.   Diego Columbus returned
with him, having effectually dispelled any doubts which
might have arisen in the minds of the sovereigns, caused
by the misstatements of the discontented deserters who
had returned to Spain.   Aguado was one of those men
whose heads are turned by a little authority.   On landing at Isabella he attempted to assume a position which
was quite contrary to his instructions, encouraged the
settlers to bring complaints to him, and gave colour to
the idea that he had come to supersede Columbus.   One
of the most striking features in the character of the
great discoverer was the patience and dignity with which
he endured the insolence of such men as Aguado.   While
firmly resisting any encroachment on his authority, he
treated the upstart with uniform courtesy and respect.
Aguado busily collected complaints against the Admiral,
and when he thought he had obtained sufficient evidence
to induce the sovereigns to supersede him and put their
butler of the royal chapel in his place, the informer
announced his intention of returning to Spain.

The Admiral held a long consultation with his
brothers.   It was known that the calumnies of Aguado
would be backed by those of other men of a like stamp,

and would be encouraged by the vindictive and envious
Fonseca.   It was therefore decided that Columbus
should return with Aguado and plead his own cause.
There were now six caravels in the port, and they were
all prepared for the voyage home.   Columbus was able
to ship 200 ounces of pure gold, including some nuggets
of considerable size, from the new diggings at Hayna.
He also collected numbers of birds of the most beautiful
plumage, and specimens of fruits and plants of all kinds,
including maize, yams, and other articles of food.   The
Adelantado Bartolomé was appointed governor and commander of the forces during the Admiral's absence.   A
servant of Columbus, an esquire from the neighbourhood of Jaen, who had shown ability on several occasions,
named Francisco Roldan, was appointed chief magistrate
of Isabella.

When the caravels were nearly ready to sail a fearful
hurricane burst over the island.   Three of the vessels
sank at their anchors, two were dashed to pieces on the
rocks.   It became necessary to construct a new caravel
from the wrecks, which was named the *Santa Cruz*.
The *Niña* alone escaped the fury of the hurricane and
was fit for sea.   The Admiral embarked in her, taking
Caonabó with him ; and about 220 sick and useless colonists were sent home as passengers.   Aguado was in the
other caravel.   The two little vessels set sail from Isabella
on the 10th of March 1496.   For ten days they were
becalmed in sight of Cape San Theramo, now Engaño,
and it was not until the 10th of April that they reached
Guadalupe, where they filled up with water and fresh
provisions, preparatory to the voyage across the ocean.

Columbus determined to take a route directly east, to
ascertain the kind of passage it was possible to make

against the trades. It proved a long and tedious one.
A Carib woman of rank, who had been captured at
Guadalupe, would have been allowed to return to her
people; but she heard from Caonabó the story of his
misfortunes, conceived a passion for the prisoner, and
resolved to share his captivity. The Admiral intended,
after the fierce chief had visited Spain and received
baptism, to restore him to his people. But Caonabó
abandoned himself to despondency. In spite of the care
and attendance of his new wife, he sickened and died
at sea, not long after the *Niña* sailed from Guadalupe.

The voyage was so long delayed by light and contrary
winds that it became necessary to reduce the scale of
provisions more and more, until the people began to
suffer from the pangs of hunger. But so accurate was
the Admiral's reckoning that, when still out of sight of
land, he ordered sail to be shortened one day, just before
sunset. The pilots had no idea of the position, but next
morning Cape St. Vincent was in sight. The two
caravels arrived at Cadiz on the 11th of June 1496.
Most fortunately the Admiral found three caravels at
Cadiz under the command of the pilot, Pero Alonso Niño,
on the point of sailing, with supplies, to Española. He
was thus enabled to announce his safe arrival to his
brother, and to send him further instructions. The
Admiral gave orders that a new town should be founded,
in a more healthy situation than Isabella, on the south
coast of the island, and that a fort should be built near
the gold mines of Hayna. On the 17th of June Niño
sailed for the Indies, and **Columbus** proceeded on his
way to Seville.

When the Admiral came to the small town of Los
Palacios, near the river Guadalquivir and about fifteen

AMB (*from Thevet's " Vies des Hommes Illustres"*).

miles from Seville. the hospitable and learned Cura came
out to meet him. Columbus remained as the guest
of the good Cura. Dr. Andres Bernaldez. until he
received a reply to the letter he had addressed to the
sovereigns.   A friendship was formed between them.
On his departure the Admiral left some of his most
important papers in the care of the Cura of Los Palacios.
Dr. Bernaldez, who was Cura of Los Palacios from 1488
to 1513, was also chaplain to Dr. Deza, Archbishop of
Seville, the old and tried friend of Columbus ; and this
probably led to his acquaintance with the Admiral. who
at that time was very deeply impressed with the mercies
he had received. and passed many hours in devotional
exercises.   Bernaldez says that the Admiral wore a dress
resembling the habit of the Franciscans. with a cord of
St. Francis round his waist : for he had always affected
that order from gratitude to the brethren of La Rabida.
It is to this visit to Los Palacios that we owe many
interesting details respecting the Jamaica voyage and
other parts of the Admiral's life, which occupy several
chapters in the " Historia de los Reyes Catolicos." by
the Bachiller Andres Bernaldez.

   Ferdinand and Isabella wrote a most cordial letter of
welcome to the Admiral. and invited him to come to
their court at Burgos.   The Queen had been to Laredo
on the north-coast, to take a last farewell of her daughter
Juana, who was proceeding to Flanders to be married to
the Archduke Philip. The King was returning from
the frontier at Girona, where he had been making de-
fensive arrangements in consequence of a war that had
broken out with France.   They met at Burgos, and
received Columbus with the utmost cordiality.   His
delightful conversation and convincing eloquence had

always had a great charm for the Queen, and he fully
and satisfactorily explained the nature and value of his
new discoveries, and the difficulties of the infant colony
in Española. The calumnies of Aguado received no cre-
dence whatever, and he was summarily dismissed. The
Admiral presented their Highnesses with the gold he
had brought home, and with many curiosities from the
Indies; while they confirmed him in his titles and
honours, and granted a licence for him to create a
mayorazgo or entail in favour of his two sons and
their heirs for ever. They also confirmed Bartolomé in
his title of Adelantado. The entail was created on
February 22, 1498. Young Fernando, then barely ten
years of age, received the appointment of page to Queen
Isabella on the 18th of February 1498, and entered
upon his duties. Diego had been a page to Prince
Juan since 1494, and continued in his service until his
death in October 1497, when the Queen received both
the Admiral's sons into her own household.

Orders were given for the equipment of a fleet at Seville, to be placed under the command of the Admiral,
both with the object of discovery and also to supply the
colony with reinforcements and provisions. This was
done in spite of the financial pressure caused by hostili-
ties with France; and the difficulties of fitting out the
expedition were materially increased by the persistent
obstruction of Dr. Fonseca, who had become Bishop of
Badajos.

At this time João II., King of Portugal, died, and was
succeeded by King Emanuel, who reigned from 1495 to
1521. One of the first acts of Emanuel was to equip an
expedition, under Vasco da Gama, to make the first voyage
to India by way of the Cape of Good Hope. Da Gama

sailed from the Tagus on the 8th of July 1497, doubled the Cape, and arrived at Calicut, on the coast of Malabar, in May 1498, returning to Lisbon in September 1499. In the following year a second expedition was despatched to India under Pedro Alvarez Cabral, who reached the coast of Brazil on his way out on the 22nd of April 1500, and named it Santa Cruz. Proceeding on their way to India a typhoon struck the ships off the Cape, in which Bartholomeu Diaz, who commanded one of them, perished; but Cabral eventually reached Quilon, and returned safely to Lisbon in July 1501.

CHAPTER X.

THE FOURTH VOYAGE OF DISCOVERY AND PACIFICATION OF THE COLONY.

THE great navigator was no longer the powerful enduring man of six years before. Exposure, months of sleepless watching, anxiety, and tropical fevers had at length done their work. The bright intellect, the vivid imagination, the great heart, the generous nature would be the same until death, but the constitution was shattered. The Admiral now suffered from ophthalmia, gout, and a complication of diseases. The last six years of his life was destined to be a time of much and cruel suffering, aggravated by ingratitude, perfidy, and injustice.

In fitting out the third expedition every petty annoyance and obstruction that the malice of Bishop Fonseca could invent was used to thwart and delay the Admiral. Each subordinate official knew that insolence to the object of the Bishop's envy and dislike, and neglect of his wishes, was the surest way to the favour of his chief. One creature of Fonseca, named Jimeno de Briviesca, carried his insolence beyond the bounds of the endurance even of the dignified and long-suffering Admiral, who very properly took him by the scruff of the neck on one occasion and kicked him off the poop of the flagship. The delays of Fonseca and his agents caused incalculable injury to the public service, as will presently appear.

The sovereigns had ordered that six million maravedis, about £2000, should be granted for the equipment of the expedition, and that eight vessels should be provided. The contractor for provisions was Jonato Berardi, a Florentine merchant settled at Seville, and, owing to his death, the contracting work fell upon his assistant, who was very actively employed on this service from April 1497 to May 1498. The dates should be borne in mind. We are thus first introduced to Amerigo Vespucci. Born at Florence in 1451, he was the son of a notary named Nastugio Vespucci, and received his education from a Dominican monk, who was his uncle. He claimed Pietro Soderini, afterwards Gonfaloniere of Florence, as his schoolfellow, and he obtained employment under the Medici. In 1492 Vespucci came to Spain, as a partner of an Italian trader at Cadiz, named Donato Nicolini, and he afterwards became the chief clerk or agent of Berardi. It was thus that Columbus first became acquainted with Amerigo Vespucci, when he had reached the ripe age of forty-five. As for his provisions a good deal of the meat turned bad on the voyage, and the contract was not very satisfactorily carried out. It is strange that this beef and biscuit contractor should have given his name to the New World. But perhaps not more strange than that a bacon contractor should be the patron saint of England and of Genoa.*

The Admiral was most anxious to despatch supplies and reinforcements to his brother, and he succeeded in sending off two caravels in advance, under the command of Hernandez Coronel, who had been appointed chief

---

* Gibbon's "Decline and Fall," ii. p. 321 (Milman's ed. Murray, 1846).

magistrate of the colony. The other vessels consisted
of two *naos*, or ships of a hundred tons, and four
caravels. After months of harassing and unnecessary
delay they dropped down the Guadalquivir from Seville,
and the Admiral sailed from San Lucar on the 30th of
May 1498. He touched at Porto Santo and Madeira,
and reached Gomera on the 19th of May.

Columbus had become aware, through information
collected from the natives of the islands, that there was
extensive land, probably a continent, to the southward.
He had also received a letter from a skilled and learned
jeweller named Jaime Ferrer, dated the 5th of August
1495, in which it was laid down that the most valuable
things came from very hot countries, where the natives
are black or tawny. These and other considerations led
him to the determination of crossing the Atlantic on a
lower parallel than he had ever done before; and he
invoked the Holy Trinity for protection, intending to
name the first land that was sighted in their honour.
But he was impressed with the importance of sending
help to the colony without delay. He therefore detached
one ship and two caravels from Gomera to make the
voyage direct. The ship was commanded by Alonzo
Sanchez de Carbajal of Baeza. One caravel was intrusted to Pedro de Arana, brother of Beatriz Enriquez,
and brother-in-law of the Admiral. The other had for
her captain a Genoese cousin, Juan Antonio Colombo.
It will be remembered that Antonio, the brother of
Domenico Colombo and uncle of the Admiral, lived at
the little coast village of Quinto, near Genoa, and had
three sons — Juan Antonio, Mateo, and Amighetto.
When these cousins heard of the greatness and renown
of Cristoforo, they thought at least one of them might

get some benefit from his prosperity. So the younger
ones gave all the little money they could scrape together
to enable the eldest to go to Spain. His illustrious kins
man welcomed him with affection, and as he was a sailor
he received charge of a caravel, in which trust he proved
himself, as Las Casas tells us, to be careful, efficient,
and fit for command. The three vessels sailed from
Gomera direct for Española on the 21st of June.

Columbus continued his voyage of discovery with one
ship and two caravels. Pero Alonzo Niño, the pilot of
the *Niña* in the first voyage, was with him. Hernan
Perez Matteos was another pilot, and there were a
few other old shipmates in the squadron. The Admiral
touched at Buena Vista, one of the Cape Verde Isles,
remaining at anchor for a few days, and on the 5th of
July he sailed away into the unknown ocean for many
days on a south-west course. His intention was to go
south as far as the latitude of Sierra Leone (8° 30′ N.),
and then to steer west until he reached land. After ten
days the vessels were in the region of calms, and the
people began to suffer from the intense heat. The sun
melted the tar of the rigging, and the seams of the decks
began to open. For days and days the scorching heat
continued, but at length there were some refreshing
showers, and light breezes sprang up from the west.
But their progress was very slow, and the stock of
water was nearly exhausted. So the Admiral ordered
the course to be altered to north-west, in hopes of
reaching Dominica. It was the 31st of July, the people
were parched with thirst, and yet no land had been
seen. In the afternoon of that day the Admiral's servant, Alonzo Perez of Huelva, went to the mast-head,
and reported land in the shape of three separate peaks.

Columbus had declared his intention of naming the first
land sighted after the Holy Trinity, and the coincidence
of its appearing in the form of three peaks made a deep
impression on his mind. The island of Trinidad retains
the name to this day. The Admiral gave heartfelt
thanks to God, and all the crews chanted the *Salve
Regina*, and other hymns of prayer and praise. Mean

GULF OF PARIA, OR "DE LA BALLENA."

while the little squadron glided through the water,
approaching the newly-discovered land, and Columbus
named the most eastern point "Cabo de la Galéra," by
reason of a great rock off it, which at a distance looked
like a galley under sail. All along the coast the trees
were seen to come down to the sea, the most lovely
sight that eyes could rest on ; and at last, on the 1st of
August, an anchorage was found, and they were able to

fill up with water from delicious streams and fountains.
The main continent of South America was seen to the
south, appearing like a long island, and it received the
name of "Isla Santa." The point near the watering-
place was called "Punta de la Playa."

The western end of the island was named "Punta del
Arenal," and here an extraordinary phenomenon presented itself. A violent current was rushing out,
through a channel or strait not more than two leagues
wide, causing great perturbation of the sea with such
an uproar of rushing water, that the crews were filled
with alarm for the safety of the vessels. The Admiral
named the channel "La Boca de la Sierpe." He piloted
his little squadron safely through it and reached the
Gulf of Paria, named by him "Golfo de la Ballena."
The land to the westward, forming the mainland of
Paria, received the name of "Isla de Gracia." Standing across to the western side of the gulf, the Admiral
was delighted with the beauty of the country and with
the view of distant mountains. Near a point named
"Aguja" the country was so fruitful and charming
that he called it "Jardines," and here he saw many
Indians, among them women wearing bracelets of pearls,
and when they were asked whence the pearls were
obtained they pointed to the westward. As many
pearls as could be bartered from the natives were collected for transmission to the sovereigns, for here was
a new source of wealth, another precious commodity
from the New World.

Columbus was astonished at the vast mass of fresh
water that was pouring into the Gulf of Paria. He
correctly divined the cause, and made the deduction that
a river with such a volume of water must come from a

great distance. His prescient mind showed him the
mighty river Orinoco, the wide savannas, and the lofty
range of the Andes; but the trammels of the erroneous
measurements of astronomers bound them to Asia, and
prevented him from picturing them to himself in the
New World he had really discovered. That the land
must be continuous appeared to be proved, not only
from the deductions of science, but also from the Word
of God. For he believed it to be established from the
revealed word (2 Esdras vi. 42) that the ocean only
covered one-seventh of the globe, and that the other
six-sevenths was dry land. Moreover, his splendid intellect was united with a powerful imagination. When
he had grasped the facts with masterly intuition, his
fancy often raised upon them some strange theory derived partly from his extensive reading, partly from his
own teeming brain. Thinking that a long and rapid
course was insufficient to account for the volume of
water and the violence of the currents, he conceived the
idea that the earth, though round, was not a perfect
sphere, and that it rose in one part of the equinoctial
line so as to be somewhat of a pear shape. Thus he
accounted for the exceptional volume of water by the
notion of rivers flowing down from the end of the pear.
One step further in the realms of fancy, and he indulged
in the dream that this centre and apex of the earth's
surface, with its mighty rivers, could be no other than
the terrestrial paradise. Writing as one thought coursed
after another in his teeming fancy, we find these passing
whims of a vivid imagination embodied in the journal
intended for the information of the sovereigns.

But time was passing on, and it was important that
he should convey the provisions with which his vessels

were loaded to his infant colony. He had seen that another narrow channel led from the northern side of the gulf, and had named it "Boca del Dragon." On the 12th of August he had piloted his vessels to the Punta de Paria, and prepared to pass through the channel. At that critical moment it fell calm, while the two currents flowed violently towards the opening, where they met and formed a broken, confused sea. But the Admiral made use of the currents, and by the exercise of consummate seamanship took his three vessels clear of the danger and out into the open sea. The islands of Tobago and Grenada were sighted, receiving the names of "Asuncion" and "Concepcion." Then the rocks and islets to the westward came in view, named the "Testigos" and "Guardias," and the island "Margarita." The latter name shows that the Admiral had obtained correct information from the natives of Paria respecting the locality of the pearl-fishery.

The Admiral now crowded all sail to reach Española, intending to make a landfall at the mouth of the river Azuma, where he knew that his brother the Adelantado had founded the new city, and named it San Domingo in memory of their old father, Domenico Colombo. But the current carried him far to the westward, and on the 19th of August he sighted the coast fifty leagues to leeward of the new capital. On hearing of his arrival on the coast, Bartolomé got on board a caravel and joined him; but it was not until the 31st that the two brothers entered San Domingo together, the Admiral for the first time. Young Diego, the third and youngest brother, welcomed them on their arrival.

The Admiral had been absent for two years and a half, during which time the Adelantado had conducted

the government of the colony with remarkable vigour
and ability. Yet, owing to the mutinous conduct of the
worst of the settlers, there was a very disastrous report
to make.

When the Adelantado assumed the command on the
departure of the Admiral for Spain in March 1496, his
first step, in compliance with the instructions he had received, was to proceed to the valley on the south side of
the island, in which the gold-mine of Hayna was situated,
and to build a fort which he named "San Cristoval." He
next, having received supplies and reinforcements, together with letters from the Admiral, by the three caravels under Niño, took steps for the foundation of the
new capital. Still following his brother's instructions,
he selected a site at the mouth of the river Azuma,
where there was good anchorage in the bay, and a fertile
valley along the banks of the river. On a bank commanding the harbour a fortress was erected and named
San Domingo, while the city was subsequently built on
the east bank of the river. It became the capital of
the colony. Before long Isabella, on the north coast,
was entirely abandoned. Trees soon grew up in the
streets and through the roofs of the houses. It presented a scene of wild desolation, and ghosts were believed to wander in crowds through the abandoned city.
Ruins of the house of Columbus, of the church and the
fort, can still be traced out by those who penetrate into
the dense jungle which now covers that part of the coast.

The next proceeding of the indefatigable Adelantado
was the settlement of the beautiful province of Xaragua,
forming the south-western portion of the island. It was
ruled over by a chief named Behechio, with whom dwelt
the famous Anacaona, his sister, widow of Caonabó,

N

but, unlike that fierce Carib, a constant friend of the
Spaniards. Behechio met the Adelantado in battle array
on the banks of the river Neyva, the eastern boundary of
his dominions. But as soon as they were informed that
the errand of the Spanish governor was a peaceful one,
both Behechio and Anacaona, who was a princess of
great ability and of a most amiable disposition, received
him with cordial hospitality. When, after a time, he
opened the subject of tribute to them, they showed
opposition. But Bartolomé proved himself to be a
masterly diplomatist, and in the end Behechio not only
consented to impose a tribute, the details of which were
amicably arranged, but undertook to collect and deliver
it periodically to the Spanish authorities. These Indians
were quite ready to submit to beings who appeared to
be superior in power and intelligence to themselves. If
the sovereigns of Spain had trusted Columbus and his
brothers fully and completely, had established trading
stations and imposed a moderate tribute, and had absolutely prohibited the overrunning of the country by
penniless and worthless adventurers, they would have
had a rich and prosperous colony. The discontent and
rebellion of the natives was solely caused by the misconduct of the Spaniards.

An insurrection broke out in the Vega Real, headed by
the chief Guarionex, who, after suffering innumerable
wrongs from the Spaniards, was at last driven to desperation by an outrage on his wife. He assembled with a number of dependent caciques; but the news was promptly
communicated to the garrison of Fort Concepcion, and
forwarded to San Domingo. The Adelantado stamped
out the rebellion with his accustomed vigour. He came
by forced marches to Concepcion, and thence, without

stopping, to the camp of the natives, who were completely taken by surprise. Guarionex and the other caciques were captured, and their followers dispersed. Always generous after victory, Bartolomé Columbus released Guarionex at the prayer of his people—a measure which was alike magnanimous and politic. But it was impossible to rule over the natives satisfactorily unless the Spanish settlers could be forced to submit to the laws, and the Adelantado was not powerful enough to keep the bad characters in subjection. The loyal and decent men of the colony were in a small minority. The consequence was that the unfortunate Guarionex was again goaded into insurrection. On the approach of the Adelantado he fled into the mountains of Ciguey on the north-east coast, and took refuge with a dependent cacique named Mayobanex, whose residence was near Cape Cabron, the western extreme of the Samana peninsula. A difficult and arduous mountain campaign followed, which Bartolomé conducted with remarkable military skill. It ended in the capture and imprisonment of both the chiefs.

Behechio now announced that he had collected the required tribute, consisting of a very large quantity of cotton, and that it was ready for delivery. The Adelantado therefore proceeded to Xaragua, and not only found this great store of cotton, but received an offer from the generous chief to supply him with as much cassava bread as he needed for the use of the colony. This was a most acceptable present, for the lazy, illconditioned settlers had neglected to cultivate their fields, and a famine was imminent. The Adelantado ordered a caravel to be sent round to Xaragua to be freighted with cotton and bread, and returned himself to Isabella after taking a cordial farewell of his native **friends.** He had shown extraordinary talent in his **government of** the native population, and his rule had been a complete success. Always moderate in victory, he had suppressed the insurrections without bloodshed, **and** had conciliated the people by his moderation. He **had** made **long and** difficult marches, had subdued opposition by his readiness of resource and energy, and had administered **the** native affairs with humanity and excellent **judgment.**

Unfortunately **his** power was insufficient **to cope** successfully with the insubordinate Spaniards. **The** ringleader of **the** mutineers was **Francisco** Roldan, a man **whom Columbus had** raised **from the dust.** He had **been a servant, and** the Admiral, noting his ability, **had intrusted** him with some judicial functions. When he sailed for Spain he appointed Roldan chief-justice of the colony. This ungrateful miscreant fostered discontent **and** mutiny by every art of persuasion and calumny at **his** command, and soon had a large band of **worthless and idle** ruffians ready to follow his lead. His first plan was to murder the Adelantado and seize the government, **but he lacked** the courage or the opportunity to put it into execution. **His next** step was to march into the Vega Real with seventy armed mutineers, and attempt to surprise Fort Concepcion. The garrison was commanded by a loyal soldier named Miguel Ballester, who closed the gates and defied the rebels, sending to the Adelantado for help. Bartolomé at once hastened to his assistance, and on his arrival at Fort Concepcion he sent a messenger to Roldan, remonstrating with him, and urging him to return to his duty. But Roldan found his force increasing by the adhesion of all the

discontented men in the colony, and his insolence increased with his power. All would probably have been
lost, but for the opportune arrival of Pedro Hernandez
Coronel in February 1498, who had been despatched from
San Lucar by the Admiral in the end of the previous
year with reinforcements. He also brought out the
confirmation of Bartolomé's rank as Adelantado.

The Adelantado was thus enabled to leave Fort Concepcion and establish his headquarters at San Domingo.
He sent Coronel as an envoy to Roldan, to endeavour
to persuade him to return to his duty; but the mutineer
feared to submit, believing that he had gone too far for
forgiveness. He marched into the province of Xaragua,
where he allowed his dissolute followers to abandon
themselves to every kind of excess. The three caravels
which had been despatched from Gomera by the Admiral
unfortunately made a bad landfall, and appeared off
Xaragua. Roldan concealed the fact that he was a
leader of mutineers, and receiving the captains in his
official capacity, induced them to supply him with stores
and provisions, while his followers busily endeavoured
to seduce the crews, and succeeded to some extent.
When Roldan's true character was discovered, the caravels put to sea with the loyal part of their crews, while
Alonzo Sanchez de Carbajal, a loyal and thoroughly
honest man, who was zealous for the good of the colony,
remained behind to endeavour to persuade Roldan to
submit to the Admiral's authority. He only succeeded
in obtaining from him a promise to enter into negotiations with a view to the termination of the deplorable
state of affairs he had created, and with this Carbajal
proceeded to San Domingo.

Such was the state of affairs when Columbus arrived

at the new seat of his government. His brother had ruled with vigour and ability during his absence, had administered native affairs very successfully, but his power had been insufficient to subdue the band of Spanish miscreants who were still in open mutiny. The Admiral was filled with grief and disappointment at the turn affairs had taken. A thoroughly loyal man himself, with no thought or desire but for the good of the colony, he was thwarted by treacherous miscreants, who cared for nothing but the accumulation of riches for themselves, and for a life of indulgence and licentious ease. After long consideration he resolved upon a policy of conciliation. The unsettled state of affairs was bringing ruin on the island, and the restoration of peace was an absolute necessity. The magnanimous Genoese was incapable of personal resentment. The men themselves were indeed beneath his contempt ; but he felt bound to treat with them, and even to make great concessions, if necessary, for the good of the public service. The welfare of the colony was his sole object, and he did not hesitate to sacrifice every personal feeling to his sense of duty. It is with some impatience that one finds the grand schemes of discovery and colonisation interrupted by such contemptible means, and the course of the narrative checked by the necessity for recording, however briefly, the paltry dissensions of vile miscreants such as Roldan and his crew.

The mutineers were most unwilling to make any agreement. They were leading the sort of lawless and licentious life that exactly suited them, and were disinclined to submit to any authority. The interests of their leaders, however, were not quite the same, and the acceptance of advantageous terms would suit them. Carbajal was employed by the Admiral to conduct the negotiations, while the veteran Ballester returned to Spain in November 1498 with the news of the rebellion, and a request from the Admiral that a learned and impartial judge might be sent out to decide all disputes.

It was finally agreed that Roldan should return to his duty, still retaining the office of chief justice; that all past offences should be condoned, and that he and his followers should receive grants of land, with the services of the Indians. The Admiral consented to these terms most unwillingly, and under the conviction that this was the only way to avoid the greater evil of civil dissension. He resolved, however, that any future outbreak must be firmly and vigorously suppressed by force. Although Roldan had now resumed his position as a legitimate official ready to maintain order, it could hardly be expected that his fatal example would not be followed by other unprincipled men of the same stamp, when the opportunity offered.

Trouble arose owing to the conduct of a young Castilian named Hernando de Guevara. Roldan was established in Xaragua, when the youthful gallant arrived at the house of his cousin, Adrian de Mujica, one of the ringleaders in Roldan's mutiny, and fell in love with Higueymota, the daughter of Anacaona. Guevara, for some misconduct, had been ordered by the Admiral to leave the island, but instead of obeying he had made his way to Xaragua, and caused trouble by this love passage, for he had a rival in Roldan himself, who ordered him to desist from the pursuit of the daughter of Anacaona, and to return to San Domingo. Guevara refused to obey, but he was promptly arrested and sent as a prisoner to the capital. When his cousin Mujica,

who was then in the Vega Real, received the news, he
raised a mutiny, offering rewards to the soldiers if they
would follow him in an attempt to rescue Guevara.
The Admiral, though suffering from illness, showed
remarkable energy on this occasion.   Marching very
rapidly at the head of eighteen chosen men, he surprised
the mutineers, captured the ringleader, and carried him
off to the fort of Concepcion.   Some severity had now
become incumbent upon the authorities, and Mujica was
condemned to death.   The Admiral regretted the necessity, but in no other way could a motive be supplied to
deter others from keeping the country in a constant state
of lawless disorder.   Guevara, Riquelme, and other dis-
orderly characters were imprisoned in the fort at San
Domingo, and by August 1500 peace was quite established throughout the island.

Thus had Columbus restored tranquillity to the colony.
By prudent and conciliatory negotiation, during which
he had exercised the most wonderful self-abnegation and
patience, he had succeeded in averting the serious danger
caused by the formidable revolt of Roldan.   But as the
habit of disorder was threatening to become chronic, he
wisely took another way with the sedition of Mujica,
maintaining order by a resort to prompt and vigorous
action, and making a salutary example which was calculated to be deterrent in its effects.

With the restoration of peace trade revived and prosperity began to return.   The receivers of grants of land
found that they had a stake in the country, and sought
to derive profit from their crops.   Similar activity
appeared at the mines, and the building at San Domingo
progressed rapidly.   The Admiral began to hope that
the first troubles incident to an infant colony were over,

and that the time had arrived for Spain to feel the advantages of his great achievement. He now looked forward to further and more important discoveries followed by colonization on the main continent.

Yet at this very time a blow was about to come from a quarter whence it was least to be expected, which was destined to shatter all the hopes of this long-suffering man, and dissipate all his bright visions of the future.

CHAPTER XI.

COLUMBUS IN CHAINS.

HITHERTO the Spanish sovereigns had kept their faith
with Columbus. They had supported him with generous
consistency, had fully acknowledged the greatness of his
services, and had understood and made allowances for
the extraordinary difficulties of his position. They had
steadily pursued this honourable and politic line of conduct in spite of the calumnies that had been poured into
their ears, at the instigation of Bishop Fonseca, by the
deserters from the colony. The change in their conduct,
after Columbus left Spain in 1498, is attributed to the
incessant repetition of new complaints against the Admiral. Crowds of discontented adventurers returned by
every ship. At one time about fifty of these malcontents frequented the court of the Alhambra, when the
sovereigns were at Granada. They declared that they
could afford to eat nothing but grapes, and brought
bunches with them, while they shouted for justice.
Their insolence rose to such a pitch that when the King
crossed the court they crowded round him, crying " Pay
us ! pay us ! " The two sons of the Admiral were then
Queen's pages, and if one of them was seen the truculent crowd called after him : " There goes the Admiral's
son, the spawn of the big mosquito who has discovered
countries of vanity and deceit for the misery and death

of Castilians;" and added such insults that the lads
excused themselves from passing near the shameless
mendicants.

But all this neither explains nor excuses the conduct
of the sovereigns. They had heard the same or kindred
calumnies before, which had been disproved to their satisfaction, and had not caused any change in their policy.
There must have been some other reason. The real
truth appears to have been that Ferdinand was deeply
impressed with the importance of the discovery, and the
vast and far reaching consequences to which it was likely
to lead. When he consented to grant the concession to
Columbus he was sceptical of any result, and believed
he was granting nothing of any value. But when he
became convinced of the true greatness of the achievement, he at the same time became anxious to curtail,
and if possible to withdraw, the concession. Fonseca, in
the hope of gratifying his malignant spite, was only too
glad to represent this contemplated breach of faith as
wise and politic. He granted permission for voyages of
discovery to be undertaken without the knowledge or
consent of Columbus, and in direct contravention of his
rights as Admiral. But it was his position as Viceroy
that Ferdinand was most anxious to assail. His super-
session, without trial or previous hearing and judgment,
would be a very shameful and dishonourable breach of
faith, but it was one to which Isabella was at length
induced to consent. It is probable that she yielded to
the plausible representations of her husband.

Francisco Bobadilla, a Comendador of the Order of
Calatrava, was selected to supersede the Admiral, and
was appointed governor and judge of the island during
royal pleasure, with extraordinary powers to investigate

complaints, and with a number of blank papers signed
by the sovereigns, which he was empowered to fill up
at his discretion. A curt letter was addressed to the
Admiral, desiring him to deliver up charge to Bobadilla, and to give faith and obedience to whatever that
official should impart. The appointment is dated May
21, 1499. No worse selection could possibly have been
made. Bobadilla had no single quality to recommend
him for such a post. His arrogance and insolence were
not more conspicuous than his incapacity. Two caravels, called the *Antigua* and the *Gorda*, were fitted out
to convey him to Española, and he was furnished with a
guard of honour consisting of twenty-five picked soldiers.
He sailed from Cadiz in June 1500.

On Sunday, the 23rd of August 1500, when dawn
broke, two strange sail were reported off the harbour
of San Domingo. The Admiral was in the Vega Real,
busily engaged in establishing order and settling the
affairs of the district. The Adelantado was absent in
Xaragua, occupied with similar administrative work.
The youngest brother, Don Diego Columbus, was in
command at San Domingo, and sent out a canoe to the
caravels, which were waiting for the tide to take them
up the river. The men in the canoe returned with the
news that from one of the caravels a man had hailed
them, declaring that he was an examining judge appointed by the King and Queen to investigate all that
had happened in the island, and desiring them to report
his approach to Don Diego. Bobadilla did not land
until the next morning. He then conducted himself in
the most extravagant manner. He first marched to the
church to hear mass, preceded by his bodyguard. He
then sent for Don Diego, and ordered him to deliver up

the prisoners in the fort, including Riquelme and Guevara. Don Diego, as well as Miguel Diaz, the governor of the fort, represented that they could not act without orders from the Admiral, and requested that they might be allowed time to communicate with him. Bobadilla would not wait. He and his bodyguard attacked the fort, although there was no resistance, broke the door down, liberated the criminals, and carried them in triumph through the street of San Domingo. This outrageous conduct was followed by further unjustifiable violence. He broke open the Admiral's house and occupied it as his own, appropriating all the private papers and other property, and all the treasure it contained. The insolent robber then seized upon Don Diego, loaded him with irons, and confined him in the hold of one of the caravels in the river.

The Admiral received the news of Bobadilla's arrival from a messenger sent by his brother, and at once commenced his journey to San Domingo, forwarding a letter of welcome in advance. Meanwhile the absurd creature, who had seized the government, gave orders of all kinds, and threw everything into confusion. Among other decrees he issued one, in order to court popularity with the mob, by which he reduced the royal fifth due from the produce of mines to an eleventh, and granted free leave for every one to use the mines and gold washings as they pleased. He also devoted much time to the collection of false accusations against the Admiral.

Columbus resolved to submit loyally and unreservedly to the orders of the Queen, as interpreted by her chosen representative. He proceeded to San Domingo almost unattended. He was arrested outside the town, loaded with irons, and imprisoned in the fort, with orders that

no one was to be allowed to speak with him. He bore
all with silent dignity, not condescending to utter a
word of complaint. He had sent to Bartolomé, who
was at the head of a large force in Xaragua, to come at
once to San Domingo. On his arrival he was treated in
the same way.

There could be no degradation to the Admiral. His
reputation was raised by the cowardly insults of the
wretch who had been so improperly clothed with a little
brief authority, for he received them with the calm dignity of a noble nature. The disgrace and degradation
fell on the Queen, and through her on the Spanish nation,
and so it was generally felt. Bobadilla must have
thought that his outrageous conduct would please Fonseca, and be approved by Ferdinand ; so that there can
be no doubt that he had received hints, which he interpreted too literally. The intense stupidity and dulness
of the outrage is its most striking feature, for if Bobadilla had been gifted with a grain of common sense he
must have known that even Fonseca would repudiate
such coarse brutality. The conviction of his successor's
incapacity must have been the hardest thing for the
Admiral to bear. Just when peace had been secured,
when orderly government was established and prosperity
was reviving, it was heartrending to see the delicate
machinery handed over to this wretched creature, with
the inevitable result that the colony would be thrown
back into confusion and ruin.

Alonso Vallejo, the captain of the caravel Gorda,
was ordered to receive Bartolomé and Diego on board,
and then to proceed to the fort with some men-at-arms
to receive the custody of the Admiral. " Vallejo,
whither do you take me ?" asked Columbus, believing

that he was about to be murdered. "Sir, I am to take you on board the ship." Still doubtful of his fate, he said, "Vallejo, is it true?" "By the life of our Lady," exclaimed the honest sailor, "it is true that I am to take you on board." The Admiral was satisfied. He soon found himself with his brothers, and early in October 1500 the caravel sailed from San Domingo. They were scarcely out of sight of land when Vallejo and Andres Martin, the owner of the vessel, presented themselves before the Admiral. Though in the employment of Fonseca they were gentlemen, and were filled with shame and sorrow at the base treatment of so great a man. Both threw themselves on their knees to remove the irons. But the Admiral would not consent. He warmly thanked his generous hosts, but he said that he had been manacled by the Queen's representative, and by the Queen's order alone should the irons be removed.[1] The voyage was a quick and prosperous one, and the Admiral was treated with the respect and attention due to his high rank and to his mighty achievements.

While at sea he wrote a letter to Doña Juana de Torres, formerly nurse of Prince Juan, and sister of the Admiral's true and loyal friend, Antonio de Torres. This lady was a great favourite of the Queen, and it was probably intended that its contents should be made known to Isabella. In reading this touching letter one is surprised at the calmness with which he speaks of his wrongs, and at his confident reliance on the justice of the Queen after all that had passed, when she really knew the truth. Columbus was firmly convinced that he was a humble instrument chosen by God to carry out His designs for the discovery of the New World. "God made me the messenger of the new heaven and the new earth of which He spake in the Apocalypse of St. John, after having spoken of it by the mouth of Isaiah." He had dreams and visions which impressed themselves deeply on his mind. On one particular occasion, when he was surrounded by difficulties, and without the means of paying the troops, it was on Christmas Day 1499, he was sitting alone and in deep dejection. Suddenly he thought he heard a voice : "Take courage. Be not afraid nor fear. I will provide for all." On that very day the discovery of a rich gold-yielding district was announced. The coincidence made so deep an impression that he mentioned it in more than one of his letters.

In his letter to his lady friend he refers to the innumerable contests he had had with the ill-usage of the world, and to his conquest in all of them until now, when he finds that neither strength nor prudence will avail, and he has been reduced to the lowest ebb. But he takes courage. Hope in Him who created us all is his support. His help he has ever found near at hand ; and he then mentions the words of encouragement he thought he heard on that Christmas Day. He believed in the special help of the Almighty because he was a chosen instrument to work out the divine will.

He then speaks gratefully of the Queen. All were incredulous when he explained his great idea, except only his royal mistress, to whom the Lord gave the spirit of intelligence and great courage, and made her the heiress of all, as a dear and well-beloved daughter. He now appeals to her for just judgment. He is judged, he says, as if he was a governor who had been sent to some province or city under regular government. He ought to be judged as a captain sent from Spain to the

Indies, where by divine will he subdued another world
to the dominion of the King and Queen, our sovereigns :
in consequence of which Spain, that used to be poor, is
now the most wealthy of kingdoms. He ought to be
judged as a captain who for so many years has borne
arms, never quitting them for an instant. He ought
to be judged by cavaliers who have themselves won the
meed of victory—by knights of the sword, not by lawyers.

He then gives a temperate account of the recent
occurrences, dwelling on his discovery of the pearl-
fishery, on the disloyalty of the mutineers, on his un-
willingness to inflict the punishment of death on Mujica,
and on his final establishment of quiet when Bobadilla
arrived. " By that time everything was quiet, the land
was thriving, and the people at peace." He describes
the conduct of Bobadilla with marvellous calmness considering the provocation he had received, alludes to the
robbery of his papers and treasure, and complains of
the false accusations and cruel calumnies to which he
has been exposed. Finally, he speaks with simple
humility of his faults, and expresses confidence in the
justice of the sovereigns. " I know assuredly that the
errors which I may have fallen into have been committed without any intention of doing wrong, and I
think their Highnesses will believe me when I say so.
If I have been in error, it is innocently and under the
force of circumstances, as they will shortly understand
beyond all doubt."

This letter is the production of a large-hearted, simple-
minded man, bowed down by injustice and wrong, but
confident in the justice of his cause. It was sure to
make a deep impression on such a woman as Isabella,
who on many points was in sympathy with her illus-

trious servant. Columbus had true friends in his noble-
minded jailers. Andres Martin, as soon as the caravel
was anchored in the bay of Cadiz, on the 20th of
November 1500, sent a messenger off to Granada with
the letters written by the Admiral during the voyage.
He thus managed that they should arrive at court
before Fonseca would have time to transmit Bobadilla's
malicious calumnies.

The discoverer of the New World had arrived at Cadiz
a prisoner, and in chains. The disgraceful news spread
through the country, and excited the most lively indignation and sympathy. The chivalrous nation was hurt
to the quick. The whole people felt shamed and humi-
liated at an outrage the perpetration of which was so
repugnant to the nature of a self-respecting and noble
race. Ferdinand, and even Fonseca, had to dissemble
and express the same feeling, if they had it not. The
Queen truly felt with her people. She shed tears over
the letter received by Doña Juana de Torres. Orders
were at once despatched to the Governor of Cadiz to set
the Admiral and his brothers at liberty, and to treat
them with all possible distinction. A sum of 2000
ducats was ordered to be paid to them for their equipment, and they were invited to attend the court at
Granada. The sovereigns also addressed a most affectionate letter of welcome to the Admiral. After a short
stay at Seville, Columbus and his brothers arrived at
Granada on the 17th of December 1500.

When the grey-headed man, bowed down by hardships
and diseases contracted in their service, stood before the
sovereigns in the royal hall of the Alhambra, they were
embarrassed for a moment, as well they might be. Then
they both rose from their thrones as the Admiral threw

COLUMBUS. (From the old engraving of the Paulus Jovius portrait.)

himself on his knees before them. Isabella shed tears, and even Ferdinand was profoundly moved. It was some time before Columbus could speak, so deep was his emotion. At length he gave expression to his loyalty and zeal, and protested the rectitude of his intentions in all that he had done. But the Queen would not suffer him to proceed. She assured him that the wrongs inflicted upon him had been without the authority and contrary to the wishes of the sovereigns, that they injured the prestige of the throne, and that the Admiral's innocence was already established. Fonseca and his myrmidons had to keep out of sight, while the letters of Bobadilla were not even read. The Admiral was treated with great consideration, the restoration of all his rights in due time was promised, and the King and Queen took frequent opportunities of showing him favour.

The recall of Bobadilla was the first and most urgent act of retributory justice. Fray Nicolas de Ovando, the Comendador of Lares, of the order of Calatrava, who was appointed to succeed him, received orders to see that all their papers, gold, and property of all kinds, were restored to Columbus and his brothers. If anything was missing it was ordered that Bobadilla should make it good. Ovando was a man of strict integrity but narrow mind, and with no administrative capacity. He is said to have been respected, if not liked, by the Spaniards. Las Casas, who was his friend, admitted that he was unfit to govern Indians. His want of sympathy or imagination made him callous to their sufferings, and his inhuman cruelty equalled anything that has been recorded of any conqueror in the New World. He went out in the largest fleet that had yet left the shores of Spain, consisting of thirty-two ships and caravels under the command of

Antonio de Torres. It conveyed 2500 men to the colony, live stock, seeds and agricultural tools, and a large supply of provisions. Bartolomé de las Casas visited the New World for the first time in this fleet. Ovando sailed from San Lucar on the 13th of February 1502, and arrived at San Domingo on the 15th of the following April. Bobadilla and the mutineer Roldan were to be sent home for trial when the ships returned.

Columbus protested against the appointment of Ovando, as infringing his rights and privileges. It was therefore limited to two years, and the Admiral was assured that as soon as numerous pending questions were settled, and the government was firmly established, his suspended rights would be restored to him. He remained for several months in attendance on the court at Granada, enjoying the society of his two sons, and the acquaintance of men of education and literary tastes. Among his new friends was Angelo Trivigiano, the secretary to the Venetian Embassy. Trivigiano had previously been secretary to Dominico Malipieri, the celebrated Admiral, who was anxious to obtain full information respecting the discoveries and maps of Columbus. Trivigiano addressed a letter to Malipieri from Granada on August 21, 1501.* He said that he had formed a great friendship for Columbus, who was then deprived of his rights, not in favour with King Ferdinand, and with little money. With the Admiral's help he had arranged to have a map of the discoveries drawn at Palos, for transmission to Malipieri. The Admiral also promised to give his friend copies of all the reports he had sent to Ferdinand and Isabella. Abstracts of two other letters

* Given by Cardinal Zurla in his edition of Marco Polo (1818), and reprinted by Harrisse, ii. p. 119.

of Trivigiano have been preserved, dated in September 1501 and early in 1502, on the same subject. They show the eagerness with which information respecting the work of the great discoverer was sought for, and also throw a pleasant light on the society in which Columbus mingled while at Granada.

The Admiral was relieved of the wearing anxieties of administration; but his active mind could have no rest. During the residence of a year at Granada his thoughts returned to the recovery of the Holy Sepulchre, and to an examination of the prophecies. He studied the latter subject with great ardour and enthusiasm, seeking for references to the discovery of the Indies, and to the expulsion of infidels from the holy places. His ardent imagination fostered the illusion that the vast riches derived from discoveries in the Indies would enable him to lead a new crusade, rescue the Holy Sepulchre from the infidels, and enable Christians to realise the passion of the Redeemer on the spot where He suffered, without fear of molestation. Such notions were quite suited to the spirit of the age in which he lived. Columbus devoted many hours of each day to the study of the Holy Scriptures, and of the most noted commentators among the early Fathers of the Church. He was guided and assisted in his researches by a great friend, who was a monk in the Carthusian monastery of Santa Maria de Las Cuevas at Seville, named Gaspar Gorricio. The result of these studies was a work which he entitled—*Manipulus de auctoritatibus dictis ac sententiis et prophetiis circa materiam recuperandæ sanctæ civitatis et montis Dei Sion.* This interesting manuscript volume, now known as the *Profecias*, is still preserved in the Columbian Library at Seville. It contains all the

prophecies in the Bible which appear to have any bearing
on the matters in hand, and is preceded by a letter
addressed to the sovereigns, in which Columbus endeavoured to stir their hearts in favour of an enterprise
which seemed to him to be for the good of Christendom.
Many thoughtful Christians of that age besides Columbus believed with him that his discoveries were made
under divine guidance, and that he was, as Jaime Ferrer,
the lapidary, puts it in his letter of August 1495, the
"Ambassador of God." Nor was the recovery of the
holy places considered in any other light than as a
practical scheme that, in the opinions of many, probably the majority of Christians, ought some day to be
undertaken. Spaniards looked upon it almost as a consequence of the fall of Granada. The *Profecias*, therefore, was no offspring of morbid fancies or hallucinations.
It was the practical work of an able and highly imaginative man, setting forth one important argument in
favour of a romantic enterprise which he had at heart,
as the complement of his western discoveries. Every
sentence written by the illustrious Genoese is valuable
to posterity; and the *Profecias* are specially interesting.
from their recording the results of deep study at a momentous period of the Admiral's life, and because the
manuscript contains paragraphs and corrections in his
own handwriting. In a letter to the Pope, dated
February 1502, Columbus regretted that he should
be unable to visit Rome, and explain his scheme for
the recovery of the Holy Sepulchre personally to his
Holiness.

After the completion of his work on the prophecies,
the Admiral reviewed the general results of all his discoveries, and was led to suspect the probability of the

existence of a strait in the western sea beyond Jamaica,
leading between continental lands direct to the Indies.
He **had** observed the existence of a continuous ocean-
current always flowing westward through the channels
between the windward islands.   He discovered the Gulf
stream.   His speculations **on** this subject are shrewd,
and fully justified by his premises.   He observed that
islands lying in **the course of the** current usually had
their length pointing east and west, and **from this** cir-
cumstance he inferred that the current was so constant
that **it had worked them into** their present shapes by
attrition on the north and south coasts.   **The** continent,
a portion **of which he had** discovered at **Paria,** formed a
southern wall **for the current, while on the** north Cuba
was assumed **to be a long promontory.**   Consequently,
as there was **no current** either to the north or the
south, it must **flow through** a strait to the westward.
The argument was invulnerable except at a single point.
The continental character **of Cuba was a** hypothesis
which might **or might not be correct,** and if not the
argument was vitiated.   **The insularity** of Cuba was not
discovered until after the death **of** Columbus.

The indefatigable explorer, although shattered in
health, fixed his mind **on the discovery** of this hypotheti-
cal strait.   **When he** submitted his **plan to** the sovereigns, **it** was received with more than complacency.
Isabella always had faith in the scientific insight of the
Admiral, **and** Ferdinand perceived **the** vast importance
of **such** a discovery.   In spite **of** the opposition of Fon-
seca and some members **of the Council,** the sovereigns
granted the application of the Admiral for four ships, to
be provisioned for two years.

Before starting **for his** last voyage Columbus devoted

FACSIMILE OF THE LETTER FROM COLUMBUS TO THE BANK OF ST. GEORGE.
APRIL 2, 1502.

much care and attention to his worldly affairs, as if he
believed it to be more than probable that he would never
return.   He possessed a number of important title-deeds,
the concession of titles, rights, and privileges, and other
documents, which it was incumbent upon him to leave in
safe custody.   These papers were thirty-six in number.
On the 5th of January 1502 the Admiral went before a
notary at Seville and obtained authorisation for a copy
to be made of them, which was duly attested.   He afterwards added a copy of the famous bull of Alexander VI.,
and his letter to Doña Juana de Torres.   Two copies of
these documents were sent to Nicolo Oderigo, the Genoese
ambassador, together with two missives addressed to
the Bank of St. George.   A third copy was intrusted
to Alonzo Sanchez de Carbajal, who was the Admiral's
agent in Española.   A fourth copy, on parchment, was
delivered to the care of the Carthusian monastery of
Santa Maria de las Cuevas, outside the Triana suburb
of Seville, where the Admiral's intimate friend, Father
Gaspar Gorricio, was one of the monks.   The originals
were deposited in an iron box, and placed in the crypt of
the chapel of Santa Ana.   They are now in the custody
of the Duke of Veragua, the heir and representative of
Columbus, at Madrid, and were published by Navarrete
in 1825.   The copy intrusted to Carbajal is lost.   The
two copies sent to the Genoese ambassador remained in
the family of Oderigo until 1670, when they were presented to the Republic of Genoa.   One is now preserved
in a *Custodia*, let into the pedestal of a bust of the
Admiral, in the town hall of Genoa.   It is a volume
beautifully written, with richly illuminated initial letters,
bound in red morocco and provided with a red morocco
case.   The binding and the case are mentioned by

Columbus in a letter to the Bank of St. George. The documents of which the volume is composed were printed by Spotorno in 1823. The other was recently discovered by Mr. Harrisse in the archives of the Foreign Office at Paris, having been carried off during the French occupation of Genoa.

Having made this wise provision for the preservation of documents establishing his rights and privileges, for the benefit of his sons, the Admiral made a will, signed on April 1, 1502, and deposited in the monastery of Las Cuevas, in the care of Father Gorricio. It has unfortunately been lost. His mind then reverted to his beloved old home at Genoa. He earnestly desired that his countrymen should reap some benefit from his success. He therefore directed that investments should be made in the Bank of St. George at Genoa, with the object of reducing the taxes on wine, flour, and other articles of food, so as to ease the burdens of the people. The sum bequeathed was one-tenth of his entire revenues. The letter to the governors of the bank was forwarded to the Genoese ambassador, Oderigo. The answer of the bank, dated December 10, 1502, gave expression to the pleasure of his countrymen at the affection and goodwill thus shown by the Admiral for his native land. There is some reason to fear that Columbus never received this answer. The original letter of Columbus to the bank was found among files of old papers in 1829, and is now preserved between two glass plates in the town hall at Genoa, together with the reply.

On a blank sheet of the letter to Oderigo * there is a spirited pen-and-ink sketch which is attributed to

* It is now fastened in the end of the volume containing the concessions.

```
        S
    S   A   S
    X   M   Y
```

.XPO FERENS. //

Segno coneta fondcffbo Colombo
Segnaua ostderfcricuenli
ſue deritteꝛ

Columbus himself. It represents a symbolical triumph of the Admiral after his great achievement. Columbus is seated in a car with Providence at his side holding a sail up by the yard, while Columbus has the sheet in his hand. The spokes of the wheels are paddles which send up spray and foam from a sea in which Envy, Ignorance, and other *monstri superati* are nearly submerged. In front of the car are Constancy and Tolerance, behind it Religion; while Victory, Hope, and Fame are flying in the air. In one corner is the well-known signature of the Admiral, and beside it an explanatory note, in a later handwriting, that it is the sign with which Columbus subscribed his letters.* The sketch may have been drawn by Oderigo, but it is more likely that it was the work of the Admiral himself. If so, it shows that he had a bold, free touch, and some artistic feeling.

The last duty of the Admiral before sailing was the despatch of a letter of advice to young Diego at court. "I leave you," wrote Columbus to his eldest son, "in my place, and I wish you to use all that is mine for your own honour. All my privileges and writings are committed to the care of Father Gaspar." He then charges the young man to attend to his devotions, and to set apart a tenth of all he possesses to the service of the Lord for the necessitous poor. "If you do this you will never want, because our Lord will provide for you." He also enjoins him "to be kind and courteous to all with whom he has to do, whether great or humble, for as you do to them so will God do to you. Serve the King and Queen with much love, and do not importune respecting the memorials I have left with their High-

* "Segno con che Cristoforo Colombo segnava e sotoscriveva le sue scritte."

nesses. Be attentive to Beatriz Enriquez for my sake; treat her as if she was your mother, and pay her 10,000 maravedis a year, besides her pension from the dues on the shambles at Cordova. Pay your aunt, Violante Moniz, 10,000 maravedis a year. Keep a careful account of your household expenses, and do nothing without the opinion and advice of Father Gaspar Gorricio. Take great care of my brother Don Diego, who remains at Cadiz, out of the money that our Lord may give you, for he is my brother, and has always been most dutiful. Endeavour to obtain from their Highnesses some preferment in the Church for him." He then explains the business on which he has sent Carbajal as his factor to Española, to collect and send home his property and all that is due to him, and to pay his debts. These final instructions were sent to young Diego with a father's blessing.

The elder Diego Columbus, the Admiral's youngest brother, was desirous of taking priest's orders, and he received letters of naturalisation in February 1504. Having entered the Church, he lived at Seville, and died there in the house of Francisco Gorricio, brother of Father Gaspar, in 1515.

On March 14, 1502, the sovereigns addressed a letter to the Admiral from Valencia de Torre, assuring him that in due time all his rights would be restored. Meanwhile he was not to touch at Española on his way out, lest his presence might cause complications. He was given permission to touch there on his return voyage. All his private affairs having been settled, Columbus busily occupied himself in the equipment of his last expedition. He was to be accompanied by his little son Fernando, then aged fourteen, and by his faithful brother the Adelantado Bartolomé, who was to be a tower of strength and support in the days of trouble and danger that were near at hand.

NOTE.

(1) *The Supposed Preservation of the Irons.*

The story of the preservation of the chains by the Admiral, and of their having been buried with him, is not mentioned by Las Casas, Peter Martyr, Oviedo, or Bernaldez. In the Italian version of the life by Fernando Columbus there is the following passage on which the story is based : " Egli avea deliberato di voler salvar quei ceppi per reliquie e memoria del premio de suoi molti servizi, siccome anco fece egli, perciocchè io gli vidi sempre in camera cotai ferri ; i quali volle che con le sue ossa fossero sepolti " (cap. lxxxv. p. 280.   Ed. Londra, 1867).   Fernando, no doubt, saw them in his father's room at Seville after his arrival in 1500.   But I agree with Mr. Harrisse that it is grossly improbable that the Admiral carried such luggage about with him, a proceeding most insulting to the King, or that the irons were carried from Valladolid to Seville in his coffin.

P

CHAPTER XII.

1. CABOT.   2. CORTEREAL.   3. COMPANIONS OF COLUMBUS.

THE first voyage of Columbus caused a very complete revolution in the minds of cosmographers and mariners. Before that great landmark in the history of the human race was raised, their ideas were confined to coasting round the shores of an old world surrounded by the ocean. After the problem was solved, after the great achievement was done, and Columbus had thrown a light across the hitherto unpassed and unpassable ocean, all was changed. Many men were ready to follow, but there was only one who could lead.

The first follower of the great discoverer of the New World was a countryman of his own, another native of the Ligurian shore. John Cabot, or Zuan Caboto in the Venetian dialect, was a Genoese who was naturalised at Venice in 1476, after a residence of fifteen years. He was a cosmographer and traveller, having extended his journeys as far as Arabia. Like all the rest of the world, John Cabot was astonished at the grand achievement of his countryman. He went to Lisbon and to Seville,* and

---

* Letter of Pedro de Ayala to the sovereigns from London, 25th July 1498. "Calendar of State Papers," Spain, i. 176 77, and Harrisse's "Cabot," p. 329. This letter was found at Simancas by Bergenroth in 1862.

heard the glorious news, with the theories of the Admiral
about the territory of the Grand Khan and the rich island
of Zipangu. It seemed to him to be "a thing more
divine than human " * to have sailed by the west into the
east. He was filled with the desire of sharing in the
work of discovery, under the auspices of some other
government. So he came to England, settled at Bristol
with his wife and three sons in about 1495, and submitted a scheme for exploration to the government of
Henry VII. On the 5th of March 1496 a patent for
the discovery of unknown lands was granted to John
Cabot jointly with his three sons Lewis, Sebastian, and
Sancius.

Unfortunately no narrative of the voyages of John
Cabot has been preserved, and there is not a scrap of
writing either by him or by his son Sebastian. It is
only possible to piece together a few meagre facts, and
reports at second or third hand, from the writings of
others, in which the Cabots are incidentally referred to.
The actual facts are very few indeed.

John Cabot fitted out one small vessel at Bristol, which
is believed to have been called the *Matthew*,† with a
crew of eighteen persons. There is no evidence that
his son Sebastian accompanied him. The *Matthew* sailed
in May, and at five o'clock in the morning of the 24th of
June 1497 land was sighted, and named "Prima Terra
Vista." We learn from a copy of a *mappe-monde*‡ drawn

---

* Sebastian Cabot, in Ramusio.

† Barrett's "History and Antiquities of Bristol" (1789), p. 172 : quoting from an old manuscript, which is not, however, now forthcoming.

‡ A map was found by Von Martius in 1843 in the house of a curate
in Bavaria, and deposited in the National Library of Paris in 1844,
which is considered to be a copy of the *mappe-monde* drawn by
Sebastian Cabot in 1544. It was reproduced by Jomard. On its sides

by Sebastian Cabot in 1544, that " Prima Terra Vista "
was the northern point of Cape Breton Island. On the
map of Michael Lok, dated 1582, in Hakluyt's "Divers
Voyages," copied from a chart of Verrazzano, the inscription, "J. Gabot, 1497," is written across the land to a
point named Cape Breton. John Cabot also discovered
an island, named St. John, because it was seen on the
same day, the 24th of June, which is identified with the
Magdalen Islands. He may also have sighted Newfoundland. These are "the Londe and Isles of late
founde by the said John" mentioned in the patent of
1498. An Italian named Lorenzo Pasqualigo, living in
London, in a letter to his brother at Venice, after
Cabot's return, said that Cabot explored the coast for
300 leagues.* But he returned in the end of July,
for he received a grant of £10 on August 10th† ("To
him who found the new Ile, £10"), so that there
would have been no time to make this 300 leagues
cruise, and barely time to return to Bristol, for a little
craft like the *Matthew*. Consequently the continent of
America was not then discovered.

are two tables with seventeen legends in Spanish and Latin. There
was a copy of this map, or part of it, prepared by Clement Adams in
1549, which was hanging in the gallery at Whitehall in Hakluyt's
time, now lost. Hakluyt copied the legend on it, which is the same as
No. 8 legend on the map at Paris. It mentions the discovery of "Prima
Vista" on June 24th and of St. John's Isle, but the year is 1494 in
both. This must be a printer's error, iiii. for vii., as Mr. Major
suggested.

 Willes (editor of "Eden's Voyages," ed. 1577) mentions another map,
which he calls "Cabot's card or table," in possession of the Earl of
Bedford at Cheynies, proving the existence of the Strait of Anian
between 61 and 64 N. It also is lost.

 * "Calendar of State Papers," Venice, I. 262.

 † "Privy Purse Expenses, Henry VII.," August 10th, 1497 : quoted
by Mr. Dean in Winsor's "Narrative and Critical History of America."

The first voyage of John Cabot in 1497 in the *Matthew* may thus be summed up. He sailed from Bristol in May, reached the north point of Cape Breton, and landed there on June 24, sighted the Magdalen Islands and perhaps Newfoundland, and returned to Bristol in the end of July. Pasqualigo says that Cabot planted on the beach where he landed the flags of England and of St. Mark, he being a citizen of Venice, and a large cross.* On his return he reported, in imitation of Columbus, that he had reached the territory of the Grand Khan. He prepared a chart of his discoveries and also a solid globe.† Great honour was paid to him; he dressed in silk, and was styled the great Admiral;‡ and in December 1497 a pension of £20 a year was granted to him, to be paid out of the customs receipts of Bristol.§

John Cabot proposed to lead a larger expedition across the ocean in the following year, and to discover the rich island of Zipangu, for he adopted all the ideas of Columbus. On February 3, 1498, a patent was issued‖ authorising John Cabot alone, there being no mention of the sons this time, to take six ships to the land discovered by him in 1497, and to enter men. He appears to have sailed in the summer of 1498. All we know for certain is that he had not returned in September. On this occasion his son Sebastian probably

* Pasqualigo *ubi sup.*

† Raimondo de Soncino (envoy of the Duke of Milan), August 24, 1497. "Calendar of State Papers," Venice, i. 260.

‡ Pasqualigo.

§ Collection of Privy Seals, Record Office, No. 4, copied by Franklin B. Dexter of Yale College, and quoted by Mr. Deane, Winsor's "Narrative and Critical History of America," iii. 50.

‖ First printed by Biddle in his "Memoir of Sebastian Cabot" (1831), p. 76.

accompanied him. John Ruysch, the eminent Dutch geographer, "whose map," in the Ptolemy of 1508, says Nordenskiold, "forms an epoch in the development of cartography," * may possibly have accompanied **John Cabot** in his second expedition. He sailed from England to the east coast of the new land, saw many islands, and reached 53', and the most probable expedition in which he could have done this was that of John Cabot. We know from a letter of Pedro de Ayala, the Spanish envoy in London,† and from Stow's Chronicle,‡ that the expedition of Cabot sailed in the summer of 1498, and that it had not returned in the following September. But we know nothing more. There is no authentic account of the proceedings of the expedition, and no record of its return. As there are no dates respecting the second voyage of 1498, and no definite facts, it cannot be said that Cabot discovered the American continent before Columbus reached Paria in July 1498. We know nothing more of John Cabot, of where or when he died, or when his ships came back.

Pedro de Ayala saw the map of John Cabot, and without doubt he obtained a copy and sent it to Spain. There is evidence of this on the famous map which Juan de la Cosa drew in 1500, and in the instructions to Alonzo de Ojeda in 1502. On the map of Juan de la Cosa, Cape Race is called "C. de Ynglaterra," there are sixteen names apparently translated from names on a

---

* Facsimile Atlas, p. 67.

† Pedro de Ayala to Ferdinand and Isabella, July 25, 1498. "Calendar of State Papers," Spain, i. 176, 177. This letter was found by Bergenroth at Simancas in 1860.

‡ Stow's Chronicle (1580), year 1498; from Fabyan. Stow gave the passage from Fabyan to Hakluyt. But there is no such passage in any edition of Fabyan's Chronicle.

map by Cabot, and beyond them to the west is written
" Mar descubierta por Yngleses."

Sebastian, the son of John Cabot, left England, and
held employment under the Spanish government from
1512 to 1547, when he was allowed to come back to
England, a very old man.   It is said that Sebastian
commanded an English expedition in 1517.   But this is
impossible.   He was then fully occupied in Spain, and
in 1518 he was appointed " chief pilot and examiner,"
residing at Seville.   Our only knowledge of the proceedings of the expedition of John Cabot in 1498 comes from
alleged conversations of Sebastian when in Spain, recorded
from memory many years afterwards at second or third
hand.   There is not a syllable direct from Sebastian
himself.   There is a statement by Peter Martyr in his
Decades, published in 1516, who says that he was intimate with Sebastian ; another recorded by Ramusio as
having been made by the guest of a friend, and which
he wrote down afterwards from recollection ; another
which Ramusio himself had received many years before
from Sebastian in a letter ; and a fourth in Gomara's
History.   Galvano, the Portuguese writer, also says
something about Cabot, but he is evidently quoting from
Gomara.

Peter Martyr's version is that Cabot sailed northwards
in July, until he met large masses of ice, and the days
were very long ; that he named the land " Baccalaos,"
because there were so many fish that they sometimes
stopped the ship, which the natives called by that name :
that he went south as far as the latitude of Gibraltar,
and so far west that Cuba was on his left hand.   The
guest of Ramusio's friend, Fracastor, said that he once
had an interview with Sebastian Cabot, at Seville, who

told him that he went with two ships as far north as 56°, then southwards as far as Florida, when his provisions failed. The recollection of Ramusio himself was that Sebastian wrote to him many years before, saying that he went to 67 30′ N., and on June 11 he found the sea still open, and expected to reach Cathay, but was hindered by a mutiny. The story in Gomara is that Sebastian Cabot fitted out two ships at his own expense, and went to the Cape of Labrador in 58° N., though he himself says much more, where there was much ice and long days in July. Turning west he refreshed at Baccalaos, and then followed the coast as far south as 38° N. Galvano gives Cabot's extreme north at 60°.

All these stories are unauthentic and unreliable, and it will be observed that everything is attributed to Sebastian, while John Cabot, who commanded both expeditions, is not mentioned. If Sebastian ignored the position and services of his father in making these statements, and took the credit to himself, his conduct forms a strong contrast to that of Fernando, the son of Columbus, whose filial piety is his best claim to remembrance. *Baccalaos* is not a native name, and it certainly was not given by Cabot. *Bacallaba* (whence *Baccalaos*) is the Basque word for stock fish, and the hardy Basque fishermen possibly frequented the Newfoundland Banks long years before the time of Cabot. With regard to the most northern latitude reached by Cabot there is no agreement. One gives 67 30′, another 60°, another 58°, another 56°, and Ruysch has 53°. But there is a general agreement that Cabot went north until he met with ice, and that then he sailed southwards until his provisions failed and he was forced to return to Bristol.

To sum up, all we know with certainty is that an

expedition commanded by John Cabot left Bristol in
1498. It is probably true that he sailed north until he
met with ice off the coast of Labrador, most likely in
53° north, as given by Beneventanus on the authority of
Ruysch, and that he then shaped a southerly course
until he was obliged to return. The Gibraltar latitude
would place him near Cape Hatteras.

It is very much to be regretted that there are no
authentic accounts of these interesting voyages of John
Cabot. When his son Sebastian returned to England
he received a pension, and as a very old man he was
Governor of the Muscovy Company. In the time of
Queen Mary he was deprived of half his pension, which
was given to one W. Worthington. This was in 1557,
when his age was about eighty-four. It is suggested
by Biddle that, on Sebastian's death, the time and place
of which are unknown, his maps and papers were delivered by Worthington to Philip of Spain, who carried
them off. This would account for the total absence of
all authentic information respecting the expeditions of
John Cabot.

The other voyages which, like those of Cabot, were
the direct consequence of the achievement of Columbus,
appear to have been undertaken by the Portuguese
Government with a less ingenuous object. The English
were under no obligation to recognise the preposterous
claims of Spain founded on the Papal bull. The Portuguese were under such obligation. By the Treaty of
Tordesillas, signed on the 7th of June 1494, the Portuguese acknowledged the binding character of the bull
on the line being moved so much further west as to fall
370 leagues west of the Cape de Verde Islands. They
were left a fair and wide field for discovery, settlement,

and commerce in the east. But they were not satisfied, and sought to enforce their **extreme** rights **on or, if possible,** beyond the dividing line.

The King **of** Portugal granted a concession **for** the discovery of lands **to** the north-west to Gaspar Cortereal, **the** youngest **of** three sons **of** Joao Vaz Cortereal, who was captain **of the islands of** Terceira and St. George in **the** Azores. **Gaspar** was about fifty years of age when he undertook **this** enterprise, and **no** particulars of his **previous career have** come down **to us.** He left Lisbon **in a well-equipped vessel, in the summer** of **1500 ;*** or **he left Terceira with** two vessels **according** to another **account,†** and, steering north, sighted the south coast of **Greenland,** observing its serrated mountains, but he did **not land.‡** It **was** supposed **to** be a point of Asia. Many icebergs **were met with,** and good fresh water was **found on them,** where the ice was melted **by** the sun. **Cortereal then coasted** along **the whole** eastern **side of Newfoundland, and** named it **"Terra Verde," because the land was covered with trees** suitable for making masts. **It was** afterwards **called "** Terra Corterealis," while **some** map-makers placed that name on the Labrador coast. **Cortereal** reached 50 N., and returned with several **natives and** some white bears.§ Only very meagre accounts of this voyage exist in the chronicle of Damien de Goes and **in** Galvano.

In the following year a second expedition was fitted **out under the command** of Gaspar Cortereal, consisting **of** three vessels, **to follow** up **the work** achieved in 1500.

---

* Damian de Goes

† Galvano.

‡ Legend on **the** Cantino map.

§ Legend on a Portuguese portolano **of the sixteenth century,** referred to by Harrisse.

They probably sailed on the 30th of April 1501.* Two of the vessels returned on the 9th and 11th of October respectively; the third, with Cortereal on board, never came back, and his fate remained unknown. His brother Miguel went in search of him in the following year, but he, too, was never heard of again.

A few details of the second voyage of Cortereal are given in two letters written by Pietro Pasqualigo, the Venetian envoy at Lisbon, on the 18th and 19th of October 1501—one to the Seigneury of Venice, the other to his brother; and in a letter written by Alberto Cantino, an Italian then at Lisbon, to the Duke of Ferrara, on the 17th of October. Cantino heard the captain of one of the vessels make his report to the King of Portugal. The account of the Italian letter-writer was that Cortereal had discovered a coast line, which he sailed along for 600 or 700 miles, bearing from Lisbon between west and north-west, about 3000 miles distant. This would be the North American coast from about Chesapeake Bay to Cape Breton. In the southern part there were delicious fruits of various kinds. Along the coast there were many large rivers, and at the northern end there was much fish; but they could not reach the land discovered during the first voyage, which was further north, by reason of the ice, or more probably the fogs. Cortereal himself pressed onwards and was lost. The two

---

* Damian de Goes says May 15th. Pasqualigo and Cantino say that one vessel returned on October 6th, after an absence of nine months, which would make January the 6th the date of sailing. But Mr. Harrisse has discovered documents in the archives of the Torre do Tombo, including a receipt for biscuits, signed by Cortereal on April 25, 1501. He no doubt sailed a few days afterwards. As one point on the land he discovered is named the Cape of the last of April, he probably sailed on April 30, 1501.

other vessels brought back seven natives, who were
minutely described by Pasqualigo and Cantino.

But the most important record of the second voyage
of Cortereal consists of a map which Cantino caused to
be prepared by a Portuguese draughtsman at Lisbon in

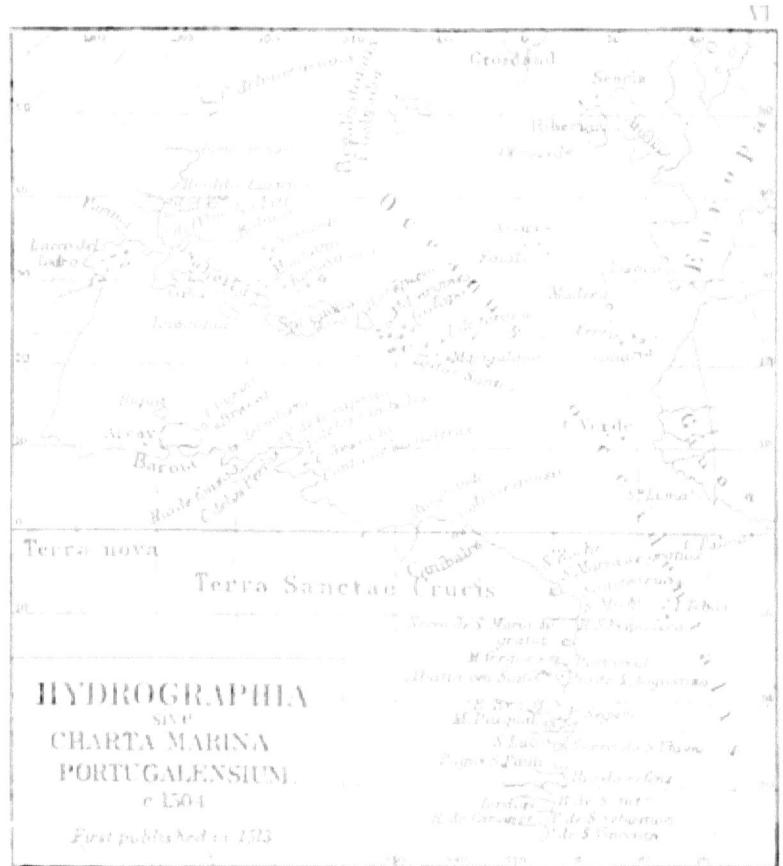

1502, and sent to the Duke of Ferrara.   It is now preserved at Modena, and a facsimile has been published by
Mr. Harrisse with his work on the Cortereal voyages.
The Cantino map is a plane chart, with the equator, the
tropic of Cancer, and the Papal dividing line down the

Atlantic as a single meridian. It shows the eastern coasts of Europe and Africa, and the discoveries of Columbus and his school of pilots, the whole richly painted and illuminated. But the object of the Cantino map was to illustrate the discoveries made during the two voyages of Cortereal. The results of the first voyage are shown by the southern part of Greenland with Cape Farewell, called "A ponta d." (Assia?), and by a line of coast, much broken by inlets, representing the east coast of Newfoundland. It is called "Terra del Rey de Portugall," and there is a legend to the effect that it was discovered by Gaspar de Cortereal, who was lost when the other vessels returned. A forest of tall trees is painted on the land. The remarkable point connected with this discovery is that it is placed just to the eastward of the Papal dividing line. This is moving Newfoundland over 300 miles too far east in the Portuguese interest; but, as longitudes were observed in those days, it may have been done without *mala fides*.

The results of the second voyage of Cortereal are shown on the Cantino map by a coast bearing from west to west by north of Portugal, and extending for 600 miles, exactly in accordance with the accounts given by Pasqualigo and Cantino. It is, no doubt, a copy of the rough chart drawn by the pilot of one of the vessels, with twenty-two Portuguese names of rivers and capes, six of which are unintelligible, doubtless owing to the original document being injured by damp or rubbing at these points. There is a " Rio de los Lagartos " (river of lizards), near where Cabot has a " Cabo de Lizarte " on the map of Juan de la Cosa. The southern point appears to be the entrance of the Gulf of Chesapeake, with the islands on the east side ; and the northern point would then be Cape Breton, where the attempt to reach New-foundland was given up by the two vessels which returned, while Cortereal himself went on into the fogs and was lost. The draughtsman placed the West Indian Islands much too far to the north, and the Cortereal coast-line is made to run north and south, to the west of Cuba. Owing to the removal of Newfoundland to the east, while the North American coast receives no eastward trend, an excessive space is left between them. This, however, was not due to Cortereal or his pilots, but to the theories of the draughtsman employed by Cantino.[1] It was felt that this coast-line examined by Cortereal in his second voyage was much too far to the westward to be claimed by Portugal, and accordingly no legend to that effect appears on this part of the map.

The Spanish voyages to the New World undertaken in the lifetime of Columbus, but in breach of his rights as Admiral of the Ocean, were for the most part commanded by men who had been trained by the Admiral himself—such as Pinzon, Niño, La Cosa, and Ojeda. The work done by them, and the discoveries made, like those of Cabot and Cortereal, are the direct outcome of his genius, and must be included among the results and consequences of his first voyage across the Atlantic. When Columbus sent home his report of the discovery of the Gulf of Paria and the pearl-fishery, accompanied by an excellent chart, Bishop Fonseca easily persuaded King Ferdinand that great gain might accrue from licensing the voyages of independent adventurers who would reap the fruits of the Admiral's discoveries. The breach of faith did not trouble either Ferdinand or Fonseca; and to the latter this perfidy was especially pleasing, because it gratified his malice.

Alonzo de Ojeda had returned from Española, and Fonseca tempted him with the prospective wealth of the pearl-fishery. The daring adventurer readily closed with so attractive a proposal, and he was furnished with the Admiral's chart in order to enable him to find his way to Paria and infringe on the privileges of his old chief. A worse man to command an expedition could scarcely have been found. Brave to recklessness, enterprising and daring, he was an admirable second, and was well fitted for the conduct of such wild exploits as the capture of Caonabó. But he had none of the qualities necessary for a leader. Juan de la Cosa, the able cartographer, accompanied Ojeda as pilot, and the provision merchant, Amerigo Vespucci, was also taken on board, probably as a volunteer. Four vessels were fitted out at the port of Santa Maria, in the bay of Cadiz, and Fonseca furnished every assistance in his power.

The expedition of Ojeda sailed from Cadiz on the 18th or 20th of May 1499, and, after touching at Gomera, the adventurers endeavoured to follow the track of the Admiral across the Atlantic, but with indifferent success. They struck a bad landfall, and, instead of sighting Trinidad, they made the coast somewhere near Surinam. They coasted along, in sight of land, finding the water quite fresh off the mouths of the Essequibo and Orinoco, until they entered the Gulf of Paria, and anchored off the mouth of the river Guarapiche. Here they found a pacific race of Indians, with whom they communicated, and who gave them a delicious fermented liquor made from fruit. Leaving the gulf by the Boca del Dragon, Ojeda passed the island of Margarita and Cape Codera on the mainland, and came to a port near Puerto Cabello, where there was an encounter with the natives, and

twenty Spaniards were wounded. The place was named
" Puerto Flechado," in memory of the arrow wounds.
The vessels moved to Coro, where they remained twenty
days while the men recovered from their wounds, and
then stretched over to the island of Curacoa, which was
named " Isla de los Gigantes," for some reason not
clearly explained. Rounding Cape San Roman, at the
north end of the peninsula of Paraguana, they entered
a large gulf, where they saw villages with houses built
out over the sea on stakes, and the communication between the different habitations effected by canoes. From
this circumstance the name of little Venice—" Venezuela "—was given to the country and the gulf. The
native name was Coquivacoa.(2) They explored the shores,
and entering a strait at the south end on the 24th of
August, they discovered the great inland gulf of Maracaibo, which they named " San Bartolomè." The Indians
were reported to be more handsome than any that had
been seen in the New World. The furthest western
point reached by the expedition was the Cabo de la
Vela, whence, on August 30th, they commenced their
homeward voyage. Entering the port of Yaquimo, in
Española, in September 1499, the presence of Ojeda
caused some trouble and anxiety in a colony where the
mutiny of Roldan had just been appeased. On the return voyage Ojeda passed through the Bahama group,
seizing 230 of the wretched islanders as slaves, and
arrived at Cadiz, in the middle of June 1500, where
he sold those who had survived the horrors of the
passage.

Alonso Niño of Moguer, the expert pilot and companion of Columbus in all his voyages, also obtained a
licence, and was fitting out a caravel of 50 tons at

Palos, with the pecuniary aid of one Cristoval Guerra, at the very time when Ojeda was sailing from Cadiz. Crossing the bar of Saltes, this second interloper followed close on the heels of the first, and was a far better seaman. He reached the Gulf of Paria only fifteen days after Ojeda. In passing out of the Boca del Dragon the caravel was surrounded by a fleet of canoes manned by warlike Caribs, who were only driven off by a discharge of lombards. Niño proceeded to the island of Margarita, and his people were the first Spaniards who ever landed on it. Some pearls were obtained, and the caravel then sailed across to the mainland at Curiana, now called Cumana. They were so well received by the amiable inhabitants, that Niño and Guerra remained at Cumana for three months, and saw the process of pearl fishing. They obtained pearls as well as a few gold ornaments during their stay. Niño sailed westward from Cumana to a place where he heard there was gold, called Cauchieto, which he reached on the 1st of November 1499. Here more gold and many fine pearls were obtained, and a further supply was got on the return of the caravel to Cumana; altogether over one hundred and fifty marcs of pearls. On the 13th of February 1500 Niño made sail for Spain, and, after a voyage of sixty days, arrived at Bayona in Galicia. Niño was arrested on an accusation of having concealed some of the treasure, but he was released, and he enjoyed the reputation of having made the most lucrative voyage to the New World up to that time.

Soon after the departure of Ojeda and Niño, a licence for fitting out an expedition was given to Vicente Yanez Pinzon, another companion of Columbus. Aided by relations and friends, Pinzon fitted out four caravels, and

Q

sailed from Palos early in December 1499. After leaving the Cape Verde Islands he sailed for many hundreds of miles to the south-west until he lost sight of the pole star. On the 20th of January 1500 he sighted the Brazilian Cape of San Agustin in 8° 20′ 44″ S., where he landed and took possession in the names of the sovereigns of Spain. Pinzon was the first to cross the equator and visit land in the New World, within the southern hemisphere. He discovered Brazil three months before Cabral, whose fleet did not reach this coast until the following April. Pinzon then followed the coast northward to the equator, and, landing on a point of land, some of his people had a fierce encounter with the natives, in which eight or ten Spaniards were killed. Forty leagues further north the water was found to be quite fresh far out at sea. He discovered the mouth of a mighty river, more than thirty leagues in width, afterwards named the Amazons.

Pinzon continued his northward course, entered the Gulf of Paria, passing out by the Boca del Dragon, and reached Española on the 23rd of June 1500, after having discovered a vast extent of the east coast of the New World. Two of the caravels were lost in a storm, but the other two arrived safely at Palos on the 30th of September. There was a great mortality in this expedition, but Pinzon had the glory of having been the first to cross the equator on the western side of the Atlantic, and of having discovered Brazil and the mouth of the Amazons. He brought home 3000 lbs. of dye-wood, and specimens of plants and animals.

When Pinzon sailed from Palos, two vessels were being fitted out there by Diego de Lepe for a similar voyage. Bartolomé Roldan, a companion of Columbus in his first

and second voyages, was pilot. Lepe sailed about a
month after Pinzon, and followed the same course, until
he sighted the Cape of San Agustin. He then doubled
the Cape, and ascertained that the coast continued to run
in a south-westerly direction. He prepared a chart of
his discoveries, but the date of his return is not recorded.
Several unrecorded expeditions appear to have sailed
from the ports of Andalusia at this time, in the hope
of sharing the good fortune of Niño and Guerra. A
comendador, named Alonso Velez de Mendoza, with two
caravels, is supposed to have followed in the track of
Lepe. Cristoval Guerra also made a second voyage with
his brother Luis, who found the means. They sailed
from San Lucar with two caravels, passed through the
Gulf of Paria, and traded for pearls and gold at Cumana.
Las Casas accuses them of having treated the natives
with great cruelty. They brought home dye-wood,
pearls, gold ornaments, and a number of Indians to sell
for slaves, arriving some time in November 1501.

A more important voyage was that undertaken by Rodrigo de Bastidas, a native of the Triana suburb of Seville.
Juan de la Cosa was his pilot, and Vasco Nuñez de
Balboa, the future discoverer of the South Sea, was one
of his crew. He sailed from Cadiz with two vessels
in October 1500, and reached the mainland somewhere
near the Gulf of Venezuela. Rounding the Cabo de la
Vela, the most western point hitherto reached by Ojeda,
he passed along the coast by Santa Marta, the mouth of
the Magdalena, and Cartagena, until he reached the
Gulf of Uraba or Darien, which he explored. Proceeding on his course he passed Capes Tiburon and San
Blas in Darien, his furthest point being the port of
Nombre de Dios, or Puerto de Bastimentos, as it was

named by Columbus. This was a most successful voyage. Intercourse with the natives was always of a friendly character, and the whole conduct of the expedition reflects great credit on Bastidas and La Cosa. The ships, however, **were much** injured by the borings of the *Teredo navalis*, **and it was not** without difficulty that they were got across to Jamaica to refit.

Bastidas **reached** the western coast of Espanola, but **encountered a** series **of** storms, and eventually lost his ships with their valuable **cargo.** A good deal of gold and many **pearls were, however,** saved, with which Bastidas **and his people** made their way to San Domingo. Unfortunately the infamous Bobadilla was in power, and the shipwrecked navigator **did not** escape from persecution and false accusations. **But** he was **fully** acquitted on his return to Spain in **September** 1502, after an **absence of close upon two years.**

During the absence of Bastidas, a licence was granted **to Alonzo de Ojeda to** fit out a second expedition, and **to** form a settlement **in the** province of Coquivacoa or Venezuela, of which **he was to** be governor. He intended to have ten ships, but he could only collect funds to fit out four. Ojeda himself was on board the *Santa Maria de la Antigua*, with Garcia de Ocampo as master. The *Santa Maria de la Granada* was commanded by Juan de Vergara, the caravel *Magdalena*, by a nephew of the governor named Pedro de Ojeda, and the *Santa Ana* by Hernando de Guevara. The expedition sailed from Cadiz in January 1502, and reached the Gulf of Paria, where **the ships** were hove down and cleaned. They then proceeded on the voyage, and after passing the island of Margarita the *Santa Ana* lost sight of the rest of the squadron. Next day Guevara went on to the port near

Point Codera, which had been mentioned as a rendezvous: but there being no signs of his consorts, he thought he must have passed them in the night. He determined to wait for them, anchoring under the shelter of two bare rocks, about three leagues from the land. The rocks were frequented by hundreds of sea-birds, and some of the ship's boys, to amuse the captain, who was ill, got leave to go and hunt the birds, bringing on board forty very large ones after a quarter of an hour.

Vergara sailed next day, though it was not until two more days had passed that he at length found Ojeda at port Codera, but only with his own ship. The other two were still missing. After about a fortnight of hide-and-seek the squadron was united. It was then arranged that villages should be attacked in the province of Curiana, which they named "Val Fermoso," and everything seized that was likely to be useful to the settlement. They took hammocks, cotton, and even some girls to be the slaves of Vergara and his friend Ocampo. Their greatest want was a supply of provisions, and it was arranged that Vergara, in the *Santa Ana*, should be sent to Jamaica to buy as much food as possible, and return either to the Gulf of Maracaibo or to the Cabo de la Vela, where the other three ships would wait for him for two months. This was in April 1502.

Ojeda, with Ocampo and Guevara, then proceeded to Curaçoa (which they called "Isla de los Gigantes") and thence to Coquivacoa, but the land looked poor and unproductive, so they went on to Bahia Honda, in the Guajira peninsula, which they named "Puerto de Santa Cruz." Here they found a Spaniard named Juan de Buenaventura, who had been put on shore at Citarma (now Santa Marta), in the province of the Sierra Nevada,

by Bastidas. He had been a year with the Indians,
learning their language. The port of Santa Cruz is
twenty-five miles to the east of Cabo de la Vela. Having fixed upon this place as the site of the new settlement,
they began to clear the ground of trees and bushes, and
to build forts, after overcoming the resistance of the
natives. These forts, three in number, were placed
under Guevara, Ocampo, and a servant of Ojeda named
Cueva. The lombards were mounted in them, and their
main object was to protect a store-house containing the
provisions, and the box of gold and pearls that had been
collected partly by barter, partly by violence. The supply
of food was running short, and, as Vergara did not return
from Jamaica after a month, the pilot Juan Lopez was
sent in search of him on board the caravel *Magdalena*.
The people were now weary of the business, half starved,
and discontented. Vergara returned at last and con-
spired with Ocampo against their chief, accusing Ojeda
of keeping most of the treasure for himself, and of having
caused the death of many Spaniards by his cruel treatment of the Indians, which made them hostile.

In June 1502 the malcontents arrested Ojeda and
put him in irons, intending to deliver him to the governor of Española for judgment. Leaving Santa Cruz in
September, the squadron arrived at the port of Hani-
gueyaga in Española, and Vergara handed over Ojeda
as a prisoner to the comendador Gallego. The box of
treasure remained in possession of Vergara. Ojeda was
sent to San Domingo, and the suit between him and
his captains commenced in December. Ojeda appealed
against the sentence to the sovereigns in Council, who
acquitted him and ordered that all his property should
be restored. It is unknown when these adventurers

returned to Spain, but the expedition was a complete
failure, and showed Ojeda's unfitness for command.

These voyages, undertaken between the years 1499 and
1504, completed the discovery of the whole coast of the
continent from Cape San Agustin, 8° south of the line,
to beyond the Gulf of Darien. The discoverers were the
companions of Columbus, men who had been trained
under his eye, and raised to their positions through
his kindly patronage.* One and all followed in his wake,
making for his discovery in the Gulf of Paria, and merely
extending a knowledge of the coast line on either side.
All this was in fact supplementary to the work of the
Admiral himself, and rightly belongs to the record of his
services to geography. To a great extent it preceded the
date of his last voyage, and falls into its place as in some
sort introductory to that final effort. A notice of the
discoveries of Bastidas is especially necessary as a prelude
to the last voyage, because the connection of the Admiral's
work with that of Bastidas completed the fruitless search
for a strait.

NOTES.

(1) *The coast-line of North America on the Cantino map.*

The Cantino map was drawn to illustrate the discoveries of
Cortereal. The two new coast-lines shown upon it, one being the
east side of Newfoundland and the other being 600 miles of the
coast of North America, must therefore be assumed to represent
those discoveries, unless some very strong reason can be produced to the contrary. The 600 miles of coast of North America
on the map fairly agree with the descriptions of the Italian letter-

---

* "Los mas que despues descubrieron eran criados, pilotos, y
marineros del Almirante." Evidence of Carbajal, Navarrete, ii. 587.

writers, as a coast 2800 miles from Lisbon, with a bearing be
tween west and north-west. This is clear enough. Yet Mr.
Harrisse maintains that this new coast, first shown on the Can
tino map, is not intended to represent the discovery of Cortereal.
He thinks that it was a discovery made between 1500, when
the map of Juan de la Cosa was drawn which does not show it,
and 1502, by some unknown navigator of unknown nationality,
but presumably Spanish. The reason which Mr. Harrisse gives
for believing that this coast-line is not intended to show a dis
covery of Cortereal is that it is placed at such an immense distance
from Newfoundland, and that Cortereal never could have made
such a blunder (*Les Corte Real*, p. 149). But the answer is that
Cortereal was dead long before the map was drawn. The chart
of the pilots were placed in the hands of the draughtsman, and
he alone was responsible for the positions of the coast-lines por
trayed on those charts, when he transferred them to his general
map of the world. He had to place Newfoundland much too
far to the east for political reasons. He placed the North
American coast too far to the west to comply with his notions
of its position with reference to the West Indian islands, which
are called "the Antilles" for the first time on the Cantino map.
But if he had given an easterly trend to the coast, instead of
giving it a north and south trend, it would not have been very
much out. The draughtsman's worst blunder was in placing Cuba
and the other West Indian islands very much too far north.

The objection of Mr Harrisse is thus fully met, and there
appears to be no other reason for doubting that this 600 miles
of the coast of North America is intended to represent the 600
miles of coast west of Lisbon, which was explored by Cortereal
in 1502.

Navarrete makes the remarkable statement that Ojeda in
his first voyage found certain Englishmen in the neighbourhood
of Coquivacoa (iii. 41). The only ground for this statement is
a passage in the instructions given to Ojeda before sailing on
his second voyage. He is told to continue his discoveries
towards the part where the English may make discoveries, and
to set up marks with the royal arms (iii. 85), that the progress

of the English in that direction may be checked. Ayala,
the Spanish ambassador in London, had sent a report of the
despatch of the expedition of John Cabot in 1498, which accounts
for these instructions, given as a precaution in the event of
encroachments on the part of the English. The vast distance
between the land which Cabot intended to seek and the coast
of Venezuela, with the Caribbean Sea and Gulf of Mexico intervening, was not then understood. Of course the English were
never within thousands of miles of Coquivacoa, but it was a
curious mistake for Navarrete to have made. See also Biddle's
"Memoir of Sebastian Cabot," p. 66, and App. B, p. 307.

CHAPTER XIII.

THE LAST VOYAGE OF DISCOVERY.

The mind of Columbus was as bright and imaginative, his intellect as clear as in the days of his prime, when he set forth on his last voyage. But his body was worn out by incessant watching, anxiety, and tropical fevers. He suffered from ophthalmia and gout in its severest form. Physically he was quite unfit to endure the hardships of a voyage of discovery, but his ardent spirit could not be restrained. The self-denying affection of his gallant brother, the Adelantado, is most touching. He did not wish to enter upon such an undertaking, but he would not allow the Admiral, in his enfeebled state, to go alone. His little son Fernando was sure to be a comfort to him, although he was also a cause of deep anxiety in times of danger and hardship.

Columbus wished to have built new vessels on a design of his own, but this was impossible owing to want of funds. He therefore bought four caravels at Seville, and provisioned them with great care, having suffered much in previous voyages from the bad condition of the food supplied by the contractors. The Admiral hoisted his flag on board the *Capitana*, a vessel of seventy tons, and sailed in her with his little son, the captain being a loyal man named Diego Tristan, and the master and chief pilot were two brothers, Ambrosio and

Juan Sanchez. The surgeon was a Valencian apothecary named Bernal, an ill-conditioned fellow.

Morales, the royal treasurer, had made a special request to the Admiral that he would find places in the expedition for two brothers of his wife, named Porras. In an evil hour Columbus good-naturedly consented, for they proved to be mutinous scoundrels. Francisco Porras was made captain of the *Santiago de Palos*, and his brother Diego accompanied him as royal inspector and accountant. Don Diego Mendez, a very gallant and loyal gentleman, sailed in the same ship as a volunteer. The worst ship was the *Gallega*, of sixty tons, and the Adelantado, an admirable navigator, went in her. Her captain was Pedro de Terreros, one of the good men, loyal and true, who stuck to his beloved chief for better or for worse. He had been with the Admiral as his steward in the first, second, and third voyages. Diego de Salcedo, the Admiral's other servant in the first voyage, was now zealously assisting Carbajal in managing his old chief's affairs in Española, and was destined to be of essential service in the coming time of trouble. The fourth ship, called the *Vizcaina*, of only fifty tons, was commanded by a Genoese friend of the Admiral named Bartolomé Fieschi, a most honourable and gallant officer of ancient lineage. Altogether there were 143 souls embarked in the four vessels—25 officers, 13 volunteers, 2 trumpeters, 41 seamen, and 62 boys, including young Fernando. Among these there were eight Genoese, countrymen of the Admiral.

On the 3rd of April the expedition left Seville, and dropped down to San Lucar, proceeding thence to Cadiz. There the Admiral joined, and when on the point of sailing he heard that the Portuguese garrison of Arzilla,

on the coast of Morocco, was being closely besieged by
the infidels.   He generously resolved to hurry to the
help of the Christians, and sailed from Cadiz with his
four little vessels on the 9th or 11th † of May 1503.
Arriving off Arzilla he found that the Moors had raised
the siege.   The Portuguese were, however, much gratified at his proffered aid, and he found among the garrison
some relations of his Portuguese wife, Felipa Moñiz, who
were very hospitable.   On the same day he left Arzilla,
and arrived at Grand Canary on the 20th of May, where
he remained for five days, filling up with provisions,
wood, and water.   He also took a last opportunity of
writing to his friend, Father Gaspar Gorricio, asking
him to watch over the welfare of his son Diego.   At
sunset of the 25th sail was once more made, and a
course was shaped for the Indies.   A most delightful
voyage across the Atlantic, running pleasantly before
the trades, brought them to an island called Martinino
on the 15th of June.   This island was probably St.
Lucia, and, if so, they anchored in Gros Ilet Bay, well
known in after years as the favourite rendezvous of
Lord Rodney's fleet.   The Admiral refreshed his people
here for three days, giving leave for men and boys to go
on shore to wash their clothes.   Thence he shaped a
course to Santa Cruz and Puerto Rico, and on the 24th
he steered direct for San Domingo.

Ovando had arrived at San Domingo on the 15th of
the preceding April, and immediately arrested Bobadilla
and the mutineer Roldan, to be sent to Spain for trial.
They were allowed to take their ill-gotten riches with
them.   Antonio de Torres expeditiously prepared his
ships for the return voyage; and he was entrusted with

* Las Casas, iii. p. 28.   † Porras in Navarrete, i. p. 283.

the largest nugget of gold that had ever been found. It weighed 35 lbs. As many as thirty-two vessels were prepared for the voyage. Bobadilla, Roldan, and the unfortunate cacique, Guarionex, who had long been a prisoner, were on board one ship, and it is believed that upwards of 200,000 *castellanos* of gold were embarked.

The great fleet was ready to sail when the little squadron of Columbus appeared off the harbour. The Admiral had no intention of touching at San Domingo on his way out, but he was compelled to seek assistance owing to the unseaworthy condition of the *Gallega*. She was a wretched sailer, and dangerously crank. Her captain, Terreros, was sent in a boat to request that Ovando would allow the Admiral to buy another vessel out of the great number in the harbour, or to exchange the *Gallega* for one better suited for the perilous service on which he was engaged. Ovando refused all assistance, and sent back Terreros with a message that the Admiral must continue his voyage with the same vessels he had brought out from Spain. Columbus received this brutal answer with the patience and equanimity which had become a part of his nature. But he found himself obliged to send in Terreros once more, and this time it was a message of warning. The great experience of those seas possessed by the Admiral, and his unerring instinct, enabled him to detect the signs of an approaching hurricane. He communicated his forecast to Ovando, and urged him to detain the fleet in harbour until the danger was over. Refused shelter at San Domingo, the Admiral then sought refuge in the little port of Azua, to the westward. During the first hours of the hurricane the four little vessels remained at anchor together.

When the force of the wind increased all but the *Capitana* were driven out to sea, and the *Gallega*, in great danger, was saved through the excellent seamanship of the Adelantado. When the storm abated they reassembled, without the loss of a man, and with slight damage to sails and rigging. These frail little boats escaped almost by a miracle. One seaman and two boys deserted, but otherwise Columbus sailed from the inhospitable shores of the island he had discovered and settled without any loss.

Very different was the fate of the returning fleet. Ovando gave no heed to the message of Columbus, and sent the fleet to sea in disregard of his warning. The thirty-two vessels sailed from San Domingo on the 1st of July, and they were scarcely out of sight of land when the full force of the hurricane burst upon them. The largest ship had not time even to shorten sail, and went to the bottom with the infamous wretch Bobadilla, the miscreant Roldan, the ill-fated chief Guarionex, and a vast amount of treasure, including the famous nugget. More than twenty vessels met the same fate, the rest were scattered and disabled. One small caravel, called the *Guchia*, was able to continue the voyage, and brought the news of the catastrophe to Spain. She also brought some of the property of Columbus, about 4000 dollars, which his agent Carbajal had succeeded in collecting. It was the only treasure that was saved. There was not a man in those days who failed to see the finger of God in this most striking retribution. The faithful servant of his Lord was preserved in safety with all his people, and even his treasure. His persecutors, with their ill-gotten wealth, were destroyed in the same furious hurricane which Columbus and his people rode out in safety.

Continuing on his adventurous voyage, the Admiral came in sight of the wooded island of Guanaja, off the coast of Honduras, on the 30th of July 1502. He gave it the name of " Isla de los Piños." While the explorers were on shore, about to return to the ship, a very large canoe came in sight, with a great number of oars, and a sort of cabin built up in the centre, roofed with palm leaves, so that the women and merchandise were protected from sea and rain under its shelter. It came alongside the *Capitana*, and its crew of twenty-five men submitted to the Admiral. They had evidently come from a long distance, and the merchandise included many things of great interest. There were wooden swords armed with fish bones, copper axes, and cotton cloths. The Spaniards here saw for the first time the nuts of the cocoa plant, and fermented liquor made from maize. The character of the manufactures indicated that the merchandise came from a country which had reached a higher state of civilisation than any that had yet been discovered. If Columbus had shaped a course westward, in the direction whence the canoe had come, he would have discovered Mexico. But he was bent on the examination of the coast in the opposite direction, in search of the supposed strait.

From the island Columbus shaped a southerly course to the mainland, and struck it where there was a cape covered with shady fruit trees, close to the modern town of Truxillo in Honduras. The natives called the fruit *carinas*, so the Admiral gave that name to the cape. Communications were opened with friendly natives on the coast, and the expedition was well supplied with fresh provisions; but from the beginning of August to the middle of September, a period of six weeks, the explorers were exposed to the most terrible navigation that any of them had previously experienced. There was an incessant downpour of rain, a succession of storms of thunder and lightning raising a terrific sea, and the wind always foul. Often they did not make good fifteen miles, and sometimes not a league in the twenty-four hours. It was not until the 12th of September that the vessels succeeded in rounding Cape Gracias a Dios, and were able to steer south along what is now known as the Mosquito coast.

Columbus had often experienced bad weather, but never of so long a duration or so fearful. The vessels had their sails blown out of the bolt ropes, anchors and boats were lost, and ropes carried away. The Admiral was very ill; but he had a small cabin rigged on deck, whence he could pilot the ship. His greatest anxiety was for the safety of young Fernando, and for the effects of such incessant toil on so young a boy; but it was a consolation to see the lad encouraging the others, and working as if he had been years at sea. His brother was another source of anxiety. " He was in the ship that was in the worst condition and the most exposed to danger," he wrote, "and my grief on this account was the greater that I brought him with me against his will. Another anxiety wrung my very heart-strings, which was the thought of my son Diego, whom I had left an orphan in Spain, and stripped of the honour and property that were due to him on my account."

When at length they rounded Cape Gracias a Dios there was a leading wind, and on the 15th of September the Admiral sent boats to a river, which seemed to have a deep entrance, to take in water. But one boat was capsized on the bar, the boatswain of the *Vizcaina*, named Martin de Fuentarabia, and a Basque boy named Larreage

being drowned. The place was called " Rio del Desastre."
On the 25th they anchored between the beautiful island
of Quiriviri, which Columbus named " La Huerta," or
the garden, and the mainland, called Cariay. Here the
Admiral rested his people until the 5th of October, held
a survey on all the provisions, condemned what appeared
to be injured, and collected information. He enforced
kindly treatment to the Indians, and won their friendship
and confidence. Sailing southwards, and passing the
sites of Blewfields and Greytown, he reached a place
called Caribiri to the south of the Nicaragua river,
where he met with people wearing gold ornaments. They
spoke of a country called Veragua, whence the gold came ;
and the Admiral, with his mind full of the eastern Indies,
understood that this gold district was not far from the
river Ganges. On 17th of October the little squadron
sailed from Caribiri in search of Veragua. Touching at
the mouth of a river called Cubiga, the natives confirmed the reports about the riches of Veragua ; but as
the wind was fair for completing the exploration of the
coast in his search for a strait, the Admiral deferred the
investigation of these reports until a later opportunity.
The acquisition of gold took a very secondary place in
the mind of this great man. whose unselfish thoughts
were ever bent on the achievement of discoveries for the
welfare of the human race. His character was noble
and generous, and this appears over and over again,
when he had to make choice between his own interests
and his duty. He continued to examine the coast eastward until he reached the harbour of Puerto Bello, but
after leaving that anchorage the wind headed him, and
he was obliged to take shelter in a bay named by him
"**Puerto de Bastimentos**," because the extensive culti-

R

vation of maize indicated the existence of abundant supplies of food. It was the "Nombre de Dios" of Nicuesa, so that the whole north coast of the Isthmus of Panama had been examined, and the question of a strait was settled. The Admiral had now connected his work with that of Bastidas. The coast of the continent was explored from Cape San Agustin in Brazil to the Bay of Honduras, and there was no strait.

Unable to proceed further towards Darien, and being in great danger, Columbus took refuge in a very small bay to the east of Nombre de Dios, which he named "Retrete." Here he refitted and collected fresh provisions, resolving to return westward to the Veragua province, and investigate its capabilities as a gold-producing district. He sailed from Retrete on the 5th of December, when a time of great suffering commenced. The provisions brought out from Spain were all consumed except the biscuit, which was so full of maggots that the people could only eat it in the dark when they were not visible. Clothes were nearly worn out, and the men were in a very unhealthy condition, owing to the want of good food and incessant rains. The ships were bored through and through by the *Teredo navalis* and were scarcely seaworthy. After leaving Retrete they encountered terrible weather, and Columbus was at the point of death. "Never," he wrote, " was the sea seen so high, so terrific, and so covered with foam. Not only did the wind oppose our proceeding onward, but it also rendered it highly dangerous to run for any headland, and kept me in that sea, which seemed to me as a seething caldron on a mighty fire. Never did the sky look more fearful, emitting flashes in such fashion that each time I looked to see if my masts and sails were not destroyed. These flashes came with such alarming fury that we all thought the ship must have been consumed. All this time the waters from heaven never ceased, not to say that it rained, for it was like a repetition of the deluge." It is wonderful that the crazy little vessels could have lived through such weather. Another danger was added to all the rest. A column of water, as big round as a wine cask, rose from the surface of the sea, joined with the clouds, and came whirling down upon them, so that escape seemed impossible.* The terrified seamen began to repeat passages from the gospel of St. John, and the waterspout swept clear of them, leaving them in the belief that they had been saved by divine favour. Then followed a day or two of calm, when the voracious sharks were so numerous round the ships that it was feared as an evil omen. Nevertheless a good many were caught and eaten. The coast on which they had encountered so many storms and contrary winds was named " La Costa de los Contrastes." On the 4th of January 1503 a ship's boy, named Diego Portugalete, succumbed to the hardships of the voyage, and there was no help for it but to throw his body to the sharks.

At length the Admiral led his battered squadron across the bar of a river which was called Yebra by the natives. It was named Belem, because they entered it on Epiphany Sunday, 1503. The river of Veragua was about a league to the westward, but the bar was too shallow for even the smallest vessels to cross it. These rivers are on the north coast of the isthmus, in the province of Veragua, between the Gulf of Chiriqui and the river Chagres. They got into this shelter not a day too soon. On the 24th of January a furious gale raged outside. There

* Las Casas, iii. 12.

was also a fresh in the river and heavy breakers on the
bar. The vessels were driven from their anchors, came
into collision, and the *Capitana* lost her foremast. But
when the storm had expended its violence and the flood
subsided, **the** river Belem, protected from the sea outside
by the shallow bar, was like a calm lake. The Adelantado
was sent **to** communicate **with the** natives at a large
village **on the Veragua river, and** entered **into** friendly

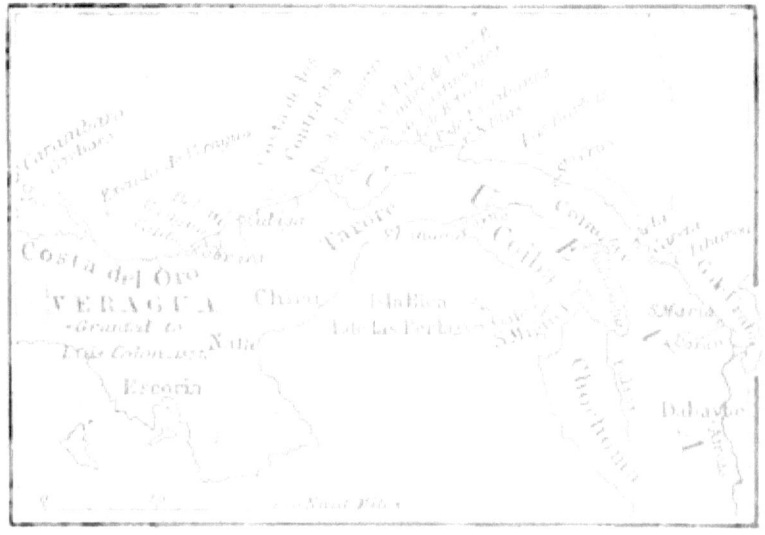

MAP OF VERAGUA

relations with a powerful chief named **Quibian,** who
afterwards visited the *Capitana*, and was entertained by
the Admiral. But from the first he was not altogether
cordial, and showed some jealousy at this invasion of his
territory.

The natives of the isthmus, comprising the region
between the two oceans, and extending from the lake of
Nicaragua to the Gulf of Darien, were a hardier and
fiercer **race than** the people hitherto **encountered** by

Columbus in the islands. Bancroft, gleaning from various
authorities, describes them as active and jealous of their
independence, always being ready to resist attempts to
penetrate into their country, which consists of deep
ravines, malarious swamps, abrupt heights, rapid streams,
and luxuriant vegetation. In the hills of Veragua and
Chiriqui dwelt tribes who received the name of " Los
Valientes," from their heroic resistance to the Spaniards.
The Indians of the isthmus are generally well built,
muscular, and of average height. Unlike most other
American races, the Isthmian has a short, rather flat
nose, dark eyes, excellent teeth, abundant coarse hair,
and skin of a medium bronze tint. They were naked,
except for a cotton cloth round the loins, the chiefs
wearing long mantles. All the Isthmian tribes were fond
of ornaments, and wore necklaces and ear-rings of gold
and silver. On going to war their bodies were painted.
Their arms were beautifully made bows and arrows
pointed with fish bone, spears, and flint-edged clubs.
They cultivated bananas, maize, and pimento, but lived
chiefly by fishing and hunting. Their huts were neatly
constructed, and many were built in the branches of
trees, and approached by bamboo ladders. Columbus
found some of the tree-top villages on the coast of
Veragua raised to a height to be clear of insects and
reptiles, and of the miasma rising from the swamps.

It was with these Isthmians that the Admiral now
had to do. On the 6th of February 1503 he sent the
Adelantado, with sixty-eight men in boats, to explore the
Veragua River. The chief, Quibian, received him with
courtesy, but was evidently jealous of the invasion.
Having offered to supply guides to show the Adelantado
the way to the gold mines, that officer left a guard with

the boats, and set out up the banks of the river with
the rest of his men. The explorers were taken through
a dense forest, where the ground seemed impregnated
with gold. Ascending a high hill, they were told that
the country yielded gold as far as they could see; but
when the Adelantado returned, he ascertained that the
guides had taken him to the territory of a neighbouring
chief, with whom Quibian was at war. On the 16th
Bartolomé Columbus set out on another expedition along
the coast, where he found proofs that there was abund-
ance of the precious metal, and much gold was collected
and brought back.

The Admiral was now convinced of the great value of
the province he had discovered. After much consultation
it was decided that a settlement should be established
at the mouth of the Belem, under the command of the
Adelantado, and that the Admiral himself should return
to Spain for supplies and reinforcements. He hoped
that Veragua would escape the fate of Española and
Paria, and that, learning from experience, a crowd of
hungry and cruel adventurers would not be allowed to
swarm into the new colony. Columbus believed that
he had reached the Aureus Chersonesus, whence, as
he had read in Josephus, the gold was obtained for
Solomon's temple. As regards latitude he was quite
right.

A small eminence was selected for the site of the
settlement, near the mouth of the river Belem, on the
right bank. All the men that could be spared from the
ships were sent on shore, and they began to build wooden
houses and magazines thatched with palm leaves, each
defended by a stockade. The garrison was to consist of
eighty men, and one of the vessels was to be left with

them, as well as all the provisions and arms that could possibly be spared. The work proceeded rapidly, and at first everything seemed favourable for carrying out the arrangement that was contemplated.

The natives, and especially Quibian, viewed these preparations with jealousy, and when they saw that it was intended to make a permanent settlement, this feeling grew into one of active hostility. An extensive conspiracy was formed, and a scheme was prepared for exterminating the intruders. The Admiral had been ready to depart for some time, but the bar was too shallow, and it was necessary to wait for the rains. Meanwhile Quibian was busily assembling his fighting men.

Suspicion of native hostility was first aroused in the mind of Diego Mendez, a valorous and loyal gentleman, and a most faithful and beloved friend of the Admiral, for whom he had been acting as secretary. With cool audacity, he determined to visit the village of Quibian and make a thorough reconnaissance. On the way he passed a great number of armed men, and heard that they were collected to burn the ships and kill all the Spaniards. He resolved, however, with a single companion named Rodrigo de Escobar, a boy on board the *Vizcaina*, to go on to the village. He found thousands of Indians drawn up in fighting array ; but he boldly pushed his way up a hill to the chief's house, and, although he could not obtain an interview with the great man, he saw and indeed was assaulted by one of his sons, whom he appeased by presenting him with a comb and looking-glass, and by making Escobar comb his hair. Returning to the Admiral, Diego Mendez reported the threatening aspect of affairs, and advised that a sudden attack on the village should be made, to secure the persons of

Quibian and his family. Without their chief he thought
the warriors would disperse.

The Adelantado urged that the advice of Mendez
should be taken. He ascended the river Veragua in
boats, with seventy-four armed men, landed at the village,
and went up to the chief's house with Mendez and five
sailors. Quibian came out, and, after a violent struggle,
was overpowered by the Adelantado, bound hand and
foot, and sent down to the boat, while the main body of
the Spaniards came up, and captured every soul in the
house. The Adelantado then returned. But Quibian
was intrusted to the custody of Juan Sanchez, pilot of
the *Capitana*, who did his duty so carelessly that the
native chief managed to slip overboard, dive, and reach
the shore in safety. He returned to the village, to find
his house desolate, and his family carried off by the
invaders. Henceforward nothing but the most relentless
hostility could be expected from him.

At this time the rains set in, the depth of the water
on the bar increased, and three caravels succeeded in
crossing it, though not without scraping the sand more
than once. They had been lying in the river for nearly
three months. The Admiral then took an affectionate
leave of his brother, promising to return with all possible
speed, and giving his final instructions.

The Adelantado had scarcely returned to the settlement, when it was furiously attacked by a large force of
natives led by Quibian. The valiant Genoese seized a
lance, placed himself at the head of his men, and fought
stubbornly in the post of greatest danger. Mendez also
organised resistance and was in the thick of the fight.
The Indians were at length driven back into the forest,
and concealed themselves in the dense underwood, with-

out losing sight of the houses of the settlement. Fortunately the Admiral had been unable to sail, owing to
contrary winds; and wishing to fill up with wood and
water, and also to communicate once more with his
brother, he sent in a boat under the command of Diego
Tristan, the captain of the *Capitana*. Tristan crossed
the bar and proceeded up the river, intending to fill up
with water before communicating with the Adelantado.
Suddenly the boat was surrounded by war canoes, coming
from both banks of the river, and their occupants poured
volleys of arrows into the crew. Tristan fought bravely
against hopeless odds, and fell covered with wounds.
Only one man escaped, a cooper of Seville, named Juan
de Noya. He jumped overboard, swam to the bank, and,
concealing himself among the trees, found his way to
the settlement. The garrison was utterly disheartened,
and, in spite of the inspiriting speeches of the Adelantado
and Mendez, the men clamoured to be allowed to return
on board. But it was very doubtful whether this was now
possible. The houses were abandoned because they were
so near the forest, under cover of which the enemy could
approach, and a bulwark was formed on the sea-shore of
a boat, casks, and planks, behind which they resolved to
defend themselves to the bitter end.

Two days passed away and the boat did not return.
The Admiral became very anxious. Most of the Indian
prisoners had broken out of the hold and jumped overboard, while those that could not effect their escape
committed suicide. A few more days passed and yet no
tidings. The saddest forebodings filled the mind of
Columbus. It was then that he heard the voice a second
time. On this occasion it was evidently in a dream, and
not in his waking moments. But the impression was so

vivid that he was able to write the words he heard in his journal. It was a compassionate voice, and it said, "O fool, and slow to believe and to serve thy God, the God of all! From thine infancy He has kept thee under His constant and watchful care. He gave thee the keys of those barriers of the ocean sea which were closed with such mighty chains, and thou wast obeyed through many lands, and gained an honourable fame throughout Christendom. Turn to Him and acknowledge thine error—His mercy is infinite. Thine old age shall not prevent thee from accomplishing any great undertaking. Thou criest out for uncertain help. Answer, who has afflicted thee so much or so often—God or the world? The privileges promised by God He never fails in bestowing; nor does He declare, after a service has been rendered Him, that such was not agreeable with His intention, or that He had regarded the matter in another light; nor does He inflict suffering in order to make a show of His power. His acts answer to His words, and He performs all His promises with interest. I have told thee what the Creator has done for thee, and what He does for all men. Even now He partially shows thee the reward of so many toils and dangers incurred by thee in the service of others." The voice paused, while Columbus remained in a trance, and its last words were, "Fear not, but trust! All these tribulations are, with good cause, recorded on marble!" He had every reason for despondency. In sinking ships, without provisions or boats, he had to cross several thousand miles of ocean, or die on the passage with his son, and all his people. But after he heard the voice he took comfort.

There was only one boat left, and the Admiral hesitated to risk its loss. At this critical juncture a young

sailor of Seville, named Pedro de Ledesma, came forward
and volunteered, if the boat would take him near the
surf, to swim to the settlement or perish in the attempt.
Columbus accepted the gallant offer, and Ledesma succeeded in swimming to shore, and in returning with the
melancholy tidings of the destruction of Tristan and all
his crew, and of the despair of the garrison.   It was a
sad but inevitable necessity that for the present the plan
of founding a colony in Veragua must be abandoned.
After eight days, by using the single boat and two canoes
fastened together, all the stores were brought back, and
the garrison was embarked. The squadron, now reduced
to three caravels, left the Belem, and arrived at Puerto
Bello on the 20th of April 1503. Here it was necessary
to abandon the *Vizcaina* as quite unseaworthy.   Only
two leaky little vessels remained to take them home, the
Capitana and *Santiago de Palos*. The Admiral appointed
the valiant Diego Mendez to succeed poor Tristan in
command of the *Capitana*.

Columbus and his brother knew it to be necessary
that they should work as far as possible to the eastward
before leaving the land, otherwise they would be carried
far to leeward by the current, in stretching across to
Española. The pilots wanted to shape a course direct
to San Domingo, and much discontent was bred among
the crew at the supposed delay. The Admiral was
unmoved. He passed Retrete and a cluster of islands
he called " Las Barbas," now known as Las Muletas,
and he did not leave the coast until he was in sight of
Cape Tiburon. Even then he did so too soon, and the
vessels were carried away far to leeward of their intended
port.

The voyage of discovery was over. Great work had

been done. The important question of the strait was solved. Columbus or his pupils had examined the shores of the continent from S. S. to 10 N., and the strait must now be sought for beyond those limits. A great extent of the new coast line had been discovered and explored, including the rich gold-yielding province of Veragua. The service had been performed in unsea worthy little vessels, in the most fearful weather, and in the face of appalling hardships. Two men had been drowned in crossing the bar of a river, a captain and fourteen men had been massacred by Indians, and six had died of disease. The rest were worn out by exposure and want of food. But their troubles were not yet over, and they had many more hardships and sufferings to endure before their service was completed.

CHAPTER XIV.

ABANDONED AT JAMAICA.

On Monday, the 1st of May 1503, Columbus lost sight of that great continent which he had discovered, but which he was never destined to see again. When we consider the pain he was suffering and his growing infirmities, and the fearful weather he encountered; when we realise the difficulties and dangers of the voyage in every shape and form, and the consummate skill with which he met them; when we contemplate his watchfulness, and his ability as a pilot and a seaman, we must come to the conclusion that his last voyage of discovery was the most admirable achievement, though not the most important, in the life of this wonderful man. If it was second to the first voyage, it was only second.

The Admiral had left the coast at Cape Tiburon against his own judgment, and as a concession to the incessant murmuring of the pilots and crew. The consequence was that, passing the Tortugas or Caymans, he only fetched the Jardin de la Reyna, nearly at the western end of Cuba. He would have to beat up, against wind and current, to Española, in vessels with hulls literally honeycombed by the *Teredo*. Suffering from hunger and exhausted by fatigue they at length reached Cape Cruz, where a supply of cassava bread was obtained. But by no possibility could the sinking hulls beat up to windward and reach Española. In despair the Admiral shaped a course for **Jamaica**, reached "Puerto Bueno," now called **Dry Harbour**, on the 23rd of June, and "**Puerto San Gloria**," the modern **Don Christopher's Cove**, on the next day. The weather was fine, and the Admiral ran the sinking vessels, **side by side**, on the sandy beach. The work of pumping and **baling** ceased, and they were soon full of water. They were securely made fast together, and huts were built on the decks to house the crew. The cabins under the poops and fore-castles could still be used.

The shipwrecked explorers were now dependent **on sup-plies from the shore for their existence.** Some friendly natives came, in the first days, with provisions to barter for any trifles the Spaniards would give them. They belonged to a small **village called Maima**, at a short dis-tance from the ships. **Diego Mendez** was a supremely capable man, as well as a **knight-errant**, and a **loyal gentleman.** He undertook to organise a system of provision supply, by means of conventions with the principal chiefs throughout the island. He travelled to the eastern cape, and formed a close friendship with a powerful chief, who sold him a good canoe, and undertook to send cassava bread, fish, and game to the ships. Similar conventions were made with minor chiefs all along the **coast.** From that time the natives came every **day with abundant supplies, and the** Admiral made strict rules **to prevent their being** imposed upon or ill-treated. **But they** were **content** with any trifling little ornament in exchange for **their provisions.** Young Fer-nando was now fifteen years **of age**, and he took great interest in the arrangements of the market. **The** Admiral purchased ten canoes at Maima **for** the use **of his** people.

The great necessity, as well as the great difficulty, was to devise the means of informing the government at Española of their predicament. The Admiral turned the matter over in his mind for a long time, and at last he sent for Diego Mendez. "My son," he said, "not one of those whom I have here with me has any idea of the great danger in which we stand except myself and you; for we are but few in number, and the natives are numerous, and very fickle and capricious. They can easily destroy us all whensoever they take it into their heads to do so. I have thought of a remedy. It is that some one should go to Española in the canoe that you have purchased, buy a vessel and enable us to escape from our dangerous position. Tell me your opinion?" Mendez replied that he saw the danger distinctly, but he doubted whether any one would be found to cross a stormy sea, 120 miles in width, in a frail canoe. The Admiral, admitting the risk and peril, denied the impossibility, and told Mendez that he intrusted the service to him. Then the gallant sailor said that if these important services were always given to him there might be a feeling of jealousy among the others. He therefore requested that the business might be placed before the whole of the people, to see if any one would volunteer. "If all refuse," added Mendez, "I will risk my life in your service, as I have done many times already."

The Admiral submitted the matter to the people, and called for volunteers. They were all silent. Then Mendez spoke out. "I have but one life, and I am willing to sacrifice it in the service of your lordship, and for the welfare of all those who are here with you." The Admiral embraced him, and he at once prepared for the voyage. Drawing his canoe on shore he fixed a false

keel on it, nailed some weather-boards round the gunwale,
and gave it a coat of tar. He also fitted it with a mast
and sail, and laid in provisions for two Spaniards and
six Indians. Everything being ready, he bade farewell
to the Admiral and all his shipmates, and made sail for
the eastern point of the island, a distance of seventy-five
miles. Here he was attacked by some hostile natives,
who made him a prisoner and were going to kill him.
Escaping to his canoe, he shoved off and made sail,
returning to the ships. It was then arranged that the
Adelantado, with seventy men, should march to the east
point, and remain as guards until Mendez put to sea.
After waiting for a few days, the sea appeared to be
calm. Diego Mendez was accompanied this time by
Bartolomé Fieschi, the Genoese, another loyal and devoted
friend of the Admiral. Mendez was instructed to proceed at once to Spain and give an account of the voyage
to the sovereigns, while Fieschi was to return from
Española and report the safe arrival of Mendez.

The Admiral wrote a most touching letter to the
sovereigns, dated the 7th of July 1503, which is full of
graphic descriptions and noble thoughts. After alluding
in temperate language to the disgraceful conduct of
Ovando at San Domingo and to the hurricane, he
describes the terrific weather off the Honduras coast and
his own serious illness, mentioning his anguish at the
condition of his brother and his little son Fernando; and
he refers to his own poverty after so many years of
service, not as a personal complaint, but to show the
destitute state in which his beloved son Diego would be left
in the event of his death. He then reports the tidings
he obtained respecting Veragua and its gold, his examination of the land, the terrible sufferings in the bad

weather off the Veragua coast, and the anchorage at
Belem. The letter describes the exploring work, the
discovery of gold, the attempt to form a settlement, and
the war with Quibian, ending with a reference to his
despondency and despair at the loss of his boat's crew
and the break up of the settlement. The solemn words
he heard in his dream, which renewed his hopes, are
then repeated to the sovereigns, followed by a narrative
of events down to the shipwreck at Jamaica. Some
account is given of the people and products of the newly
discovered country, and especially of the gold mines of
Veragua, with the grounds he has for identifying Veragua
with the Golden Chersonese. The Admiral concludes
his letter with an earnest appeal for his men. "The
people who have sailed with me have passed through
incredible toil and danger, and I beseech your highnesses,
since they are poor, to pay them promptly and to be
gracious to them." Finally, he refers with grief to the
condition of Española and Paria, overrun with greedy
adventurers, to his own wrongs, and in making a final
appeal for justice he prays for the prosperity of the
sovereigns. This most interesting letter was accompanied by one to Father Gaspar Gorricio, with messages
to young Diego and another to Ovando, requesting him
to send vessels to convey the people to San Domingo.

With these letters Mendez embarked in one canoe
while Fieschi accompanied him in another, each having
five Indians, who went with them voluntarily at the
risk of their own lives. They bade farewell to the good
Adelantado one bright night, and the Indians impelled
the canoes over the smooth sea with their paddles during
the whole of the next day, occasionally jumping overboard to cool themselves by swimming. On the second

night the Indians were exhausted with fatigue **and** thirst, so Mendez and Fieschi hoisted their **sails**. On the **second day** there was **no** land in sight. The Spaniards took **their** spells at the paddles, but all began to suffer terribly from thirst.

> " Water, water, everywhere
> Nor any drop to drink.

The calabashes were now all **empty**. The sun poured down its scorching heat, and **by noon** the Indians had lost all power to work. Mendez and Fieschi kept giving the poor fellows short drinks from their breakers from time to time, and so **kept them up until** the cool of the evening, when they revived a little. They were making for a small island called Navasa, **about** twenty-four miles from the west point of Española, and they began to fear they had been taking a wrong course. They were almost in despair when night overtook them, and **they were still out of sight of land**. As the moon rose, Mendez noticed that he could only see half, when the whole disc ought to be visible. It was **rising** behind the islet, and this blessed sign was their salvation. The Indians were all **given drinks and shown the land**. They exerted their final strength, and soon the canoes reached the shore. It was a mass of barren **rocks, but some** rain water was found in the clefts, and they all obtained welcome rest. One Indian had died **that afternoon**. Cape Tiburon, the western point of Española, **which the Admiral** had named **San Miguel**, was in sight, **and** at sunset they resumed the voyage, reaching land **at dawn**. Fieschi wished to return to Jamaica, in obedience to the Admiral's instructions, but the natives could **not be** induced to undertake another **such voyage**. After resting for two days Diego

Mendez proceeded to Xaragua, where he found the
Comendador Ovando, and reported what had happened,
and the critical position of the Admiral and his people.

Ovando deliberately put off the despatch of any help.
He was ever in dread that the Admiral's rights might
be restored. He hoped that, if he left him to starve
at Jamaica, he would die, and that all danger from
that quarter would be removed. Mendez found him at
Xaragua engaged in work so diabolical that it requires
the unanimous testimony of all contemporary writers
to make it credible. The chief Behechio had died, and his
sister Anacaona had succeeded him. Ovando announced
his intention of paying her a visit, and she summoned all
the under chiefs of Xaragua to assemble at her residence,
to do honour to the comendador. That officer's plot had
been arranged beforehand. In the midst of festivities
in his honour, he caused the caciques to be seized and
fastened to wooden pillars within the house, which was
then set on fire. They were all burnt alive. An indis-
criminate massacre was then committed, neither age nor
sex being spared. Finally he ordered Anacaona to be
hanged—the good and bountiful princess, who had ever
been a firm friend of the Spaniards, and with whom the
Adelantado had had such pleasant relations. Ovando
then carried desolation into Higuey, the eastern province
of Española, and hanged its noble and gallant chief,
Cotabanama. He was rapidly exterminating the native
population. His friend Las Casas admits that he was
unfit to bear rule over natives, but maintains that he
was a good governor of his own countrymen. Yet he
deliberately left 130 Spaniards to starve at Jamaica, in
the expectation that his own private interests might
thereby be advanced.

The months passed on, and no tidings came to Puerto la Gloria of Diego Mendez. Sickness began to appear among the people, who were crowded in the huts on the ships' decks, although excellent arrangements were made by the Admiral for their general comfort, and for exercise on shore. Want of employment, and the long-deferred hope of relief, were telling upon them, and many were becoming discontented and demoralised. The two brothers to whom Columbus had been induced to give appointments for which they were quite unfit, by the treasurer Morales, began to stir up a mutiny. Francisco de Porras was captain of the *Santiago*, and Diego was accountant. They were joined by Juan Sanchez, the pilot who allowed Quibian to slip through his fingers; by Pedro de Ledesma, the intrepid swimmer; by Juan Barba, the gunner of the *Capitana*, and about fifty others. Their intention was to seize the Admiral's canoes and follow Mendez to Española.

On the 2nd of January 1504 Porras and his followers broke out in open mutiny. Porras entered the cabin where the Admiral was laid up with a severe attack of gout, made violent complaints, and accused him of never intending to return to Spain. Columbus reasoned with him, but he refused to listen, and rushed out of the cabin, calling upon the mutineers to rally round him. The Admiral limped out but was induced to return, and the Adelantado confronted them with a drawn sword, ready to defend the approach to his brother's cabin with his life. The loyal men, of course, included all the sick, and they were too weak to resist the followers of Porras, who seized what stores they chose to take, and the ten canoes, and departed in the direction of the east point. They made several attempts to put to sea, but always returned.

There was no Diego Mendez among them. At last they gave up all hope of crossing to Española, and wandered over the island, robbing and ill-treating the natives.

The Admiral and his brother consoled the loyal men who stood by them in their need, gave them hopes of speedy relief, and attended to the comforts of the sick. But the misconduct of the mutineers began to tell against the Admiral's adherents, for the natives did not distinguish between the two parties, and the cessation of supplies began to threaten actual starvation. Something was necessary to avert a famine, and the Admiral's readiness of resource saved his people. He hit upon a stratagem which served its purpose admirably. They had entered upon the month of February, and the Admiral knew, from the ephemeris of Regiomontanus, that there would be a total eclipse of the moon at a certain hour. Young Fernando tells us that his father sent for the principal caciques of the district, and told them, through a native who had acquired sufficient knowledge of Spanish, that he and his people were servants of the God of Heaven, who would reward the good and punish the evil. God was angry with the people of the island for failing to bring provisions according to their agreements, and he would punish them with great evils unless they fulfilled their promises. As they might not believe his words, God would show them a sign that very night, by making the moon dark before them. When the eclipse commenced the Indians were terrified, and came to the ships with great lamentations and laden with provisions, entreating the Admiral to pray to his God that His anger might be averted from them. Columbus waited until the eclipse began to wane, and then told them that they were forgiven, and that the sign of God's anger would disappear. They went away **full of** awe and wonder, and from **that time** the **supplies** came **in** with **great regularity.**

The month of March arrived, and it was eight months **since** the departure of Mendez and Fieschi. Fears began **to be** entertained that they had perished **in** the passage. Even some **of those who** had hitherto remained loyal began **to entertain** mutinous **thoughts,** which the Catalonian **apothecary named Bernal, and** two seamen, his accomplices, **named Alonzo de** Zamora and **Pedro de** Villatoro, strove to fan **into a flame.** At this juncture, **late one afternoon towards the end of April, a** caravel hove in sight. **All despondency** disappeared, **and** the people **were filled with joyful hope. But** she **hove to** outside the **port.** Then a boat was **seen** to be pulling in, and when **she came near enough a man** named **Diego** de Escobar **was** made out **in the stern sheets.** He came alongside, **handed up a letter from Ovando, and** a present of one bottle **of wine and a** piece **of bacon, and** then shoved off, **the boat's** crew laying on their oars.

Escobar was **a** main supporter of Roldan, and one of **the** most **infamous** miscreants in Española. **He had been** selected **for this mission** as **one of the** Admiral's most bitter enemies. His orders from Ovando were merely to leave the letter and receive an answer, but to allow **no** further communication, and to take no one back with **him.** In his letter Ovando condoled with the Admiral **on his** sufferings, and regretted that no vessels could be spared to convey him and his people to San Domingo. Escobar was evidently sent as **a** spy, in the hope that he would find the Admiral dead **or** in extreme distress, and to report on the condition of affairs. **The** Admiral at least got the news that his faithful friends arrived safely at Española, so he knew for certain that sooner or later they would arrange for his relief. Columbus wrote a dignified answer to Ovando, calling upon him for assistance, and Escobar's caravel departed again that very night.

The disappointment was very bitter, but the Admiral consoled his people with the reflection that they were now certain of the safety of Mendez, and that succour was only delayed. He also sent a message to the mutineers with the same assurances, and an appeal to them to return to their duty. But Porras prevented his followers from seeing the missive, sent back an insolent reply, and commenced a march on Maima, with the intention of attacking the ships, and making the Admiral and his brother prisoners. The Admiral was too ill to move. He intrusted another mission to his brother, who, if it failed, was to reduce the mutineers to obedience by force. Bartolomé Columbus was a man rather of action than of words, and he was justly indignant against Porras. He collected and armed all the men who were not disabled from sickness, and advanced beyond Maima until he confronted the mutineers. Much against his will, but in obedience to his brother's instructions, he sent messengers to propose terms. Porras saw that his numbers were superior to those of the Adelantado, and he reckoned upon an easy victory. He and six others swore to keep together and make straight for the Admiral's faithful brother. They feared him more than all the rest put together, and his death would secure their victory. Giving no answer to the messengers, Porras and his friends made a desperate rush upon the Adelantado. But he was a match for the whole of them.

The doughty Genoese, with feet firmly planted, dealt

blows right and left. Sanchez the pilot fell dead at his feet. Next fell Barba the gunner. Pedro de Ledesma dropped under the third blow, desperately wounded. Porras himself aimed a furious stroke at the Adelantado, which was caught in his shield, and went so deep into the leather that the mutineer could not free it. Bartolomé quickly closed on his antagonist, threw him to the ground, and with some help bound him hand and foot. The other malcontents, seeing the fate of their leaders, fled in all directions. Porras was brought on board a prisoner. He ought to have been hanged, but the Admiral's humanity intervened. Ever loth to proceed to extremities, he granted this ungrateful miscreant his life. The defeat of the mutineers took place on the 18th of May, and on the 20th they sent an abject letter to the Admiral, praying for forgiveness, and expressing repentance for their rebellion. With his invariable kindness the Admiral sent them his pardon, the brothers Porras alone remaining in custody.

Nothing remained but to wait for the succour which Mendez and Fieschi were sure to send. During this period of suspense, one of the Admiral's oldest and most faithful friends succumbed to the hardships of this severe service. Pedro de Terreros, who had been captain of the *Galleya*, died on the 29th of May 1504. He had been steward during the first voyage, and witnessed the memorable landing at Guanahani; and he had served with his beloved commander in every subsequent expedition. While one faithful old friend passed away, another was hurrying to the rescue. Towards the end of June 1504 two caravels at length hove in sight. Diego Mendez, after overcoming the numerous obstacles and delays caused by Ovando, succeeded in freighting a small vessel,

the command of which he gave to the true and loyal
Diego Salcedo. Servant of the Admiral during the first
voyage, it was Salcedo who told the sailor of Lepe that
Columbus was the first to see the light. Ever faithful
to his beloved master, he had been employed for some
time at San Domingo, as one of the Admiral's agents to
recover the property robbed by Bobadilla. The shameful conduct of Ovando at length aroused the indignation
of the colonists, and he was even attacked from the
pulpit for leaving the great Admiral, the discoverer of the
New World,* and his people to their fate. To save
appearances, he sent a caravel to accompany the vessel
commanded by Salcedo.

At length the long-suffering explorers were rescued.
Many had never expected to leave the island. In nearly
all the lamp of hope had sunk very low, and their joy
was proportionately great. They all embarked in the
two caravels on the 28th of June 1504. It took them
three weeks to beat up to San Domingo against the trade-
wind, and during that time Salcedo gave the Admiral full
particulars of the government of Española by Ovando.
He heard with grief and indignation of the murder of the
good and gracious Anacaona, of the cruel burning of the
caciques, of the massacre of the people, and the depopu-
lation of the island. On reaching San Domingo, the
colonists crowded to the beach to greet the illustrious discoverer, saved from so many perils and dangers almost by
a miracle. The force of public opinion obliged Ovando to
receive him with outward courtesy and hospitality, but
the real feeling of the man was shown by the infliction
of many petty annoyances on his noble-minded guest.

* This appropriate name was first used by the Admiral himself in
1500.

San Domingo was now a melancholy place for the
Admiral and his brother, and they hurried the preparations for their departure. Most of their people were
sadly in want of clothes and money, and the majority
elected to remain in the colony. They had received no
pay from the government, but their generous leader
distributed money among them from his own slender
stock. On the 12th of September, after a residence of a
month at San Domingo, the Admiral sailed for Spain.
with his brother and young son Fernando. On the 19th
they encountered a fearful storm, the mainmast went by
the board, and the little vessel was left at the mercy of
the waves. The Admiral, although suffering tortures
from the gout, showed his accustomed seamanlike qualities
in rigging a jurymast and getting the vessel under control again. Soon afterwards the mizenmast was carried
away, and there was bad weather for many days. After
fifty-six days the coast of Spain was at length sighted,
and on the 7th of November 1504 the Admiral crossed
the bar of the Guadalquivir and anchored at San Lucar.

Thus ended the naval career of the greatest navigator
in history. His mind was still full of schemes for the
settlement of Veragua, and the extension of further discovery, but the worn-out body could bear the strain no
longer. He had come home to die. If a few more years
of work had been permitted, the whole magnificence of
his discovery would have been revealed to him. The
errors of astronomers and mathematicians respecting the
length of a degree were still the data on which he based
his speculations. He had no others, and the dark veil
they drew before his eyes could only have been removed
by actual discovery. The revelation of a great South
Sea would probably have torn it away. The absence of

a strait must even then have revealed to him the insularity
of Cuba and the true course of the Gulf Stream. But
the glass was run out. He knew that he was the
chosen Christopher destined to bear Christ across the
ocean. He knew that he was the discoverer of a New
World, as he had called it in one of his letters, and
that his idea of sailing westward had borne such fruit
that all civilised Europe resounded with it. He knew
that he had done his duty faithfully and loyally as a
Christian man, and with such knowledge he was prepared to die. But while he had breath he was bound to
claim his rights and privileges, not for himself, but for
his dearly loved son who would inherit them. His
duty was done, and done in a way that no other man
could have done it. His brief span of remaining life
must be devoted to his love. Full of such thoughts the
old hero, old before his time, was carried out of the
tempest-tossed vessel and conveyed up the river to Seville.

After the Admiral's return from his last voyage, his
old follower, Vicente Yanez Pinzon, agreed with another
pilot, named Juan Diaz de Solis, to take up the thread
of their great master's discoveries at the island off the
coast of Honduras, which he had named, " Isla de los
Piños," and to follow up the clue in an opposite direction.[1] According to Oviedo, they took the young
mutineer, Pedro de Ledesma, with them, and they set
out in the autumn of 1506,* or possibly in a subsequent
year, 1507 or 1510. Sailing late in the autumn, they
reached the Gulf of Honduras at about Christmas, and
Pinzon therefore gave it the name of Navidad. They
returned after having explored a great part of the coast

It appears from documents in the collection of Navarrete that
Pinzon was in Spain during 1505 and until August 23, 1506.

of Yucatan, and, according to **Peter Martyr,*** Pinzon afterwards claimed that he established the insularity **of Cuba.** He may have **conjectured** that Cuba was an **island, but the credit of the actual** discovery of that geographical **fact is due to the voyage** of Sebastian de Ocampo **in 1508.**

NOTE.

(1) *Date of the Yucatan voyage of Pinzon and Solis.*

With the object of detracting from the credit of Columbus, Oviedo tried to make out that "the pilots Vicente Yanez Pinzon, Juan Diaz de Solis, and Pedro de Ledesma, with three caravels," discovered the Honduras coast before Pinzon was off the mouth of the Amazons. The alleged voyage would, therefore, have been made in 1498. His mention of Ledesma enables us to detect the misrepresentation. This young native of Seville was an inexperienced ordinary seaman in his twenty-seventh year, when he sailed in the last expedition of Columbus in 1503. He was entered as a seaman on board the *Vizcaina* by her captain, Bartolomè Fieschi. If he had sailed with Pinzon six years before, he would have been a lad in his twenty-first year. It is not to be believed that he was then in a position to have his name coupled with those of Pinzon and Solis as a pilot in command of a caravel, while six years later he was only an ordinary seaman. But in 1506 or 1507, when Ledesma was thirty, Pinzon would be likely enough to take a man who had previously served with the Admiral on the coast for which he was bound, as a pilot. Thus this mention of Ledesma defeats the object of Oviedo to mislead, and brings us to the truth. Gomara, as was his wont when there was a chance of injuring Columbus, adopted this mis-statement of Oviedo. He, however, only ventured upon an insinuation. "But some say that Pinzon and Solis had been there three years before." This is certainly false, for "three years before" Pinzon was engaged on a voyage in quite a different direction.

* Dec. II. lib. vii.

These statements may be set aside as attempts to deprive Columbus of his right of priority in discovering the Honduras coast, which are shown to be false from internal evidence. They are more completely disproved by a historian whose perfect fairness and means of obtaining accurate information cannot be doubted. Las Casas was a contemporary, and had an intimate knowledge of these events, and an acquaintance with the actors in them. He alone gives any details of the voyage of Pinzon and Solis to Honduras, and says that it was undertaken after the return of the Admiral from his last voyage, and with the object of following up his discoveries (Lib. ii. cap. xxxix.). He denounces the conduct of men like Oviedo and Gomara, who unjustly attempted to detract from the work of the Admiral, "as if Columbus had not been the first to open the gates of the ocean, which had been closed for so many thousands of ages, and as if it was not he who showed the light by which all might see how to discover, . . . and who put the thread into the hands of the rest, by which they found the clue to more distant parts."

Herrera copied his account of this voyage of Pinzon and Solis word for word from Las Casas, adding that it took place in 1506. If so they must have sailed late in the autumn of 1506, for Pinzon was certainly in Spain in August of that year. This is very likely, as, from his having given the name of Navidad to the Gulf of Honduras, he does not seem to have reached the coast until Christmas. However that may be, it is certain, from the unimpeachable evidence of Las Casas, that this voyage of Pinzon and Solis was undertaken after, and not before, the last voyage of Columbus. The evidence of Rodrigo Bastidas in the trial is equally conclusive. He bore testimony that the coast discovered by Pinzon and Solis was all one with the coast which the Admiral discovered *first*. Bastidas was a trustworthy honest man, as Las Casas tells us, and was personally acquainted with all the facts.

CHAPTER XV

DEATH OF THE ADMIRAL.

THE Admiral arrived at Seville in November 1504, and was very anxious to proceed to court and report himself to the sovereigns. A litter was even got ready for him by order of the municipality, but he proved to be much too ill to be moved for many months. At Seville he was attended by both his brothers, and was surrounded by many warm friends, chief among them being Fray Gaspar Gorricio, and the Fathers of Las Cuevas. The vast Carthusian monastery of Santa Maria de las Cuevas stood on the right bank of the Guadalquivir, near the north end of the suburb of Triana. Rich in architecture, in its library and pictures, it was further enriched in after years by the labours of Zurbaran. But its greatest ornaments were its delicious groves of orange and lemon trees along the banks of the river; and here no doubt the illustrious invalid passed much of his time in conversations with Gorricio, the Cura of Los Palacios, and other friends.

The faithful Diego Mendez had preceded the Admiral to Spain, had presented his letter from Jamaica to the sovereigns, and was still at court with young Diego. The Admiral wrote to his son on November 21st expressing a wish that he should remain at court and superintend his affairs; and in another letter, dated the 28th, he wrote of his delight at the promised payment of his poor people

who served in the last voyage, and who had passed
through such fearful dangers and hardships.   His chief
hope of support at court was from Dr. Deza, now Bishop
of Palencia, his old and staunch friend ; and he also
anticipated help from the exertions of his agent Carbajal,
of Diego Mendez, and of his son.   Writing again on the
1st of December, the Admiral expressed great anxiety
for the health of the Queen.   He was sending his brother
the Adelantado and his son Fernando to court, to kiss
hands on their return.   " Make much of your brother,"
he wrote to Diego ; " he has a good disposition, and is now
leaving his boyhood.   Ten such brothers would not be
too many.   Never have I found better friends, on my
right hand and on my left, than my brothers."

Alas ! the good Queen had breathed her last in Medina
del Campo six days before the date of the Admiral's letter.
Her constitution had been undermined by the strain of
hard and constant physical and mental work exacted by
her position as reigning Queen of Castille.   Before her
death, she was horrified at the news of the atrocities per-
petrated by Ovando, of the burning of caciques, the
murder of Anacaona, and the massacres of the people in
Xaragua and Higuey.   One of her last requests to
Ferdinand was that Ovando might be recalled, and that
order might be taken for the better treatment of the
natives.   Ferdinand did not comply with it.   Ovando
suited him.   He sent plenty of gold.   When Ovando
had nearly exterminated the natives of Españolæ, Ferdinand authorised him to fill their places by kidnapping
the unfortunate inhabitants of the Bahamas.   Isabella
died at noon of the 26th of November 1504.   Her loss
was deeply felt by the Admiral, for she had upheld him
in his adversity, had adopted his great scheme, and had

ever been a warm and consistent friend. She had no
more sincere mourner than the illustrious Genoese, whose
grief was deep and genuine.

The Adelantado, with young Fernando and the
Admiral's agent Carbajal, left Seville on the 5th of
December, to kiss the King's hand and give an account
of the voyage. Columbus himself was still unable to
move; but he wrote frequently to Diego, and in one
letter, dated January 18, 1505, he sent a playful message to his old friend the Bishop of Palencia. "I must
lodge with him whether he likes it or not, for we have
to go back to our first brotherly love, and he will not be
able to deny me." Diego Mendez had been at Seville,
and started again for the court on the 3rd of February.
The Admiral was happy in still having true and faithful
friends in all ranks of life. He deserved to have them.
Amerigo Vespucci, who came to him at this time,
enjoyed his good will. "He always," writes the Admiral, "showed a desire to please me; he is a very respectable man, but fortune has been adverse to him, as it has
been to many others, and his labours have not been so
profitable to him as he might reasonably have expected.
He expresses himself very desirous to serve me, and to
do all he possibly can for me." The Admiral sent this
letter to his son, dated February 5, 1504, by Vespucci,
and desired Diego to do what he could to help him and
further his wishes at court.

The Admiral had obtained license to ride a mule, and
as the tortures of the gout, aggravated by the cold and
damp of a very severe winter, were less unbearable when
warm weather set in, the journey was commenced in the
middle of May 1505. Ferdinand was at Segovia, and
thither the Admiral journeyed by short stages, accom-

panied and fondly cared for by his brother Bartolomé.
The King received him with feigned delight, and listened
to his account of the events of his last voyage, probably
with real interest. But nothing came of the interview, and after a time the Admiral submitted a memorial
for the restitution of his rights. The King's reply was
that a matter of so much gravity and importance should
first be considered by some councillor of experience and
probity. Columbus concurred, and suggested that no one
could be better fitted for such a task than Dr. Deza, who
had just been translated from Palencia to be Archbishop
of Seville. That true friend said that he was willing to
arbitrate respecting the amounts due to the Admiral,
but not on the question of his rights, for concerning
them there could not be any doubt.

The Admiral remained with the court at Segovia from
May to the end of October, and he then followed it to
Salamanca, waiting for a definite reply to his memorial.
Here the severe cold of the early winter brought on fresh
attacks of illness, and he determined to go to Valladolid,
leaving the care of his business in the hands of his two
sons, under the friendly protection of Cardinal Ximenes
de Cisneros. The court was shortly expected at Valladolid also, and in anticipation of the King's arrival the
Admiral addressed a letter to him, praying that his son
Diego might be allowed to take his place, as the recipient
of royal justice. He asked for no favour, only for bare
justice. He also pleaded for the unhappy natives of
Española. "They were, and are," he wrote, "the wealth
of that country. It is they who dig and produce bread
and other food for the Christians. It is they who extract
gold from the mines, and perform all other services not
only of men but also of beasts of burden."

T

Soon afterwards the court arrived at Valladolid, but Ferdinand went on to Laredo, to meet his daughter Juana, the new Queen of Castille, who was expected with her husband, the handsome young Philip I. of Austria. Leaving the port of Weymouth, after a visit to Henry VII. at Windsor, they arrived, not at Laredo but at Coruña, on the 28th of April 1506. The news revived all the hopes of the Admiral, and he received it with delight. He trusted in the justice of Isabella's daughter and her gallant young husband. His illness kept him confined to his bed in a hired lodging at Valladolid, but he sent his brother the Adelantado to present himself to the new sovereigns in the name of the Admiral, and to deliver to them a letter of congratulation. Las Casas considered it as certain that if the Admiral and Philip had both lived, full justice would have been done at last.

Bartolomè bade farewell to his brother, whom he was never destined to see again. There remained with the Admiral his two sons, the ever faithful companions of his last voyage, Mendez and Fieschi, and several servants and mariners, humble but loyal friends, who had continued true to their old commander, and remained by him to the end. That end was now near at hand. The Admiral had written a codicil to his will at Segovia on the 25th of August 1505. Feeling that he had but a short time to live, he sent for the notary and several witnesses, who assembled in his room on the 19th of May 1506. He was unable to move, but his mind was as clear as ever when he formally ratified his last will and the Segovia codicil.[1] He then became tranquil, and he was quite at rest with regard to his temporal affairs. His mind indeed was buoyant and full of hope from the result of his brother's mission. He devoted his last day

on earth to thoughts of eternity. At his own request
he was attired in a Franciscan habit, an order to which
he had been warmly attached since he formed the old
friendships at the convent of La Rabida. A Franciscan
named Gaspar acted as his confessor, and administered
to him the sacraments of the Church. Surrounded by his

HOUSE AT VALLADOLID IN WHICH COLUMBUS DIED.

weeping sons, and by many faithful and attached friends,
the great man expired peacefully on the eve of Ascension
Day, the 20th of May 1506. His last words were, " In
manas tuas Domine commendo spiritum meum."

   The brightest light of that age was put out. The
beacon round which had centred its great aspirations, its

enterprise and its science, was dimmed for a time, but only to burn still brighter in the ages to come, as a glorious example for all future generations. Four centuries, far from having dimmed the memory of the great discoverer's achievement, have impressed it more deeply on the minds of men.

After the funeral ceremonies at Valladolid, the Admiral's body, in accordance with his own wish, was translated to Seville, and deposited in the convent of Santa Maria de las Cuevas, where he had found such true friends, and which he had loved so well. We may assume that the coffin was attended by the Admiral's brothers and sons, in the long journey from Valladolid. The remains of Columbus remained in the chapel called Santa Ana, in the Carthusian convent at Seville, from 1506 to 1544. In the latter year the widow of Diego took the bodies of the Admiral and his eldest son in her own ship to San Domingo, and, by permission of Charles V., interred them in the chancel of the cathedral church in that city. There they remained in peace for 250 years. But when Española was ceded to France by the treaty of Basle, in 1795, the Spanish Admiral, Don Gabriel de Aristizabal, resolved that the venerated ashes should not remain in a foreign land. They were disinterred, put on board the Spanish line-of-battle ship *San Lorenzo*, and conveyed to Havana, arriving in the harbour on January 25, 1796. The precious remains were placed in a niche on the right hand side of the high altar of Havana cathedral.[1]

No monument was erected in the chapel at Las Cuevas, consequently King Ferdinand never caused the lines to be engraved on it—

> " A Castilla y a Leon
> Nuevo Mundo dió Colon."

It was indeed a most unlikely thing for that unsym-
pathetic matter-of-fact personage to do. The lines were
used as a motto encircling the arms of the Admiral's
heirs, and may be seen on the tombstone of his son Fernando, in Seville Cathedral.

There is only one authentic portrait of Columbus.
It was painted when the great discoverer was advanced
in years, and was in the villa at Como of the Italian
historian Paulus Jovius, who made a collection of portraits
of the worthies of his time. This picture is still at Como,
the property of the Nobile Alessandro de Orchi, whose
grandmother was a Giovio; and it has never left the
family. It is the head of a venerable man with thin
grey hair; the forehead high, the eyes pensive and
rather melancholy. The face is oblong, without beard
of any kind, and there is a small swelling on the left
side of the nose, which is one indication of the picture
having been painted from life. Over the head are the
words "Colombus Lygur, novi orbis reptor." Only
half the bust is shown, the dress being a gown laced
at the throat. In an edition of a book called "Elogia
Virorum Illustrium," published in 1575, there are
woodcuts of the portraits in the villa of Jovius, including
one of Columbus, but it is quite different from the
original. The engraving in the "Elogia" is half-length,
representing an elderly man with hair inclined to curl,
and a thoughtful, melancholy, but rather pleasing expression. The dress is a cape and hood fallen back, of some
religious order, one hand drawing in the folds of the
cape, and resting on the other. A copy was made of
the picture of Jovius in about 1550, which is now in the
Uffizi gallery at Florence; but the artist, though copying the features exactly, made a much younger man,

with dark hair. The picture in the National Library at
Madrid is a copy of the Florence picture. The engraving
published by De Bry in 1595 claimed to be from a portrait painted by order of Ferdinand, stolen from the hall
of the council of the Indies and brought to the Nether-

ENGRAVING OF COLUMBUS IN DE BRY.

lands. It has no resemblance to those taken from the
portrait of Jovius. The De Bry engraving represents a
round face with masses of curls on each side, large eyes
without expression, and a blunt nose: all these features
being entirely different from the descriptions of Las

Casas and Oviedo. The picture attributed to Parmigiano at Naples is generally considered to be merely fanciful. A portrait which is said to have belonged to the Cuccero family, was purchased by the Comte Rosselly de Lorgnes, and is attributed by him to Antonio del Rincon, the artist who painted Ferdinand and Isabella, and who lived between 1445 and 1500. But the authenticity of its history is more than doubtful. It is engraved in the Count's life of Columbus. Another portrait has recently been brought to light at Venice by the archæologist Antonio della Rovere, which is said to have been painted by Lorenzo Lotto, possibly by order of Angelo Trivijiano, for transmission to Malipieri in 1500, with the letters and charts of the Admiral.

The portrait at Como alone has any claim to be a likeness, so that the only authentic materials for picturing the appearance of Columbus in our minds are the Como picture and the detailed descriptions of his features recorded by Las Casas and Oviedo.

The character of Columbus was deeply tinged with religious enthusiasm and strong devotional feeling from his earliest youth; and when, probably at a much earlier age than is generally supposed, he became possessed by his one grand idea, his religious feelings became entwined in every worldly thought, and he was impressed with the belief that he was a humble but specially selected instrument for the fulfilment of an Almighty design foretold in prophecy. He strove to keep these thoughts in his memory by day and night, and to bear them in mind, so that they might influence the transactions of each day. The Admiral's invariable signature is an indication of the way religious thoughts pervaded his life. It was an invocation to Jesus, Maria, and Joseph above the words "bearing Christ," and it is seen at the end of every document under his hand.

He left instructions for the way it was to be written: first X, and S above it for *Christus*, M with A above it—*Maria;* and S above that—*Salve !* then Y with S above it—*Yosephus;* below χ℈º FERENS, for *Christopher.*

Columbus had a very active and imaginative brain, the bright thoughts following each other in rapid succession, and his enthusiastic and impressionable nature produced visions and day-dreams which often impressed him with all the force of reality. Like Joan of Arc, and other gifted beings who have been the instruments to work out great events, Columbus heard voices, which had the practical effect of rousing him from despondency and bracing him to his work. He has recorded two occasions on which this happened, but probably "the voices" made themselves heard at other critical turning-points of his life. Yet there was no danger of his becoming a mere visionary. His clear penetrating intellect saved him from that; and it was this unrivalled power, combined with a brilliant imagination, which constituted his genius. He prepared himself for his great work by long study, by the acquisition of vast experience, and by a minute knowledge of every detail of his profession. But this would not have sufficed. He added to these qualifications a master mind endowed with reasoning powers of a high order; and an ingenious, almost subtle, way of seizing upon and utilising every point which had a relation to the subject he was considering. His forecasts amount to prevision. Assuredly the discovery of the New World was no accident. "His genius and lofty enthusiasm, his ardent and justified previsions, mark the great Admiral as one of the lights of the human race."*

Apart from his genius, Columbus was a very simple-minded man, full of love for his fellow-creatures and a desire for their welfare. He was absolutely devoid of any vindictive feeling, although few men ever received greater provocation. Fonseca, Roldan, Bobadilla, Porras, were to him merely obstacles injurious to the public service, nuisances to be removed if possible. But he bore them no ill-will: partly from the natural magnanimity of his disposition, partly from the influence of religion on his thoughts and actions. He was naturally hasty and quick-tempered, but he succeeded almost completely in restraining this tendency by watchfulness and self-restraint.

His powerful intellect and habitual attention to details fitted him for the work of administration, although he was easily imposed upon by plausible villains like Roldan: and some of his greatest difficulties were the consequences of this trustfulness and simplicity. Yet, if he had been firmly supported from home, the government of Española by the Admiral and his supremely able brother would have been a success. The feeling of the age, which in the time of Columbus was absolutely universal, was that infidel prisoners of war might be treated and sold as slaves. Prince Henry and the Portuguese went much further, and systematically seized upon any natives they could secure. In acting in the spirit of the age, and

* Colonel Yule, "Marco Polo," Introd. i. 102.

advising the sale of Caribs and prisoners of war, Columbus
hoped that the slaves themselves might receive benefit
from conversion to Christianity, while the administrative
necessities of the colony were cared for. He had seen
how Ferdinand and Isabella acted when the people of
Malaga were sold into slavery, with the full sanction of
the Church. He had never heard any doubt expressed
on the subject, and on this point he was not three cen
turies in advance of his contemporaries. Las Casas,
with no responsibility and no administrative anxieties,
advocated views which were three centuries in advance
of his age. He was in advance of Wilberforce and
Clarkson. But he was not a contemporary of Columbus,
being thirty years his junior. He had not yet raised
his voice when the great discoverer died, and much that
he urged would have found a warm response in the heart
of the Admiral.

After the revolt of Roldan, Columbus had allowed a
repartimiento of Indians with great reluctance, and under
extreme pressure, but he imposed various restrictions,
with a view to the prevention of ill-treatment. Apart
from these administrative necessities which were forced
upon him by the exigencies of his position, the relations
of Columbus with the natives were friendly and cordial.
The men taken as interpreters were kindly treated, and
we hear of one at least who had a prosperous career in
after life. The Admiral never allowed the people to be
ill-used when he could prevent it. Guacanagari was his
devoted friend ; and the last letter of Columbus to Ferdinand contained an earnest appeal in favour of the
natives. In order to show how far Columbus and his
brother were in advance of their contemporaries as regards the treatment of the Indians, it is only necessary

to compare their conduct on all occasions with that of
Ovando; who is a fair average specimen of the colonial
governor of the day.

It was, however, as a navigator that the genius of
Columbus found the most suitable field for its display.
He was a consummate seaman, and without any equal
in that age as a pilot and navigator; while his sense of
duty and responsibility gave rise to a watchfulness which
was unceasing and untiring. His knowledge of cosmography, of all needful calculations, and of the manipulation
of every known instrument was profound; but he showed
even greater power in his forecasts of weather, in his
reasoning on the effects of winds and currents, and in
the marvellous accuracy of his landfalls, even when
approaching an unknown coast. He had that capacity
for taking trouble without which even genius is but a
doubtful blessing. It was in the preparation of charts
and journals, in the diligence with which he recorded all
useful observations day by day, that Columbus set such
a valuable example. His genius was a gift which is only
produced once in an age. But his reasoning power carefully trained and cultivated, his diligence as a student,
his habits of observation, and the regularity of his work,
especially in writing up a journal and taking observations,
are qualities which every seaman might usefully study
and imitate. He has been accused of carelessness and
inaccuracy in his statements: but every instance that
has been put forward can be shown to be consistent with
accuracy. The blunders were not those of the Admiral,
but of his critics. Considering the circumstances under
which many of his letters were written, his careful
accuracy of statement is remarkable. It is another proof
of a mind long trained to orderly and methodical habits.[3]

The Admiral was a man of dignified bearing, fascinating in conversation, and endowed with great eloquence and power of exposition. He was amiable and of a most affectionate disposition, and made many and lasting friendships in all ranks of life. Among his warmest friends were Queen Isabella, Archbishop Deza, the great Cardinal Cisneros, the Cura of Los Palacios, and the Fathers of La Rabida and Las Cuevas. We find his shipmates serving under him over and over again. Terreros his steward, Salcedo his servant, were with him in his first voyage and in his last. Diego Mendez and Bartolomé Fieschi were ready to risk life and limb in his service, and attended on him to the end. Several faithful sailors never left him until the last scene at Valladolid. He was blessed with two loving and devoted brothers, and Bartolomé was his trusty defender and counsellor in his darkest hours of difficulty and distress, his nurse in sickness, and his helpful companion in health. The enduring affection of these two brothers, from the cradle to the grave, is most touching. Columbus was happy too in his sons, who were ever dutiful, and whose welfare and happiness were his fondest care. He never forgot his old home and the companions of his childhood; as is shown by his bequest to the Bank of St. George, and by the provision for poor relations in his will. The last words he ever wrote were, "In the city of Genoa I was born." We reverence and admire his genius, we applaud his large-hearted magnanimity, we urge the study of his life on all seamen as a useful example, but his friendships and the warmth of his affections are the qualities which appeal most to our regard. Columbus was a man to reverence, but he was still more a man to love.

The work of few men in the world's history has had

such a lasting influence on the welfare of the human race as that of Columbus. It created a complete revolution in the thoughts and ideas of the age. It was a landmark and a beacon. It divided the old and the new order of things, and it threw a bright light over the future. In ten years he discovered the way across the Atlantic, he explored the Gulf stream and the regions of the trades, of the westerlies, and the calms; he discovered the Bahamas and the West Indies; he inspired the work of Cabot and Cortereal; and he or his pupils discovered the coasts of the new continent from S S. of the equator to the Gulf of Honduras. But the greatest achievement was the first voyage across the ocean. It broke the spell and opened a new era. All else he did, and all that was done after his death for the next fifty years, followed as a natural consequence. The originator and supreme leader of all, was Christopher Columbus.

NOTES.

(1) *The Will of Columbus.*

Columbus was authorised to establish an entail or *mayorazgo* by letters patent dated April 23, 1497. On January 22, 1498, he accordingly executed a deed of entail in favour of his son Diego, which was confirmed by the sovereigns on September 28, 1501. In 1502, before sailing on his last voyage, he executed a new entail of his goods, which he deposited in the monastery of Las Cuevas. This document is lost. On August 25, 1505, the Admiral wrote a codicil at Segovia, and two days before his death, on May 19, 1506, he ratified it before witnesses. Another codicil was executed at Valladolid.

In the Segovia codicil he appointed his sons to be executors, and confirmed the entailing deeds, settling his rights, privileges, and estates on Diego and his heirs male, then on Fernando and his heirs male, then on his brothers in succession, and failing all these, on his nearest relation. If his rents are ever recovered in the Indies, his son Fernando to receive one cuento and a half annually, his brother Bartolomè 150.000 maravedis, his other brother 100,000 maravedis. His eldest son Diego to inherit all his offices and estates, one tenth part to be given to poor relations who appear to be most in need, and in works of charity. Of the other nine parts, two to be set apart and divided into thirty-five parts, of which twenty-seven parts to belong to Fernando, five to Bartolomè, and three to Diego the brother. His eldest son to maintain a chapel with three priests, to say masses for the souls of the Admiral, his father, mother, and wife: the chapel, if possible, to be at Concepcion, in the Vega Real of Española. Diego to pay the debts contained in an accompanying list, and any others that appear to be honestly due; and Beatriz Enriquez is commended to the care of his son. The creditors in the list are Genoese and a Jew living at Lisbon.

The other codicil, concerning the authenticity of which there has been a doubt, is believed to be authentic by Mr Harrisse. In it Diego and the heirs of the entail are desired always to maintain a person of the Admiral's family at Genoa, who has a house and a wife, so that he may live honourably, "that our lineage may have a root in that city, for from it I came, and in it I was born."

(2) *Question of the removal of the Admiral's body.*

In the year 1877, during the work of repairing the pavement of the chancel of the cathedral of San Domingo, two lead coffins were discovered, containing the remains of Luis and Cristoval Colon y Toledo, grandsons of the Admiral. A story was spread abroad that when the Spaniards removed the ashes to Havana in 1795, they had mistaken the coffin, and that the real coffin of the Admiral was still at San Domingo. The clergy of the cathedral made an attempt to establish their case, by concealing the leaden inscription on the coffin of Don Luis, because that of Cristoval was exactly like it as regards the lettering, which was German-Gothic. The Admiral was interred on the gospel side of the altar. The coffins of his grandsons are on the epistle side.

(3) *Note on the alleged inaccuracies of Columbus.*

There are three passages in the writings of Columbus on which the charge of habitual carelessness and inaccuracy is

based. One occurs in a letter written in a vessel of 20 tons in a
furious gale of wind in the Atlantic; the other in a letter written
from a bed of sickness in the midst of the Jamaica hardships;
and the third when he was dying. This is a small basis on which
to found a general charge; yet it can be shown to be without
anything to sustain it, in all three instances.

The first is that he dated his letter "*Canaria* 15*th Febrero*
1493," when he was off the Azores. The quotation is from a
careless copy of the letter at Simancas. "*Stamaria*" was read
by the copying-clerk as "*Canaria*," and 15 for 18. The correct
version, found by Varnhagen, is "*Santa Maria* 18 *Febrero* 1493."
Columbus was quite accurate.

The second is that, in the letter from Jamaica (*Nav*. i. 311), he
said, "Yo viné a servir de veinte y ocho años." Rossi, Navarrete,
and even Major think this is a mistake. All assume that he
intended to say, "I came to serve your Highnesses (of Spain) at
the age of twenty-eight," when he was really at least thirty-
eight or forty when he came to Spain. But he did not say so,
and he did not mean it. He said, "I came to serve at twenty-
eight years," that is, "I left my home and came to serve (in this
business of discovering the Indies) at twenty-eight." He is
not alluding to Spain especially. That is exactly what he did
do. He left his home at the age of twenty-eight, and from that
time until he was wrecked at Jamaica, he was constantly
serving. He is perfectly accurate.

The third is that in a letter to King Ferdinand (*Nav*. ii. 527)
without date, but written a few months before he died, he said
that in fourteen years he could not get the King of Portugal to
understand what he said. The critics point this out as a gross
blunder, for Columbus was only about ten years in Portugal,
and not fourteen. He came to Portugal in 1474, and left in 1484;
but he was at Lisbon again in 1488, when he no doubt once
more tried to make the King of Portugal understand. From
1474 to 1488 is exactly fourteen years. Again he is perfectly
accurate.

The logical conclusion is that true criticism should assume so
able a man as Columbus to be correct, when an apparent difficulty occurs in his writings, and that the blunder is on the side
of the fault-finders.

CHAPTER XVI

THE ADMIRAL'S SONS.

I.— DIEGO AND HIS DESCENDANTS.

THE two sons of Columbus lived to see the completion of their father's work by the circumnavigation of the globe. The *Victoria* arrived at San Lucar on the 6th of September 1522. Diego succeeded to the Admiral's titles and recovered some of his rights. Fernando devoted his life to the study of his father's professional work, and to the preservation of memorials of his deeds. Both were tall, handsome young men: Diego being twenty-eight and Fernando eighteen years of age at the time of their father's death. Diego succeeded at once to the title of Admiral of the Ocean Sea. In their uncle Bartolomé they had a wise and experienced counsellor. He had already made a favourable impression on the new sovereigns, and Philip I. issued an order that what was due to the deceased Admiral should be paid to his heir. But Philip died very suddenly in September 1506, after a reign, in his wife's name, of little more than four months. He was the same age as Diego, the recognition of whose rights would again be dependent on the will of the faithless old king. Ferdinand was absent at Naples until the following year.

Very soon after the young king's death Bartolomé Columbus undertook a journey to Rome, in the hope of

inducing the Pope, Julius II., to recommend the pro-
priety of another colonising expedition. His efforts
were fruitless. He appears, however, to have written
an account of Veragua for one of the canons of the
Lateran, a résumé of which is preserved in the Maglia-
bechiana Library.* Bartolomé had returned to Spain
in 1508.

The young Admiral continued to urge the restitution
of the rights inherited from his father, with importunate
vigour. He had the advantages of an intimate acquaintance with the court, of youth, health, and popularity.
Once Ferdinand said to him, "Look here, Admiral! I
would confer it on you, but not if I am only to grant it
for your sons and successors." "Sir," replied Diego,
"is it reasonable that I should be punished for the sins
of heirs who perhaps will never exist?" But the old
fox continued to delay and evade a direct answer, until
at length Diego asked for permission to bring a suit
and obtain a decision from a court of justice. The King
was induced to give his consent to such a trial, and
it was a fortunate thing for posterity that this legal
process was sanctioned and recorded. Many most interesting details appeared in the evidence that are not
found elsewhere, including incidents in the Admiral's
career and in those of his companions. It was as a
witness in this trial that the good physician of Palos
related the touching story of the arrival of Columbus at
the convent gate of La Rabida with his little son. Las
Casas expresses indignation at the attempts of the judge
to diminish the glory of the great Admiral's services;
but the testimony that was collected rather tended to

* Published by Mr. Harrisse in his *Bibliotheca Americana Vetustissima*, p. 471.

U

make the light of his fame to shine more brightly. The judgment was in favour of the Admiral and his heirs.

Diego Columbus was a handsome and gallant young courtier, and he won the love of a lady of very high rank. Doña Maria de Toledo y Roxas was the daughter of Don Fernando de Toledo, Lord of Villora, Comendador Mayor of Leon, and Grand Huntsman of Castille. Her uncle was the second Duke of Alva. Her grandmother was Maria Enriquez, sister of King Ferdinand's mother. This near relation of the King was a young lady of spirit and energy, and devoted her life to the interests of her husband and children. She never rested until the influence of her uncle and father had extorted the long-sought act of justice from their cousin the King. There can be little doubt that the marriage, and not a sense of abstract right, explains the character of the sentence and its acceptance by Ferdinand.

On the 9th of August 1508 the young Admiral, Diego Columbus, was appointed Governor of the Indies. A fleet was equipped at San Lucar, and in the end of May 1509 he embarked with his wife Maria de Toledo and many ladies of her household, his uncles Bartolomé and Diego, and his brother Fernando. Arriving at San Domingo in July, the young Admiral assumed the government of Española, superseding the cruel Ovando, who went home, and died four days after he landed in Spain. Young Fernando also went back, as captain-general of the returning fleet, as he was desirous of completing his studies. Juan Ponce de Leon had been made governor of San Juan or Puerto Rico; Esquivel, one of the most ruthless of Ovando's bloodhounds, was sent to reduce Jamaica; and in 1511 the young Admiral sent Diego Velasquez to

RUINS OF THE PALACE BUILT BY DIEGO COLUMBUS AT SAN DOMINGO.

colonise Cuba, its insular character having been determined by Ocampo in 1508.

When Diego Columbus arrived in Española, there were four personages already residing there, one of whom was destined to record his great father's achievements, and the other three to complete them. These were Bartolomé de Las Casas, the defender of the Indians; Vasco Nuñez de Balboa, the discoverer of the South Sea: Hernan Cortes, the conqueror of Mexico; and Francisco Pizarro, the conqueror of Peru.

Diego did not find the colonists of Española much easier to govern than had his father. They had nearly exterminated the native population, the kidnapped victims from the Bahamas were rapidly following their predecessors, and the denunciations of slavery by the Dominican monks fell on deaf ears. With the approval of Ferdinand, negro slaves were beginning to replace the Indians, who were dying by thousands. In October 1511 a Court of Appeal was instituted for San Domingo, called the *Audiencia*, and the new governor met with enemies and fomenters of trouble among the lawyers, while the conduct of the treasurer, Miguel Pasamonte, was hostile and insubordinate. The young Admiral found it necessary to make voyages to Spain in 1512 and 1513, to defend his conduct, and again in 1515. King Ferdinand died on the 23rd of January 1516, and the government of Spain was conducted by Cardinal Cisneros until 1520, when Charles arrived from the Low Countries. Diego Columbus returned to Española in September 1520, and commenced the building of a stone palace of some architectural pretensions, the ruins of which may still be seen. It was destined to be the abode of his Vice-Queen Maria for many years, and here most of his children were born.

Bishop Fonseca continued to hold office, and to mis-
manage the affairs of the Indies. One of his worst
blunders was the selection of Alonzo de Ojeda and Diego
de Nicuesa to colonise the coast of the mainland discovered by Bastidas and the Admiral. The territory of
Ojeda was to extend from Cabo de la Vela to Darien,
to be called "Nueva Andalusia"; and Nicuesa was to
be governor of a province including Veragua, to which the
name of "Castilla del Oro" was given. Ojeda had already
shown himself to be unfit for separate command, but he
was a favourite of Fonseca. The appointment of Nicuesa
was a slight to the young Admiral whose father had
discovered Veragua, and a great injustice to his uncle
Bartolomè, whose claims had been passed over, although
his proved courage and ability pointed him out as the
proper man for the place.

Ojeda was nearly penniless, but he was supplied with
funds by the famous pilot Juan de la Cosa, who was to
accompany him; and by a lawyer named Martin Fernandez
de Enciso, who was to follow with reinforcements. Nicuesa
was accompanied by an officer named Rodrigo de Colmenares, as his second in command. The two expeditions
arrived at San Domingo, where it was agreed that the
river Atrato should be the boundary of their respective
jurisdictions. Ojeda sailed from San Domingo with four
vessels and 300 men, on the 12th of November 1509, and
Nicuesa started about ten days afterwards with five
vessels and 650 men.

The hot-headed and incapable Ojeda landed at Cala-
mar, near the present town of Cartagena, and immediately made an unprovoked attack upon an Indian
town, called Turbaco. He was entirely defeated by the
valiant natives; upwards of seventy Spaniards perished,

including Juan de la Cosa, and Ojeda himself only
escaped by hiding in the forest, where his people found
him after a long search, half starved, and in a miserable
condition. Meanwhile Nicuesa's squadron arrived, and
the two commanders took their revenge by a horrible
slaughter at Turbaco, men, women, and children being
indiscriminately massacred. The body of Juan de la
Cosa was found, but in a shocking state, owing to the
effect of poisoned arrows. The rival governors then
sailed for their respective territories, Ojeda arriving in
the gulf of Uraba or Darien, and founding a town on its
eastern shore, named San Sebastian. Ojeda made no
provision for obtaining food, and famine soon made its
appearance, while the condition of the settlers was aggravated by frequent attacks from the natives, armed with
poisoned arrows. He determined to return to Española
for supplies, leaving Francisco Pizarro as his lieutenant,
with instructions to return himself with the rest of the
people, if they were not relieved within fifty days. Ojeda
quarrelled with the crew of the vessel in which he took
a passage, and was put in irons. The vessel was wrecked
on the coast of Cuba, and the crew succeeded in reaching
Jamaica, whence Ojeda was sent to San Domingo by the
governor Esquivel, where he lived for some time. He
died there in extreme poverty in 1515.

Pizarro embarked the starving settlers of San Sebastian in two brigantines and sailed for Española, but he
had scarcely left the bay when he encountered Enciso
bringing reinforcements in two small vessels. Soon after
Enciso had left San Domingo, a stowaway was found
headed up in a cask, who had adopted this means of
escaping from his creditors. Enciso was furious, and
threatened to maroon him, but he was pacified after some

time. The escaped debtor was Vasco **Nuñez** de Balboa, one of **the companions** of Bastidas, **a** soldier aged about thirty-five, who afterwards proved **himself to be** a valiant **and most** capable leader of men. They all returned to San Sebastian ; **but Enciso's** ship, through bad seamanship, **was run upon** a rock and became a complete wreck, **a great part of the** provisions being lost. **The** people landed, **both the new-comers** brought by Enciso, and the **old settlers under Pizarro ; but** they found the fort at **San Sebastian destroyed, and** themselves exposed to the **hostile** attacks **of the brave** natives. They were in despair. The lawyer Enciso was incapable **and helpless.**

Vasco Nuñez de **Balboa** naturally came to the front. **He cheered up the desponding, and** provided a remedy for **their misfortune. Using the experience** he had gained **in the voyage of Bastidas, he** told **his** comrades that the **natives of** the western side **of the gulf had** no poisoned arrows, and that they **would be comp**aratively safe on that **side. They crossed the gulf of** Uraba, defeated the hostile **natives, got supplies from** their villages, and founded a settlement und**er the invocation of** the well-known image **at Seville, Nuestra Señora de** la Antigua. Enciso was deposed as incompetent, and Vasco Nuñez would have been **made governor if,** just at that time, Colmenares, **the lieutenant** of Nicuesa, had not arrived with supplies. Colmenares persuaded the settlers to accept Nicuesa as successor to Ojeda, and governor of both the provinces.

Nicuesa had, meanwhile, **shown** greater incapacity than either Ojeda or Enciso, if that were possible. He lost his ship and all his provisions by blundering on to a river bar, suffered fearfully **from** hardships caused by want **of** forethought, and when at last he collected the **remnant** of his people at Nombre de Dios, in December

1510, there were about seventy left, out of the original complement of over six hundred. Starvation led to the cutting of all the bonds of discipline, and Colmenares found his chief at last, being merely one of a little band of famine-stricken wretches. To such a condition had his incapacity reduced the well-equipped expedition which left San Domingo only a year before. In his adversity he had shown neither temper nor sympathy for his comrades, and when he reached Darien the settlers refused to receive him. He sailed away in a small brigantine, and was never heard of again.

Vasco Nuñez de Balboa became the undisputed governor of Darien. He was a handsome man, cheery and good-humoured, with great natural ability, patient, enduring, and full of resource, and endowed with all the qualities needed in a commander. He sent Enciso home, accompanied by two leading settlers, named Zamudio and Valdivia, who were to give a true account of the course of events. Enciso had given Vasco Nuñez a very low opinion of lawyers, and he entreated the King not to allow any more to come to the colony, because "they are devils and lead the lives of devils, and not only are they themselves evil, but they give rise to a thousand lawsuits and quarrels."

But Enciso, although incapable of leading men, was an author of some merit, and his work on navigation, entitled "Suma de Geografia," is one of the earliest books of the kind. Besides tables of the sun's declination, it contains curious accounts of the various countries of the world, including some notices of Darien or Uraba.

The first act of Vasco Nuñez was to fetch the starving remnant of Nicuesa's people from Nombre de Dios, and on his way he captured a cacique of the isthmus named

Careta, who became a firm ally, and whose daughter he married. The policy of this elected ruler, to whom chance had offered such grand opportunities, **was** humane and prudent. There is more of diplomacy and negotiation than of massacre and oppression, in the history of his dealings with the natives. His sympathy for the sufferings of his own men ensured him just popularity among the wild and reckless spirits who formed his colony. He cheerfully shared their hardships, and attended to the comforts of the sick; while his measures usually combined energy with prudence. His chief lieutenants were Colmenares, Pizarro, and Alonzo Martin. His alliance with Careta, the chief of Cueva, was a wise and statesmanlike measure. His treatment of the cacique of Coiba secured the little colony of Darien a most valuable ally. The visit to the wealthy chief of Comogre, from whose son the first news of the existence of the great South Sea was received, added another nation to the list of the allies of Vasco Nuñez. His romantic expedition to Dabayba was unstained by the atrocities which usually marked the proceedings of Spanish explorers. These achievements quite established his position as a wise and successful governor; and in January 1513, before setting out to discover the South Sea, he wrote a long and very interesting despatch to King Ferdinand, reporting the course of events, and very fully explaining the position and needs of the colony.

In the following September Vasco Nuñez de Balboa set out to complete the work of the great Admiral in one direction by discovering the South Sea. Columbus knew it was there, but sought to reach it by a strait. His successor revealed the dividing isthmus. Vasco

Nuñez went by sea to the territory of Careta, with 190 well-armed men. Routing the hostile forces of a hill chief named Quarequa, he obtained guides and ascended the mountain range until, after a tedious and difficult journey of twenty-five days, he attained the summit ridge on the 25th of September 1513, seven years after the death of Columbus.

Vasco Nuñez told his men to rest themselves, while he walked up to the summit alone. The wide expanse of ocean was suddenly spread out before him. He fell on his knees and gave thanks to God, then beckoned to his followers to come up; and they all sang the "Te Deum." A great cross was formed out of felled trees, and set up on high, by piling stones round its base. Descending the mountain, the discoverer made friends with a chief named Chiapes, whose territory was on the southern slope, and he sent forward Francisco Pizarro, Alonso Martin, and Juan de Escaray, with twelve men, to find the shortest way to the sea-shore. Alonso Martin, accompanied by Blas de Atienza, came to a place where there were two canoes, and as soon as the rising tide floated them, they got in and called upon their comrades to bear witness that Martin was the first, and Atienza the second man that ever embarked on the South Sea. Martin returned with the news, and Vasco Nuñez requested the cacique Chiapes to accompany him with some of his people, and went down to the beach. Advancing into the water up to his thighs, with a sword and shield, he took possession of all that South Sea, and of all that appertained to it, in the name of the sovereigns of Spain. He afterwards made an expedition in canoes to explore the Gulf of San Miguel, and returned to Darien in January 1514, after an absence of four months.

It would have been wise if King Ferdinand had confirmed the appointment of Vasco Nuñez de Balboa. But he had been prejudiced by Enciso and others, and he selected an arbitrary, ill-tempered old man, a sort of second Bobadilla, named Pedrarias de Avila, at the recommendation of Bishop Fonseca. The new governor came out accompanied by the Bishop Quevedo; the future historian Oviedo; Enciso, burning for vengeance on Vasco Nuñez; Hernando de Soto, the future discoverer of the Mississippi; Belalcazar, the conqueror of Quito; Pascual de Andagoya, and other men of note. In the end of July 1514 Pedrarias arrived at Darien. Violent and incapable, he undid all the good that the wise and conciliatory policy of Vasco Nuñez had wrought on the isthmus. Expeditions were sent in all directions, led by savage and cruel adventurers, who spread devastation and ruin wherever they went. The historian Oviedo is not considered to have been a very humane man, but the horrors of Darien were too much for him, and he returned to Spain. In 1517 Pedrarias caused the discoverer of the South Sea to be beheaded, on false charges, and thus destroyed one of the ablest leaders in the New World. It was a melancholy fate, and the more to be regretted because, if the few men possessed of the good sense and ability of Vasco Nuñez had been entrusted with power, the history of the native race might have been different. Ferdinand, guided by Fonseca, invariably selected the very worst and most unfit men that could be found in Spain for high commands, such as Margarit, Bobadilla, Ojeda, Nicuesa, and Pedrarias. Really great and able leaders, like Columbus and Vasco Nuñez, were either forced upon him or rejected.

The discovery of the South Sea solved one of the great problems that presented themselves to Columbus; the

passage to the strait far to the south, and the circumnavigation forming a natural sequence of events. The
arrival of Sebastian del Cano* at San Lucar in 1522, forged
the last link of the chain which had its origin in the
port of Palos in 1492, an interval of only thirty years.
Meanwhile the Admiral's work was extended westward
and northward from his landfall on the Honduras coast.
His own pupil, Vicente Yanez Pinzon, accompanied by
Juan de Solis, had carried on the discovery thence to the
Yucatan coast, in the very year of their old commander's
death; but it was not until ten years afterwards that
Hernandez de Cordova accidentally hit upon the same
country, near Cape Catoche. His report induced Velasquez, the governor of Cuba, to send a small expedition
under Juan de Grijalva from Santiago in May 1518,
accompanied by the more famous Pedro de Alvarado.
They touched at the Tabasco river, and explored the
Mexican coast as far as Panuco. The conquest of Mexico
by Hernando Cortes followed in 1519, and thus was the
work completed, which the great Admiral left for a successor, when he gave up the alluring suggestion of going to
the land whence the richly freighted canoe had come, at
the Isle of Pines. His duty, as he then saw it, called him
to explore the coast in search of a strait, in the opposite
direction.

After the complete failure of Ojeda and Nicuesa, the
government of Veragua was at length offered to the Adelantado Bartolomé Columbus. The young Admiral had
watched the blunders of the incapable adventurers who
unjustly occupied his uncle's rightful place, with anger
and contempt. At length justice was done, but it was
too late. The Adelantado had received a grant of land

* *Not* Deleano, as the name is sometimes erroneously written.

around Fort Concepcion, in the Vega Real, and had
resided for some years in Española under his nephew's
rule. The island of Mona, between Española and Costa
Rica, was also ceded to him. He died in December
1514. He had probably just returned to Seville, for his
body was placed, with that of the Admiral, in the chapel
of Santa Ana, in the monastery of Las Cuevas. The
two brothers rested side by side.

Harassing accusations were continuously brought
against the young Admiral, as they had been against
his father, and in 1519 he was obliged to return to Spain
to disprove them, leaving his wife and children at San
Domingo. He was present at the grand assembly summoned to Barcelona by Charles V., and accompanied the
Emperor to Cologne. He triumphantly disproved all the
slanders against him, and received the title of Viceroy,
which had been withheld by Ferdinand. In 1523 he
was again in Spain, having first made his will at San
Domingo on the 8th of September. He once more
cleared himself of all charges, and the Emperor held
him in high esteem. The young Admiral started from
Toledo, to be present at the marriage of Charles V. with
Isabella of Portugal, but he was taken seriously ill on
the road, and stopped at the house of a friend named
Alonzo Tellez Pacheco, at Montalban. He died there
on the 21st of February 1526, and was interred with his
father and uncle, in the monastery of Las Cuevas at
Seville. He survived his father twenty years, and had
governed Española for eighteen years.

He left four daughters : Felipa, who never married ;
Maria, wife of Luis de Cardona, Marquis of Guadaleste
and Admiral of Aragon ; Juana, married in 1537 to
Luis de la Cueva, brother of the Duke of Albuquerque ;

and Isabel, wife of Jorge de Portugallo, Count of Gelves ; and three sons. Luis was his heir, Cristoval continued the line, and Diego died before his father.

The Vice-Queen, Maria de Toledo, was in San Domingo with her children when her husband died. She did not return to Spain until 1529, when she came to urge the claims and protect the rights of her son Luis, who was born in 1522. Courageous and devoted, this noble lady fought her son's battle during fourteen years. In 1542 she returned to San Domingo with the bodies of the great Admiral and of her husband. Dying there on the 11th of May 1549, she was buried in the cathedral by the side of her husband. Her son Luis succeeded his father in 1526, and, owing to a judgment pronounced by Cardinal Garcia de Loaysa in 1536, he had to renounce the Viceroyalty and other great hereditary rights and privileges granted to the Admiral his grandfather, receiving in their place an annuity of 10,000 ducats, the island of Jamaica in fief, and the dukedom of Veragua. He retained the title of Admiral of the Ocean Sea. In 1540 he returned to Española with the title of Captain-General. After occupying that post for ten years, he went back to Spain in 1551, and was married at Valladolid in 1554, when he had two wives still living at San Domingo. In 1556 Philip II. deprived him of his Jamaica fief, and reduced his pension. Soon afterwards his matrimonial irregularities led to a criminal prosecution, and he was banished to Oran, where he died in 1572, aged fifty years. His remains were conveyed to San Domingo, and buried in the cathedral. He left two legitimate daughters by his first wife, named Maria and Felipa. The eldest became a nun. Felipa was married to her cousin Diego, son of Cristoval and nephew of Luis. Diego's father, Cristoval, died in the same year as his brother Luis, so that Diego became the second Duke of Veragua. He was the last male of the family of Columbus. He died in 1578, leaving a daughter named Maria, who married an obscure Creole in Española.

Diego, the second Duke of Veragua, had a sister named Francisca, who lived at Panama, and married the licentiate Diego Ortegon, a judge at Quito. Her daughter Josefa was the wife of Paz de la Serna, and mother of Josefa, who, in 1651, married Martin de Larreategui of Eybar, in Guipuzcoa. The Larreateguis were thus the nearest heirs of the great Admiral, and to the dukedom of Veragua.

But from 1578 to 1790, for upwards of two centuries, there was a usurpation of the title by descendants of the daughters of Diego Columbus, the second Admiral ; the Larreateguis having a prior right as descendants of one of his sons. The rightful heir, when the second Duke died, appears to have been poor and resident in the Indies, while the usurpers were powerful noblemen who could push their claims at court. Cristoval de Cardona, Marquis of Guadaleste and Admiral of Aragon, was recognised as third Duke of Veragua, when Diego Columbus, the second Duke, died in 1578. He was a son of Maria, the second daughter of Diego, the second Admiral. When he died in 1583 without children, the title remained in abeyance until the Council of the Indies adjudged it to Nuño de Portugallo, Count of Gelves, in 1608. He was grandson of Jorge de Portugallo, Count of Gelves, who married Isabel, fourth daughter of the second Admiral. Nuño became fourth Duke of Veragua, and received possession of the iron box containing all the title-deeds and other documents deposited at the monas tery of Las Cuevas. The titles of Duke and Admiral remained in the male line of Portugallos, Counts of Gelves, for five generations. The heiress Catarina was Duchess of Veragua, and she married James Stuart, second Duke of Berwick and Liria, and died in 1740. The Stuarts enjoyed the titles for three generations, although an almost interminable lawsuit had been brought against them by the rightful heirs.

At length the lawsuit terminated, in 1790, in favour of Don Mariano Larreategui, descended from Francisca Columbus, who married Diego Ortegon. He became Duke of Veragua and Admiral of the Ocean Sea, and also received the custody of the iron box, containing the title-deeds and letters of the great Admiral, which are now in the house of his grandson at Madrid. They were published by Navarrete in 1825.

His Excellency Don Cristoval Colon de la Cerda y Larreategui, Duke of Veragua and Admiral, ex-Minister of Public Works, and Vice-President of the International Congress in 1892 for celebrating the four hundredth anniversary of the discovery of America, is the heir and direct descendant of the Admiral, Cristoval Columbus. Born in 1837, he succeeded to the dukedom on the death of his father in 1866, and has a young son and heir named Cristoval, born in 1878.

It is pleasant to know that the great Admiral still has heirs and representatives who religiously preserve his archives and revere his memory.

X

CHAPTER XVII.

THE ADMIRAL'S SONS.

II.—FERNANDO, AND THE OTHER AUTHORITIES FOR THE LIFE OF COLUMBUS.

FERNANDO, the second son of Christopher Columbus by Beatriz Arana y Enriquez, was born at Cordova on the 15th of August 1488, and continued to live with his mother until he became a Queen's Page, at the age of ten, in February 1498. After being at court for four years, he went to sea with his father, and passed through all the terrible hardships and sufferings of the last voyage, off the coast of Veragua and at Jamaica. He performed this service between the ages of fourteen and sixteen, taking his full share of the work, cheering and encouraging his shipmates, and making himself useful to the Admiral, to whom he must have been the greatest possible comfort. On returning home, his father sent him from Seville with his uncle Bartolomé, in June 1505, to kiss the King's hand and report himself. Diego and Fernando nursed their father in his last illness, and attended him on his deathbed. The younger son was left very well off, receiving an independent fortune. But the two brothers were warmly attached to each other; and when Diego recovered some of his inheritance, and went out to Española as Governor in 1509, he

was accompanied by Fernando, who rejoiced to see one
of the most cherished desires of his father accomplished.
Fernando remained for a few months at San Domingo,

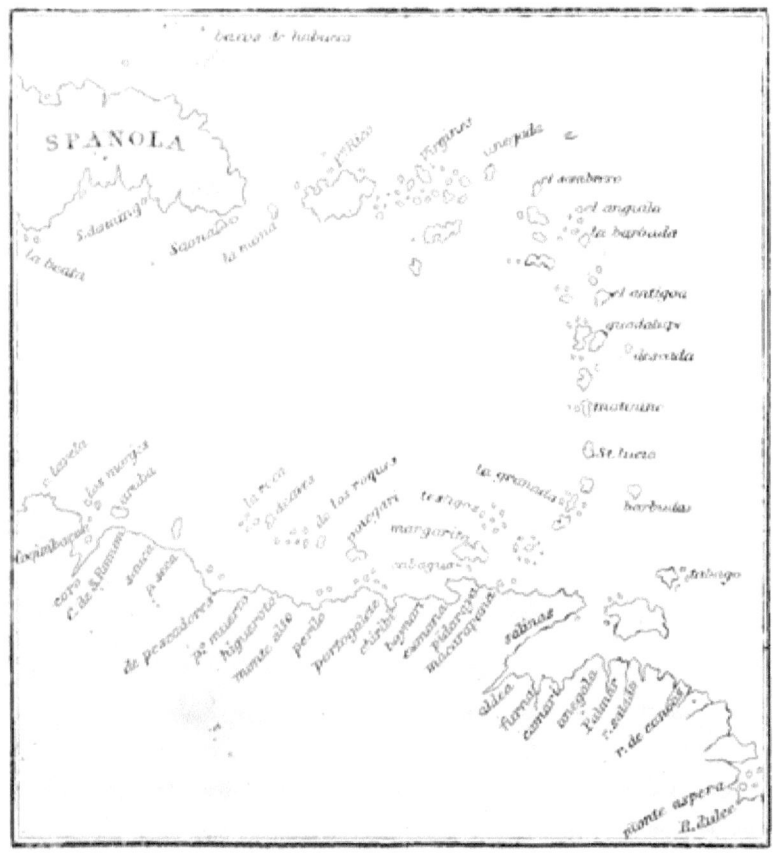

PORTION OF THE WEST INDIES.
(*From the Weimar Map of 1527, ascribed to Fernando Columbus.*)

and then returned to Spain with the object of completing his studies.

Fernando Columbus devoted considerable ability and
learning, combined with great industry and a love of
literature for its own sake, to the grateful task of

honouring his great father's memory. He acquired a practical knowledge of navigation as a boy, and he mastered the science of cosmography in after life, becoming an accomplished mathematician and a draughtsman. The Weimar map of 1527,* and a chart showing the dividing line of the Papal Bull, have been attributed to him. When only twenty-two years of age he wrote a Latin treatise on circumnavigation, called "Colon de concordia," which he presented to his father's friend, the famous Cardinal Ximenes de Cisneros, and received a grateful letter of acceptance.　Fernando was also a poet and a jurist; but his favourite occupation was the collection of books for the formation of a large and permanent library at Seville.　He was thus engaged, at intervals, for more than a quarter of a century, visiting all the chief book marts of Europe, and, as he always made an entry of the date and place of purchase, his travels can be accurately traced by reference to his books.

In 1512 Fernando Columbus paid the first out of several visits to Rome, and resided there for a year; and in 1515, when he was again in Italy, he visited Genoa, and must have examined all the old haunts of his father in the city and at Savona with intense interest.　In the following year he was at Rome and Florence, returning to Spain on the death of King Ferdinand.　Fernando's worth and fine qualities were appreciated by the new sovereign. Charles V., with whom he appears to have been a great favourite.　He attended the Emperor to the Low Countries, and was present at the coronation at Aix-la-Chapelle.　At Louvain he made the acquaintance of Erasmus, who presented him with one of his works; and he formed a friendship with two learned

* Facsimile published by J. G. Kohl, Weimar, 1860.

Flemings, Johan Vœsius and Nicolas Cheynaerts, who afterwards joined him at Seville. Fernando was with the Emperor at Worms in 1520, and extended his travels to Genoa and Venice, to Nuremburg, Frankfort, and Cologne. In June 1522 he went to England with the Emperor, visiting London, and returning thence to Spain by sea.

Fernando rested at Seville for about a year, probably engaged in writing memoirs relating to his father, and treatises, such as that on the reasons for the belief in a westerly voyage. But in 1524 he was summoned from his retirement, and nominated one of the arbitrators to meet at Badajoz, and adjudicate the respective claims of Spain and Portugal on the Moluccas. He was the author of four memoirs on the subject. He spent the autumn of 1525 at Rome, and during the four succeeding years he was superintending the building of a handsome house at Seville, with a fine portico of marbles brought from Genoa. It was situated in the centre of a beautiful garden planted with trees and shrubs sent to him from the Indies. The house, where his splendid library first found a resting-place, has long since disappeared ; but one of the trees of the garden remained until quite lately—a star appletree (*Chrysophyllum Cainito*). A cutting was taken from it, and is now growing in the garden of Don José M. Ascensio, the historian of Columbus. Fernando was well able to afford the necessary expenditure on his house, library, and garden, for his two pensions from the Emperor, added to his revenues from the Indies, brought him in an income equivalent to £7500 a year at the present day.

In 1526 Fernando was charged with the presidency of a commission of cosmographers and pilots to correct marine charts, and to construct a *mappe monde* showing the countries lately discovered. In the following year he was requested, during the absence of Sebastian Cabot in the River Plate, to preside over the examinations of pilots, assisted by Diego Ribero and Alonso de Chaves, two learned mathematicians and cosmographers.

These useful labours were interrupted, in 1530, by visits to Perugia and Rome, and to Bologna to be present at the Emperor's Italian coronation. Fernando resided for some time at the university of Alcala de Henares, and, in 1535, made a tour into France, visiting Montpellier and Lyons. From that time he did not leave his house at Seville, and in 1537 he founded a school of mathematics and navigation there, which was called " El Colegio Imperial." He made his will on July 3rd, 1539, and at the time of his death, in the same year, he was engaged on a catalogue of his library.

Fernando Columbus is described as a tall handsome man, and in his later years he became very stout. He was learned and eloquent, with pleasing manners and very agreeable in conversation. Never married, he led a blameless life, and devoted his time to his library, to work connected with the public service, and to recording the deeds and preserving memorials of his beloved and revered father. The Admiral was happy in both his sons. Diego fulfilled the wishes nearest to his father's heart, by recovering his rights and privileges. Fernando did more than any other contemporary to make the deeds of the great discoverer known to posterity. Fernando was buried in the cathedral of Seville, where his tomb may still be visited by those who respect true worth and devoted filial piety.

The library of Fernando Columbus comprised from

12,000 to 20,000 volumes. By his will he left it to his nephew Luis; and, if the legacy was declined, it was bequeathed to the Chapter of Seville Cathedral. Luis resigned his right, and the chapter received possession of the library in 1552. It has since been called "La Biblioteca Colombina." For a century and a half it was shamefully neglected; and, when a new catalogue was made in 1684, only about 5000 volumes remained. Its value is now better understood, and it occupies two long rooms over the cloister of Seville Cathedral. Next to the authorship of the Admiral's life, the greatest service done by Fernando Columbus to posterity is the preservation of some of the most interesting of his father's books, containing his marginal notes.

In the inner library there is an ebony table made as a stand for a glass case containing the most precious relics of the great Admiral—the books with marginal notes in his own handwriting. They are four in number. The first is the closely studied "Imago Mundi" of Cardinal Petrus de Alliaco or Pierre d'Ailly, with several interesting marginal notes by the Admiral. The second is a Latin copy of Marco Polo, printed in 1485, with marginal notes, which belonged to the Admiral, as Fernando had another copy in his library. The third is the "Historia Rerum ubique Gestarum" of Pope Pius II. (Æneas Sylvius), printed in 1478. The Admiral quotes from this work* in his letter from Jamaica, so that he probably had it with him in his last voyage. In a fly-leaf the original letter in Latin, from Toscanelli, was found. The fourth is the manuscript of seventy leaves, containing the "*Profecias de la recuperacion de la santa*

---

* Navarrete, i. p. 307.

cindad de Hierusalem, y del desenbrimiento de las Indias,"
by Columbus himself.

The existence of these treasures is due to the pious
care of Fernando, who also completed a memoir of his
father in 107 chapters, written at different times, and
often probably with long intervals. Unfortunately the
Spanish original is lost. An Italian translation by
Alfonso Ulloa, was published at Venice in 1571, thirty-
two years after the death of Fernando Columbus, and a
second edition at Milan in 1614. Other editions have
followed, the latest being that by Dulau, published in
London in 1867. The original title was " *Historie del
Signor Don Fernando Colombo nelle quali s'ha particolare
e vera relatione della vita e de i fatti dell Ammiraglio D.
Christoforo Colombo suo padre.*" A pamphlet, published
by Mr. Harrisse at Seville, in 1871, raised a doubt as to
the authenticity of the Italian version, which was stoutly
defended by D'Avezac, by Duro in his " Colon y Pinzon "
(1883), and by Dr. Prospero Peragallo, who wrote a considerable book on the subject, published at Genoa in 1884.
The controversy has raged for twenty years. The question
is, however, settled by an examination of the history by
Las Casas. The whole of the first ten chapters of the
Italian translation will be found, almost word for word,
in fifteen chapters of Las Casas, and Las Casas frequently
quotes Fernando Columbus in other places. As all these
passages agree with the Italian version, both must have
been correctly copied from the original manuscript of
Fernando. It may, therefore, be assumed that the
remainder of the Italian translation is fairly reliable.
There is, however, reason for thinking that Ulloa took
some of the earlier chapters from Las Casas, and not
from the original. This work has been the chief source

whence materials have been obtained for the early life of
Columbus down to 1492, and for some details of the last
voyage. But it must be used with caution, for Fernando
himself raises a warning. He says (cap. iv.) " Di quali
viaggi, e di *molte altre cose* di quei primi di, io non ho
pena notizia ; perciocchè egli venne a morte a tempo che
io non aveva tanto ardire o pratica, per la riverenza filiale,
che io ardissi di richiedermi di cotale cose : o, per parlare
piu veramente, allora mi ritrovava io, como giovane,
molto lontano da cotal pensiero." This accounts for such
mistakes as those respecting the Perestrelo connection,
and the command of King René's galley.

There were four other historians who were personally
acquainted with Columbus or his sons, and whose works,
together with the writings of the Admiral himself, complete the sources for the life of the great navigator. Of
these, Bartolomé Las Casas is by far the most important,
from his intimate personal knowledge of many of the
actors in the scenes he describes. Bartolomé, when very
young, witnessed the entry of Columbus into Seville,
when he returned from his great discovery. His father
accompanied the Admiral on his second voyage. Las
Casas himself went out with Ovando to Española, where
he took orders, and eventually joined the Dominicans.
He was many years in the Indies, and devoted them to
endeavours to ameliorate the condition of the natives and
to indignant protests against their cruel treatment by
the Spaniards. There was much in common between
Las Casas and Columbus. If Columbus, pressed down
by the heavy responsibilities of office, recommended and
consented to measures which were condemned by Las
Casas, it must be remembered that the good bishop never
himself felt the burden of responsibility. Columbus had

the same regard for the Indians and admiration for their simple life and good qualities, the same desire for their **fair** treatment, and felt the same indignation at the cruelty of Ovando, **as was** so loudly proclaimed by Las Casas. The bishop **would not** only have found a sympathising **listener, but also** an active supporter, in the Admiral. **Columbus, on** the whole, was fortunate in his historian, **for Las Casas was** a generous admirer of the Admiral's genius, **as well as** an excellent narrator of the events of his life. He also had the advantage of knowing the country, and of being able to describe the scenery. He thus supplied colouring to his narrative; and he never omitted to give the correct pronunciation of native names. But his greatest advantages were his personal acquaintance with Columbus, his brothers and sons, with Dr. Deza, with Vicente Pinzon, Ledesma, Ojeda, Diego Mendez, Vallejo, and Bastidas; and his access to the letters and other papers of Columbus. He gives thirty-one documents, seventeen of which are to be found nowhere else; and to him is due the preservation of the precious abstract of the journal of the first voyage, and the full report of the third voyage. Las Casas commenced his "Historia de las Indias" in 1527, when he was in Española, and worked at it during many years. Returning finally from the Indies in 1547, he took up his residence in the monastery of San Gregorio at Valladolid in 1550, and there he finished his book in 1561. He died at the great age of ninety-two, in 1566. This most important historical work remained in manuscript for more than three centuries after the death of its author. At length it was printed and published at Madrid, in five volumes, in the year 1875

Dr. Andres Bernaldez, the cura of Los Palacios from

1488 to 1513, and chaplain to Dr. Deza, Archbishop of Seville, received Columbus as his guest, when he returned to Spain in 1496. The good cura was intrusted with the care of several documents by the Admiral, and he had also seen the letter of Dr. Chanca, relating the events of the second voyage. Bernaldez was the author of the "Historia de los Reyes Catolicos," which, like the work of Las Casas, remained in manuscript for more than three centuries and a half. At length it was printed at Granada in 1856, and published, in two volumes 8vo, at Seville, in 1870. Bernaldez devotes thirteen chapters to Columbus, and the account of the second expedition, including the voyage during which Jamaica was discovered, is particularly valuable.

Gonzalo Fernandez Oviedo was born at Madrid in August 1478, and became a page to Prince Juan at the age of twelve. He must have been intimate with both the Admiral's sons during their life at court, and was present at the reception of Columbus at Barcelona in 1493. Shortly afterwards he went to Italy, and was secretary to Gonsalvo de Cordova. When Pedrarias was sent out as Governor of Darien in 1513, Oviedo accompanied him, and was, at different times, a Regidor of Darien, Governor of Cartagena, and Alcalde of the fort at San Domingo. Oviedo had a love for writing and recording events from his youth. He eventually became Chronicler to Charles V., and, in 1533, he was appointed Historiographer of the Indies. The "Historia General de las Indias," by Oviedo, is incomplete. It covers the period from 1492 to 1548. The early editions are rare, but the work was well edited by Don José Amador de los Rios, in 1851–55. Oviedo died at Valladolid in 1557. He had conversed with the sons of Colum-

bus, with Vicente Yanez Pinzon, Father God, Margarit,
and Ovando. The work is valuable in many respects,
though the author sympathices with his countrymen,
and has no feelings for the sufferings of the natives.
Moreover, he made more than one attempt to depreciate
the Admiral's services by misrepresenting facts and dates.
Las Casas denounces him for injustice and inaccuracy,
and he was certainly prone to listen to gossip, without
any sense of proportion in regard to the value of different classes of evidence. Yet we have to thank Oviedo
for many details not to be found elsewhere; and, although
he was the first to tell the fable about an old pilot dying
in the house of Columbus, who told him the way to the
Indies, yet he adds, "For me, I hold the story to be
false." * Gomara and others copied the story from
Oviedo, omitting his belief that it was an invention.

Pedro Martyr d'Anghiera was born at Arona in 1455,
took orders, and came to Spain in 1487. He was chaplain to Queen Isabella, tutor to Prince Juan, and, in 1511,
a member of the Council of the Indies. Martyr loved
to retail the freshest news to friends in Italy; but, out
of hundreds of letters written between 1488 and 1525,
only a dozen relate to Columbus. The "Opus Epistola-
rum" appeared in 1530. His "De Orbe Novo," more
generally known as the Decades, is in the form of more
carefully prepared epistles to important correspondents
in Italy, and was printed in 1511 and 1530. Although
Pedro Martyr narrates events connected with several
periods of the Admiral's active life, his letters contain
little or nothing that may not be found elsewhere. The
ancient letter-writer died at Valladolid in 1526.

There are two Spanish historians whose works were of

* Parci ui yo lo tengo por falso.

importance in studying the life of Columbus a century
ago, but which have lost their value, owing to the authorities they relied upon having since become more accessible. Francisco Lopez de Gomara, who wrote a " Historia de las Indias," flourished a generation after the
Admiral's time, and had great advantages in the collection of information. His narrative is agreeably written
and well arranged, but he was an unconscientious writer,
and his statements cannot safely be accepted unless they
are corroborated by more reliable authorities. His treatment of the story about the pilot, who had been to the
Indies, dying in the house of Columbus, is a good example
of his method. It is given by Oviedo, with the important
addition that he believed it to be false. Gomara copied
the story from Oviedo, omitting his opinion that it was
false, but admitting that the name of the pilot was
unknown. Others copied from Gomara, until at last one
of them invented a name. This is a good example of
the way in which fables grow.

Antonio de Herrera, the chronicler of the Indies, was
born more than forty years after the Admiral's death.
He held the office of historiographer, with a good salary
and access to all official documents, throughout the reign
of Philip II., and until that of his grandson, Philip IV.
He died in 1625, aged seventy-six. His great work,
" Historia General de las Indias Occidentales," in eight
decades, covers the period from 1492 to 1554. Its publication, in five folio volumes, was completed in 1615.
Herrera's narrative is composed in strict chronological
order, so that it is tedious and sometimes confusing.
Since the publication of Las Casas, the work of Herrera
has ceased to be of any value as an authority for the life
of Columbus, for that portion is copied from the bishop's

history with scarcely **any** additions. Neither Gomara
nor Herrera were **ever in the Indies.**

The enormous accu**mulation of** materials for history
in the receptacles for Spanish archives at Simancas and
Sevill e, attracted **the attention of** Charles III., the best
of the Bourbon kings of Spain. In 1781 he appointed
the learned Juan Bautista Muñoz to investigate the
sources of information, with **free** access **to all the
archives, and to found a more complete and** authoritative
history on them than had yet appeared. Muñoz col-
lected a mass of documents with excellent judgment,
and completed the first volume of his " Historia del
Nuevo Mundo," which brings the narrative down to the
landing of Bobadilla at San Domingo in 1500. Muñoz
was a man endowed with great literary talent and almost
inexhaustible power of work. He possessed critical in-
sight of a very high order, and, through a maze **of
contradictory statements, discerned the** correct date of
the birth of Columbus, and his true landfall in the
Bahamas. **It is a cause of deep regret that** his untimely
death, **in** 1799, **in the midst of his** labours, deprived the
world **of the** remainder **of his** history.

Martin Fernandez de Navarrete, an accomplished naval
officer, commenced **his historical** researches **in** 1789, and
worked for some years **in concert** with Muñoz, both being
assisted **by the talented and industrious archivist** Tomas
Gonzalez. His labours were **interrupted by** the French
war, but they were resumed **at the** peace, and extended
over a period of thirty years. In 1825 he published
four volumes of the collection **of** voyages **and** travels
made **by the** Spaniards at sea.[*]   For the first time the

---

[*] "Coleccion de los Viages y Descubrimientos que **hicieron por**
mar los Españoles," **tom. i., ii., iii., iv.** (Madrid, 1825.)

actual texts of the Admiral's reports and letters became accessible. Navarrete collected them, with great labour and care, from the royal archives at Simancas, and, from the archives of the Dukes of Veragua and Infantado, had deciphered and arranged them, and edited them with admirable skill and judgment, together with numerous other documents throwing light on the great events comprised in the life-story of Columbus. Navarrete published a fifth volume in 1837. A French edition of the earlier volumes, with many valuable notes, appeared in 1828. Navarrete died in 1844. A few letters of Columbus have since been printed, two in a volume brought out by the Spanish Government in 1877, called "Cartas de Indias," one by Mr. Harrisse in his "Christophe Colomb." The materials published by Navarrete furnish by far the most important sources for the Admiral's life, as will be seen by the following brief abstract of the actual writings of Columbus himself, thus brought to light :—

First Voyage—
    Letter to the Escribano de Racion (Santangel), 18th February 1493.
    Abstract of the Journal, in the handwriting of Las Casas.
Second Voyage—
    Memorial to the Sovereigns, 30th January 1494.
    Letter to the Sovereigns without date (in "Cartas de Indias").
Third Voyage—
    Report in the handwriting of Las Casas.
    Letter to Fonseca as to pay of Coronel and Carbajal, January 1498.
    Deed of Entail, 24th February 1498.
    Letter to Roldan, 26th October 1498.
    Safe-conduct for Roldan, 26th October 1498.
    Letter to the Nurse of Prince Juan.

Before Last Voyage —
> Letter to the Sovereigns, 1500.
> Letter to the Sovereigns, April 4, 1502.
> Letter to the Sovereigns, February 6, 1502 (in "Cartas de Indias").
> Letter to Pope Alexander VI, February 1502.
> Letter to Oderigo, Genoese Ambassador, 21st March 1502.
> Letter to the Bank of St. George, 2nd April 1502.
> Memorial for his son Diego.
> Four letters to Father Gorricio.

Last Voyage —
> Letter to the Sovereigns from Jamaica, 7th July 1503
> Fragment of a letter to Ovando, sent by Escobar.
> Letter at Beata, to Ovando.

After Last Voyage —
> Eleven letters to his son Diego.
> Letter to Oderigo, the Genoese Ambassador, 27th December 1504.
> Memorial to the King, in favour of his son Diego, January 1505.
> Letter to the King, May 1506.

Will —
> Codicil written at Segovia, 1505.
> Codicil at Valladolid, 1506.

In Books -
> Libro de las Profecias.
> Marginal Notes in "Imago Mundi,"
> Marginal Notes in "Marco Polo,"
> Marginal Notes in "Æneas Silvius,"
> in the "Biblioteca Colombina" at Seville.

The important publication of Navarrete enabled a satisfactory biography of Columbus to be written, which had not previously been possible. When Robertson wrote in 1777, his authorities were the Italian version of the memoir by Fernando, Peter Martyr, Oviedo, and Herrera. As soon as the work of Navarrete appeared, Washington Irving undertook to write a complete life of the illustrious discoverer of the New World. Born at New York in 1783, this charming author had passed some

time in Spain, had visited Palos and La Rabida, and
had had access to the manuscripts of Las Casas and
Bernaldez.   He must have completed his " Life of Columbus " within twelve months, for Navarrete's collection was
published in 1825, and the preface of Washington Irving's
book was dated 1827.   The work was published by
Murray in 1827; another edition in 1838, and was
translated into Spanish by José Garcia de Villalta.   The
" Vita di Cristoforo Colombo," by Luigi Bossi, appeared
at Milan in 1818, but that author had not the advantage of access to the documents published by Navarrete.
The life of Columbus by Washington Irving is as remarkable for careful research, and for the soundness of
its judgments, as for the charm of its style.   He has
drawn a picture of the great Admiral which is based on
a critical study of his character, and on a careful consideration of the varied motives which influenced his
actions.   It is a true and accurate portrait, showing the
man's character as it really was, and it is not likely to be
affected by later criticism.   Irving's " Life of Columbus "
will continue to be, as it has been in the past, the most
popular and most widely read biography of the great
Admiral for all English-speaking people.   This most
delightful of American authors died at Tarrytown in
1859.

For a critical examination of the numerous biographical
and geographical questions involved in the life-story and
discoveries of Columbus and his companions, all students
are indebted to Humboldt's " Examen Critique de l'Histoire et de la Géographie du Nouveau Continent," which
was published at Paris in 1836-39.

The French lives of Columbus, by the Marquis de
Belloy and the Comte Roselly de Lorgues, are more

Y

eulogistic than critical, and the works of the latter author
were prepared mainly with the object of advocating the
canonisation of the man who bore Christianity across
the Atlantic to the New **World.** Roselly de Lorgues
published his "Christophe **Colomb**" in 1864, and the
"Histoire Posthum **de Colomb**" in 1885, which was
answered by Captain Duro **of the Spanish** navy in his
"Colon y la Historia **Postuma.**" "Christophe Colomb,"
by Charles **Buet,** appeared **in** 1886.

Mr. R. H. Major, the bio**grapher of** Prince Henry the
Navigator, has the merit **of having** brought the principal
writings **of Columbus, in the work of** Navarrete, within
reach of English readers by his **excellent** translations.
His "**Select Letters of** Columbus" formed the volume
printed for the Hakluyt **Society in** 1847, and the second
edition appeared **in** 1870. **The** 1870 introduction is **an**
ad**mirable** memoir **on the life** and discoveries of the
Admiral, and contains the most **closely** reasoned argument
that **has** been yet written, on the date of his birth. **Mr.**
Major also made a careful study of the question of the
landfall, and established the exact position off the
south-east cape **of** Watling Island, where Columbus
anch**ored.** This excellent geographer and most amiable
man, **who was** for so many years Keeper of the Maps at
the British Museum **and** Secretary to the Royal Geographical Society, died in May **1891.** The "Landfall of
Columbus," by Admiral Becher, **with** whom Mr. **Major**
is in close agreement, was published in 1856. An official
of the Hydrographer's Department in the English
Admiralty, Becher, both by his occupation and his
previous life at sea, had an excellent training for the work
he undertook. His book is one of considerable merit,
and he gives a translation of the abstract of the journal

of the first voyage, which is not included in Major's
volume. His account of the life of Columbus, previous
to the first voyage, is a translation from the work of the
Baron de Bonnafoux.

By far the most valuable and important researches
relating to the life of Columbus, since the publication of
Navarrete's work, are those which have been made
during many years, by the eminent American author
and critic Henry Harrisse. His magnificent work,
entitled " Bibliotheca Americana Vetustissima," containing notices of the earliest books relating to the New
World from 1492 to 1551, was published at New York
in 1866; and Mr. Harrisse had previously published
translations of the letters of Columbus describing his
first voyage, with the original texts. Mr. Harrisse has
since published numerous treatises on various questions
relating to the Admiral's life, and to the authenticity of
the memoir attributed to Fernando, but his great work
is the "Christophe Colomb" in two large volumes,
published at Paris in 1884. It is based on inedited
documents in the archives of Genoa, Savona, Seville, and
Madrid. It evinces immense research, and a critical
faculty of a very high order. Aided by the recent researches of the Marchese Marcello Staglieno* and others
in the notarial records of Genoa and Savona, Mr. Harrisse
has given a more complete and detailed view of the family
of Columbus at Genoa, and of his early life, than has
ever appeared before. He has also established dates of
the greatest importance, with reference to the birth and
early movements of Columbus and his brothers. With
the same elaboration and exhaustive research Mr. Harrisse
has discussed the previously obscure questions relating

* Giornale Ligurtino.

to the marriage and **life in** Portugal, the transactions during the residence in Spain, and other disputed points ; and **has** furnished new particulars **respecting** the lives of all **the** relations **of** the Admiral. In the course of inquiries extending over many years, and in the light of **new discoveries.** Mr. Harrisse has sometimes found **it necessary** to alter or modify previously formed opinions, but his knowledge of all subjects bearing on the **life of the** great Admiral is unrivalled, and the value of his researches **places him in the very first** rank as an authority. His labours, as regards the light they throw on the true history of Columbus and his discoveries, are second in value only to those **of Navarrete.**

Mr. Justin Winsor, **the** accomplished librarian of Harvard College, published a work entitled, " Christopher Columbus, and how he received and imparted the Spirit of Discovery," **in** 1890. His extensive and **accurate** knowledge of literature, especially of the literature of the Columbian period **in its** relation to navigation **and discovery,** was sure **to** result in a valuable addition to the library of works on Columbus, for their number is now so great that the name of library is quite applicable. In his early chapters, Mr. Winsor exhaustively reviews the authorities for the Admiral's career, and he supplies the latest information respecting the family and early life at Genoa, giving full acknowledgments as to the value of Mr. Harrisse's assistance. His narrative of the discoveries is based on better-known authorities, and the work concludes with an interesting chapter on the geographical results, which very few scholars would have been competent to compile, and the value of which is enhanced by numerous illustrations. Mr. Winsor's **view** of the character and motives **of Columbus is** not one which

is likely to recommend itself to critical students, for it
ignores considerations without which a sound judgment
cannot be formed.   But there can be no question of the
value of his work as a comprehensive digest, as well of
former knowledge as of the latest researches and discoveries.

The Italian biographers of Columbus, from Spotorno
to Staglieno, give the best information respecting the
birth and early life of their illustrious compatriot.
Among other valuable memoirs, the Marchese Marcello
Staglieno has published a most interesting pamphlet
on the Admiral's early home "Sulla casa abitata da
Domenico Colombo" (Genova, 1885).   Cornelio Desi-
moni is another eminent authority; while Guiseppe
Pescia has very ably contended for his native parish,
comprising Terrarossa, as the hero's birthplace.   Peragallo has maintained the authenticity of the life by
Fernando Columbus with considerable warmth, and the
advocate Dondero, in his "L'Onesta di Cristoforo Colombo" (Genova, 1877), defends Columbus from the
imputation of immorality in relation to Beatriz Enriquez.   The best Italian lives of Columbus are by Angelo
Sanguineti (1846, 2nd ed. 1891) and Francisco Tarducci
(1885), the former being an excellent biography, critical,
judicious, and very agreeably written.

The most complete and, on the whole, the best life of
the great Admiral that has yet appeared, was published
at Barcelona in 1891, in view of the fourth centenary of
the discovery of America on the 12th of October 1492.
This is a monumental edition, with coloured illustrations
from the works of the best modern Spanish artists, and
with every page enriched by allegorical borders.   The
type is clear, the engraving of head-pieces and vignettes

excellent, and the whole work reflects great credit on the
typographical art of Barcelona. The accomplished
author, Don José Maria Asensio, has bestowed years of
research and of thought on the composition of a work
which should do credit to his country, and he has been rewarded with complete success. The "Life of Columbus"
by Asensio is, without doubt, the best and most complete
that has yet appeared. Perfect master of his subject,
acquainted alike with the older chronicles and the results
of the latest researches, Asensio had the further advantage of writing at Seville, within a stone's throw of the
"Biblioteca Colombina." In a pleasantly written narrative, he describes the events of the Admiral's life in
full detail, discusses the points in dispute with critical
insight and sagacity, and corrects several misconceptions
of his predecessors. On the other hand he has adopted
an untenable date for the birth of Columbus, and has
reverted to the exploded theory that Cat Island was his
landfall. He, however, furnishes an antidote to the
latter mistake, by printing among the notes and illustrations, which conclude each division of his work, an
admirably argued memoir on the true landfall by Don
Juan Ignacio de Armas of Cuba. These comparatively
unimportant errors are more than compensated for by
the good sense and sound judgment with which all the
various difficulties connected with the Admiral's life are
approached and discussed. Asensio, while far from blind
to the weaknesses and blemishes in the character of
Columbus, fully appreciates his genius, his magnanimity,
and the amiable qualities which so endeared him to his
friends and relations. "Humanity," he says, "has
placed his name on the highest column of the temple of
immortality; and for close upon four centuries his

memory has been exalted, praised, and loved by successive generations." The value of this splendid edition is very much enhanced by the number of original documents that are printed at the end of each book. They include the texts of nearly the whole of the letters and reports contained in Navarrete, besides many others, some of them being printed for the first time. Such a mass of documentary illustration necessarily swells the work to considerable dimensions, and the two large volumes of the "*Cristoval Colon, su vida, sus viajes, sus descubrimientos por Don José Maria Asensio*" comprise 1643 pages of letterpress. This great work very aptly commemorates the celebration of the fourth centenary of the discovery of America, while it is not too much to say that it is an addition of permanent value to the literature of Europe.

Several other cultured Spaniards have devoted their time and abilities to the study of portions of the life-story of Columbus within the last few years. Tomas Rodriguez Pinilla, in his "Colon en España" (Madrid, 1884), has very ably explained the true nature of the conferences at Salamanca in the winter of 1486-87, at which Columbus assisted; and the accomplished naval captain, Don Cesareo Fernandez Duro, in his "Colon y Pinzon." and in several parts of the volumes entitled "Disquisiciones Nauticas," has thrown light on various questions relating to the life of the great Admiral. All Spaniards and Italians unite to do honour to the memory of the illustrious Genoese navigator, and their feeling of veneration and love receives an answer of warm sympathy from every nation throughout the world.

CHAPTER XVIII.

It is the strangest accident in the history of geographical discovery that the great continent discovered by Columbus should not have received his name, nor even the name of any other discoverer, but that it should for ever be known by the Christian name of a provision merchant whose short experience of the sea began in advanced middle life, and who never even commanded an expedition of discovery.

Amerigo Vespucci came of a respectable Florentine family, and was born on the 9th of March 1451. He was brought up to mercantile pursuits in the house of the Medici, and came to Spain at the age of forty. There he obtained employment in the commercial house of the Italian Juanoto Berardi at Seville, whose business was to contract for equipping and provisioning ships. Berardi died in December 1495, and Vespucci had to complete the engagements of his deceased employer. He was the contractor for the ships of the second and third voyages of Columbus. The learned Muñoz examined the official records of expenses incurred in fitting out the vessels. They show that Vespucci was at Seville or San Lucar from April 1497 to the end of May 1498. The Admiral always found him civil and obliging, but his meat soon turned bad, and his biscuits appear to have been

abominable. In 1499 Vespucci went to sea for the first
time at the age of forty-seven—much too old ever to make
a sailor. He was on board one of the vessels of Ojeda's
expedition, probably in the capacity of a merchant or
volunteer. He returned in 1500, and went to Portugal
in the following year. His own account was that he proceeded to Lisbon at the invitation of the king, conveyed
to him through a countryman named Giuliano Giocondo.
It would seem, from his conversation with Columbus
afterwards, that the object of his journey was to make
money, and that he failed. After four years, Vespucci
returned to Spain and visited Columbus at Seville in 1505,
on his way to court. In a letter to his son Diego, dated
February 5, 1505, the Admiral wrote —

"Diego Mendez left Seville on the third of this month.
After his departure I spoke with Amerigo Vespucci, the
bearer of this letter, who is on his way to court on
matters relating to navigation. He always showed a
desire to please me, and he is a very respectable man.
Fortune has been adverse to him, as to many others, and
his labours have not been so profitable as he might
reasonably have expected. He goes for me, and is very
desirous of doing anything that would be useful to me,
and he is in your hands. He sets out with the determination to do all that he possibly can for me. See in
what way he can be of service, and work for him, as he
will tell you all."

In the same year Vespucci returned to his old trade,
and again obtained a contract to supply provisions for
ships. On March 22, 1508, he was appointed Pilot-Major
of Spain. He was a very clever, plausible man, and he
must have picked up some knowledge of a pilot's duties.
Still this was a strange selection, with such tried and ex-

perienced men as Pinzon, Solis, and Cosa ready to serve. But appointments made without reference to qualifications were characteristic of Fonseca, and indeed of Ferdinand. Vespucci never went to sea until he was forty-seven, and had since made three voyages at the outside.* A pilot should have learnt his business from his youth afloat and at sea. Vespucci was a landsman, and no true pilot. This is all that is certainly known of him, apart from his own letters. He died on February 22, 1512.

Vespucci wrote a letter from Lisbon, dated September 4, 1504, to his schoolfellow Piero Soderini, who was Gonfaloniere of Florence in 1504, describing four voyages which he alleged that he had made, two with Spaniards and two with Portuguese. He also wrote a letter to Lorenzo di Pier Francesco di Medici in March 1503, describing the third of these voyages along the coast of Brazil. Except in the case of Coelho, the names of the commanders of expeditions in which Vespucci claimed to have served, are carelessly, or perhaps carefully, omitted.

Vespucci stated that his first voyage was undertaken by order of King Ferdinand, and that it occupied from May 10, 1497, to October 15, 1498. His story is that he sailed to the Canaries with four vessels, and thence steered west and south, making a thousand leagues, when a landfall was made in latitude 16° N. He saw a village, with long houses built out over the sea on piles, like a little Venice. He next came to a place, in 23 N., called *Parias* in the Latin, and *Lariab* in the earliest known Italian edition. Thence he sailed 870 leagues

---

* His supposed voyage with Juan de la Cosa in 1505, referred to in the letter of Vianello, is not possible. There is proof that Vespucci was in Spain up to the end of August 1506, and the letter is dated December of the same year.

north, and came to the finest harbour in the world. There was an island called *Iti* inhabited by cannibal savages, a hundred leagues from the coast. Here the Spaniards captured 222 slaves, and took them to Cadiz, where they arrived in October 1498.

No such voyage was undertaken in 1497, and Vespucci was employed as a provision contractor during the alleged period of the absence of the ships. As the chief events in Vespucci's story also happened in the voyage of Ojeda, it was naturally suspected that the story of this imaginary voyage was concocted from incidents which really occurred during the voyage made by Vespucci under the command of Ojeda in 1499-1500. There was the village called Little Venice by Ojeda. There was the finest harbour in the world, being Ojeda's idea of the Gulf of Caraico. There was an encounter with natives, in which exactly the same number of Spaniards were killed and wounded as in the encounter during Ojeda's voyage.* There was the attack on islanders and the capture of over 200 slaves, which was the last event of the voyage of Ojeda. Vespucci merely altered the latitudes, and made such a gross blunder respecting the difference between his dead reckoning and the observed position of his landfall (over 900 miles!) that this alone stamps his tale as apocryphal. He also added the impossible additional voyage northwards for 870 leagues, which would have taken him overland to British Columbia.

Humboldt, unwilling to believe in a fraud with regard to the four voyages of Vespucci, and aware of the evidence that he was in Spain during 1497 and 1498, suggested an explanation. It was that the dates were the results of clerical and typographical errors; that the voyage of Ojeda

* Las Casas, i, 392.

may have been the first voyage of Vespucci; that the Florentine provision dealer left Ojeda at Española and got back to Spain in time to go out with Pinzon in 1500, and that the voyage with Pinzon was his second voyage. But no one was allowed to leave Ojeda's ships at Española.

Varnhagen took **a** bolder course **in** his attempt to rehabilitate Vespucci. Entirely ignoring the evidence that he was in Spain all the time, the Brazilian advocate adopts **the story of his client** *au grand sérieux*. His landfall **in** latitude 16° would have taken him to Honduras if his **run of** less than 1000 leagues had not landed him at the eastern end of **Española**. Varnhagen passes **over this some**what **serious** obstacle, and takes Vespucci to Honduras, suggesting a " little Venice " for him on the coast of Tabasco. Vespucci **gives a second** latitude of **23°**, which takes him to Tampico, **on the Gulf** of Mexico; and assuming that *Lariab* was the form in which the name was originally written by Vespucci, **it appears that**, although there is no such name, yet the Huasteca Indians round Tampico have names of places ending in *ab*. But **it** is qui**te** impossible to tell whether *Parias* or *Lariab*, or either, was the word in the original manuscript. Varnhagen is **unable to** follow his client for 870 leagues northwards overland from 23° **N.**, so he makes him steer in a different direction. By this means Varnhagen takes Vespucci along the coast of America, round Florida, and **as far as Cape** Hatteras, discovering nearly 3000 miles of new coast-line. The finest harbour in the world is not in that neighbourhood ; but *Iti*, where there were cannibals, and where Vespucci alleged that he carried off 222 slaves, is identified with Bermuda. It is well known that Bermuda was uninhabited before the arrival of Europeans but that fact is set aside to make the theory complete.

It was, however, necessary to find an expedition with which Vespucci could embark in 1497, for he did not pretend that he commanded one. His admirers have suggested that he sailed in the expedition of Pinzon and Solis to Yucatan ; but it has already been shown that this theory is quite untenable.*

Pinzon and Solis were alive when the lawsuit was in progress between Diego Columbus and the Crown. The Crown prosecutor exerted himself to collect proofs that some of the discoveries were not made by the Admiral but by other navigators. If Vespucci had been in an expedition which discovered thousands of miles of coast-line between Honduras and Cape Hatteras, a report must have been made to the king, and that report would inevitably have been produced at the trial. Pinzon and Solis, too, must have given evidence. But there is not a word about it. No such discoveries are shown in the map of Juan de la Cosa (1500), who was intimate with Pinzon and Vespucci. Peter Martyr was intimate with Vespucci and his nephew, yet there is no sign of the discoveries suggested by Varnhagen, on the map drawn for the Decades, which appeared in 1511. At least one copy of Vespucci's story, which was printed in 1507, had reached Spain in 1515, namely, that in the library of Fernando Columbus. If the first voyage had not been known to be a fabrication, it would have been eagerly brought forward as evidence at the trial against the Admiral. But it is not mentioned. Ponce de Leon obtained a concession to discover this very coast in 1511, on condition that it had not been discovered before. It is incredible that Pinzon, Solis, and Vespucci would still

* See note at end of Chapter XIV.

have kept silence without any conceivable reason. **More-over, it** would have **been** officially known that the coast referred to by Ponce de Leon had already been explored. The inevitable **conclusion is that no** such discovery was **ever made, and that there** was no expedition with which Vespucci **could have sailed** in 1497. Even if there had been, **it does not follow** that he was in it. The evidence **that he was then working as a** contractor at Seville stands **in the way.**

On these grounds the alleged first voyage **of Vespucci must be pronounced to have** been apocryphal. Respecting **the second voyage with** Ojeda there is **no doubt.** Ojeda **gave evidence, in the lawsuit of Diego** Columbus, to the effect **that he took with him** "Juan de la Cosa the pilot, **Morigo Vespuche, and other pilots.**" In this sentence the words **"other pilots" are** to be coupled with the pilot **Juan de la Cosa, not with** "Morigo Vespuche." For Vespucci went to sea at the age of forty-seven **for the first time,** and cannot therefore have been a pilot. **He may have** possessed some theoretical knowledge **of astronomy,** but this would not constitute **a pilot, who must have** learnt his business afloat **and at sea.** It is, therefore, very unjust on the part of those writers **who** try to rehabilitate Vespucci, to speak **of him as** the chief **pilot** and director in any expedition **in which** he is alleged to have served. The whole **credit of** any discovery belongs to Pinzon, Solis, Ojeda, Coelho, or **whoever the theory places in command,** not to the Florentine merchant. Vespucci was a landsman, **and** had no experience **as a sailor,** much less as a pilot, before he **sailed with Ojeda.**

The evidence against the first voyage throws doubt on the two which Vespucci asserted that he made from

Lisbon. The Viscount de Santarem searched all the Portuguese records in the Torre do Tumbo, from 1495 to 1503, and the name of Vespucci does not once occur. This makes it very improbable that he was ever in command of a Portuguese vessel. But it does not preclude his having sailed in one in some subordinate capacity. Moreover, while his first voyage must be condemned as unreal from internal evidence alone, there is much in the account of his third voyage which bears the stamp of having been written by an eye witness. Peter Martyr had heard that the Florentine contractor made one voyage with the Portuguese.

In the letter to Medici, describing the Portuguese voyage of 1501, Vespucci spoke of the Brazilian coast as "novum mundum appellare licet." This letter hence received the heading of *Novus Mundus.** It was first published in Latin at Paris in 1503, then in German at Augsburg in 1504, at Dresden and Strassburg in 1505. It next appeared at Vicenza in 1507, in the book called "Paesi novamente Retrovati," and went through several other editions.

But it was owing to the publication of the letter to Soderini, describing the four voyages, that the name AMERICA was first suggested. A copy of this letter in French was sent to René II., Duke of Lorraine, from Lisbon. It was translated into Latin by Jean Basin de Sandacourt, a canon of a small cathedral town of Lorraine called St. Dié, at the request of another canon of St. Dié named Walter Lud, who was also the Duke's secretary. Lud had founded a college at St. Dié under the auspices

* It has been erroneously supposed that the expression "New World" was first used by Vespucci. It was used by Columbus himself in his letter to the nurse of Prince Juan.

of Duke René, and had even established a printing-press, appointing a youth named Ringmann (called Philesius) as corrector of proofs and teacher of Latin. Walter Waldseemüller (called Hylacomylus) came to St. Dié in 1504, as teacher of geography.

Walter Lud wrote a little book of four leaves, entitled "Speculi Orbis Declaratio," which was printed at Strassburg. It is a work of extreme rarity, but there is a copy in the British Museum. It is from this little book that we learn that the letters of Vespucci were sent from Portugal to the Duke of Lorraine in French, and translated into Latin by Sandacourt. In April 1507 Waldseemüller (or Hylacomylus) produced, from the St. Dié printing-press, a little work entitled "Cosmographiæ Introductio," to which was appended the Latin version of the four voyages of Vespucci. It was in this little book that the first suggestion of the name of America appeared. Waldseemüller wrote : —

"And the fourth part of the world having been discovered by Americus, may well be called Amerige, which is as much as to say the land of Americus or America."

In another place, a few pages on, the suggestion is more fully stated as follows :—

Nũc v̄o & hẹ partes sunt latius lustratæ/& alia quarta pars per Americũ Vesputiũ(vt in sequenti bus audietur)inuenta est/quã non video cur quis iure vetet ab Americo inuentore sagacis ingeñy vi

Ameri- ro Amerigen quasi Americi terrã / siue Americam
ca dicendã:cũ & Europa & Asia a mulieribus sua sor tita sint nomina. Eius situ & gentis mores ex bis bi nis Americi nauigationibus quæ sequunt̃ liquide intelligi datur.

"But now these parts are more extensively explored, and, as will be seen in the following letters, another fourth part has been discovered by Americus Vespatius, which I see no just reason why any one should forbid to be named Amerige, which is as much as to say the land of Americus or America, from its discoverer Americus,

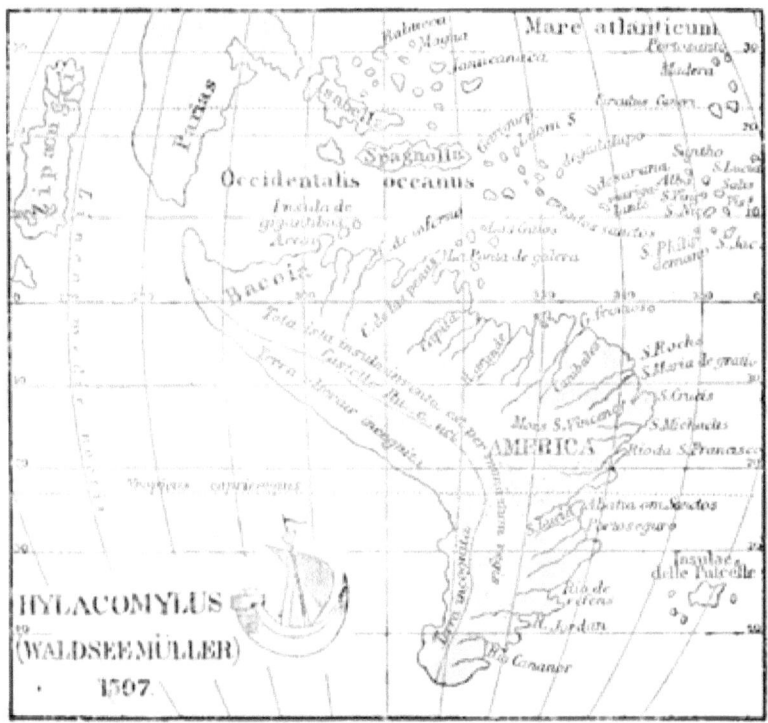

PORTION OF THE HAUSLAB GLOBE.

who is a man of shrewd intellect; for Europe and Asia have both of them taken a feminine form of name from the names of women."

A new edition of the "Cosmographiæ Introductio" appeared in September 1507, and another at Strassburg, in 1509. A copy of the Strassburg edition was in the

z

library of Fernando Columbus, who probably looked upon the proposal to give the name of America as intended to apply only to part of the coast of Brazil discovered by the Portuguese in 1502. In the Pomponius Mela of 1518 there is a letter dated Vienna, 1512, in which the expression occurs "America, discovered by Vesputius." It has recently been shown [*] that Waldseemüller made a map of the world and a globe in 1507, when he wrote the "Cosmographiæ Introductio." The map has not been found, but the globe is that formerly the property of General Hauslab, and is given by Gallois. Upon it the name of America is inscribed. This is the first time that the name appeared on a map. In 1509, the name was placed on a manuscript map now at Vienna. In 1511, the following passage appeared in an English play, called "The New Interlude":

> "But this newe lande founde lately,
> Ben callyd America by cause only
> Americus dyd first them find." [†]

In 1515, the name America appeared on Schoner's globe, and on the gores at Windsor Castle, which were attributed by Mr. Major to Lionardo da Vinci. The earliest engraved map bearing the name of America is the map of the world by Peter Apianus, in an edition of Solinus of 1520. The name was placed along the coast of what the Spaniards called Tierra Firme. It was first applied to the whole continent by Mercator in 1540.

America was a convenient and euphonious word, and was gradually adopted by map-makers throughout Europe; but it was long before this inappropriate and

---

* Gallois. *Les géographes allemandes de la renaissance.* Paris, 1860.
† Quoted by Harrisse.

intruding name took root in Spain. Las Casas declared that the continent ought to be called Columba, and Herrera also raised a protest. But habit and the map makers eventually overcame justice, even in Spain, although the continent of Columbus was there always officially known as the Indies.

René II., Duke of Lorraine, died in December 1508. The printing-press at St. Dié was broken up, and the little knot of professors was dispersed. It would seem that Waldseemüller afterwards became better informed, when he was engaged on the Ptolemy of 1513. It contains a map on which there is no name of America, but on the new continent there is the following inscription : —" Hæc terra, cum adjacentibus insulis, inventa est per Columbum Januensem, ex mandatis Regis Castilliæ." It was too late. The mischievous suggestion in the "Cosmographiæ Introductio" had taken root, and rapidly bore fruit.

There is no reason for supposing that Vespucci himself connived at the suggestion of the name America, and it is most probable that he never heard of it. Vespucci merely wrote his romance for the admiration of his friends at Florence, seeking for credit at home by magnifying his exploits, as many another has done before and since. He can have had no other object, nor could he have foreseen the notoriety his letters acquired. Nevertheless America is now the name of the great continent discovered by Columbus.

The Admiral's name is confined to a few localities. The country of Veragua, all the coast thence to Cabo de la Vela, and a great inland territory, comprise the United States of Columbia. The city at the Atlantic terminus of the Panama railway, where the Admiral hoped to find a strait, is the city of Colon. British

Columbia is an extensive province in North America, and the capital of the United States is situated in the territory of Columbia; but the name of the whole continent was filched from its great discoverer.

That name has a securer abiding place. Monuments and columns at Genoa, Madrid, Barcelona, at Mexico and other Spanish-American towns, are the outward evidence of the firm hold that the mighty achievement of the Admiral has taken on the imagination of mankind. The love and reverence that is universally felt for his noble character will be manifested by the enthusiastic celebration of the fourth centenary of the discovery of the New World, and the story of his life will continue to be studied by generations yet unborn. For it teaches many a lesson of devotion to duty, of perseverance, of loyalty, and of faith. The great work of his life has long been completed, but his example will remain for ever to incite the youths of each succeeding generation to emulate his example, and to impress upon them the qualities which enable men to rise from the humblest rank of life to the height of worldly ambition. The name of a new continent is a small thing compared with the enthusiastic veneration with which the civilised world, for ages to come, will treat the name of Christopher Columbus, the weaver of Genoa and Admiral of the Ocean Sea.

INDEX.

THE END.